Pen
and
Plow

a novel by

Harry F. Casey

A *Scribe* Book

PEN and PLOW

A *Scribe* Book

Published by
Scribe Publishing
PO Box 913, King City, CA 93930

ISBN 0-9659184-1-6

Library of Congress Catalog Number 97-61769

For my daughters, Sharon and Patty,
and my sons, Richard and Bill.

Also by Harry F. Casey

Land of the Eagle

Forty-Three Years of "Casing,"
a collection of newspaper columns and editorials

Jo Jo and Other Stories
for children

ACKNOWLEDGMENTS

The Salinas Valley, King City and its environs, and the other communities in this novel, are real. So, too, is the historical background of this central coast of California. But the events which take place, except for the obvious, are imaginary, and the main characters are fictitious. However, some of the storekeepers, cowboys, officials, townspeople, sheriffs, and other such minor roles, have the names of people who actually lived the times, brought to life to roam the background.

For those names, for the business places and institutions, for the events and the atmosphere of the period, I relied on the files of the *King City Rustler* and thank South County Newspapers for their availability. I also appreciate the excellent cooperation from Liz Checke-Ewing and the staff of King City and Monterey County Libraries. The Monterey County Agriculture and Rural Life Museum at San Lorenzo Park in King City was a treasury of information on agricultural and pioneer life.

I am also indebted to Elmer Eade for his guidance on farming practices, to Attorneys James Sweffle and Edward Foley for legal references, John McCarthy on banking, and to Matt Gildersleeve for sharing his University of San Diego thesis: "San Lucas—History of a California Cattle Town." Many others were of great help, including K.L. Eade, Father Larry Kambitsch, Al Garcia, Dr. Duane Hyde, Dr. Robert Hostetter, Michael Barbree, Father Bill Clancey, and my daughters, Sharon Ruth Casey and Patty Casey Griffin.

I also thank my daughters-in-law, Holly Casey, who drew the map, and Sharon Jane Casey for her fiscal advice, my son, Richard, who checked my horsemanship, and my son, Bill, who unlocked the mysteries of this damn word processor.

But, most of all, I thank my wife, Peggy, whose encouragement, patient criticism, character analysis, creativity, and editing made *Pen and Plow* her novel as much as mine.

— *Harry F. Casey*

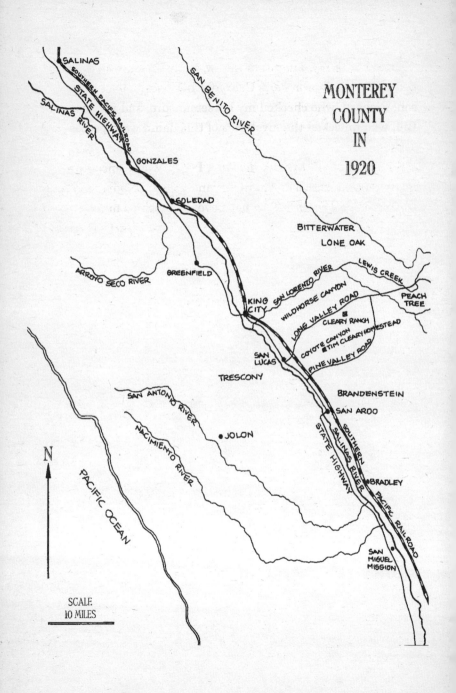

MONTEREY
COUNTY
IN
1920

SALINAS

SOUTHERN PACIFIC RAILROAD

STATE HIGHWAY

SALINAS RIVER

SAN BENITO RIVER

GONZALES

SOLEDAD

ARROYO SECO RIVER

GREENFIELD

BITTERWATER

LONE OAK

LEWIS CREEK

SAN LORENZO RIVER

WILDHORSE CANYON

LONG VALLEY ROAD

PEACH TREE

KING CITY

CLEARY RANCH

COYOTE CANYON

TIM CLEARY HOMESTEAD

SAN LUCAS

PINE VALLEY ROAD

TRESCONY

SAN ANTONIO RIVER

BRANDENSTEIN

SAN ARDO

NACIMIENTO RIVER

JOLON

N

PACIFIC OCEAN

STATE HIGHWAY

SALINAS RIVER

SOUTHERN PACIFIC RAILROAD

BRADLEY

SAN MIGUEL MISSION

SCALE
10 MILES

CHAPTER ONE

"SAW IT OFF RIGHT ABOUT HERE." Fred Godfrey held out the shiny, double-barreled shotgun to the blacksmith. Joe Wasson stopped pumping the bellows for his glowing forge. He took the weapon, turned it over in his hands and admired it.

"Hell, Fred. This is brand new. Why you want to wreck a good piece like this?"

"Just do it, Joe."

"Won't be much good for birds, Fred."

"Not for birds, Joe. Blowhards!"

Joe Wasson's eyes widened in disbelief as he shook his head. "Holy hell, Fred. If I cut it off there, it'll blast a hole a yard wide in whatever you're shooting."

"That's the idea, Joe," Fred Godfrey said. His calm voice belied his inner turmoil.

He stood by as Wasson shrugged, inserted the shotgun into a vice, squeezed it down, and began to cut. Godfrey noticed a few townspeople standing by the open door, looking in, curious. Good, he thought. Just what he wanted. He'd waited until almost noon, to make sure there'd be more people on the street, before locking up the newspaper office, hanging out the "Be back in 15 minutes" sign and stepping onto the board sidewalk that ran the three-block length of Broadway.

He'd gone into the Ford and Sanborn store and asked the clerk to show him the shotguns. "Just got two in stock, Fred," the clerk said, bringing out a lever action ten gauge.

"Winchester came out with these just two years ago. The latest thing."

Godfrey shook his head. "Not what I want. Looks too much like a rifle. I want a double barrel, side by side."

"How about this?" The clerk laid a Remington twelve gauge on the counter and Fred hefted it, checked the steel barrels and dual hammers. He shouldered it, swung it around, sighted it through the window, and nodded.

"How much?"

"Fifteen dollars!"

Fred whistled, realizing that Sarah would have a fit. They were barely getting by. "I'll need a box of twelve gauge, too," he said. "Put it on my account."

"Sure, Fred," the clerk agreed, but he was puzzled. He and Fred had hunted doves together last fall so he knew Fred already owned a decent double barrel. What did he want another for? The young newspaperman was brusque as hell this morning, too — no jokes, no hunting stories. The clerk followed Godfrey to the front door, and then watched him walk to the middle of the main street of the little town and head right up the center, shotgun in one hand and box of shells in the other. Something had the editor of *The Salinas Valley Settler* all lathered up.

Others watched, too, and the word quickly spread. Godfrey felt the eyes on him as several riders reined aside their saddle horses, and drivers stopped their wagons to follow his progress. He strode purposefully the length of Broadway and turned into Wasson's blacksmith shop.

When he came out a short while later, carrying his newly sawed-off shotgun, Godfrey stopped in the middle of the street, broke open the breech and inserted two shells, snapped it shut, cocked the hammers and headed back to his office, holding the gun in front of him. People stopped on the sidewalk, gathering in small groups telling each other, "The editor's on the prod about something." Heads appeared at the windows and travelers along Broadway pulled over their rigs to watch and wonder what Godfrey was doing. He marched to the small building that housed his newspaper and stopped at the door. He released the hammers, propped the shotgun against the build-ing, and reached for his bandanna to wipe the beaded sweat from his face and neck, glancing up and down the dusty street baking in the August heat.

He unlocked his office door, picked up the shotgun, went directly to his roll-top desk and stood the shotgun beside it, in easy reach. He shrugged out of his coat and vest, hung them and his derby hat on the wall hook, loosened his tie, and sat down to wait. He had five hours.

The note he'd found pinned to his door that morning had advised the "smart-assed editor" that he'd better "get heeled" because his press was going to be smashed if he hadn't packed up and left town by five that afternoon. Well, Godfrey thought, he was heeled, dammit, and it won't be long before Josh Gibbons knows it, too. He'll come riding into town and word gets around fast. He'll hear that this editor has some sand in his craw. Let's see what he thinks of that shotgun.

Fred Godfrey was thirty-two years old, stood only about five foot seven, but he was feisty. People noticed that when Fred got angry his face turned as red as his rust-colored hair. He had a temper, to be sure, but he wasn't foolish.

He'd put on quite a show there, Fred thought, allowing him-self a wry grin. He hoped to hell it worked. He hoped Gibbons was the big bully he had him figured to be, and that he'd ride back to his ranch and stay there. But if he'd read Gibbons wrong, Fred worried, he'd show up, and there'd be a con-frontation. *Will I have to shoot him? Will he shoot me? How do I keep getting into this pickle barrel? But, holy Jehoshaphat, nobody's going to tell me what I can write and what I can't write. I want that settled right now. This is my newspaper, by God, and I'll write what I think is true and proper.*

Josh Gibbons had ridden into town with some of his cowboys the week before and they'd all gotten liquored up in Locatelli's Grand Saloon. They'd started a fight, broken the mirror, crashed through the window, and generally wrecked the place. Gibbons had dropped some greenbacks on the bar to pay for the damages and thought that was the end of it. It always had been in the past. But the next issue of *The Salinas Valley Settler* had some pointed advice for him and his hands: *Most of the men who tend the cattle and do the farming in this region are gentlemen and a credit to themselves and their employers. But there is a certain element which comes into town and comports itself in a disgraceful manner.*

We refer particularly to the group of uncouth rowdies who wrecked Locatelli's saloon last week, smashing furniture and glass and endangering the other patrons as well as some ladies, who happened to be passing on the street outside. They may wear big hats and boots, but they are not cowboys, not in the true tradition of those Knights of the West. It is past time that the decent people of King City warn those punks and hoodlums to act like gentlemen or stay out of our town.

Now Fred Godfrey had been warned to "get heeled" to back up his editorial, or pack up his press and type cases, and move on. Not on your tintype, would he! He might not be very big, but Fred Godfrey backed down to no man. He'd proven that up in Angels Camp on his first job editing a newspaper in California, *The Angel's Voice*. He'd made a big show of sawing off a shotgun to stand by his desk up there, too, and it had worked. No one bothered him after that, and he wrote any damn thing he liked. And he'd continued that way in King City, ever since he'd arrived with his press and his type, two years back.

That was 1888 when King City was three blocks long and four blocks wide. It still was. Its sidewalks were board planks, and the streets were either a foot of mud or six inches of dust. Behind the false fronts were two hotels, two general stores selling everything from groceries to suits and plows, a livery stable, harness and saddle shop, a blacksmith, a barbershop, five saloons—it seemed a new one opened every other day—a variety of dwellings, a few boarding houses and one church.

The Salinas River Valley, depicted on some maps as the Great Salinas Desert, had few inhabitants who realized that there was abundant water underneath, and that the valley awaited only the magic of irrigation to bring it to life, fertile and green.

Fred Godfrey knew the water was there—it was part of his vision—it was why he started his newspaper here.

Fred sat back in his oak swivel chair. And sweat. It got mighty hot in his office in the summer. Again he wiped his face. Holy Jehoshaphat, he thought, it was a good thing Sarah was attending the Ladies' Social Club tea in the lobby of the new Vendome Hotel. Nobody would dare interrupt that. She might not hear the gossip about his sawed-off shotgun. At least he hoped not. He wouldn't have to face Sarah until tonight.

By that time he'd have pulled off this bluff. Or he'd have shot Gibbons. Or he'd be dead. Fred didn't pray much, but this was a time for it. "Lord," he murmured, "Don't make me use this shotgun."

When Sarah found out what he'd just done, Fred knew she'd be mad as hell. Word spread fast in a town of two hundred. She had wanted him to tone down the editorial when he told her about it. "Why make enemies, Fred? It's hard enough to keep this newspaper going without you raising such a fuss."

"What kind of town do you want, Sarah? Isn't this where we'll stay, make our home, have our kids? We can't let it be run by a bunch of hoodlums." The editorial was printed over Sarah's' objections.

But usually Sarah had her own way. Nearly thirteen years younger than her husband, she was two inches taller, slender, and carried herself regally. She was spoiled and accustomed to having the last word. Sarah came from a large and wealthy family. Her father had struck it rich in the Sierras during the California gold rush. He'd bought a large farm on the eastern shores of San Francisco Bay and married Sarah's mother, a poor Irish immigrant who never quite recovered from the surprise of her suddenly affluent circumstances.

"My children will be having everything that I wasn't having," she'd say with grateful pride.

So Sarah was spoiled and Fred did little to change her. He was eternally amazed that she'd agreed to be his wife, and he adored her. Sarah had her mother's wit and a temper to match, with her long, auburn hair, green eyes, and a patrician nose that had no place in an otherwise Irish face. She could scorch him with a frown or turn on her radiant smile when she wanted to charm him into giving her whatever it was she wanted. Except for the newspaper. She could never tell her husband how and what to write.

Fred had been a newspaperman since he was fifteen years old. Or rather, he'd been a compositor, one of those highly-skilled typesetters who'd form the news stories one letter at a time on a composing stick from a type case. His father was a doctor, but Fred had no desire to follow him into medicine, not after getting a taste of the newspaper business. That had happened on his first job, running errands for the printers on *The Alexandria Post* in his native Minnesota, mostly to the nearby saloon for gallons of beer in a lard bucket.

By the time he was eighteen, he was touring the West as a compositor. He'd drop into a daily newspaper office and pick copy off the extra board, getting paid well based on the amount of type he set. He worked on just about every major daily paper west of the Mississippi, and then realized that his was a dying trade. First the Simplex was developed to mechanically set type, and then a man named Otto Merganthaler had invented the Linotype. Fred, whose formal education ended with the sixth grade, but who had an excellent command of the English language from his years of typesetting, became a reporter for William Randolph Hearst on the *San Francisco Examiner*. He was hired from there to edit *The Angel's Voice* in Angel's Camp, a small mining town in California's Sierra Nevada mountains. He built up that paper from scratch. But when it was sold "out from under him," as Fred lamented, he vowed that from that point on he'd be his own man. He took all his savings and bought four hundred dollars worth of cast-off type and a press. He had it shipped to the fledgling town of King City, California, which was growing up in the middle of Charles King's grain fields.

The town sat near the junction of San Lorenzo Creek and the Salinas River, both roaring cataracts in the rainy season, but bone dry, dead ribbons of sand and willows in the summer. King's was one of a series of tiny commercial centers created by the railroad, and the needs of the farmers and cattlemen, now settling both the main valley and the many smaller ones radiating from it. There was Gonzales to the north and then Soledad, twenty-two miles up the track, and nine miles south was San Lucas, then came San Ardo, and then Bradley, each spaced like beads on a necklace strung together by the rails of the Southern Pacific. And each little town was convinced it was on its way to becoming a metropolis as they competed with each other to be the main shipping point for the burgeoning grain and cattle industries of the Salinas Valley.

They gave their three-block-long business streets names such as Front and Main and Central, or, in a fit of pretentious optimism, Broadway. In the other towns these streets ran parallel to the railroad, so that all the business houses faced the tracks. But King City's Broadway was different. It ran perpendicular to the tracks so that its main thoroughfare could have business enterprises on both sides of the street. This gave townspeople a feeling of superiority whenever comparisons were made.

* * * * *

Fred Godfrey dug out his pocket watch and again checked the time. It wasn't moving very fast. He snapped the lid shut and shuffled the papers on the big roll-top desk, tried to organize them, stack them neatly, but they just didn't cooperate. He tried to write, his soft lead pencil crawling in his tiny, cramped squiggles across the foolscap. But slowly. Too slowly.

7

cramped squiggles across the foolscap. But slowly. Too slowly. The words wouldn't come.

He resisted the temptation to go outside and have a look up and down the street, then opened a window to let in what little breeze was moving the warm air. He admitted to himself that he was a bit frightened. But he'd made his play and he had to back it. A man, and a newspaper, by God, had to stand for what was right.

He fidgeted as he looked around the small office. In the back was the little, two-page, hand-operated Messenger newspaper press, and his hand-fed Challenge clapper for printing envelopes, tickets, business forms, billheads and posters. Two California job cases, holding his entire assortment of type, stood backed against the wall beside his small, lever-operated paper cutter. On the other wall were the shelves for paper, and next to them the counter that held the little cans of different colored ink, and black, of course. All the shelves were nearly empty. It took money to keep up an inventory.

He sighed and stood up, put on his apron and rolled up his sleeves. May as well set some type while he was waiting. No customers were coming by this afternoon. No one dropping in just to visit. They were steering clear of the newspaper office. Fred wished some of the law-abiding citizens would stop by to help, or just offer encouragement, particularly those who had urged him to write the editorial. But Fred Godfrey really knew better. Sometimes this newspaper business could be a lonely affair.

If only Sarah would help. She could learn to set type and he could spend more time out on the street rustling up business. But she'd flat out refused. Fred set his composing stick for one column and pulled out the tray of eight-point Caslon. He picked out the letters for a patent medicine ad. "What crap this is," he muttered to himself, as he set the words, *Is Your Liver Out of Order? Do you go to bed in an evil humor and get up with a bad taste in your mouth? You need something to stimulate your liver. You need Herbine, the liver regulator, a positive cure for Constipation, Dyspepsia and all liver complaints. At Ford and Sanborn Co.* As a doctor's son, Fred put little faith in patent medicine claims, but these ads helped pay the bills.

Fred took another look at his watch. It was almost five. But Holy Jehoshaphat, it was still hot in here. The sweat was dripping into his typestick. He mopped himself with the bandanna, finished setting the ad, transferred it to a galley and was just hanging up his apron when the front door opened.

"Mister Godfrey! Mister Godfrey!" A young boy yelled to him from the doorway. "Gibbons and his hands just left the Grand Saloon and they're headed this way. They're all boozed up. I was sent to tell you to skedaddle." The boy breathlessly delivered the message and ran off.

Fred Godfrey straightened his tie, buttoned his vest and pulled on his coat. He noticed his hands were shaking. He took a deep breath and picked up the shotgun from beside his desk, cocking both triggers. He opened the front door and stepped onto the board sidewalk just as a huge man, his belly sagging over his saddle horn, rode up on a bay gelding and stopped in the street in front of the newspaper office. Four cowboys lined up beside him, two on each side, swaying in their saddles.

"You the pipsqueak that runs this rag?" the big man roared, his mouth working in the center of a long, stained handlebar mustache. He leaned over and sent a stream of tobacco juice in the direction of Godfrey. "Thought I told you to get your junk the hell out of town."

The shotgun wavered in Fred's hands, but he managed to bring it up to his hip, pointing it directly at Gibbons' gut. He hoped his voice wouldn't crack, but his mouth was so dry he could hardly make his tongue work. He finally croaked, "You get the hell out of town yourself, Gibbons! And take those clowns with you!" Fred gestured with the shotgun to include all five men.

"Well, I'll just show you," Gibbons shouted and swung himself out of the saddle. When his foot hit the ground, he stumbled and had to grab onto the saddle to right himself. He bled and had to grab onto the saddle to right himself. He straightened up and staggered toward the boardwalk.

"Don't!" Fred cried. "Stay where you are."

Gibbons drew his pistol and moved forward.

"Stop!"

Fred lifted the shotgun. But Gibbons kept coming, stumbling along, lifting his foot to step up on the walk. "Get you, you goddamn pencil-pushing pipsqueak," he cried.

Gibbons brought up his pistol. It wobbled and waved from side to side, but then steadied on Fred.

As the huge man stepped up on the edge of the board sidewalk there was a loud crack. Gibbons fell over backwards into the dust and horse manure of Broadway. A splintered board flipped high into the air, turned over in an arc and landed down the boardwalk with a clatter.

Gibbons' cowboys looked at the cracked board and then down at their floundering boss. He was on his back making grunting noises and trying to regain his footing. But one foot was caught in the hole in the sidewalk. Each time he almost lifted out his foot, he got tangled up and fell back again.

"Gotcha, didn't he, boss?" one of his men said.

"Yep, dead center," another said with a grin.

"Drilled proper," a third said between giggles.

Now they were all chortling as they watched their boss flop around in a pile of fresh manure. "Watch out for them horse apples," a fourth cowboy advised as his widening grin broke into a laugh. The mirth spread to the others and grew into guffaws and they roared and snorted and almost choked with laughter. One of them laughed so hard he fell off of his horse, which created a whole new round of hilarity. He struggled to regain the saddle, fell back himself and triggered another wave of mirth.

"One of you goddamned hyenas get down here and help me!" Gibbons bellowed. His face was blooming bright red from the liquor, the heat and his struggles. But mostly from embarrassment.

He gave a mighty heave and yanked his foot from the hole, falling free onto the street. But his boot stayed caught. Gibbons yanked furiously on the boot and it suddenly gave way, again throwing him over backwards onto the street. Swearing at his men in particular, and the world in general, Gibbons hopped around on one leg, struggling to put on the boot.

Finally another cowboy dismounted and joined the one already on the ground and their laughter eased off enough to boost their cursing boss into his saddle. Without even turning to face Fred Godfrey, who still stood in front of his office door, Gibbons rode off with his cowboys.

Fred watched them trot their horses down Broadway and out of town to the east. Then he looked wonderingly down at the shotgun that was still gripped tightly in both his hands. He pried his finger off the trigger guard and lifted one hand to his face. He rubbed his jaw, which hurt from clenching his teeth so tightly. Fred finally looked down at the wooden sidewalk in front of him. There was a gaping hole. His eyes traveled down the walk to the splintered board.

"Holy Jehoshaphat," he muttered to himself. "I told them to fix that board."

He hadn't noticed the people gathering. They came from everywhere. From the stores, from the houses, from down the street and they circled around him. Quiet at first, their voices lifted and increased in volume. "By God, you showed 'em, Fred" — "We got us an editor with some sand, I'll tell you" — "Faced up to 'em, Fred. Knew you would!" The clamor grew and they slapped him on the back. "Come on, Fred. Buy you a drink."

"No thanks," he said. He breathed a sigh of relief, uncocked his shotgun and locked up for the night. "Best I get home to Sarah."

CHAPTER TWO

FRED WALKED SHAKILY the short distance to the alleyway that led to the back stairs of the Vendome. He climbed up the steps, bracing himself to face Sarah Godfrey, his bride of six months.

She greeted him with, "Well, I see you're still alive."

Fred propped up the shotgun in the corner of the room and went to the basin, poured it full of cool water from the pitcher and mopped his face and neck. There, that felt better. He turned to Sarah, ready to tell her what had happened.

Then he noticed it. There on the floor by the bed was her suitcase, packed.

"Fred, I'm taking the morning train. Going home." Sarah had that stance, legs firmly planted, hands on hips, and the stubborn set of her jaw. Fred had seen it enough times to know he didn't have any words, no matter what he said, to change her mind.

"A visit, Sarah?"

"I don't know, Fred. I'll have to think about it. I'm tired of just scraping by, not having anything. It was embarrassing for me, wearing the same old dress to the Social Club this afternoon. The other ladies have seen it a dozen times." Sarah sighed. "And they all have homes to go to and I just walk upstairs in this ratty hotel like some third-rate drummer's woman."

Sarah had let Fred know more than once that she considered herself a "lady." She refused to work on the newspaper with him because "ink-stained hands aren't for me," she'd say. She wouldn't even play the mandolin any more. It would be great if she'd fill in with the dance orchestra, Fred had tried to cajole her. But she didn't want to develop new calluses on her fingers. It didn't make sense to her husband. That's how he'd met Sarah, at a musical afternoon in San Leandro near her home. He'd been smitten by the stately young woman who played the

12

mandolin so well, star of the string ensemble featured that afternoon. A musician himself, Fred had used that excuse to stay after the program and talk to her. Music had been their shared interest while they courted.

Now Sarah wouldn't even pick up the mandolin for fear of ruining her fingers. Fred had wanted her with him in the orchestra he'd organized to earn a little extra money playing at the country dances. He gave guitar and mandolin lessons, sold musical instruments for a San Francisco company, represented a business school and peddled real estate, investment bonds and burial insurance and did the job printing for the few local business houses. Every nickel made a difference until the newspaper was on it's feet. And it would be, if he could just hold on. But right now the advertising in the four-page newspaper didn't quite pay all the bills.

Fred shook his head. "Sarah, you know this is only temporary. We'll rent a place and then build our own house, just as soon as we get a little bit ahead. Holy Jehoshaphat, give me time." Fred was used to expressing himself with saltier language, practiced extensively during his travels across the West in his bachelor days. But in deference to his young wife, he'd toned it down.

"You'll never get ahead," Sarah responded. "You insist on alienating all the business people with your editorials. They're sick of hearing your harping on incorporation and taxes. And you've made all the big landowners sore by urging irrigation and cutting up the large ranches. Now this stunt today. I heard all about it. Oh, didn't those women just love to tell me. It's just not fair."

Maybe Sarah thought her husband was making a mistake, but Fred knew there'd be hundreds of farm families moving in once the big tracts were cut up and the land was under irrigation. And his newspaper, *The Settler,* would be its booster, playing a role to make that happen. Now if the two hundred subscribers who were in arrears would just pungle up the one-fifty each that they owed him, Fred thought, he'd have some breathing room, maybe even buy Sarah the new dress she wanted. Even start saving for the house they both wanted. But right now every dime went into the business.

"But, Sarah — " Fred tried not to plead, but he couldn't help himself. "I love you. I need you."

"What I don't need," Sarah said, with a stubborn toss of her long auburn hair, "is to be a nineteen-year-old widow."

There wasn't anything left to say. Fred, who made a living with words, desperately searched his mind for the right ones. But it always came down to the fact that he'd never let anyone tell him what to write, not even this wife he loved.

So the Godfreys ate a silent supper, sent up from the hotel kitchen, and went to bed. It was a long night. Neither slept much, laying stiffly side by side, careful not to touch one another.

In the morning Fred carried Sarah's valise down the back stairs and out front where he placed it in the hotel's rig. He helped her up and sat beside her, neither speaking, as the driver took up the lines and the team trotted along Broadway to the depot where the morning train sat huffing and puffing on the track. Fred took Sarah's arm and silently, grimly escorted her to the train steps, handed up her small bag, and sadly stepped back. Sarah tossed her head, looked down the length of town, and sniffed before disappearing into the passenger car.

"Wife leaving, Fred?" one of the bystanders asked with a grin.

"San Leandro," he answered. "Visiting her folks."

* * * * *

Fred kept busy during the day, but the nights were bad. That's when he remembered the things Sarah had said and done, what he'd said, how he might have handled things differently. He anguished through the long nights, hating to think he'd lost his wonderful bride. And it was during those dark hours that he mulled over in his mind the remarks he heard around town. "Hi there, Fred. Haven't seen your wife around lately." "Wife gone somewhere, Fred?" "Eating alone again tonight, Fred?"

Why were there people who always had to get in a small dig, an innuendo? Was there some petty pleasure to be had out of another's troubles? Some thrill out of gossip? Oh, well, can't fight them all, he thought. So he just smiled and kept quiet. But he was deeply hurt, and very sad, and there was no one in whom he could confide, so he kept to himself.

There was also no mail from Sarah and it had been three weeks now since she'd left. Fred's post office box was filled with bills, a few orders for advertising, a number of puff pieces and so-called news releases from government agencies, some articles from country correspondents and the usual outright junk mail. But no letter from his wife.

He tried to write to her, but couldn't find the words she'd want to hear. He couldn't promise to change his editorials, compromise his beliefs. Good thing Sarah wasn't there last week, Fred thought, when a contingent of five saloon owners arrived at his newspaper office. Sarah wouldn't have approved of his response when they backed Fred up against his own desk, shaking their fists at him.

"You're wrecking business, Godfrey. You and your damn newspaper!" Tito Morales, owner of Tito's Cantina, exclaimed. He was referring to a recent *Settler* editorial stating that King City had eleven saloons and only two churches and that it was time for more churches and fewer saloons unless the town wanted a reputation as a haven for rowdies. "The cattle outfits are going to ship out of San Lucas or Soledad if their cowboys aren't treated right in King City," Morales warned.

"Yep, and the stores will lose money, not just the saloons," Kurt Schmiddle, the German who owned the Bavarian Bar, said angrily. He shook his finger in Fred's face. "You'd better tone down that stuff about needing a constable to keep the cowboys under control. Those boys work hard. They're just cowboys under control. Those boys work hard. They're just blowing off a little steam."

"Now look, Kurt, I know the majority of the cowboys are no trouble. It's just that Gibbons outfit. That's who I meant. Him and those three or four hard cases who work for him. The others, the boys off the other ranches, they're no trouble. But that bunch, shooting off guns just for the hell of it — "

"Nope, you can't soft soap us, Fred," Henry Locatelli interrupted. "All of us agreed—you put any more stuff like that in this paper and we're all pulling out our ads."

That did it. Fred's face turned crimson. He shook his own fist at the group. "I'll print what I think is right. I'll not cave in to any damn threats. To hell with all of you. Keep your damn ads!"

No, Sarah wouldn't have liked that response at all. It had probably cost Fred some business. Every one of those saloons had a card ad in the paper at a dollar fifty a month. He'd just told them he didn't need their damn business. Well, Sarah didn't know about it. Maybe she never would. But he missed her terribly. And wondered what she was doing.

* * * * *

Williams Farm near San Leandro, with its orchards of huge walnut trees, apricots and peaches, offered Sarah the shady retreat she needed during the August heat. She walked out every day among the trees. And thought. When she first arrived home, she didn't anticipate that she'd miss Fred. But she did, and she finally admitted it to herself.

Her mother and father had assumed she was homesick and had come back for a brief visit. But when a week went by, Maggie Williams asked her daughter, "What is it, Sarah? It's moping around like a sick cat, you are." Maggie put down her needlepoint and patted the velvet sofa beside her. "Sit down here and tell me the trouble."

Sarah sat down beside her mother. "It's Fred," she cried. "He doesn't love me. He won't do anything I ask him, and we don't have a thing. I'm tired of living in two tiny rooms in that crummy little hotel, eating in that restaurant all the time, and never having any money to do anything. I can't buy any new dresses. There's no room for my own things. It's always scrimp, scrimp, scrimp. The newspaper is doing no better now than it did when he started it two years ago. We'll never get ahead because all he does is make people mad with his stupid editorials. He's so bull headed!"

Sarah paused, then said in her most imperious voice, "And he expects me to learn typesetting and help around the print shop. Can you imagine that?"

"Well now, help him, is it?" Maggie asked. "And you have nothing, you say?"

Maggie rose and walked around the room. Her brow was furrowed and she seemed deep in thought. "Have nothing, is that what you're saying?" She was silent a moment and then seemed to come to a decision. "Sarah, quiet yourself. I'm going to be telling you things that you don't know. Things your brothers and sisters aren't knowing. Oh, they may have been hearing bits and pieces, but there's been no need to tell them. But now, I'm thinking, there is a need to tell you."

Maggie sat down again and patted her daughter's hand. She began quietly, looking down at her own hands twisting themselves on her lap. "Sarah," she said, "it's myself I'm blaming for raising you the way I did. It's me that was always wanting the best for all of you. I wasn't wanting any of you to suffer for the lack of anything you wanted, and your father, God bless him, let me do it. And why was that important to me?

"I was born in Ireland. You're knowing that." As she spoke, Maggie's brogue got thicker. "It was in County Donegal, near a tiny town called Ardara. There was my ma, and my da, and two older brothers, and there was my little sister, Rosie. Ours was a one-room cottage like all the rest, not far from the Owentucker River. We shared it with our pigs at night, and

17

when we had chickens they roosted inside in the loft with Rosie and me."

Sarah's eyes widened. "Pigs and chickens in the house? Mother!"

"It was glad we were to be having pigs and chickens, and a cow to be giving milk. And the *praties* to eat. You're not knowing what it is to be poor, and you've never known what it is to have the hunger upon you. I've been keeping it away from you like it's something to be ashamed of. But I can't be ashamed. Because it was not our fault, you see. No one had much, no matter how hard they worked, my da and brothers, the neighboring men, the women in the fields. All we earned went to pay the rents and there was nothing left, nothing but the *praties*. We ate potatoes every meal, and that was about all. But we fared well on them and that was all we knew."

Maggie took a deep breath and plunged ahead with her story. "And then the famine struck us down. The blight came over the potatoes and people starved. There was no help from the landlords, none from the authorities. They let the people starve. My mother and da went without, so what there was could be shared by the children. But the famine continued for another year, and soon there was nothing to share, and sickness came into our cottage. We'd sold all we had, the cow and the pigs, the hand cart, our table and chairs, even our clothing, to pay the rent. And then the potato crop blighted again and the famine continued. My brothers went off to seek work. But there was no work and then they took the fever and fell by the wayside. My mother and father starved to death right there in our cottage." Maggie was silent for a moment, staring into space.

"I didn't know what to do. I was sixteen, and Rosie but fourteen. I took her by the hand and left the cottage, left my poor ma and da there, dead by the cold fireplace with no one to bury them, and went to the manor house. The servants were about to chase us away, but the lord himself came out. It was me, sobbing out my story, that reached his heart. He sent his servants

18

to burn the cottage. It was because of the fever, he said, and the putrefied bodies.

He gave me the money to buy passage to America for Rosie and me. I was trying to thank him, when he said he intended to do it anyhow. Clear the land, he would, to put his sheep to graze."

"Oh, Mother, how terrible!" Sarah exclaimed as she put her hand on her mother's shoulder, but Maggie shrugged it off, rose and walked to the window.

She stood looking out, envisioning for the first time in many years those terrible days. "We made our way across to Liverpool, England, where the ships were leaving for America. Those were awful, horrible ships. Some would sink before they got out of the bay. Coffin ships, they called them. And so filthy and crowded, Rosie and I could but cling together in a tiny space. There was never enough to eat. They ran low on water so we had little to drink. There was no way to keep clean and the privies were overflowing. The ship stank. The sailors made vulgar remarks to the young girls and we were frightened. The passage was so very long—six weeks—and sickness broke out. It seemed forever. Finally we arrived in Boston harbor. And there a terrible thing happened!"

Maggie stopped talking for a moment. She turned back from the window and Sarah could see tears gathered in her mother's eyes. Maggie brushed them away and plunged ahead with her story. "Health authorities came aboard the ship and examined all the passengers. Rosie was burning with fever, and they tore her from my side, and sent her to the hospital on Deer Island. I never saw her again, your Aunt Rosie, my dear little sister."

"Oh, Mother!" Sarah got up and tearfully threw her arms about Maggie. But Maggie, her head up, her eyes dry now, pulled away, and her voice steadied.

"I went off the ship with the others, pushed we were, like cattle being herded, down the gangway and onto the dock. A man approached me, said he was from the Irish Immigrant Association, and said he had a good job for a likely Irish lass if I wasn't afraid of work. I didn't know what to do. There I was, on the dock of a strange city in a strange country. I knew no one and had no prospects. So I went with him.

"Afterwards I realized what terrible trouble I could have been in. So young and stupid was I. But he took me into the city, to a fancy district with big houses and fenced-in yards, and there delivered me to the door of a huge mansion. 'Clean this one up a bit,' he told the head housekeeper, 'and put some decent clothes on her and she'll make a presentable maid.' He held out his hand and some greenbacks were placed in it. 'There's a good lass,' he said to me. 'Mind yourself now and you'll be having a grand position.' I was an indentured servant. Sold, I was, like a slave.

"And there I worked for seven years," Maggie said as she sat down again on the sofa and looked at Sarah. "It wasn't so bad, really. I had enough to eat and a little room high up in the house. Sunday morning they gave me off to go to Mass, and in the afternoon I could walk in the park across the way. Sometimes I would take the children there for play. It was there I met your father. He was sitting on a park bench, when a ball rolled his way. One of the children ran after it, but it was to me he tossed the ball." Maggie smiled at the memory.

"I had no idea who he was, but he was in the park each day that I was there. We started talking and he told me that he'd been a sailor, captain of a ship out of Boston, and that his crew had deserted in San Francisco Bay to go to the gold mines. With no crew to sail his ship, he'd gone to the mines as well. He was successful. How successful, I wasn't knowing at the time. When he asked me to marry him, I was dumfounded. Your father was Boston gentry. His family lived in one of those big houses about. After those years in California, he'd come home for a visit, and, of course, his family hoped he'd take one of their kind for a bride, not an unlettered Irish servant girl. But it was me he wanted. And so we married despite his family's objections, and our honeymoon was in a stateroom on the

20

ship to Panama. A train took us across that neck of land, and another ship carried us first class to San Francisco. I never dreamed there was such wealth. He installed me as mistress on this grand estate, and all these years I've tried to forget my past and where I came from."

Maggie looked into her daughter eyes. "And now I'm ashamed of myself for not telling you, Sarah, and for spoiling you in the raising."

It was quiet in the big room when Maggie finished her story. Mother and daughter sat very still, looking straight ahead for some minutes. Then Maggie shook her head, stood up, lifted Sarah and took her daughter's face in her two hands. "Be thinking about your own life, girl. Have nothing, you say? You have too much. And you don't appreciate any of it.

"You have a grand husband," Maggie said. "It was you, right here in this very room, pleading with your father and me to bless your marriage. You said he was such a fine, gentle, kind man, so understanding. A man of high principles, righteous and courageous, you said. A brave man, making his own way. He refused to take any help from us when it was offered and you said that was right. You were proud of him and told us that it didn't matter if you were poor, that you two would make it on your own. And he loved music, and he loved you so, and would cherish you, you told us. It mattered not, you insisted, that he was thirteen years older. 'Look, Mother,' you said, 'how much older Father is than you and your marriage worked out wonderfully,' Maggie reminded her.

"And so you were married. And in the church, it was. You're a Catholic and marriage is forever. Be thinking of that, Sarah, and go back there and help that husband of yours." Maggie held her daughter firmly by the shoulders. "And if he wants you to be getting ink on your hands, you be doing it."

CHAPTER THREE

H E'D RECEIVED THE TELEGRAM last evening. It had been delivered to *The Settler* office just before he left to go back to another desperate lonely night at the hotel. "Arriving tomorrow afternoon train. Stop. Sarah." It didn't say "Dear Fred." It didn't end, "Love, Sarah." It didn't tell him if she was coming home to stay, or if it was just to pick up the rest of her things. It didn't tell him anything he really wanted to know. Except that she was coming. That was enough to keep him awake all night.

The next morning, as Fred waited anxiously for the hours to pass until he could go to the train station, George Cosgrove came into the newspaper office with a scowl on his face. He was just dropping by, he said, "for a friendly visit, a little chat, Fred. Let you know what some of the boys are saying around town."

"What's that, George?"

"Well, that you should tone things down a little, Fred. This is still a small town. Maybe we're not quite ready for incorporation. Takes taxes to pay for all those things you're pushing in the paper."

"What are you getting at?" Fred was trying to remain calm. "Lots of people are telling me we need to gravel Broadway, keep down the dust, and fix the sidewalks. And the ladies complain about the drunks coming out of the saloons cussing and fighting. Just last week Missus Jerkins was knocked down in front of the Grand. Luckily she wasn't hurt. Some of the women are afraid to come up town to do their shopping. And all those hogs shouldn't be allowed to run around town on the loose. We need some laws and some enforcement. Don't you agree that we need a constable here, George?"

"Oh, now, Fred, be reasonable," Cosgrove said. "There's nothing here that the sheriff can't handle."

"The sheriff? Holy Jehoshaphat, George! The sheriff is fifty miles away. By the time he'd get here from Salinas, the rowdies could wreck the whole town."

"Now, Fred, take it easy," Cosgrove soothed. Fred knew why he'd been the one sent to talk to him. Cosgrove had a reputation as a smooth one, a great talker. Besides, he owned the largest general merchandise store in town and had a hand in other things, real estate, insurance, investments. Cosgrove always seemed to have money to lend.

"Just let up a bit on pushing incorporation, Fred. Times aren't so good right now. Nobody wants to pay more taxes, you know that. By the way," Cosgrove said, reaching in his pocket and pulling out a sheet of paper, "here's the copy for next week's ad. Usual size."

The "usual size" was Cosgrove's half-page every week in *The Settler,* a big part of the newspaper's revenue. Fred understood, all right. Cosgrove didn't have to say it. His request to "let up a bit," amounted to an order. But the red-headed editor didn't take to such intimidation. He held his temper and managed a weak smile for the departing Cosgrove.

The hour finally came to meet the train, Fred adjusted his tie, pulled on his coat and his derby hat. Filled with conflicting emotions, Fred strode up Broadway toward the depot wondering if Sarah would greet him that derisive sniff. Was she only coming back long enough to pack up everything and leave forever? Or was she coming back to be a loving wife and partner? Fred thought he'd be able to tell by his first glimpse of her. He stood back on the station platform and waited.

Sarah Godfrey was excited. The closer the train rolled toward King City, the more excited she became. She fussed with her hair, re-arranged her hat, smoothed her skirts and pinched some color into her cheeks. In less than an hour she'd be with her husband and she'd make it up to him, make up for all the difficult times she'd caused him, be a real helpmate to him. She'd learn to set type, or run the press, and she'd even sweep up the place, if he wanted her to. And she'd take up the mandolin again, play in his orchestra. Whatever it took to prove to Fred that she truly loved him.

And she'd be a good wife, she told herself. Sarah blushed so red there was no need to pinch her cheeks. She knew she hadn't always pleased him in bed. But she'd try. And she'd learn. And she might even like it. That thought sent another rush of heat through her body.

But would he forgive her? Did he want her back after all? He'd never written and begged her to come home. Well, begging wasn't his style. But could he still love such a selfish, spoiled little girl? *He'll wonder what brought me to my senses. Sometime I'll tell him my mother's story.*

The train whistle jarred Sarah from her reverie and the conductor announced, "King's Station. King's." The train jolted, backed up a bit and came to a hissing, squealing stop. A porter took her bag, set it on the platform and placed the little steps by the car door. Sarah stood in the doorway, anxiously looking up and down the platform.

Fred spotted her first and waved. She gave him a shy, quizzical smile. Fred hurried to help her down the train steps. They stood together on the platform and Sarah bent slightly forward to kiss him. A quick, questioning kiss. The same question was in her deep green eyes.

Fred knew. It was going to be all right. His heart jumped into his throat and he could hardly say the words, "Welcome home, Sarah."

She said it. "I love you, Fred. I missed you."

She put her hand in his and he used his other to pick up her suitcase. Funny, he thought, it felt so heavy when he was carrying it to the train the day she left. Now it felt as light as his heart. They ignored the waiting rig to the Vendome Hotel. They walked hand-in-hand the three blocks of Broadway, nodding and smiling to people they knew. They didn't speak, not even to each other. But they smiled at each other with a new-found intimacy, and when they reached the hotel they went immediately upstairs to their rooms.

Sarah took off her hat and threw it on the bed. Fred threw his bowler there, too. But Sarah gave Fred a sideways smile, and a look from the corner of eyes that were sparkling, and she retrieved the hats from the bed, placing them on a chair. Sarah unpinned her auburn hair and let the long, wavy tresses cascade down her back. She started to unbutton her blouse.

Fred's eyes were on her as he shrugged out of his coat, threw off his vest and fought the knot in his tie. Sarah came into his arms and pressed herself against him. They kissed and Fred knew this was unlike it had ever been before. She wasn't tense, and stiff, all sharp angles. This Sarah was soft and pliable, and melted against him. This was a warm, inviting woman, willing and eager. Fred's spirit soared. He heard her murmuring into his ear how happy she was to be back, how much she'd missed him, how glad she was to be his wife. "And Fred, darling. I want you to teach me to set type."

"Holy Jehoshaphat, Sarah! Not right now."

* * * * *

"Take a rest, Fred. Don't kill yourself." Sarah was inserting the sheets of paper into the press and removing the printed pages as fast as Fred could ink the forms, lock the clamp, and pull down the lever.

"No time, Sarah. Have to keep at it or we'll miss the mails." Fred, working in shirt sleeves, without a tie, stopped long enough to remove his bowler hat, mop his forehead, tug at his sleeve garters, hitch up his trousers, and then went back at it. Now with nearly four hundred subscribers that meant eight hundred impressions, doing two pages at a time on the little Messenger hand press. It was not only physically hard and tiring, it was time consuming.

Fred pulled down the lever to finish the run and they started bundling the papers. He looked at his wife and grinned. Since Sarah's return from San Leandro the Godfreys' marriage had taken a happy turn and so, too, did *The Salinas Valley*

Settler. A better relationship was forming with the business people and the subscription list was growing. Fred and Sarah were finally able to move from their rooms in the Vendome Hotel to a cottage behind the hotel, five rooms that rented for only ten dollars a month. Sarah had learned to hand-set type, and revived her mandolin skills to help fill out the orchestra. And once she let herself, Sarah even enjoyed the trips "to drum up a few subscribers" around the countryside, meeting the people that Fred would then write about in the paper.

"Some day we'll have a regular drum press with a motor," he told Sarah. "But in the meantime, I'll think I'd better hire some muscle on press day. I need to spend more time out on the street."

Each week he'd make his rounds of the town, picking up ad copy, making notes for his local "Chat" column and getting feedback on his editorials. Often he was stopped on the street, or by groups gathered in Cosgrove's Department Store, talking about Fred's latest editorials for local improvements.

"You're right, Fred," George Cosgrove agreed. "We need a volunteer fire department. But we don't have enough water here to do any good."

So Godfrey wrote about the fire-fighting chemicals that were on the market, about ways they could harness what water was available from each private well with storage tanks and pipes, and stressed the serious fire danger to a town of wooden buildings. He estimated the cost of the high insurance rates and the money to be saved with a fire fighting system. And he urged incorporation and a town council, or, at least, formation of a group of concerned citizens who could discuss ideas to make the town better. Fred advocated planting trees along the streets, a sewer system, a high school, a constable, and he regularly wrote in glowing terms about the value of irrigation.

"I read your editorial, Fred," Tito Morales said. "You're right. Someday we'll be ready for those things. But just now we can't afford the taxes."

"Go slowly, Fred," Cosgrove cautioned one day as he sat across from Fred's roll-top desk in *The Settler* office. "It all takes time. People appreciate your ideas, but they're a bit premature, don't you think? Especially a sewer system."

"Holy Jehoshaphat, George. If we want this town to grow we've got to make it desirable for people to live here." Godfrey's face took on its familiar reddish hue as he tried to make his point. "All these damn privies and septic tanks are carbuncles on our community."

"Well, you're talking about a lot of money there, Fred. This little town just doesn't have it. Someday, maybe. By the way," Cosgrove said, "why don't you tone down your editorials about cutting up the big ranchos. The small farmers might like the idea, but the big landowners don't. They're the ones with the money to spend in town. That fellow Josh Gibbons is talking to them, trying to work them up against you, telling them not to come to King City."

"Oh, that guy." Godfrey snorted at the name, waved his hand and shook his head. "I tell you, George, there's something fishy about Gibbons. I hear he's spending money in San Lucas, shipping steers out of there, raising hell at The Mint like he's some big, high-rolling cattleman. He only has a little place back east of Wild Horse Canyon somewhere. That can't be making big money for him."

As Cosgrove left the office, Fred sat at his desk fuming. What the hell was Gibbons up to now? Bad mouthing him, huh? But at least he wasn't coming into King City any more, making trouble. And *The Settler* was running the saloon ads again.

Fred glanced at the proofs on his desk of those Sarah had set this morning. One caught his eye. *Reward of $100 will be paid for information leading to the arrest and conviction of anyone stealing cattle from the Miller and Lux Peachtree Ranch.* That was marked "tf", meaning "till forbidden," a newspaper term for an ad that is scheduled to run indefinitely. Fred had a half column of such ads running in the paper now from the Dunphy Estate, Jake Gamboa, Cleary Ranches, Bill Brinan, Andy

Copley, Breen's Topo and others. Now Henry Miller wanted one.

But he didn't have much time to dwell on it because he had to finish up and hurry. He made a final correction on the proof, spiked it and rushed over to the Blackhawk stables to pick up the rig he'd hired. Fred and Sarah were playing that night for the Harvest Ball in San Lucas so he had to get home and freshen up, load up the instruments, and get on up the road.

It was a warm August evening, not quite dusk and the last vestiges of a red sun still peeked over the coast mountains as Fred, his derby hat set securely against the jolting, guided the blacks along the dusty road toward San Lucas. Sarah, a brown dust coat over her yellow party dress, its hood covering her hair, sat beside him on the buggy seat, worrying about her appearance. She'd just be another member of the orchestra, but that was no reason not to look her best.

"Do you have to hit every bump on the road, Fred," Sarah complained as she tried to file her nails despite the rough ride.

"Don't blame me. Blame our county supervisors," he responded, with a chuckle. "I'll speak to Will Cleary about it tonight."

"Humph," Sarah sniffed. "Maybe he should spend more time supervising and less time giving these big parties. How did he start doing this, anyhow?"

Fred was inwardly amused at his wife. He knew her bite didn't measure up to her bark. "Now Sarah," Fred said, "good thing for our pocketbook he does put on this party." He reined the trotting team around the biggest chuck holes and smiled as he looked over at her. "The Clearys have always been famous for their hospitality. They feed just about everybody that comes along the Long Valley road. Remember how hospitable old Jeremiah and his wife were that time we visited them?"

"Yes, they sure were, Fred." Sarah recalled that Jeremiah had seemed to her to be the epitome of the successful rancher and his wife was a dear. "And Catherine was so nice. She had a brogue just like my mother's. But what about this son of a brogue just like my mother's. But what about this son of theirs and his Harvest Ball? How did this all come about?"

"Well, I heard they used to give a party at the end of harvest up at Jeremiah's place, invited all the employees. But when Will went out on his own and leased that big chunk of the Trescony grant, he became so successful the party just grew." Fred checked the team to a walk and went on with his story. "You know he runs a big custom harvesting business. By the time he invited all the employees and all the farmers he harvests for, I guess he didn't want to leave anybody out. So he put an ad in the paper," Fred said with a laugh, "and invited the whole kit and caboodle. Wasn't room at either his place or the home place, so he rented Bunte's Hall. Will does things up right, I'll tell you. He's very progressive and well liked. And Will's respected. He was elected supervisor in a landslide."

"I guess so," Sarah said with a sniff. "No wonder, if he throws a party for the whole countryside." Then she looked over at her husband and smiled. "And I thought it was just because *The Settler* supported him."

Fred pulled into the main street of San Lucas in front of Bunte's Store where there were already several rigs parked and some saddle horses tied to the hitching rail. He brought the buggy to a halt, but Sarah wasn't ready to get out. She fussed with her hair and then sat there looking at her hands.

"Oh, Fred," she said, holding up her hands for his inspection. "My poor hands, see what playing that mandolin does to my fingers. Just look at those calluses. And I'll never get the ink out from under my finger nails."

Fred took her hands in his and raised them to his lips. He kissed each finger tip in turn. "Yes, Sarah. I see. And I love every one of them, ink and all. And those calluses are very special because you got them for me."

Sarah's frown turned into a radiant smile and she began to help unload the mandolins and banjos and Fred's guitar. The other orchestra members arrived and they all helped carry them upstairs to the hall.

29

CHAPTER FOUR

I F THE WHOLE COUNTRYSIDE wasn't at the Harvest Ball, nobody could tell who was missing. Bunte's hall was crowded, and the dancing was in full swing with schottisches and reels, mazurkas, polkas and waltzes, music to satisfy every taste. Sarah, Fred and the other musicians hardly had a break. But when enough dancers were worn down for a while, the orchestra stopped playing and Sarah had a chance to look around.

"Fred," she asked, "who is that beautiful, blond girl with that tall, lanky fellow over there?"

Fred looked over the crowd of people and located the couple. "That's Tim Cleary, Will's younger brother. He's a tenant farmer on the Brandenstein. Doing well, I hear. And the girl is Amy Barnes. She belongs to that Barnes family, the ones that no one ever sees there in Pine Valley. But I heard she moved to San Francisco. Must be visiting."

"Well, don't let her get too near you," Sarah said in mock warning. "I watched her between dances. She's a flirt, Fred."

He laughed. "Now what would I want with her when I've already got the prettiest girl in all of California?"

Sarah smiled at her husband and then looked again in the direction of Amy Barnes.

Amy was looking up at Tim Cleary, her long eyelashes bordering blue eyes that sparkled in the lamplight. She had a half smile on her full, red lips as she reached up to pat him on the cheek. "Come on, Tim. Let's get some air, let's get away from all these people. I'm positively suffocating."

She took his arm as they left the hall and hurried down the stairs onto the main street of San Lucas and quickly walked away into the shadows. They stopped behind the blacksmith shop and Amy turned to him. Tim pulled her into his arms, her head against his chest, and felt her push against him. He tipped her blond head back and kissed her, softly, lovingly at first, then roughly, hungrily. Amy had her arms around Tim's neck and, with one hand stroked the hair at the back of his head. She twisted her hand in his hair and pulled down his head. Her tongue darted into his mouth. Amy moaned and moved against him.

Tim was breathing hard when they pulled apart. His voice was hoarse with emotion when he could finally speak. "Oh, my God, Amy, Amy. I've missed you so. I love you, Amy."

"Tim, you dear boy, you wrote such beautiful letters. I kept every one."

"Will you stay now, Amy?" He kissed her again and then held her by the shoulders and looked into her eyes. "I'm doing well on the Brandenstein. I wrote you about it. I can afford to build you a big, fine house, and fill it with everything you want. We can take trips to the city, stay at the Palace. Please, will you marry me, Amy?"

Amy put her finger across his lips to stop him. "Shh," she murmured. "I don't want to think right now, Tim. I just want to feel. Hold me." She moved inside his arms, pulled his head down and kissed him again.

Tim had been in love with Amy since she was sixteen and he'd ridden regularly across the hills to Pine Valley from the Cleary place in Long Valley. When she was eighteen, Tim had just filed for his own homestead on the spring in Coyote Canyon, and he asked her to marry him, but she'd refused. "You'll always be a farmer, Tim," Amy had scoffed. "I think you're sweet, but I can't be a farmer's wife. And Coyote Canyon, Tim? You must be joshing. No, I can't stay here. I'm going to the city to live with my aunt."

That was six years ago. Six long, lonely years for Timothy Cleary. But he never stopped loving Amy. He wrote to her regularly, but received only occasional letters in return. They were, however, all signed, *"Love, Amy,"* and that kept hope alive that someday Amy would be his. Tim had taken the Brandenstein lease with the intention of improving his standard of living and had done so over the past few years. He'd written to Amy about his success. And he'd seen her during her infrequent visits to her parents in Pine Valley. She'd let Tim escort her to parties and the local dances, even let him kiss and caress her. But she always laughed and put him off with another kiss when he talked of marriage. Now she was home for a week's visit with her parents and Tim had brought her to the Harvest Ball.

He'd been as happy as he'd ever been in his life, entering Bunte's Hall with this beautiful girl clinging to his arm. And he watched with pride as she whirled around the floor in the arms of the other young men who begged her for a dance. But no matter who she danced with, each time she caught Tim's eye she gave him her dazzling smile. And now they were alone and she was in his arms.

She stayed there, tight against him in the curl of his arm as he guided the horse up the Pine Valley road. Tim turned the horse into the deep shadows by the side of the road and kissed her. Amy strained against him. Then she pulled away, reached for the lap robe and folded it, carefully placing it on the floorboards in the back of the buggy. She rose and stepped across the seat. She knelt on the robe and Tim turned to watch her, puzzled. Amy locked her eyes on his and held her hand out to him. Slowly, he stepped into the back and knelt beside her. Amy smiled at him, sank to the floorboards and gently pulled Tim with her.

An almost unbearable joy and ecstasy filled Tim's entire being as he and Amy made love that night under the stars. It was almost dawn when he drove the buggy into the yard at the Barnes place. As he kissed Amy goodnight and she pressed herself against him, Tim, his voice choked with emotion, asked her again. "Marry me, Amy. I'll make you so happy. You'll never want for a thing."

"You silly boy," she said with a little laugh. "Be sure to write."

Amy's throaty chuckle rang in his ears all the way home to his place on the Brandenstein near San Ardo.

Later that morning Amy was on the northbound train when it pulled out of San Lucas. As she took her seat in the coach she blew a kiss southward in the direction of San Ardo. Then she reached into her purse and took out her wedding ring. She slipped it back onto her finger.

* * * * *

Will Cleary drove a handsome pair of matched grays with his surrey, a spanking new vehicle, black with red trim and red wheels. The wheels flashed in the early morning sun as he took the turn from his lane on the Trescony and put the grays into a trot on the county road. It was about nine miles to San Ardo and he wanted to say hello to his younger brother before Tim left his place on some errand or other.

A big man, not fat, but solid, Will stood five-feet-ten and had been described as a sturdy oak tree. He was only thirty-two, but his brown hair had already turned mostly gray. He had the reputation in this part of the country as a responsible man, a man of his word, and he was a leader. A progressive farmer, Will was among the first to switch from wheat to barley, and was in the forefront of summer fallowing, the practice of farming a plot every other year to increase yield, and his thirty-five sacks to the acre, now in storage in the Trescony granary in San Lucas, held the record.

Will settled his bulk in the surrey's seat, his capable hands, which had been driving and training horses since he was jackrabbit high, managed the team without conscious thought, so his mind was free to wander. He was very pleased with the harvest season just completed, the best ever. He'd used the new Holt combine for the first time, not only for his own seven hundred acres, but also for many farmers on the west side of the Salinas River between San Ardo and King City, a distance of eighteen miles. If they'd get some decent bridges at this end of the county, Will mused, he could be custom harvesting for ranches on the east side, too. But then he'd need another harvester. And, he laughed to himself, he'd better not be cutting his dad out of customers. Will's father, Jeremiah Cleary, had a stationary machine, which did most of the harvesting on the east side of the Salinas River. Tim Cleary ran the harvesting operation for their father, in addition to farming his own lease on the Brandenstein. Will hadn't seen his brother since the Harvest Ball, a month ago.

He shook his head over the memory. If only that Barnes girl hadn't shown up. She always got Tim into such a crazy state. He wished Tim would forget her. My God, she'd been gone five or six years. But she shows up again and Tim acts like he's on loco weed.

He turned the grays into the yard where Tim was living in a little house that went with the farming lease, and was surprised to find Mike Hoalton, the San Ardo carpenter, nailing in some framing on the house and Tim sawing away at a board.

"Good morning, big brother," Tim said, a wide grin of greeting on his face.

"Hi there, young feller. Hello, Mike." Will climbed down from his rig and shook hands with Hoalton. He gave his brother's shoulder a squeeze. Hoalton noticed the obvious affection between the two. But they were as different as brothers could be. Tim was tall, at least six foot one, and thin, with a supple, sinewy look that suggested strength. His hair was black in contrast to his brother's gray. Will wore a suit, minus a tie today, an expensive Stetson and shiny, black, custom-made boots. Tim, as usual, was dressed in bib overalls and hatless.

Tim nodded approvingly at the new surrey. "Fancy outfit you've got there, Will."

"Just bought it." Will glanced at his buggy with pride, then turned back to his brother. "What's going on here?"

"Putting a new room on the house, making it bigger," Tim explained. "Amy will be coming back soon and we'll need more room."

"Oh, I see," Will muttered. "Tim, come over here a minute. There's something I need to talk over with you." He drew his brother aside, over by the parked surrey, out of Hoalton's hearing.

"Look, Tim, I've just got to talk straight to you. Don't waste your life on Amy Barnes. She's not coming back. She's not going to marry you. Hell, she's just been flirting with you all these years." Will took his brother by the shoulders and looked into his eyes. "She's not worth it. Dammit, Tim, you could have just about any girl you want around here, if you'd just forget Amy."

Tim shook him off, anger and hurt in his eyes. "Will, you don't know a damn thing about it. Amy loves me. My God, Will—if you only knew what's between us! All she needs is to get a little of that big city excitement—get it out of her system. Then she'll come back and we'll be married. I just want to have things ready. You'll be the best man at my wedding. You'll see."

Will realized there'd be no convincing his brother of anything when it came to Amy. He turned away and got back into his buggy. "Well, I'd better be getting on, got work to do. Honora would like you to come to dinner anytime your down our way."

Tim nodded. "Thanks. I'll be there soon. Tell her hello. I miss seeing her and the kids."

Will snapped the reins and put the team into a quick trot out of the yard. "Good luck," he called back.

Tim watched his brother disappear down the road, then went back to his carpentry, quickly shrugging off whatever little seeds of doubt Will's words had planted. He'd show his brother. He'd show everyone. He and Amy had a future together.

CHAPTER FIVE

"I'LL BE OUT ON THE STREET A WHILE," Fred called to Sarah, who was busy at the type case. She waved to him and said, "Be back in an hour or so. I have do the shopping or we won't have anything for supper."

Fred tucked a note pad in his pocket and checked for a pencil. It was time to make his rounds, see if he could collect a few ads for next week's paper. Fred crossed Broadway and silently cussed the dust. He stepped up on the wooden sidewalk in front of the Peerless just as the door swung open. Fred recognized Jasper Riley, one of the Miller and Lux ranch hands.

"Hello, there, Mister Godfrey," the young cowboy said. "Big news for your paper, huh?"

Fred hated to admit he didn't always know all the news. But this one had him stumped. "What's that, Jasper?"

"Oh, didn't you know? Everyone's talking about it. Big cattle rustling deal back of Wild Horse. Caught some guy dead to rights."

"Holy Jehoshaphat!"

Fred whipped out his notepad and wrote furiously as Jasper gave him whatever information he knew. Then Fred went off to check the facts with more reliable sources. Within an hour he had the story pieced together and was back at the office to get it into type.

* * * * *

Seamus Cleary sat on his sorrel mare atop a ridge and tried to figure out the land below him. He didn't know this country, somewhere high up between Wild Horse and Lonoak. He was there with Buck O'Keefe to help gather cattle. Buck was his brother-in-law, married to his sister, Kitty, and he'd do anything Buck told him. Buck was his friend and it wasn't easy for Seamus to make friends. He was a thirty-year-old man whose mind had stopped somewhere around the age of ten when the boy had been near death with scarlet fever. Although his emotions were childlike, he was a good cowboy and worked hard and Buck had taken him under his wing.

Buck had rousted him out way early this morning, and they'd saddled up by lamp light, and ridden for hours before it was even dawn. About the time the sun showed up behind them they'd met a bunch of men, and Buck had talked things over with them. They split up to make some wide sweeps, and bring the cattle they found back to the center for a hold.

Seamus had done this lots of times, so when they split off and Buck had pointed him in this direction, he knew just what to do. But now he wasn't so sure. This was strange country, not a bit like Long Valley. Seamus thought he'd rather be home playing with Bucky, making sling shots, or kicking the can, or playing mumbly peg the way they used to do. But Bucky didn't want to do that kind of stuff any more, said he was too old for kid stuff. But Seamus still liked it. No use trying to play with his niece, Julie, any more either. She said those games weren't ladylike, and when she did play she always wanted him to pretend he was daddy to her dolls. Nuts to that. Buck told him he was thirty years old and had man's work to do.

Seamus headed down a long draw. Maybe there'll be some cattle down here some place, he thought. He wondered where Buck was. The draw got steeper and steeper, and his sorrel mare had to slide, but she was a good one to keep her feet under her in rough country. Suddenly there was a brush patch, and on the other side it dropped right off, a cliff. And below that was a little valley filled with cattle.

Gee whiz, that's a big bunch, Seamus thought. And how would he get down there? And how would he get that bunch started back toward the holding place? Where exactly was the holding place from here?

There were so many steers Seamus couldn't count them. But then, he never was much for keeping a good count. But there must be a zillion and all steers. Steers? Where are all the cows and calves? They must have cows and calves in this country. But he couldn't spot any. Seamus was puzzled. Wonder why these are just steers?

Seamus was trying to figure out a way to work his horse down below the bunch of steers, and a way to drive them out of that little valley, when he noticed something else strange. That roan steer. The one with the right horn tipped down. What was he doing there?

That was a Cleary steer! Seamus was sure of it. He'd seen that steer many times. Buck said it was a three-year-old, and ready to ship, but it was a wild sucker, and when it turned back they couldn't find it again. That happened back at the head of Long Valley, way up toward Peachtree. So what was it doing way over here?

Seamus wrinkled his brow, trying to decide what to do. Guess he'd better go tell Buck. Turning his horse, he climbed out of the draw and headed off looking for his brother-in-law.

"Are you sure, Seamus?" Buck asked skeptically. "You saw our big roan steer, or one just like it? Did you see our brand?"

"Naw, I wasn't close enough to read any brands. But honest, Buck. I know that steer." Seamus got off his horse to reset his saddle, which had slipped back from the steep climb.

"Okay then," Buck agreed. "Let's go find some of the other fellows, and let 'em know what we're doing, and go have a look. Think you can find your way back there?"

Seamus frowned, thought a minute and nodded. "Sure, Buck. We can follow my tracks, if you'll help me."

The sun was high up and the horses were sweating as Seamus and Buck topped out above the cliff, and looked down on the cattle below. They were all laying down, most of them in what shade they could find, and it was hard to tell anything from high up. Buck put his black gelding on a narrow trail around the side of the canyon and Seamus followed as they worked on down onto the flat. That's when Buck spotted the big roan steer.

"By God, Seamus, you're right!" he exclaimed. "That's our steer. He sure as hell drifted a long way."

The cattle were beginning to get to their feet, facing the two horsemen, and then started milling around as Buck and Seamus rode closer. Buck noted there were more than a hundred-fifty head of steers in the canyon. Sorta boxed in, too. He saw fencing below and wondered why it was there. Buck stopped his horse and squinted against the hot sun, looking over the brands. All had Josh Gibbons' double box arrow. Buck edged around to where he could see the left hip of the roan steer.

It should have had a quarter circle triangle, the Cleary brand. But that wasn't what he saw. Damn if there wasn't a full circle around the triangle. The brand didn't look new, though. None of them did. Something funny was going on here, Buck decided. He needed a real look.

"Come on, Seamus, let's dab onto that old roan steer," he called out as he uncoiled his *riata*, and built a loop. Seamus followed as Buck swung in behind the steer, which ran off looking for a hiding hole. There wasn't any, and a quick chase down the side of the box canyon brought Buck's horse right up on the steer. His loop settled over the horns, and the stout black turned off, bringing the animal up short. The big steer swung around to face the sliding horse. Seamus came in behind, and threw his loop on the ground, just in front of the steer's hind feet. As they crossed over, Seamus deftly lifted the rope, picking up both feet, and took his turns.

"Good shot, Seamus," Buck shouted. "Hold him tight." Buck stepped off his black, and the horse backed and strained, keeping the rope tight, while Seamus backed his mare. She planted her front feet and hunkered down to stretch the big, bellowing steer. Finally, he toppled over, left side up, fortunately. Buck was on him in a second, and pulled out his pocket knife. He deftly scraped the hair off the brand. There underneath was the quarter circle triangle, an old scar.

"Well, I'll be damned," Buck muttered. He remounted, and moved his horse forward, easing up on the rope. Seamus did the same, and the steer shook off the loops and ran toward the the herd.

"Let's check another one," Buck said. They dropped a second steer, and Buck again scraped off the hair, and found a perfect double H underneath. The H H belonged to Miller and Lux and it, too, had been altered into the double box arrow, Josh Gibbons' brand.

He must be holding these steers here, planning to sell them as his own, Buck decided. But what the hell was he going to do with a full circle triangle? That Cleary steer must have drifted over onto the Peachtree, and mixed in with Miller and Lux cattle. Gibbons' men probably picked him up when they drove off a bunch and never noticed until they branded, Buck figured. If they'd just turned our steer loose, they might have gotten away with this. Just shows what greed will do.

"What's it all about, huh, Buck?"

Seamus didn't understand, so Buck, always patient with him, carefully explained. "They drove these Miller and Lux cattle off the Peachtree Ranch, and they changed the brands, used a running iron to make it look like the Gibbons brand, just burned the hair so the brands wouldn't scab and look new. They picked up that roan and changed our brand, too. Good thing you spotted it. Good job, Seamus."

Seamus grinned his little boy grin. He was proud as could be when Buck said stuff like that.

Buck left Seamus to watch the cattle while he rode back to bring over some of the other men as witnesses. One of them headed cross country for King City to telegraph the sheriff. The next day Buck and a few of the hands, including the rep from Miller and Lux, met Sheriff John Matthews when the morning train rolled into the King City station. They had a horse already saddled for him, and they headed out for the canyon where Seamus had found the stolen cattle.

The men cut out a couple of steers and threw them and the sheriff bent over to read the altered brand. He straightened up and sadly shook his head. "Sure as hell," he agreed. "Let's go get 'em. But first I have to deputize you boys. Raise your right hands."

With Buck and Matthews in the lead, they headed out for Gibbons' place, an old *adobe* on the little ranch just a half hour ride away. As they trotted up, they saw two men working afoot in the corral, and another was fixing the axle on an old buggy propped up in front of the house. "Who are you?" Matthews asked in a flat voice.

The man looked up and spotted the star. "Jim Riggleman," he said. "What you want with me, sheriff?"

"Don't know," was the laconic answer. "Looking for Gibbons right now."

Riggleman jerked a thumb in the direction of the house. Matthews motioned for the others to keep an eye on Riggleman and the men in the corral, who had come over to the fence to see what was going on. "You fellows all stay put right where you are," Matthews quietly ordered. Then, in a loud voice, he called out, "Hey, Gibbons. It's the law! Come on out."

A moment later Josh Gibbons appeared at the door. Unarmed, he stepped onto the porch and greeted the visitors. "Hello there, sheriff. What can I do for you?"

"You're under arrest for stealing Double H cattle," Matthews declared vehemently.

"What? Not me, sheriff." Gibbons feigned surprise. His voice remained calm, conciliatory. "There's some mistake. I don't know anything about any stolen cattle. I just have this little place here. Farm a bit, run a few cows."

"Hah!" Matthews snorted. "If this is such a little place, how come you have all this help around?"

"That's it. Must be them." Gibbons pointed to the ranch hands. "If anybody stole any steers, it must be them."

"Steers, huh?" Matthews retorted. "How'd you know they were steers? Nobody mentioned any steers," he said, looking sideways at Buck and the men with him. "Did they? Any of you mention steers?" Buck and the others shook their heads as Matthews kept his eyes on the man on the front porch. "Cut the bullshit, Gibbons, and put up your hands."

Gibbons suddenly became frantic, glanced around into the house, and then started back through the door. Matthews pulled out his big Colt and let loose one shot. It crashed into the door frame. Splinters flew. Gibbons stood stock still.

He put up his hands and stepped down off the porch. "It was them," he cried. "They did it!" He pointed toward the cowboys at the fence, and to Riggleman standing stock still by the buggy. "They forced me to let them use this ranch. They threatened me. I had nothing to do with it." His voice became a pathetic whine.

"Why you dirty bastard," Riggleman yelled back. "You hired us on for this! You said it was easy, so many cattle around that Miller and Lux didn't even know how many they had. Some other ranchers, too. That's why you bought this place. You told us all about it, how you been getting away with this for years. You thought you were so damn smart!"

Matthews turned his pistol on the three at the fence and waved them toward him. They climbed over slowly and stood in front of him, all obviously hard cases, but with hands raised to show they had no weapons. One of them spit in the direction of the porch. "Gibbons, you son of a bitch. We're not taking any rap without you. You're the boss of this crap-up," he shouted. Just then a fourth rough-looking hand came riding into the yard.

"Step down and join the party," Matthews ordered. He cuffed Gibbons and tightly tied three of the cowboys. "Keep your eyes on these bastards," he instructed Buck, handing him the Colt. Matthews took the fourth cowboy aside. "You show me what you used for a running iron," he demanded. When he'd located the iron for evidence, all five were mounted, hands behind them, and on their way across the hills to King City.

Josh Gibbons and his accomplices were loaded aboard the northbound train out of King City that evening, headed for the county jail in Salinas. Even as they were being boarded, Gibbons remained defiant, shouting his innocence on the station platform, trying to put the blame on his hired hands and vowing to get the sheriff for this outrage.

Fred Godfrey wrote it all down. Cattle thieves. Not just rowdies. Real crooks. And, evidently, Gibbons had been getting away with this for years, but only a few head now and then. But he'd gotten greedy and went after a huge herd. And he'd become careless.

So Josh Gibbons is a crook, thought Fred. *Holy Jehoshaphat, I knew it all the time.* He finished writing his story and gave it to Sarah to set. He'd included a good plug for Seamus Cleary, the hard-working cowboy with the mind of a ten year old. *Settler* readers would know Seamus was a hero. Fred closed up his notebook and sat at his desk, grinning.

CHAPTER SIX

EARLY ONE MORNING, after the addition to his house was finished, Tim Cleary hitched up and drove in to San Ardo. He
needed a few supplies and would pick up his mail. He tied up
at the corner of Main and Jolon streets and entered the store.

"How's it going, Tim?" The owner, Harry Gimble, greeted
him.

"Good enough, Harry. Here's a list of a few things I need,"
Tim said, handing him a sheet of paper. "I'll be right back. Just
going over to the post office."

Tim accepted his handful of mail from the postal clerk, sorting it as he walked back outside to his buggy. He went through
a week's collection of bills and circulars then came across an
envelope postmarked from Salinas, but with no return
address. He ripped it open and found a clipping inside. It was
from the society page of the *San Francisco Examiner,* dated
March 23, 1891. Curious, Tim thought, turning it over in his
hands. Why would someone send me this? And then he saw the
photo and the headline. It sprang off the page and stabbed him
in the heart.

*Miss Amy Barnes Becomes Bride of Mr. Michael Vincent
Fabray —*

*Gala Wedding of Season — Hundreds of Guests — Bride
Beautiful*

And there, two columns wide, was a photo of Amy, *his Amy,*
all in white, her lovely face framed by the lifted bridal veil, her
lips parted to receive the kiss of her new husband.

Tim was staggered. His knees felt weak and his heart pounded. It wasn't possible. A mistake, his frantic mind decided. It
had to be a mistake. Or a joke. Somebody must have made up
this elaborate joke. He turned the clipping over again and
stared at the date, March 6, 1891, more than six months *before*
the Harvest Ball! And then he noticed the handwritten message scribbled in the margin, "You should know. A friend."

Tim was shaking so badly he could hardly hold the clipping. Tears clouded his eyes and he could barely read. *Miss Amy Barnes, the talented and lovely niece of the socially prominent Mr. and Mrs. Elbert Whitney, became the bride of Mr. Michael Vincent Fabray III, heir to the Fabray Iron Works of this city and mining interests in Nevada. The wedding was performed in Grace Episcopal Church by the Episcopal Bishop of California, the Right Reverend William I. Kip, before hundreds of guests, all of them leaders of Bay Area society.*

Miss Barnes, radiantly beautiful in her wedding gown of slipper satin, with an overskirt of antique lace, entered the church on the arm of her uncle, the Honorable Mr. Whitney, who gave her away. She paced the aisle to the traditional strains of Richard Wagner's Wedding March from his opera, Lohengrin, preceded by ten lovely attendants, her long train carried by two charming children, Adeline and Georgette du Bonnet, daughters of the renowned Gregori du Bonnets of Atherton — Tim could read no more. He crumpled the clipping and threw it violently to the floorboard of the buggy.

Stunned, he stood there for many minutes. Then he reached in and retrieved the clipping. He smoothed it and slowly refolded it. He returned it to the envelope, and placed it in his pocket. Tim wiped his eyes and stared off into space. No, he thought, no. He said aloud, "No! It can't be. She loves me." He stayed there, leaning against the buggy for a long time.

Passers-by hailed him, "Hi, Tim." "Good morning, Cleary." "How you doing, Tim?" When he didn't respond, they looked at him curiously, puzzled that this usually friendly man seemed so preoccupied.

Finally, Tim gathered himself and went back into the general store. Gimble nodded to him. "There's your order, all put up," he said. "I put it on your bill."

Tim stared blankly at Harry Gimble for a moment, it was almost as if he'd never seen him before. Then, in a barely audible voice, he said, "Give me a case of whiskey. Add it to the bill."

"What's your brand?" Gimble asked. Tim Cleary waved his hand to indicate it didn't matter.

* * * * *

It was more than a month later, after the first rain, that Will Cleary ran into Meyer Brandenstein in San Ardo. "Say there, Will, what's become of your brother?" Brandenstein asked with concern.

"Timothy? I haven't seen him lately. Why do you ask?"

"He hasn't been around. He isn't working up his ground. I stopped by the place, but he wasn't there, horses all turned out, house empty. Did he go somewhere."

"I'll be damned," Will said. "I'll sure find out."

Will had a good idea where to look for Tim. He headed north out of San Ardo, and turned right up the Pine Valley road, his grays trotting at a fast clip. Tim was probably working on the cabin on his homestead. He hadn't spent much time there, but he'd finished the necessary improvements and proved up last year. If he wasn't there, Will didn't know where to find him.

The narrow road, just seldom-used wheel tracks, from the upper end of Pine Valley, cut across Jeremiah Cleary's land, where cows with young calves were grazing. At the end of it, by the boxed spring, stood Tim's one-room cabin.

It was just past noon when Will reached it. Tim was sitting on the stoop, watching his brother come up the canyon. "Well, hello there, Brother Will. How the hell are you?" Tim's greeting was too effusive. Getting unsteadily to his feet, he bowed deeply and gestured around him. "What brings you way up here?"

He picked up the bottle from the steps beside him, and waved it at Will. "Come on up. Have a seat. Have a snort."

Will shook his head. "Too early in the day for me, Tim. Should be for you, too. What the hell is going on?"

"Whaddya mean, what's going on? I'm just sitting here contemplating my domain, having a quiet, little drink. That's

46

"Whaddya mean, what's going on? I'm just sitting here contemplating my domain, having a quiet, little drink. That's what's going on."

"Come on, Tim. You know what I mean." Will tried to control his growing anger at his brother. "I saw Brandenstein this morning. He's worried about you. Said you hadn't started working up your ground. Wonders if you're going to plant now that it's rained a bit."

"Oh, worried about me, is he?" Tim retorted. "If he doesn't like the way I farm he can get another tenant." Tim took another big swig from his bottle. "You can tell him that for me. To hell with him. To hell with farming. To hell with everybody!"

"Tim, what's the matter? What's gone wrong?" Will asked.

"None of your damn business." Tim's boozy eyes narrowed. "I'm tired of you always fussing over me. Think you're some kinda mother hen. If you're not going to have a drink with me, get the hell out! I can take care of myself."

Will stared back at his brother, but said nothing. He sadly returned to his rig and drove off slowly down the canyon. This must have something to do with Amy Barnes, he thought. That had to be it.

* * * * *

Amy Barnes Fabray stepped from her huge porcelain tub and stretched like a cat. She moved across the room, her wet, naked body dripping on the thick Persian rug, to stand in front of her full length mirror. The image she saw pleased her from her tiny feet and long tapered legs ending in a triangle of soft blond hair below her flat stomach to the swelling roundness of her hips, narrow waist, and full, upthrust breasts, the nipples a deep pink from the hot bath. She shook out her long, luxurious hair and ran her fingers through it, then cupped her breasts and smiled at herself in the mirror.

Amy ran her hands down the curve of her hips and across her flat stomach. She studied her image in the mirror with a critical eye. No, she decided. If she was two months pregnant it certainly didn't show.

But she was sure she was pregnant. She caught her under-lip with her bright white teeth and frowned. She'd missed her monthly period twice now since the Harvest Ball. Then she smiled remembering the surprised, silly look on Tim Cleary's face when she invited him to lie down beside her in the back of the buggy. Her patient, ever-adoring Tim never expected that much from her. Amy chuckled recalling his fumbling, his haste and his ardor. "Poor Tim!" she told the mirror, "That little taste of heaven will just have to hold him."

But she would love to see his face if he ever learned he'd fathered her child. And Amy had no doubt about that. Her husband, Michael Vincent Fabray III, had been on an extended business trip visiting the family mining interests in Colorado and Nevada. He'd been gone since before her escapade at the Harvest Ball and he wouldn't be back for yet another week.

Amy smiled again. Oh, won't he be pleased by the loving she would give him when he returned. He'd never guess. Not Michael Vincent Fabray the Third. He'd be so sure his absence had made her heart grow fonder. Amy laughed outright. She knew how to handle him, the pitiful goose. She wasn't worried!

She tossed her long, blond hair again and reached for a robe. Then she pulled the bell chord and sat at her dressing table. When her personal maid answered she commanded, "You may brush my hair."

CHAPTER SEVEN

A<small>S FAR AS</small> F<small>RED</small> G<small>ODFREY</small> <small>WAS CONCERNED</small>, there were only two major events in 1894. One made front page headlines in *The Settler*. The other was a small item on page three. The headlines went to Will Cleary, who was re-elected county supervisor by an overwhelming majority to represent the fourth district of Monterey County, an area south of King City. Fred thought Will had done a good job and deserved re-election and had said so often in his editorials. But the item on page three was the one that burst the editor's buttons. *Editor Godfrey is walking on air these days. The reason is Millicent Virginia Godfrey, six pounds, four ounces, born to Mrs. Godfrey at the family home Wednesday last with Doc Brumwell in attendance. Mother and baby are doing fine, and Doc says the father is going to pull through.*

It wasn't long before Sarah was back in the shop, typestick in hand and baby Millie in a rocker beside the type case. The couple resumed their trips into the country, with Millie sleeping peacefully, lulled by the rocking motion of the buggy. Fred, who doted on his baby daughter, would laughingly suggest a buggy ride whenever she started to cry.

One weekend they'd been invited to a picnic in Lockwood, which was a few miles south of King City in the coast mountains. It would have been a wonderful day, except Millie was colicky and cried all afternoon, but Fred made the trip pay off by signing up many of the farmers for newspaper subscriptions. He wrote about the day in the next edition of *The Settler*.

The hardy pioneers of Lockwood Valley brought with them from their native Island of Fohr, Germany, the jovial social life of their homeland. Sunday they treated the editor and his family to a festive picnic. Served on tables set out-of-doors, under great, shady oaks, were many delicacies, and also an abundance of solid, delicious German food, enough to satisfy the entire populace with plenty remaining. Here and there among

49

*the tables were stationed barrels of beer, and placed conve-
niently at hand were an assortment of gaily-decorated beer
steins inviting all to drink their fill. They sang the songs and
did the dances of their homeland some 6,000 miles away, and
managed to prevail upon the editor and his wife to join in the
fun. We are indebted to the Paulsen, Wollesen, Heinsen,
Johnsen, and Martinus families, and many others, for their
convivial demonstrations of hospitality.*

Sarah sniffed as she typeset this. Fred made it all sound
wonderful, but he hadn't been the one to deal with a crying
baby all day. Nor was she all that thrilled to spend the day in
company with so many foreigners.

As soon as the paper was printed, Fred carried the bundled
newspapers to the post office for distribution the next morning. *The Settler* circulation had grown so much that now it took
him several trips to carry all the papers. Fred was on his way
back up Broadway when he heard the cry, "Fire!"

He looked around for some sign of the blaze. But all seemed
normal along the street. And then he saw it, to the north, a
black cloud boiling up from the grain field that bordered King
City. And he could smell the smoke.

People were running in every direction now, and yelling.

"My God, it's burning this way!" "It'll wipe out the town!"
"What'll we do?" "Get everybody out of the buildings!"
Everyone was shouting orders. King City was suddenly in
chaos.

Fred ran into the newspaper office and grabbed a frightened
Sarah. "Get Millie. Stay out of the buildings. Be ready to run
for it!"

Then he dashed for Ellis Street, joining scores of other anxious men from Broadway. Ellis was on the north edge of town,
which faced the coming fire. What Fred Godfrey saw sent chills
up his spine. Smoke billowed up about a mile away from the
grain field. Great gray and black clouds filled the sky. Even at
this distance he could see flames licking at the standing
wheat. They were fanned by the north wind, pushing the fire

wheat. They were fanned by the north wind, pushing the fire straight toward town.

Panic and pandemonium was spreading fast. People screamed and shouted to one another, but no one was in charge. Fred didn't know what to do, either. But they had to do something, somehow to try to save the town. All its wooden buildings stood in the path of the rapidly approaching fire.

"You men over there!" The call rang out with authority and got attention. It was Bob Irwin, a man Fred knew well, who shouted, "One of you run over to the milling company and tell Steinbeck to send every empty sack he has in the place. You others spread out through town and get somebody stationed at every well." He pointed to a young livery stable hand, "Johnny, get some rigs hitched up. Start hauling water over this way in whatever you can find." He sprinted off toward the Blackhawk Stable.

Fred, too, ran as fast as he could to the other side of town, to Pearl Street, where he found Bill Curran, the town's new constable, a close friend and neighbor. Together they organized the residents to haul water up out of their wells and store it in barrels, buckets, whatever they could find. Women and children joined in running the winches, hauling on the ropes, working the pump handles, raising the precious water from the wells. Johnny drove up with a wagon and everyone began loading the barrels and buckets. Some others quickly got the idea and hitched up wagons and buggies to carry water. As they worked, they kept nervously glancing toward the giant cloud of gray smoke, growing and spreading over the town.

Fred ran as fast as he could back across town to Ellis Street. There was a line of men, and some women, spread out along the street facing the fire. Al Carlson was organizing a back fire, a tricky thing against the prevailing wind. Some others had arrived with plows and harrows, and worked feverishly, driving their teams back and forth trying to create a fire break. Thank God, Fred thought, it wasn't later in the afternoon. By then the wind would be raging and it would be impossible.

then the wind would be raging and it would be impossible. There'd be a firestorm and the town would be lost for sure.

The people on the fire line were being handed wet sacks, and the water was starting to arrive from all parts of town. Every one of the city's forty-three wells was in use and, although half the water splashed out as it was jounced around by the jolting wagons, enough arrived to wet the sacks. They advanced on the fire.

Fred used his coat to fight the flames until it was a shredded crisp, and somebody handed him a wet sack. He beat it against the advancing flames. He swung it again and again until it smoldered from the blaze. And then somebody handed him a new one, freshly wet, and he continued. Still the fire advanced, slowly, but steadily, unwavering in its purpose, like a dreadful tide about to engulf the vulnerable town in its destructive path.

Sweat poured from every part of Fred's body. His clothes were soaked with it, but still sparks ignited and burned holes in his pants and his shirt. Now his breath came in harsh gasps, his throat was raw from smoke, and his eyes stung. Around him were many others, blackened by the burning chaff flying in the wind, and hardly discernible through the dense smoke. Fred couldn't even make out the person swinging a sack just next to him. He blinked his smarting eyes, peered into the smoky haze and recognized his wife.

"Sarah, Sarah — !" he shouted over the noise of the crackling blaze. "What the hell are you doing here? Where's Millie?"

"She's safe. I left her with Missus Curran!" Sarah shouted back. Her face was smudged with charcoal, her dress was burnt, her long hair was singed, flying wildly about her head, but she kept up a steady beat with her sack. Fred was never more proud of her.

But as the group worked they had to keep falling back as the fire made its steady advance. It was now only a hundred yards from the city's edge. Suddenly, Fred felt a fierce heat behind them. Were they caught between two blazes? He looked behind and saw Carlson's back-firing group setting small fires, moving them about, using the areas being hurriedly plowed, pitting one blaze against the other, fighting the wind, engulfed in smoke, and then appearing out of it, apparitions.

Fred and Sarah, and the others in the long line, had their backs against these new fires. Soon they were retreating into a burned-over area and began frantically beating their sacks against the back fires to keep them from encroaching on the outbuildings along Ellis Street.

Heads down, sacks swinging, arms aching, the exhausted fire fighters were startled out of their rhythm by cheering. A great yell of jubilation swelled from hundreds of throats. Fred and Sarah straightened up, rubbed their aching backs, and looked around. The fire was burning itself out, taking last, feeble licks at the edges of the field. The great fiery monster was dying. And King City was saved.

The next day an exhausted Fred Godfrey sat at his roll-top desk, just staring blankly at the papers piled there. He was too tired to do anything else. Sarah had stayed home with Millie. Typesetting could wait. He looked up as the front door opened and in came George Cosgrove, smiling.

"Fred, you look all done in."

"Don't we all?" Fred grinned back at him.

"Well, they must have lost about eight hundred acres of wheat, but we've sure got one helluva fire break now north of town. How'd it start?"

"Harvester," Fred said. "I talked to the foreman. Must have been sparks from the chaff they were burning for the steam engine."

"Close call." Cosgrove paused. "Fred, the boys and I were talking this morning, and we'd like you to put a notice in the paper next week. We're calling a mass meeting at the Opera House on Friday night. Bob Irwin and Al Carlson, and some of the others think it would be a good idea to form a volunteer fire department. What do you think?"

Fred looked up at Cosgrove, careful to hide his real feelings. "Holy Jehoshaphat, George. Now that's a great idea!"

"Look forward to seeing you there, Fred," Cosgrove said as he left the newspaper office.

Fred smiled wryly to himself. Hope it doesn't take another near disaster before they get around to a sewer system, he thought. But he knew better than to expect improvements to happen soon.

CHAPTER EIGHT

ST. JOHN'S CATHOLIC CHURCH WAS FULL that warm February day in 1899. Neighbors had come from ranches in every canyon and valley for twenty miles around, and all the townspeople and Cleary employees, the cowboys and harvest hands, were there. All had come to pay their last respects to Catherine Cleary, sixty-six-year-old wife of Jeremiah Cleary and matriarch of the Cleary family.

Fred Godfrey joined Sarah in her pew, just behind the first three benches, which were saved for the Cleary family. Fred, who wasn't Catholic, didn't usually go to church, except for Christmas, Easter, weddings and funerals. But Sarah never missed. Each Sunday would find her there, in the fourth pew on the right side, with five-year-old Millie, her honey-brown hair caught in tight braids, a starched dress of calico print, and Bobby, now three years old, scrubbed clean of his usual grime, even his red hair combed, and in the knickers he hated. But the children weren't with them today for Mrs. Cleary's funeral. They'd been left in the care of Mrs. Curran.

They all stood as the pastor, Father Garriga, entered the church with Jeremiah's son, Father Dan Cleary of San Francisco, followed by the altar boys, the pall bearers with the casket, and the bereaved family. Jeremiah walked alone behind the casket. Tall and ramrod straight, he carried his seventy-three years well. A lean man with a full head of gray hair, he stared grimly ahead, looking at no one, lost somewhere deep inside himself. Behind him came Will Cleary with his wife, Honora, and their daughters, Mary and Nora, now young women, and the boys, Patrick and Matthew, called Spud, nicknamed by his grandfather when Jeremiah found him as a baby gnawing on a potato. "It must be the Irish in him," Jeremiah had said with a chuckle. Now the boys, usually hellraisers, were quiet and subdued for their grandmother's funeral.

Seamus walked down the aisle, tears pouring from his eyes, looking like a little boy who realized his mama had left and was never coming back. The eldest daughter, Kitty, in her mourning black, still beautiful behind her veil, held his arm and with them came her husband, Buck O'Keefe, also trying to comfort Seamus. Their children, Bucky and Julie, followed. And then came the rest of the Cleary family, Jeremiah's other daughters, Annie Phillips and Peggy Carrigan, with their husbands and children, and Connie Cleary Baxter, a cousin who had been raised by the Clearys, married to a wealthy San Francisco lawyer.

The only Cleary missing was Timothy. Three years earlier he'd headed for the gold mines of Alaska and no one had heard from him since. Will and Jeremiah had tried to talk him out of going when the news of the gold strike first reached California in 1896, but now that Will thought about it, he decided Tim was better off up there doing something, rather than sitting in Coyote Canyon grieving over his loss of Amy Barnes.

All was quiet in the church as the two priests prepared to celebrate the Requiem Mass. Fred was always amazed that there was so little wailing and crying at these Catholic funerals. Perhaps they got it all out beforehand, particularly the Irish with their wakes, he thought. Perhaps there was something to this faith that gave them so much solace. Fred wondered and planned to look into it more deeply. Someday.

"*Dominus vobiscum,*" Father Dan intoned, turning to the congregation. "The Lord be with you." He saw his father kneeling in the front, controlling his emotions with a mighty effort, his features drawn in tight, lips moving in silent prayer, making the response "and with thy spirit" in Latin, *Et cum spiritu tuo.*

Jeremiah was following the Mass by rote, but his mind wasn't on it. He was thinking of Catherine's last day, of the stroke that struck her down as she appeared in the best of health. He'd found her unconscious on the kitchen floor. They'd sent for Doc Brumwell, who came out from King City as quickly as he could. But there wasn't anything he could do.

Catherine had regained consciousness, but she couldn't talk. Her lips were drawn up in a horrible grimace and she couldn't move her arms or legs. Her blue eyes moved, though. They followed Jeremiah wherever he went around the bedroom. When he held her hand and called her "Cauth darlin'," he was sure she tried to smile with her eyes.

Doc Brumwell left some medicine and Jeremiah had trouble giving it to her. But he insisted on doing it himself, though it dribbled down her chin, and he had to massage her throat to help her swallow. He lay down beside her and held her through the night. He felt her shudder, and then grow cold in his arms.

He stayed there, beside her, holding her, until dawn. And then he said a prayer of thanksgiving. "Thank you, Lord, for taking her. She'd not want to be staying here as she was." Then he got up, gently laid her back on the bed, and kissed her one last time. "Ah, Cauth, Cauth darlin. It's a grand girl you were." Then he went outside, by the corral, to let go of his grief.

Mass was over and they were leaving the church, filing out as they had entered, onto Bassett street. Jeremiah climbed into the buggy with Will and Honora and the rest followed, some in buggies or buckboards, some on horseback, up Russ Street to Broadway and down toward the river to the cemetery. Jeremiah wanted it over, but he knew even after the last shovels full of dirt had covered her up, it wouldn't be over. There'd be a time for condolences and handshaking and then folks would all come out to the ranch. He'd hear it over and over again, what a wonderful woman she'd been. He knew that. Oh, how he knew that.

* * * * *

After the funeral they all stood around in the cemetery in little groups, visiting—the women spoke of illnesses such as Sadie Conway's boy, who'd caught malaria in the Army in Cuba and nearly died, and they talked of coming weddings and of new babies. They especially enjoyed hearing about new babies at the time of a funeral. The men spoke of the peace treaty with Spain and thought some of the local boys would be coming home soon. And they talked of horses and cattle, of crops and the weather. Always the weather.

This February seemed more like late summer than late winter and they were all worried about it. There hadn't been any real winter yet. Little rain had fallen and that had been a month earlier. Grass was short in the hills. Early rains had started it, but now it was already starting to turn brown. If it didn't rain soon there'd be scant feed for the cattle and the grain crops were already struggling.

Nels Svensen, a San Lucas farmer in his bib overalls and holding a goose bone, stood in the center of one group. "Well Nels, when's it going to rain?" Fred asked as he stepped into the circle of ranchers.

"Right after this little dry spell," Svensen cackled, pleased with himself for dredging up that old joke.

"Come on, Nels. Don't give us that one. Is this another dry year like ninety-four? We had less than five inches back then. So far this season all we've had is a little over three inches. What's your goose tell us?"

"Tell you what, Fred, you can put it in the paper that it's going to rain within a week. See there," he said, indicating the markings on the goose bone. They all craned their necks to look where Nels was pointing. "Yep, stake my reputation on it!"

"Well, that's good news, Nels," Fred said. "I'll quote you in this week's paper. I'd better be getting back to work or there won't be a paper." He joined Sarah and they left the cemetery together. By the time they got to the newspaper office, Fred was feeling the heat. At least his face was getting redder and redder. He slammed the office door as soon as Sarah was inside.

She jumped at the noise. "What's that all about, Fred?"

"Holy Jehoshaphat, Sarah. What is it going to take to wake up some of these damn dunderheads?" Fred threw off his coat, unbuttoned his vest, pushed his derby to the back of his head, and flopped down at his desk. "That damn George Cosgrove. He'll be the death of me."

"What's wrong, Fred?"

"Well, I was just talking with him and some of his cronies there after the funeral and the sewer idea came up. At least I brought it up. Cosgrove jumped all over me. 'No money,' he said. And the others joined in. 'Can't afford the taxes,' they said. 'The time is not quite ripe yet.' Cosgrove claims I'm always premature, no matter what I write."

Sarah picked up her typestick, half listening to her husband, but watching out the window, where she saw Mrs. Curran returning Millie and Bobby. She waved thanks to her neighbor. Sarah watched her daughter immediately climb the hitching post and start swinging around it. Good grief, Sarah said to herself, she'd have to make that girl some black bloomers. What a handful Millie was becoming. There was nothing she could say or do that would make her act like a proper little girl. She was a tomboy, that's all there was to it. Bobby, the three-year-old, was escaping down Broadway, trotting after some older boys and a motley assortment of dogs. About time she reeled him in for a bit, Sarah decided.

"Sarah, are you listening to me?" Fred demanded.

"Yes, dear. You were talking about the dunderheads."

"Right," he agreed, "Well, remember the fire department thing, Sarah? They had to wait until the town damn near

58

burned down before they'd organize a fire department! Now what will it take to get rid of those cesspools and all those stinking privies? A typhoid fever epidemic?"

"Yes, dear," Sarah said, absently, her mind still on Millie and Bobby. Beside she'd heard this all before, many times.

"And if it happens, somebody will come to me and say, 'Hey, Fred, we've got a great idea. What do you think about forming a tax district and bonding to build a sewer plant? Or, better yet, Fred, maybe we should incorporate the city and tax ourselves for it. What do you think?' It's like they haven't read the damned paper for the past five years."

"Now Freddie," she tried to soothe him. He hated it when she took that tone of voice, as if he was a child with a bad temper. And he hated her to call him Freddie. "Freddie, you've always said there's no telling how much good can be done, if you don't care who gets the credit."

"I know, I know," Fred was muttering as Sarah went out the front door to round up her children. She came back with Bobby by the hand and gave him some wooden type blocks to play with on a table in the back shop. Millie promised to stay right by the hitching rack.

Fred was still grumbling when Sarah came back into the office to resume her typesetting. "Pretty skimpy edition this week," he said. "Nobody wants to advertise. They all say its no use because the farmers are so worried about the crops they won't spend any money. It's going to get worse if it doesn't rain."

"I thought Nels Svensen assured you it was going to rain soon," Sarah said.

"Oh, Nels — !" Fred muttered something about hogwash. "If those damn fools would only put their land under irrigation they'd not have to live from rain storm to rain storm. The water's there, Sarah. Plenty of it, just underground. All they have to do is — " His voice trailed off as he locked up the forms and got the press ready.

It didn't rain until March that year. But Nels Svensen still took the credit, claiming he just hadn't read the goose bone correctly. They called it "Miracle March," and the rejuvenated barley headed out after all and the feed in the hills grew tall and strong.

Farmers nodded to each other and smiled. "This country," they said, "it may scare the hell out of you, but it always comes through."

CHAPTER NINE

FRED'S BACK ACHED, the way it always did on paper day. He'd just finished carrying the last of the bundles of newspapers to the post office, and was about to close up and drop by the Bavarian House for a cold glass of Old Joe Steam Beer. He was thinking about just how good that would taste when Sarah swept into *The Settler* office. He could spot the fire in her eyes before she got through the door.

"Fred. You must talk to that boy of yours," she commanded.

Fred was mystified. "Well, sure, but what about, dear? Where is Bobby?"

Sarah sputtered, "In his room, and you'd better give him a good hiding, and explain some things to him, and wash his mouth out with soap."

"What on earth did he do?"

"Do?" Sarah sniffed. "Why, I've never been so embarrassed in my life. Do? My goodness! It was terrible."

"I see," Fred said calmly, and then waited for his wife to stop sputtering and get to the point.

Sarah took a deep breath as if she was about to plunge into an icy lake. "I was in the parlor of the Vendome for the usual Friday afternoon tea with the ladies of the Social Club and in rushes Bobby — your son — " Fred nodded. "He's got that awful McBride boy — Buster — with him. His mother is there with all of us, you know the group, Fred — " again he nodded. "And Buster cries out to his mother, 'Dad's going to the whorehouse and we're going with him!'

"It was awful! The ladies were shocked. We all turned red. Mabel Haskins dropped her tea, spilled it all over herself. And then Bobby asks me, in a voice I am sure was heard all over town. 'Can I go to the whorehouse, too, Mama?'" Fred nodded, trying not to laugh.

"Fred, I was so mortified, I couldn't speak," Sarah said, not noticing her husband's attempts to stifle his urge to laugh. "I didn't know what to do, so I just grabbed that boy of yours by the ear and marched him right back to the house."

Fred's nose twitched. His eyes started to tear. His lips curled. His entire face contorted as he tried to stop it. But he couldn't. It started deep in his stomach, spread through his chest, nearly choked him as it passed his throat, and then erupted from his mouth in a loud burst. He was laughing so hard he had to clutch at his desk to keep from falling to the floor. Sarah stood with hands on hips and watched him.

"And, may I ask, just what is it that's so funny, Mister Godfrey?"

"Oh, Sarah — " Fred wiped his eyes and caught his breath. "Old Cobb McBride runs the rig for the Vendome. You know, he meets all the trains with that surrey and gives rides around town to his guests. I'll bet some of those drummers wanted to go out to the Apple Orchard, or one of the other places, and the boys heard them. They don't know what those places are. They just wanted to go for a ride."

"Well," Sarah sniffed. "I'm not letting my son go to a place like that. I think you'd better have one of those fatherly talks with him."

"Holy Jehoshaphat, Sarah! The boy's only seven years old."

"Well, obviously it's never too soon in this town. If we're not going to live in a decent place, and I have to bring him up on the streets, the very least you can do is teach him good manners." Sarah was still angry. "And not only that, Fred. I think it is time that the decent people of this town did something to rid King's of those horrible places. You should be writing editorials about that!"

Fred didn't want to remind her, but the memory was still with him, of nearly losing her because his editorials against the rowdy cowboys had once cost him the saloon advertising. Now she wanted him to take on the houses of ill repute. Well, at least they weren't advertisers.

Fred was still chuckling to himself when he and Sarah stepped out on Broadway just in time to see Johnny Leonard, driving the Blackhawk's team of spanking blacks at a swift clip up the street. Doc Brumwell was on the seat beside him, hanging on with one hand, the other holding onto his hat. Fred watched them speed to the depot and then take a right turn toward San Lucas.

Slim Smith, a teamster and handyman who could always be counted on to know what was going on, was standing in front of Doc Brumwell's office. "What's the fuss about, Slim?" Fred asked.

"Shooting in San Lucas. Some fracas at The Mint," Slim responded. "Telegraph message. Man badly wounded. Supervisor Cleary sent it."

Fred hit his fist into his hand. "Damn, why does the big news always break right after the paper's out?"

"What are you going to do, Fred?" Sarah asked as they continued walking.

"Nothing I can do, dear. No use chasing down to San Lucas. I can't print the story until next week. I thought the days of the Wild West were over. We'll just wait and find out what happened. I've got plenty of time to write the story. I sure hope Will Cleary wasn't involved."

But he was.

Will had come in on the evening train from Salinas where he'd attended to some county and some personal matters. At the livery stable he picked up his rig, which had been in the care of Joe Carrigan, his brother-in-law. Joe had the surrey hitched and ready to go, and Will was anxious to get across the river to his home on the Trescony. But first he had to leave off a package and some money with Sam Bunte, owner of the general store. Will often did the banking, and other business around Salinas, for various local people when he made his regular trips to the county seat.

"Buena serra," Juan Bravo had greeted Will as he parked his rig in front of Bunte's store. Bravo was a man of considerable standing in southern Monterey County. He was recognized as one of the champion bucking-horse riders in the West and won big money from time to time in bronc-riding matches with challengers from other areas. In the meantime he worked as a cowboy and broke horses for several ranches in the region.

"Como esta, Juan? How's she go?"

"Oh, *poco poco.* I was wondering, *Señor* Cleary, if I could take a few turns on the gray mare? I need the practice. Going to match up to Ned Neely from San Jose at the Fourth of July celebration in King City."

"Sure, you can, Juan. Come out to the ranch. Tinkerbelle's not working right now. I'll tell 'em you're coming." Will Cleary had a big, gray work mare that was gentle as a pussy cat in harness, but she became a roaring hellcat if anyone tried to put a saddle on her. She'd bucked off every cowboy for miles around, even Juan Bravo a few times. She was a test for him, kept him sharp.

Will waved goodbye to Juan and was heading into Bunte's store when he heard a shot. He stopped in his tracks and looked toward The Mint saloon, the source of the sound, just as a second shot roared. Will swiftly bounded up the walk, threw open the doors, and stepped into The Mint.

He was in the middle of it. There on the floor, moaning and bleeding, was a young ranch hand, a Colt revolver in his limp hand, and the other man, a few feet away, held a gun on him. Will Cleary was between them. Stools were tipped over, and several other patrons stood, immobile, at the bar, or crouched, frozen in their places by the tables. Will looked at the man with the smoking pistol and held out his hand.

"Hand me the gun, Ray," Will commanded in a cool, calm, decisive tone.

Will recognized the first cowboy as Raymond Brisco, and the wounded man on the floor as Hector Romero. He knew there had been bad blood between them for some time.

"Get out of my way, Mister Cleary. I'm gonna finish off this sonofabitch right now! "

"No, you're not, Ray. That'd be murder. You're not a murderer, Ray. It's all over now. Take it easy. Give me that gun." Will spoke soothingly, but Brisco, agitated, wild, continued to wave the pistol at Will, at the wounded man, and at the men standing rigid by the bar.

"I don't wanna hurt you, Mister Cleary, but I gotta end this between us. He's not gonna treat my sister that way and get away with it."

Brisco took his eyes off Will and aimed again at the wounded man. The pistol shook in his hand, and his eyes grew wide, his finger tightening on the trigger. Will moved, quickly and deftly. He swung his left hand downward and struck the gun, knocking it aside, and hit Brisco alongside the head with his right, a powerful punch that staggered the man. The pistol discharged, the bullet harmlessly plowing the floor, as Will lifted Brisco in both arms and crashed him down into a chair.

Now the room came alive. Everyone began to breathe again. Several men helped Will hold Brisco down and others attended to Romero. Townspeople hurriedly crowded into The Mint to see what had happened. Everyone was talking at once, shouting orders, giving advice.

Will again took command. "Charlie, you get over to the depot and have them telegraph King City for Doc Brumwell. Tell him to hurry. And then send out a message for Sheriff Matthews. Lay that man there on the pool table. Put something down so he doesn't bleed all over it. Make him comfortable as you can."

Will called for some rope and tied Brisco tightly to the chair. "And all of you who were in here when that happened, give your names to Tito there and he'll write them down. You're all witnesses." Will indicated Tito Domingos, who was behind the bar, still watching, bug-eyed.

Will turned back to the man trussed up in the chair. "Raymond Brisco," he said, "in case I haven't mentioned it, you're under arrest for attempted murder."

"My God, Will, can you do that?" Domingos asked.

"Beats the shit out of me," Will said. "They give supervisors all sorts of authority, but I'm damned if I know what. This'll have to do until the sheriff gets here."

Ray Brisco was sentenced to ten years in San Quentin. Hector Romero recovered completely thanks to the tender and loving care of one Sadie Brisco in a room at the Pleasant View Hotel. And The Mint became famous, or infamous, depending one one's point of view, as the scene of California's last great gunfight.

Readers of *The Salinas Valley Settler* thought it made a helluva story, good for several issues, when Fred was finally able to print it.

CHAPTER TEN

TIMOTHY CLEARY CHECKED INTO THE PALACE HOTEL in San Francisco, signed the register with a flourish and added the date, Tuesday, April 17, 1906. He ordered a suite and put cash on the counter, oblivious to the surprised look of the desk clerk, the stares of other guests in the opulent lobby, and the curious glances of the bellboy, who carried Tim's one, tattered carpet bag to his rooms. Tim peeled off some bills for the bell-boy, who left wondering about this lanky, roughly-dressed man with the weathered face behind a black beard and shaggy hair.

Tim had just stepped off the steamer from Seattle. He had a plan and making his headquarters at the Palace Hotel was part of it. The next move was to buy new clothes, the latest fashion, whatever that was, get his hair cut, and his beard stylishly trimmed, and replenish his wallet.

That wasn't going to be any problem. He would find the bank and draw on the funds he had transferred. Tim wasn't sure how much money was in his account at the Pacific Savings and Trust in San Francisco, but he knew it was plenty. Tim allowed himself to exult. He had gone up to the Yukon practically broke and had come back a wealthy man. Now he could pursue his dream.

Tim sat in his elegant hotel room, slowly sipping from a glass of the finest whiskey that room service could provide and gazing out the window at the city. It had changed a lot in the nine years Tim had been away. He'd changed a lot, too.

Tim had grown tired of sitting up there in Coyote Canyon on the stoop of his little cabin, sucking on his jug and nursing his mad at the world. He'd lost interest in farming, finally gave up the Brandenstein lease. It wasn't the hard work. But what was the point? There'd been no need to get ahead, not after that clipping came about Amy being married. And he knew it was-n't fair to his landlord to be doing a half-assed job. So Tim had moved up to his "squat," which is what he called the homestead cabin on his one hundred and sixty acres in the middle of the Cleary ranch. Now and then he rode horseback over the hill into Long Valley to visit his father and Aunt Cauth. He loved her very much even though she wasn't his real mother. Jeremiah's first wife was mother to six of the Cleary children and when she was gored to death by a bull, Jeremiah sent to Ireland for her sister Cauth to help raise the family. They'd married for propriety's sake and later fell deeply in love and had two more children, a girl and the retarded Seamus.

Once in a while Tim made it in to San Lucas for his mail and the newspaper. *The Salinas Valley Settler* gave him all the news he wanted of the outside world. Will came by occasionally to check on him and scold him for drinking and brooding. How could Amy do what she did? Why? He knew she loved him! After what there was between them, how could she have married someone else?

Or could it be that she regretted her marriage and that's why she had come to him? Tim was sure that was it.

Three years went by that way and then Tim saw an article in *The Settler* about the gold strike in the Yukon. No one could stop him from going. Will tried to talk him out of it and his father was aghast when he heard. Jeremiah feared for his son just as he had once feared for his brother, Matthew, who'd gone to the California gold fields forty-five years before, only to become a penniless drunk. But Jeremiah and Will just didn't understand, Tim thought. He was different. He'd strike it rich and that would surely impress Amy. He'd come back to San Francisco with more money than she'd ever imagined and he'd win her back. She'd leave her husband and they'd be together forever.

Tim was thirty-four years old when he took the steamer out of San Francisco, traveling steerage class to Seattle and on to Dyea, at the foot of Chilkoot Pass, with hundreds of gold seekers, each chasing his own dream. They carried more than their hopes up over that treacherous pass. The Canadian government insisted each have at least one thousand pounds of supplies on entering Yukon Territory, and the red-coated mounties were there at the top to check. It took nearly three months and countless trips up the trail and the frozen steps, struggling with sixty pounds on his back each time, but Tim was wiry and strong, as soon as the liquor boiled out of him. He arrived at Lake Bennett and partnered with others to build a boat for the five-hundred-mile trip down the Yukon to Dawson when the ice broke up. Many didn't make it. If Chilkoot Pass hadn't killed them, the long, hazardous trek by water did.

Tim Cleary made it through and wound up on a tributary to Bonanza Creek panning for gold. But bad luck seemed to be his partner, always at his side, and he had little color to show for his hard work. Throughout it all, the vision of beautiful, blond Amy, the feel of her that last night in his arms, her rippling laughter, the promise in her eyes and on her lips, drove him on. When word reached Dawson of the strike in Nome, Tim joined the rush.

He learned about freezing. He knew hard work. He traveled by dog sled and spent many lonely days and nights in a snowed-in cabin. But the solitude didn't bother him. He'd grown accustomed to that. And the dream of Amy was his company—it kept him warm. But the sought-after gold eluded him.

Tim finally had to abandon his claim near Nome. He joined the next rush, the one to Fairbanks. It was 1902 when he found Tanana Valley and froze there while he lived on moose meat and beans. And it was then that bad luck and Tim Cleary split up partnership. The luck of the Irish, they called it, when he finally hit it. But Tim knew how long it had been in coming. Now gold dust filled the bottom of his pan with every sluice. Nuggets as big as barley heads began showing up, some as big as peanuts, and even a few as big as his thumb. He found them in his pan, spotted them in the stream, mucked them from the frozen tundra, picked them out of the gravel. He dug into the bank and chased a ledge of gold-bearing quartz. Even when his pokes were full to bursting, he wouldn't quit. He had to get enough for Amy. If he were a rich man, she would surely be his!

Finally, he sold out to a placer mining company and transferred that huge chunk of money to join the rest he'd been sending regularly via Wells Fargo to the Pacific Savings Bank of San Francisco. He strapped on a belt weighted down with two pokes of gold dust and a few nuggets, along with his ready cash, and headed back to the states, leaving behind a creek named Cleary. Now here he was, in the spring of the year, ready at last to realize his dream.

He entered the lobby of the bank and stepped up to a teller's cage. But the moment he made his intentions known, the manager was called. Tim was ushered into an office, where the bank official politely explained the various options available to him. Tim could take his one million three hundred and forty-seven dollars in cash, of course. But there would be some delay. And that much cash would be cumbersome and subject to theft, now wouldn't it? Or he could convert it to government bonds, or perhaps, he would prefer a letter of credit?

Since he couldn't take a suitcase full of cash with him to impress Amy, Tim settled for the letter of credit. He tucked it into the inside pocket of his new suit coat. Yes, that's what he'd show her!

Tim walked jauntily out of the bank, proud of himself in his new suit, white shirt with a high, celluloid collar, stickpin holding his tie, gold watch chain across his vest, bowler hat at a rakish angle, button shoes on his feet. He hailed a hack and gave the driver the address on Green Street. Tim had no idea where Amy lived, but he'd start with her aunt, Mrs. Elbert Whitney, who lived in one of a row of imposing homes on a street recognized for the importance of those who dwelt behind the elegant facades. Tim paid the driver with gold coin and dropped a small nugget in his hand for a tip. The driver was duly impressed as Tim nodded confidently and got out of the hack. He adjusted his hat and stepped jauntily to the door. But it was all bravado. Underneath, he was nervous, anxious, and unsure of what he was about to do.

After the butler had escorted Tim to the drawing room and he'd waited for what seemed an interminably long time, Mrs. Whitney entered the room and offered her hand. Tim didn't know quite what to do, so he took her hand and shook it. "How do you do, Missus Whitney."

"What can I do for you, Mister Cleary?" Despite her regal bearing, her voice was friendly, almost motherly.

"I'm looking for Amy Barnes, uh — er — ah — Amy Fabray," Tim felt suddenly embarrassed.

"And why is that, Mister Cleary?"

"I'm an old friend," Tim explained. "I haven't seen her in years and I want to pay my — ah —"

He was interrupted by a young girl, who burst into the room calling, "Aunt Addie, Aunt Addie. I must tell — "

"Please, Clara, don't interrupt. I have a guest. I'll call you when Mister Cleary leaves."

Tim stared in shock at the girl. She was blond and blue-eyed, no more than fifteen years old, but the bloom that would make her a beautiful woman was already there. It was Amy. The likeness was fantastic. Even the way she offered a pouting smile and excused herself with a rippling laugh. Tim's eyes followed her from the room and he stood, speechless.

"Yes, I know, Mister Cleary," Mrs. Whitney said softly. "She does resemble Amy." She paused. "I do recall your letters for Amy coming here. But that was so many years ago. What could you want of Amy now?"

"Well, I just — uh, I wanted — ah, I'd like to see her," Tim stuttered the reply. He felt childish, even stupid. How could he tell this woman that he longed to see Amy, to make her realize he was capable of giving her everything she wanted, the kind of life she'd craved, and then take her away with him. Mrs. Whitney would probably think him mad and have him thrown out.

Mrs. Whitney stared at him for a long moment, appraising him, and then seemed to come to a decision. She gestured to one of the Chippendale chairs across from the sofa upon which she was sitting. "Please, Mister Cleary, do sit down."

Tim sat on the edge of the chair, too nervous to get comfortable, too fearful of what she might say. "Mister Cleary, let me explain to you about Amy," Mrs. Whitney said, looking directly into Tim's eyes "There are things you should know."

She studied him a moment and then said, "First, I do remember you, and I once knew your father. A fine man, Jeremiah Cleary. I met him a long time ago at a social function in a San Lucas hotel when I visited my sister and her husband on their dreadful little ranch — " she grimaced ever so slightly, but Tim caught it — "in Pine Valley. You were one of the many young boys who were attracted to Amy like bees to honey. Your letters for her came here while she was my ward. But they continued to come long after Amy had married and moved into her own home. I can only surmise that you did not know of her marriage?"

Mrs. Whitney stopped to look closely at Tim, and just as he started to speak, to say he had no knowledge of the marriage, she interrupted, "Yes, Mister Cleary. I'm sure you didn't."

She was silent for a moment, then leaned forward and spoke softly. "Mister Cleary — Timothy — Amy is gone. Gone from San Francisco. Gone, I have no idea where."

"Gone?" Tim was puzzled. "Gone?" He didn't understand.

"Yes, Timothy. I'm sorry to tell you. My niece left her husband and her child and ran off with a New York lawyer. Ran off without a word, in the dead of night. Took the transcontinental train and left her poor husband, and her two-year-old baby girl, and the rest of our family. It was a terrible scandal." Mrs. Whitney paused again and looked at Tim.

He was shaking his head, unable to accept it. "No, no," he said. "Amy couldn't do that. Amy wasn't like that."

"Oh, let me tell you all of it," Mrs. Whitney said, sadness and resignation in her voice. "There were other scandals before

71

that, other men, a series of them. But her husband, a patient soul, claimed he loved her, forgave her each time, and faced down the terrible gossip. But when she ran off, it was just too much for him. He couldn't face it and moved away, to Nevada, and left the child with me. I'd be alone if it weren't for Clara. She is such a pleasure. Having her around makes up for the hurt caused by her mother. Amy hasn't been heard from in more than ten years now."

Tim sat frozen, staring without seeing, unresponding. How could a mother leave a child? Amy and all those other men? Amy doing all those things with other men? Tim had accepted a husband in Amy's life, but that wasn't real to him, and he was ready to win her away from Michael Vincent Fabray. He'd been convinced he could do so. He'd deluded himself to the point of appearing on this woman's doorstep, expecting to be told where Amy lived and going there so he could whisk her away with him. What kind of a wild idea was that? What sort of a fantasy world had he been living in?

Mrs. Whitney continued speaking and Tim fought through a haze of emotion and tried to give her his attention. "I was so very hurt and bitter about Amy. I'd given her so much and saw to it that she made a suitable marriage. I hated what she became, but perhaps there's an explanation. Her mother was my younger sister. We were raised with every privilege here in San Francisco. I married well, as you may note. My late husband was a wealthy man. But my sister married that dirt poor farmer, and then resented her lot for the rest of her life. She filled Amy with romantic notions of city life and wealthy men — and turned her daughter into a spoiled, selfish, young lady with grandiose ideas. My sister begged me to let Amy live with Elbert and me so that she might have the so-called finer things in life. She became my ward and we certainly gave her everything. And I've just told you what she gave in return.

"Now I can only pray that Clara has not inherited her mother's frivolous attitudes and scandalous behavior!" Mrs. Whitney took a deep breath and let it out in a sad sigh. "Now

Whitney took a deep breath and let it out in a sad sigh. "Now you know it all, Timothy. Put Amy out of your mind."

Tim stumbled from the house on Green Street. He walked for hours. Up and down the streets of San Francisco. At first he was too numb, too empty, too defeated to think coherently. He wandered into a bar and sat on a stool, staring at himself in the mirror at the back of the bar. The bartender had to ask several times before Tim ordered a drink. The whiskey jolted his mind awake, realization hit him, and he saw his image staring back at him in the mirror.

Portrait of a fool, damn fool, he thought. Tim Cleary, a roaring idiot over a worthless woman. *You've wasted half your life, and Will was right. Your father was right. Your friends were right. But you never saw it!*

Tim glared at his image in the mirror. His reflection glared back — a frown of derision, of self-loathing on its face.

Oh, how they must have laughed at you, Tim Cleary. You must have been the laughing stock of the entire Salinas Valley. And now you're back with your tail between your legs. A wealthy man. And for what? And who cares? You've lost Amy. Hah! You never had Amy. The girl you loved wasn't real. She only existed in your silly fantasy. Amy Barnes was only an unreal dream. It was your dream, Tim Cleary. Not hers. Never hers.

Tim looked up again at his image in the mirror. "You stupid, stupid loser," he cried, and he threw his whiskey glass against the mirror. It shattered loudly, cracking the mirror and knocking several bottles to the floor. A few patrons jumped up, startled, and the bartender grabbed for him. But Tim stepped back, took a handful of greenbacks from his pocket and threw them on the bar. He hurried out before the police were called.

He walked and walked through the city streets, stopping at saloons here and there for a drink. But at first, the whiskey had little effect on his pain. Tim's head was clear, and the truth continued to pound into his brain, how foolish he'd been, how deluded he was, the life he'd missed. All because of Amy

Barnes. What an object of pity and scorn he'd become to his relatives and friends. The realization was eroding his very soul.

The stops for whiskey became more frequent and lasted longer. He staggered from place to place. Finally, about two in the morning, he stumbled into the bar at The Palace Hotel. Slumped in a chair, sodden with drink, he was at first accorded courtesy by the bartender only because of his attire. Then Tim was finally recognized as a guest of the hotel and a bellhop helped him to his suite on the third floor. His coat was removed and hung on a hanger, his collar loosened, and his inert body laid out on the bed. Tim lay in a stupor.

CHAPTER ELEVEN

THINGS WERE BUSTLING AT THE GODFREYS' little rented house in King City. The day was spent in packing. Everything had to go into boxes and suitcases. Fred knocked together some crates for Sarah's lamps and flower vases, and for the huge, ornately-framed photographs of her mother and father. Only enough dishes and utensils, and pots and pans for supper were left out. In the morning Slim Smith's wagon would arrive and they'd load it for their move across town to their new home.

"Millie," Sarah called. "You run over and tell Lon Sing to make his delivery to our new home tomorrow."

"Can I go, too?" Bobby asked.

"Sure, run along. But be back for an early supper."

Millie and Bobby dashed off to Lon Sing's grocery store to deliver Sarah's message. "We'll be in our new home tomorrow, Mister Sing, and Mama wants you to deliver her vegetables there."

"New home, missy? What new home? Where new home?" Lon Sing shrugged his shoulders and seemed bewildered. But his eyes twinkled. He knew exactly where the new house was. Everybody in town had watched it being built. It stood all by itself on the outskirts of town, toward the river.

"Stop teasing me, Mister Sing. You know."

"All light, missy. Gleat, nice house. Sing bling. You terr Missy Salah."

The old Chinese grocer had a plot of vegetables behind his store and each morning he'd hitch old January to his little wagon and make the rounds of his customers. The poor old horse, mostly skin and bones, never out of a slow walk, seemed to hardly make it from street to street. But Lon Sing made a big show of pulling him up with a flourish at each stop. He'd tug on the reins and cry, "Whoa, Januelly, whoa. You some wild thing, you go rike a hotcake." He'd climb down slowly from the wagon and skinny, old January would stand quietly, head down, while the sack of vegetables was delivered. When Lon Sing was seated again, January would slowly move off to the next house with his master yelling, "Whoa, you wild son of bitch, whoa." But Lon Sing pronounced it "wide" instead of "wild," playing to his audience and the merriment of his listeners. And the wily old man sold a lot of vegetables.

Today Millie was full of news about the new house. "I'll have my very own room, Mister Sing," she said, with a glance at Bobby. "And my mother says I can put my own things wherever I want them." Millie didn't think it proper for a young lady of twelve years to share a room with a younger brother, even with a curtain between them.

"Yeah, me, too," Bobby added. "And I won't have some silly girl in the way, either, always mad if I leave something on the floor. And we're gonna have a bathroom, right there in the house, too."

Lon Sing listened, smiled and nodded, his parchment-like skin crinkling at the corners of his eyes and around his mouth. And, as always, when the youngsters left his store, a piece of rock candy had been slipped into each of their hands.

Millie and Bobby skipped out of Lon Sing's onto the board sidewalk to cross the street, but Millie cried, "Watch out." She grabbed her brother's arm and pulled him back against the store front. A herd of bawling cattle came trotting up Broadway, their hooves churning up the dirt, already dry in early April. Cowboys kept them moving and their shouts and whoops added to the din and dust billowing up behind them. It wasn't an unusual sight as cow outfits occasionally drove right through town, but business activity halted, and pedestrians became spectators until the herd passed. Millie and Bobby chewed on their hard candy and watched.

"Wow, look at that!" Bobby exclaimed, pointing to a cowboy whose young cowhorse, overly excited by city life, bowed its head and bucked across the street, jumped up on the sidewalk and through the swinging doors of Stan Hill's saloon. After a few seconds, the horse bucked back through the doors and rejoined the cattle drive, the cowboy still in the saddle. Millie and Bobby cheered with other bystanders. But several saloon patrons poked their heads out the doors, scratched them in bewilderment, and then returned to their libations, asking each other, "What the hell happened?"

"What took you two so long?" Sarah asked when Millie and Bobby finally got home. "Lollygagging downtown? And look at you, covered with dirt. You get in there and scrub up for supper."

Sarah was especially excited about this being their final night in the rented house. She'd squeezed every coin, gone without things she'd formerly thought were necessities, scorned every luxury and watched the hoard of gold coins and greenbacks grow. When Fred wanted to spend the money on an automated typesetting machine, Sarah refused. She simply put in longer hours at the type cases herself. She'd not live in a rented house behind the Vendome Hotel any longer than absolutely necessary.

When her father died, just a few months after her mother's death, Sarah's inheritance—two lots in San Leandro—she gladly sold to one of her brothers for five hundred dollars. She then announced to Fred that she'd put it with the three hundred they'd saved, and that it was time to talk to the building contractor. Fred thought the windfall might be better spent on improving the newspaper equipment. "If we put out a better paper, subscribers and advertisers will respond," he argued. "We'll make more money and then we'll have the house." Sarah just sniffed.

She was the one who picked out the lot on the far edge of town, made the arrangements with the builder and proceeded to drive the poor man to distraction with changes during construction. When the house was finally completed, it stood well back from the street on a large lot with a long sweep of front yard where Sarah intended to plant trees and flower beds. Fred claimed the back yard in which to grow vegetables and build a run for the hunting dogs he hoped to have one day.

Millie had a hard time falling asleep just thinking about moving in the morning. But she was finally sleeping soundly when the lamp fell off her night stand. The crash startled her awake. Her bed was rocking. She heard Bobby yell when he slipped to the floor and landed with a thud. The room was swaying and she heard Sarah cry out, "Earthquake!"

The quake jolted the house again, harder this time. And they could hear objects falling, chairs toppling, dishes, pots and pans from last night's supper clattering and banging to the floor. Fred and Sarah ran into the children's room. "Millie, Bobby, are you all right?" Sarah called, grabbing Bobby. Fred held Millie and all four of them stood in the doorways, under the frames, the safest place to be as every Californian knew.

"This is a whopper," Fred said as another wave of motion moved the house. When it subsided, he fumbled in the dark for a lamp, but the chimney was shattered. Sarah felt for a lantern hanging from a hook and they got that lighted to survey the damage.

Everything that wasn't packed for the move was scattered on the floor. Furniture tumbled over, and Sarah's big flower vase, forgotten in the living room, was shattered. All the boxes and crates were intact. But the thought struck each of them at the same moment. The new house!

"It'll be fine," Sarah promised.

"We'd better go see," Millie said.

"Right now," Bobby agreed as he leaped into his clothes.

"You stay right here," Sarah ordered. "It's still too dark."

* * * * *

The sleepy night operator at the Southern Pacific railroad depot, dozing in his chair as he awaited his relief, was jolted awake. He felt the building moving and hurried outside where he could hear the cries and a few screams as the people of King City were shocked from their beds. He felt the earthquake send shudders and waves of motion along Broadway and the station building swayed and then stood still.

Suddenly his telegraph machine startled him, clattering to life with the terrible message: *S.F. sends — Emergency — Huge Earthquake — Buildings fall — Many deaths — trains halted —* And the clicks stopped.

Word quickly spread throughout King City and soon scores of people had gathered at the depot, hovering over the telegraph operator, waiting for more news.

Those with relatives in San Francisco spoke in hushed whispers. More than an hour went by before the telegraph lines were repaired and reports again brought the clattering messenger to life. Each bulletin was more frightening than the last. *Thousands killed! San Francisco destroyed! Population fleeing!* Roads had been ripped up, train tracks destroyed. Rumors and counter rumors tumbled out of the clacking telegraph machine, each one more terrible than the last.

* * * * *

It was just about dawn, twelve minutes after five, to be exact, as the newspapers later recorded, that the San Francisco earthquake struck.

The Palace Hotel shuddered and then swayed. Plaster cracked and fell in chunks, windows blew out, raining down shards of glass. And just as the building settled, a second, more severe quake hit with an immense jolt.

Now people were screaming and running about, and rushing into the street in whatever clothes they were able to put on. Thousands of terrified, frantic men, women, and children spewed forth from toppling buildings throughout the downtown. Bricks crashed to the street as walls and chimneys cracked, caved in and became instant, enormous piles of rubble. Huge jagged gaps appeared in the city streets, sidewalks and gutters twisted, water mains burst, gas lines exploded, streetcar rails along Market street writhed and bent into contorted knots of steel.

The Palace Hotel swayed and shuddered with each aftershock, and then, with a final quiver, amazingly stood still, severely damaged, but upright.

Tim Cleary slept through it all.

It wasn't until later that a bellboy, charged with checking every room to insure that the hotel was evacuated, found him, rousted him, and led him in a daze from the building. Tim stood on Market Street, fully dressed, except for his coat, bewildered and confused. What was going on around him had to be some horrible dream — a nightmare from which he'd awaken. But instead, his head painfully throbbed and his eyes wouldn't focus. Slowly he came to realize he was amidst hundreds of people, some just standing there, numb like Tim, unable to comprehend the tragedy. Some were searching through the crowd, looking for relatives and friends. Others were crying out for their children, for wives and husbands. Here and there was a body, crushed by a fallen object, lying on the sidewalk, some covered by a blanket or a coat. The wounded and bleeding were everywhere.

Tim found an overturned bathtub, flung through some upstairs window to the center of Market Street, and sat down on it. Looking about him at the devastation, he kept trying to clear his head. It took time for his bloodshot eyes to focus and his brain to function. The cold, early morning air helped the sobering process as much as the shock. Tim shivered with the cold. He needed his coat.

My God, my coat! My letter of credit, all my money is in that coat pocket. Where is it? Where is my coat? In the hotel room? It must be! Tim jumped to his feet and frantically rushed through the crowd to the front door of the Palace. But he was stopped by guards, posted by the police for safety and to prevent looting.

"I'm sorry, sir. We can't let any one enter the building. Orders."

Tim ran around to the other street, searching for another entrance. But it was the same, locked doors, guards. "But I'm a registered guest," he protested. "I must get something from my room. It's important."

"Sorry, sir. No entry now. The building isn't safe. Perhaps later we'll be allowed back in."

Tim, in despair, gave up for the moment. He'd have to wait, he decided, surely they'll let him in after while. He returned to his seat on the bathtub. Then a new clamor began around him, its fierce suddenness as terrifying as the quake itself.

"Fire!"

"Fire!" was the cry. And the fire spread throughout the downtown area. But there was no water and firefighters were helpless. Building after building burst into flame. Gas escaping from broken pipes fed the hungry blazes. The brick buildings still standing were smoldering inside and suddenly ignited.

Tim again tried to enter the Palace to retrieve his coat with the precious letter of credit tucked into the inside pocket. But again he was driven away. He looked up to see smoke billowing from the windows of the hotel.

Now the nearby Grand Hotel erupted in flames, and so did the *Examiner* and *Chronicle* buildings and the building on Third Street, which housed the *San Francisco Call*. The entire Mission district was burning. The boom of dynamite punctured the roar of the flames as firefighters tried to blow up entire blocks of buildings to create fire breaks. But the raging red tide continued to engulf the city.

Tim watched in horror as the Palace exploded into flames. Then he remembered. The Pacific Bank. There'd be a record there. There had to be. He'd surely be able to get a receipt or something, to prove his money was there. Tim turned from Market Street where soldiers now were ordering the people to safer locations. He raced up Montgomery Street, his hopes fading as he passed the burned-out buildings, the charred, smoldering wreckage, the vacant spots where yesterday the city's financial firms had flourished. The Pacific Bank had been reduced to a smoking pile of rubble.

Tim turned away, heartsick. His nine years of hardship and struggle in the Yukon and Alaska had gone up in smoke. In one short night, all his dreams were forever destroyed, his money gone and his dream of Amy shattered by reality. He began to walk, not knowing where he was going, not caring. He walked for hours before he became aware of the weight around his waist, his money belt. He almost laughed at the irony of it. That's something, he thought. It held more than he had when he headed for the gold fields. The hell with the rest of it. What good was money to him without Amy?

He was trying to figure out what to do when he thought of Connie, his cousin, Mrs. Christopher Baxter. She and her husband lived in a mansion on Nob Hill. He knew that much. Tim would find his way there, make sure they were all right— maybe they needed help, maybe they would help him. But when he reached the address and climbed the granite steps to the house set back behind a formal garden, the place was empty, doors swung open, windows were broken, and the badly damaged mansion had been gutted by looters. There was no sign of Connie or her husband or any of the servants. Tim stood before the once-splendid home, utterly drained and hopeless.

Never in all his years in the north, no matter how many mining dead ends and disasters he encountered, had he ever felt so totally defeated. And lost.

He walked away from the Baxter mansion, downhill and away from Nob Hill and made his way west. Tim was fed and slept on the ground at a camp for refugees that had been hastily set up in the Mission District at 17th and Castro. In the morning he joined thousands of others leaving San Francisco, heading south onto the peninsula, where they found more devastation. Near San Mateo, Tim bargained for a horse and buggy, paying five times the value, taking the money from his belt, not caring how much the rig cost. All that mattered was where the rig would take him, and the only place he could think of was the one place he didn't want to go back to: Home.

CHAPTER TWELVE

A T FIRST LIGHT OF DAWN the Godfrey family rushed over to San Lorenzo Avenue and found their new home intact. It was unharmed, inviting, the just-completed red brick chimney rising solidly at the side. Relieved, they all hurried back to *The Settler* office to see what had happened there. "Holy Jehoshaphat!" Fred exclaimed when he opened the front door and saw the mess.

Ink cans had tumbled to the floor, some had spilled amid the paper which had slipped off the shelves, books had fallen and work tables were knocked over. But worst of all were the type trays, which had slid out from their stands and scattered hand-set type all over.

"All that type is pied. We'll have to redistribute it before we can even start setting again," Fred said, looking at the mess with a helpless expression. "We'll never get a paper out."

"Oh, for Godssakes, Fred," Sarah admonished him. "Let's just get to work." She started putting the letters back into their little compartments and Millie, who had been learning to handset type, quickly gave her mother a hand. Bobby went with his father to check over the presses. "At least, there's no damage that I can see," Fred said, relief in his voice. He and Bobby set about putting things to rights.

By the time more news of the San Francisco catastrophe commenced to arrive over the telegraph wires, Fred was at the train station, ready to write it down and they were ready to set up their edition.

But with no trains leaving San Francisco, Fred Godfrey's usual shipment of pre-printed paper for the two inside pages of *The Settler*, could not arrive. Fred had to publish just one sheet, printed both sides. The front page, in end-of-the-world type, told the story:

MOST APPALLING CASUALTY IN WORLD HISTORY – Earthquake Has Spread Devastation in its Path – Following

Coast Line — Many Cities Lie in Ruins — FIRE ADDING TO HORROR — S.F. Burning in Rubble

Conservative estimates of loss of life in San Francisco placed at 500, but harrowing reports arriving by telegraph each hour. Reports have kept the populace of this usually tranquil town hovering about the telegraph office.

Although the rocking of buildings here lasted fully a minute and a half, and was described as greatest earthquake ever felt in this area, not a dollar's worth of damage was done in King City, nor in places to the south. But to the north it was different. Many buildings fell in Salinas and Hollister, and much damage was reported, but no loss of life.

Without the San Francisco papers coming in by train, the only real news of the tragic event was that printed in *The Settler*.

"Fred, you did a great job getting your paper out in a hurry, but it sure didn't amount to much," Cosgrove chided Godfrey several days later, as both men were having their hair cut in Tom Himmah's barber shop. Several other businessmen were there, waiting their turns and commenting on the earthquake.

"That'll have to do for a while, George. I can't get my pre-prints. They're out of business in San Francisco," Fred explained.

Another customer said, "Good job on the quake, but tell me, Fred, why do you print all that stuff on your inside pages?" one of the men asked. "I never look at that crap."

"Yeah, neither do I," another man chimed in, "but my wife thinks some of it's okay. She likes that *Trimmed Lamp* stuff by O. Henry. Says he's a good writer."

The Settler followed the practice of many small, rural newspapers, which purchased newsprint already printed on one side with ads for Peruna, *the tonic for worn out systems,* Hoods Sasparilla *for pure blood* and Swifts Specific, *the purifier for every skin disease.* These were interspersed with sayings by Mark Twain, columns of farm and home hints, the Jolly

Jokester, and news of general interest about new inventions, women's fashions and calamities the world over.

"Sure would be better if you'd put local news in that space, Fred. I like your Chat and all the items from the other country places," Himmah said, snipping the hair around Fred's ears.

"I'd need more ads to support more local pages. And I'd have to buy one of those new typesetting machines to set enough type to fill them, and then I'd need a drum press to print it on. Can't afford it," Fred said, wishing to himself that all these opinionated men would stop trying to tell him how to run his newspaper. But at least they were interested. He got out of the chair and shrugged into his coat and fastened his tie pin. "Meanwhile, those patent medicine ads, and the other stuff you call junk on the pre-printed pages, they bring in some money for me and supply the paper I print on."

"Aw, c'mon, Fred," Cosgrove chided. "You got piles of money. Big new house like you just built."

Fred nodded. "That's just it. Spent it all on the house. The builder sort of insisted on it." Godfrey laughed and they all joined in. Then the talk returned to the earthquake.

It was several weeks later when George Cosgrove dropped into the newspaper office. Fred was never really sure if he was pleased or not to see George coming. But it wasn't to criticize or offer an unwanted opinion this time.

"Fred," Cosgrove said, sounding more friendly than Fred could ever remember. "I've been wondering. Just how much would that new equipment cost to get you set up to put out a bigger paper for us?"

"More than I've got, George," Fred replied. "And if people don't pay up their overdue subscriptions damn soon, I won't have enough to print anything at all."

"Ever thought of borrowing?"

"Well, sure, I have, but without a bank here and no credit record in Salinas, I haven't given it a try."

"None of my business, of course, Fred. But I heard you paid cash for your new place. You could put up the house," Cosgrove suggested.

"Oh no!" Fred shook his head. "Sarah would never allow that."

"Well, maybe not with a bank, Fred. Maybe there's private money around waiting to earn some interest," Cosgrove hinted. "How much would you need?"

Godfrey thought for a moment. "Oh, about three thousand."

Cosgrove nodded. "Think on it, Fred," he said as he smiled and walked out of the office.

Fred hurried home from the office, anxious to tell Sarah, but he found Slim Smith's delivery wagon in front of the new house and Slim in conversation with Sarah. "Hi, Fred," Slim greeted him. "Got here just in time to help me unload your new furniture. Just came in at the freight office."

Slim lowered the tail gate, climbed into the wagon and slid out the crated dining room table. "Careful, Fred it's a mite heavy," Slim said. Fred took the end of the crate and the two men lowered it carefully to the street where Slim knocked the crate apart. "Hey, she's a beauty," he said, admiring the polished finish on the oak table. "Must seat eight or ten, huh?"

The two men carried the table to the house, working it sideways through the door and set it along the living room wall where Sarah admired it while they returned for the chairs and then the small desk, given as a premium by the furniture company.

When Slim left, she surveyed the room with a critical eye. "Fred, don't you think the sofa should be over there? It would face the fireplace better." She pointed across the room where Fred's rocker sat.

"Holy Jehoshaphat, Sarah, why didn't you say so when Slim was still here? He could have helped move it." Fred began tugging on the sofa, sliding it across the room, Sarah helping to lift one end. "There," he said. "That better?"

They sat side by side on the couch, a bit threadbare but still serviceable, and smiled at each other. "Our own home, Sarah." Fred took her hand and leaned over to kiss her cheek. Sarah was smoothing a worn spot on the couch. Fred noticed and said, "Eventually we'll get all new furniture. That's a promise."

"That'll hold us for a while," Sarah said, nodding at the new table across the room. "It's worth the cost. And our own home. Finally!" She paused a moment and then started to rise. "Well, I'd better get busy in my new kitchen and fix something for supper." But Fred's arm on her shoulder held her back. "Wait a minute, Sarah. I came home early to explain something to you — "

"Explain what?"

"You know how badly we need a new press and a typesetter — " Sarah nodded warily. " — and now I've got a way to pay for them."

"You do?" Sarah raised an eyebrow and got up from the couch. She looked down on Fred. "Well — "

"Cosgrove will lend us three thousand for three years at eight percent. I know where there's a Brower drum cylinder press available and a Simplex typesetter. I can get them both for under three thousand total. Then we could put out a real newspaper."

At the mention of Cosgrove's name, Sarah's eyes narrowed. "I don't trust that Cosgrove." She sniffed as she said it. "There's something in it for him. What's he got up his sleeve?"

Fred had come home filled with enthusiasm and hoped Sarah would be, too. But she wasn't. Fred rose from the sofa and started pacing the living room. "Of course, there's something in it for him, Sarah. The interest. He'll make plenty on the interest and he says it's a civic venture, too, for the good of the community."

"Humph," Sarah sniffed with scorn. "Civic venture, my eye! Good of the community! He's a wily one. Probably wants to own *you*. Figures you'll be his puppet and only print what he wants in the paper."

"No, Sarah. It's nothing like that," Fred protested. "I asked him and he assured me. No strings attached."

"Oh, Fred, you trust everybody. You're so honest yourself, you don't understand that everybody else isn't that way. You're going to get taken again, just like you did in Angels Camp."

"Holy Jehoshaphat, Sarah!" Fred insisted, "We'll never get ahead unless we take a risk. And this isn't even a risk. It's a sure thing."

"Well, maybe so. But I think we should wait until we've saved some money toward it."

Fred waited until after supper when the dishes were done and after Millie and Bobby had gone to bed before he brought up the subject again. "Ah, Sarah," he began, "about that loan — "

"Not now, Fred." Sarah turned from the kitchen sink and walked up to him, put one hand on his shoulder. "Shhh," she said, placing two fingers of the other hand across his lips. "No more talk about equipment and loans and business, Fred. Not tonight. We haven't properly christened our new home yet."

And Sarah took the willing Fred by the hand and led him into the new bedroom.

CHAPTER THIRTEEN

T HE MORNING OF THE CLEARY BRANDING was fresh and clear
after the rain. A few days of sunshine had dried out the
corrals enough for working the cattle.

Fred had arranged with Joe Carrigan to have a rig waiting
in San Lucas, so when the noon train pulled in the Godfrey
family lost no time in heading up the Long Valley road. They
weren't alone. The road was crowded with traffic, all headed
for the Cleary ranch. Everyone had been invited—Jeremiah
Cleary had stopped in at the newspaper office to give Fred
Godfrey a personal invitation. Millie was excited. She'd been to
a few brandings, of course, but that was when she was
younger. Her girlfriend, Teddy Irwin, who had been to a lot of
them, told her that sometimes somebody would let her ride a
horse, if it was tame enough. Millie hoped she'd get a chance
this beautiful March day.

Bobby didn't care. At age eleven, he wasn't much interested
in horses, but he thought those new horseless carriages were
"pretty swell." His father had called them "smoke snorters,"
and said that their only purpose on earth was to frighten horses and scare the hell out of innocent people. Bobby knew that
Mr. Will Cleary had one of those gas buggies, a Reo Runabout,
and that he was the county supervisor so he should know what
was best.

"See, see, Millie, there it is!" As they pulled into the Cleary
yard, Bobby didn't even wait for his dad to stop the surrey
before jumping out, landing on his backside, and quickly getting up to run over to the automobile, where a crowd of admir-
ers were gathered.

"It's called a Reo Runabout," Bobby said excitedly to anyone
who would listen. "See the top, and the gas lamp headlights,
and it has twelve horsepower with a one-cylinder motor, and
planetary gears. See that crank there? That's to start the
motor. Betcha it'll go thirty miles an hour if he wants it to."

"Nope. That'd be too fast," a rancher in the crowd said adamantly. "Man ain't built to go that fast." Several others nodded in agreement, but Bobby laughed.

The Godfreys left Bobby behind to admire the auto and expound his wisdom and started for the big house just as Jeremiah Cleary came down the steps, hailing guests with his words of welcome. Jeremiah lived alone, although there was a cook living in the room just off the kitchen and ranch hands in the nearby bunkhouse. Now eighty-one years old, he was still active in community affairs, still a director of the First National Bank of Salinas. He kept abreast of all the local news and supervised his cattle ranching and farming enterprise, with the assistance of his son-in-law, Buck O'Keefe. Jeremiah still sat his horse with ease. But despite his good health and being surrounded by his large, loving family, he was constantly fighting off terrible bouts of loneliness since his wife Catherine had died seven years before.

"Glad you could make it, Fred," Jeremiah said, shaking Fred's hand and tipping his big Stetson to Sarah. "Nice to see you, Missus Godfrey. I see you've brought one of your delicious cakes. Take it right on in there to the kitchen."

Jeremiah put an arm on Fred Godfrey's shoulder and led him toward the cattle corrals. "Let's go see if they're getting the right brands on my calves," he said. But Jeremiah was stopped often to exchange greetings and visit with other guests, so Fred drifted to the corrals, which were well below the house, just off the long lane from the county road.

The large Cleary home sat on a rise against the foothills and was surrounded by huge eucalyptus and pepper trees, and the path to the house led through a well-tended rose garden. Team bells mounted above the garden gate announced the entrance of visitors. Off to one side of the main house sat an adobe building with a vine-covered porch, which served as a bunkhouse for the cowboys and harvest hands. A huge barn, equipment sheds, chicken coops, hog sheds, a blacksmith shop, and other buildings stood across from the house at the end of a large horse corral. The freshly white-washed buildings and fences gleamed in the morning sun. The house, although painted white, had green shutters, doors, and trim.

Millie, too, was drawn to the corrals where she could hear the calves bellowing, and the cows bawling, and the shouts of the cowboys, the cheers for a good throw, and the catcalls when somebody missed with a loop. Dust from the milling cattle and smoke from the fire, where the branding irons were heating up, floated up and hung in a cloud over the corrals.

To the side, under the shade trees, she could see that tables had been set up, and behind them were the men preparing the barbecue fire. People were everywhere, dipping into the punch bowl on the table, a few drifting over to gather beside a buggy and drink something a little stronger from a bottle or a flask. Some were bringing food—potato and macaroni salads, cakes and pies—from their buggies into the kitchen, carrying benches, laughing, talking. A few of the girls she knew called out to her. They were sitting in the shade, probably playing with dolls or something, Millie decided. But that didn't hold much interest for her. So Millie smiled politely, waved, but shook her head. She dashed off to watch the branding. Thirteen-year-old girls weren't supposed to do that, but she didn't care. Besides her mother was in the house and couldn't see her. Millie hiked up her long skirt and climbed onto the corral fence.

Cows were on one side of the fence, calling to their babies, and the calves were bunched up in the branding corral where the cowboys were catching them with their ropes. She watched as one man on horseback chased a calf and swung his rope. The loop settled over its head, and the calf bucked and bellowed, and spun around to face the cowboy. He wrapped his rope around his saddle horn and turned his horse, dragging the calf toward the branding fire as a second cowboy rode in behind and threw his rope on the ground by the calf's hind feet. As the calf stepped forward, the cowboy pulled up his rope and tightened it, pulling the calf's legs out straight toward his backing horse. Other men ran to the calf. One grabbed it by the

91

tail, and threw it to the ground, another sat on it, and still another man ran up with the branding iron. Millie turned her head away as the smoke curled up and she could smell burning hair.

"Bull or heifer?" somebody asked, and when the answer came, "Bull," a man detached himself from the group by the fire and approached the calf with a knife in his hand. He knelt down by the calf and Millie stopped watching. Teddy Irwin had told her what was going to happen and she didn't like that part even more than she didn't like the branding.

Whatever they cut out of there they threw into the branding fire. Millie could see it was something to eat because the men were dragging the things out of the fire. She heard somebody call, "Mountain oysters, boys! There, that one's ready to pop!" and he pulled one of them out of the fire, and cut it with his knife, and passed it around. It made Millie feel kind of sick and she was ready to climb down off the fence, anyhow, when she felt two strong hands go around her waist.

Millie was lifted off the top rail and plunked down in a saddle, on top of a large, brown horse. "There, young lady, this is a better place for you," an old man said as he handed her the reins. "Ever ride a horse before?"

"No, sir. I never had a chance," Millie replied, "but I always wanted to. Thank you, mister. What do I do?"

Millie looked down at the man. He wasn't so old as she first thought. He just had a lot of wrinkles on his weather-beaten face. And he was tall and skinny, as if he was all shrunk up. But he seemed awfully sad, and sort of mad, but not at her. She could tell that. He smiled and it was a nice smile. But Millie somehow knew he didn't smile often.

"Oh, just kick old Beauford a little bit and he'll go off that way. If you want to turn him, move your hands and pull the reins over here. If you want to go the other way, just put the reins on his neck on the other side. Got it?"

Millie nodded. She hitched up her skirts and settled herself in the saddle. Her feet didn't reach the stirrups, but she prodded Beauford into a slow walk, away from the corrals and down the lane.

"Didja see that?" Pat Cleary, Will's oldest son, asked his cousin, Bucky O'Keefe. Pat and Bucky were waiting their turn to enter the branding corral and do some roping.

"Yeah," Bucky answered. "Uncle Tim never let anybody ride his horse before. He hardly even talks to anybody, let alone be nice to them. Wonder what came over the old geezer."

"Who's the little girl?"

"I think it's that newspaperman's kid," Bucky replied as they rode through the gate, shaking out their ropes, and building their loops.

Millie sat confidently on old Beauford as she kicked him down the lane. After a bit she even got up enough courage to prod him into a jog. She was bouncing along when she noticed several cowboys bringing cattle through the field toward the corrals. Millie pulled Beauford to a halt to watch. That was all right with Beauford.

The cattle were getting closer, nearing the gate, when suddenly the leaders turned back. The rider on a gray horse broke out after them, made the turn and headed them off. But as the horse came in low out of the turn, the gray dropped his head and started to buck. He went into the air with all four feet and, stiff legged, struck the ground with a jolting thud. Dust flew into the air. The other cowboys yelled and whooped. "Hang with him, Spud!" and "Stay in there, cowboy!"

Millie nudged Beauford closer so she could watch. The gray squealed, snorting froth, spraying it around as he bucked high in the air, changed directions and whirled. But he couldn't shake the young cowboy. Millie was thrilled.

When the horse finally settled down, the cowboy was still solidly in the saddle, his feet firmly in the stirrups. And he was laughing. Why, he could have been thrown to the ground and killed, Millie thought. And there he was, sitting up there, grinning, ready to get on with driving in the cattle.

93

He'd lost his hat in the fracas, and Millie was remembering a thatch of black hair as she rode over to pick it up. She'd find him and return it. But once on the ground she was having a terrible time getting back into the saddle. Beauford stood patiently still and gave her every opportunity. She got one foot in the stirrup, but it was the wrong one, and she started to climb up backwards. Then realizing what she was doing, she stopped, took a deep breath and tried again. But then she discovered that with the hat in one hand, she didn't seem to have enough hands free to grab what she needed to pull herself up.

Just as Millie was praying that no one was noticing her clumsy attempts, she felt a strong hand on her bottom giving just enough of a boost for her to reach the saddle. Millie swung around to face the young, lanky, black-headed cowboy. A wide smile broke below a chiseled nose and dimples dented his cheeks. His brown eyes twinkled as he said, "Thank you, young lady, for saving my hat from getting stomped."

She handed it to him and he jammed it on his head. With a flash of white teeth, he smiled again, touched the brim of his hat, and put his horse into a sudden gallop toward the branding corral. Millie watched in awe as he rode off, seated in the saddle as if he were a part of it and the horse.

That must be Spud Cleary, Supervisor Cleary's youngest son, she thought as she watched him gallop from sight. Millie sat atop Beauford wishing her skirts weren't all hitched up and that her hair wasn't in pigtails. Oh well, she decided, he's so much older, he'd never notice her, anyway. And she probably wouldn't see him again so what was she making such a fuss about? She slowly rode Beauford back to the corrals, taking her time, savoring the image of the tall cowboy whose eyes twinkled when he smiled.

Later in the afternoon Millie's mother found her, in the bedroom set aside for female guests. Millie had taken down her girlish pigtails and fixed her long, honey-brown hair into a single braid, hanging down her back. Somewhere she'd found a red ribbon to tie it up.

Good grief, Sarah thought. She looks so much older. But she didn't say anything. After all, her daughter was starting to grow up.

CHAPTER FOURTEEN

F RED HELD THE EAR PIECE close to his head and shouted into the mouthpiece, "Hello? Hello?" The sounds crackled over the line and into his ear. He couldn't make them out. "Hello —? Is this Bunte's Store?" There was no answer. He clicked the receiver several times and cranked the handle again.

"Central," a voice finally responded.

"Dorothy, this is Fred at *The Settler*," He had to shout to be heard over the static that crackled on the line. "I'm trying to get through to Bunte's Store in San Lucas. I just get a buzzing when you ring there."

"Oh dear, I know, Mister Godfrey. There's been a fire."

"Holy Jehoshaphat, Dorothy." Fred was impatient. "I know there's been a fire!" He paused for a second. "Sorry, Dorothy. I didn't mean to yell at you. I'm trying to get the news about it. Nobody seems to know what's been burned and I have to get the paper on the press."

"Hang on, Mister Godfrey, I'll try to get through to somebody else in San Lucas."

Fred heard some more cranking on the line and distant ringing. But no one picked up the phone. "Damn telephones," Fred grumbled to himself. They were fine as long as they worked. But you couldn't depend on them. No time left now to chase down there to San Lucas; he had to start printing the paper or he wouldn't make the mails. So he had Sarah set up a simple head in forty-eight point, *Fire in San Lucas This Morning* and under it Fred reported that *no further information was known at press time.*

It wasn't until the next day that he learned the extent of the latest fire. Half of San Lucas had burned in a series of fires over the past two years. Bunte's Store was saved, the Pleasant View Hotel and the favorite saloon, The Mint, but the blacksmith shop, the saddle shop, and several houses burned to the ground.

It was enough to prompt Editor Harris of the *San Lucas Herald* to load up his press and cases of type, turn over his subscription list to *The Settler,* and leave in search of a town that had a better fire rating.

Fred Godfrey welcomed *The Herald's* two hundred thirty-seven names to his own list of five hundred and eight subscribers, but the added number stretched press day even longer. Fred doubted that he could get *The Settler* off the press on time each week. He convinced Sarah that it was time to accept Cosgrove's offer of a loan.

Her first reaction was what Fred expected. "I don't like it, Fred," Sarah protested. "We can't trust that man. He's too smooth. I wish we'd get that bank here." But after thinking it over for a few hours, Sarah reasoned, "I guess there's no use you killing yourself and the rest of us."

So Fred Godfrey made the deal with George Cosgrove for three thousand five hundred dollars and they agreed on five years at eight percent with low payments on principle, which would be easy to make, the first four years, and a fifteen hundred dollar balloon payment at the end.

Fred felt rather important when he took the train to San Francisco to visit the printing equipment dealers and look over the Simplex typesetter and the Brower drum cylinder press.

"King City's growing a bit, huh?" The salesman at American Type, which had a list of used equipment for sale, was a trifle patronizing, Fred thought.

That made Fred's hackles rise and he couldn't help bragging a little. "You bet we're growing. Great little town. Water works. Telephones. Brick factory. New sewer system one of these days. Be incorporated soon. And it will really boom when we get

Be incorporated soon. And it will really boom when we get more irrigated farms."

"You'll be back up here ordering a Hoe for your daily pretty soon, Mister Godfrey," the salesman kidded.

"Well, we are moving into a new building," Fred said. "It'll be ready September first, and that's the date I'd like to receive the equipment. Set it up and get it running. What'll you give me on a Messenger hand press?"

"Not much." The salesman laughed.

When Fred got back to King City, it seemed at least half the population was on hand to watch the unloading of his new press and the typesetter at the Southern Pacific depot. They had to make two trips with Slim Smith's wagon to haul the equipment to *The Settler* building, which is what Paul Talbot decided to name his new brick edifice on Broadway when he first rented the downstairs to Fred for his newspaper. Upstairs were the classrooms for the new high school.

Millie loved the proximity of the two. Now a high school freshman, she'd finish her classes and then hurry down the stairs and into the world she really loved. Writing stories, learning the new typesetter, smelling the ink, and hearing the thump of the press, all of it excited her. She loved being there when the last form had been carried to the flatbed and locked into place, and the gas motor kicked in. Her father would climb up to the platform, wet his finger and flip the stack of paper on the feed board. He'd throw the lever to engage the motor, the warning bell would ring and the belts would start to whine. He'd smoothly slide the sheet into the grippers, which would pull in the paper, and Millie would hear the clunk-clunk of each impression as the paper rolled around the drum and onto the delivery arms, which set the sheet atop the stacking table.

Millie's job was to catch the folded papers as they came off the Brown folder, which her father operated after the press work was finished. Millie and her mother were grateful that they no longer had to hand fold the newspapers. Then they'd stamp the subscribers' names on each paper with the Mustang mailer, put them into bundles, and carry them to the post office.

Bobby wasn't very much help. It was a ruckus just to get him to sweep up and his rebellion was a greater source of irritation to Millie than it was to their parents. But ever since Joe Carrigan had moved his livery business from San Lucas to King City, and combined it with an automobile garage, Bobby was constantly sneaking off to Carrigan's to inspect and marvel over the gas buggies.

Millie's favorite place in the new *Settler* shop was at the back window, where she could observe, undetected, the older boys coming back from baseball practice. Spud Cleary, and his brother Pat, and their cousin Bucky, were all on the team. Millie often wondered if Spud could play ball as well as he rode a horse.

Despite Millie's help in the new *Settler* office, Fred and Sarah were now having serious second thoughts about the move into larger quarters and the debt they'd assumed. Fred even wrote his concerns in an editorial: *Just as The Settler's owner has begun to expand with the dollars that some other editor might put to his own use, just as he purchased new equipment to publish a larger paper to better serve the community, a few of his advertisers have withdrawn their patronage. Their reason, as they put it, is that 'all my customers know me and what I sell. That money is just thrown away.'*

To which the editor must reply, 'That $1.50 per month ad in the town business directory is important. Scarcely a week passes that someone doesn't send for a sample copy of The Settler as his way of sizing up our town. What would he think of us if he received a measly little sheet, devoid of news and ads, because there was no income from the latter to support a good paper? He wouldn't think much of our town.

It is very hard to prove that ads in a country paper either do, or do not, bring direct return to the advertiser. But there is no question that a good local paper is the greatest institution for its welfare and advancement that any town can have. Thus everyone enjoys the benefit.

Next time on his rounds, Fred was stopped on Broadway by several business owners who said, "You know, Fred, I just hadn't thought about it that way. Put my ad back in the paper. And you keep plugging for us."

This response fueled Fred's editorial efforts for civic improvement and particularly his crusade for irrigation in the valley. He often filled the front page of the paper with stories of successful projects, such as Cleary's, called for mass meetings on the subject, and suggested formation of irrigation districts. Some of this was over the objection of the large landowners, mostly absentees, who resisted cutting up their grain fields or grazing land, to attract small farmers, even though it had been proven to be profitable. But Fred kept pounding at it.

The Settler's editorial columns continued to advocate incorporation as the cure for what Fred deemed to be King City's major problem: Lack of a sewer system, and other social necessities, such as an ordinance to control cows.

There are many King Cityians, he wrote, such as this writer, who would own a cow if we could afford the luxury. There are others who maintain this luxury at the expense of our peace and happiness. We allude to those who tie their bovines with a rope in the middle of the side street, moving them about from end to end, and to other side streets, when the cows have chewed off all the grass and rendered pedestrian traffic extremely unpleasant, to say the least. Then, for dessert, these ruminants lean against the fences, after breaking them down, to nibble the budding leaves of fruit and ornamental trees, and the flowers of those too poor to own cows for themselves. If we were incorporated, we'd have a poundmaster to enforce ordinances against this practice."

Sarah didn't even know that one of the ladies of her social club, Mrs. Jamison, owned a cow until that lady cut her dead at the Friday afternoon social in the Vendome Hotel. Later she discovered that Mrs. Jamison was insulted because she thought that the editor had referred to *her* as a ruminant. When somebody explained to Mrs. Jamison that it meant a cud-chewing cow, she was still sure the editor was implicating her personally.

Sarah had become accustomed to the occasional snubs. She'd learned that those upset by today's news were pleased by tomorrow's, and most of the grudges were short-lived. But she had to suffer through months of frosty stares from mothers whose daughters were the subject of some social commentary in another issue of *The Settler*.

We would like to make a protest, the editor wrote, *against some of our young ladies concealing a very pretty forehead behind a lot of loose hair. It may be fashion, but hang fashion if it is going to damage the looks of a pretty woman or girl. A fine forehead is something of which to be proud, and they must not spend so much time, and waste so much ingenuity, trying to make it appear that the Almighty had made them destitute of a forehead.*

Because Sarah didn't set all the type since the Simplex machine had come into the family, she didn't always know what her husband had written, and her role as censor was diminished. "I'd just like to know, Fred, a bit in advance," she said one day, "what to expect when I go out on Broadway or visit with my friends."

Millie added her complaint. "Dad, sometimes my teachers find fault with me over something you wrote. Or my friends can't play with me on orders from their parents."

"That's the way it is being in the newspaper business, Millie," her father explained. "That's the price you pay for being part of this family."

Millie laughed, gave him a hug, and said it was worth it. But sometimes she wondered. She remembered when her father criticized the county road department because of the pot holes on Broadway, and Margaret Benchley, whom she'd befriended when no one else would and thought of as a true friend, crossed the street rather than walk with her because Margaret's brother worked on the road crew.

There were always conversations around the Godfrey supper table about the events of the town and the lives of its people and the Godfrey children learned what was for publication and what wasn't and that what they heard was not to be discussed outside. Occasionally they were privy to sensitive information and never betrayed the confidences.

But Bobby's question one night at the dinner table brought conversation to a sudden halt. "What's a cuckold, Dad?" Fred looked at Sarah, but she just shrugged so Fred looked back at Bobby and asked, "Where did you hear that word?"

"I heard one of the fellows over at Carrigan's say that Mister Benton is wearing horns," Bobby said. "Somebody said that means he's a cuckold."

"Well, that means that some people haven't anything better to do than gossip," Fred said. Then he decided that Bobby should be properly informed so he explained. "A cuckold is a man whose wife has taken up with another man. The saying is that the man is wearing horns."

"Well, they said you wouldn't put it in the paper because Mister Benton runs an ad in the paper."

"Gee, Dad, I heard the same thing," Millie added.

Fred had heard the same gossip, that Felicia Benton had gotten on the train for San Francisco with the drummer who peddled ladies' undergarments to Cosgrove's store. Benton was not the most popular man in town and had made a number of enemies who would have enjoyed seeing his marital problems made public. *The Settler* was criticized for not printing the news, and Fred Godfrey was accused of cowardice.

"That type of news is just scandal and there's no place for such things in our family newspaper," Fred explained to his children. In the next issue he responded to the critics: *We would rather build up, than tear down. We print things that help and encourage and uplift, rather than hold up mistakes of some unfortunate to scorn and ridicule. Decency is not lack of courage. If it were, we'd rather be decent than courageous.*

Millie was proud of her father when she read that and that night at the supper table she said, "You know what?" When her mother and father and brother gave their attention, Millie announced, "I think I'll be in the newspaper business when I grow up."

CHAPTER FIFTEEN

TULLY HALL IN BITTERWATER, which sat way off by itself near the junction of the Lewis Creek and Lonoak roads, came alive on dance nights. Of all the country dances, this one had the reputation of being the best. It wasn't that the hall was so big, dancers were always bumping into each other when the serious dancing started, and sometimes the music could hardly be heard over the sound of stomping boots and all the loud laughter and talk. Certainly the location wasn't the reason for its popularity. It was remote and took planning and effort to get there. Maybe it was the great midnight supper served by the friendly Bitterwater people. But whatever it was, Tully Hall dances had a certain charm and appeal and anybody who could ride, walk or crawl was usually there.

They came out from King City, from San Lucas and San Ardo, from the Oasis country and Paris Valley, from the Topo, Wild Horse, Peachtree, and all the way from Priest Valley. They arrived in buckboards and surreys and errand wagons, and in horse-drawn freight wagons that brought entire families who camped nearby for the night. Parked in the yard among the buggies and wagons were Model-T Fords and a few Olds runabouts, Reo touring cars and Overlands. Many young bucks came by saddle horse and the hitching rails were full.

Light shone through the cracks in the walls and glinted on the dust particles which floated out, along with the sounds of guitars and fiddles, accompanied by the bass and the drum, banjos, mandolins and the piano. The hall pulsated with the lively beat of the music. And it was all played by the orchestra Fred Godfrey had put together years ago in King City.

Millie arrived at Tully Hall with her parents, but they were minus Bobby, who hated dances and had stayed at home with a friend.

Millie, on the other hand, loved everything about the evening's festivities. At sixteen, she'd taken on curves in all the right places, and her long, honey-brown hair bounced in a thick braid across her shoulders as she danced. Her smile was warm and her nose crinkled up when she laughed, which was often. Millie had no difficulty attracting boys and, although she enjoyed the attention, she had no serious interest in any of them. Nevertheless, her mother, who was playing second mandolin in the orchestra this evening, looked up often enough to keep tabs on her pretty daughter.

The dance was going full force when the "terrible trio," as they were called by some local residents, came down the Lonoak road, their well-broke, gray horses at a swinging trot. Bucky O'Keefe and his cousins, the Cleary boys, Pat and Spud, turned into the fenced-off yard of Tully Hall and sat on their horses, looking things over. Everyone was inside as those so inclined had not yet worked up the thirst that would later drive them to their caches of liquid refreshment hidden in buggies, saddlebags or beneath the seats of their cars.

The three young cowboys went everywhere together, bound tight by blood and friendship since they were ankle high. Spud was now nineteen years old and, though younger than his brother and cousin, he was considered the leader. The three young men worked hard as harvest hands on Will Cleary's combines, and as cowboys for Bucky's father, Buck O'Keefe, who ramroded the cattle operation for the Cleary ranches. They played hard, too, never missing a picnic, a fiesta, or a dance within twenty miles. If they could reach it by horseback, and still make it home by daylight in time for work, they'd be there.

All three had completed King City high school and had gone to college at University of Santa Clara for two years—the exact length of time it had taken Spud, Pat and Bucky to decide that the Jesuits had nothing more to teach them, and that they preferred ranch life. But the Santa Clara experience had given them an appreciation of urban life—in small doses—and instilled in them the necessary social graces. The boys were as comfortable in the elegant ballroom of the Palace Hotel in San Francisco as they were on horseback in Long Valley.

Their education and civilized veneer, however, weren't the virtues which had earned them characterization as the "terrible trio." That had happened back when they were much younger, when Pat and Spud were pupils in Alberto School on the Trescony, the days when their mother had insisted they wear suits to school, although their classmates were clad in bib overalls. To compensate for the indignity of being dressed as their mother said "young gentlemen must dress," they played harder than any other boys, got their clothes torn and dirty more often, had more playground fights, and were involved in more pranks than all the rest of the Alberto school population put together. In response to the consequences for their actions, they just smiled. Teachers meted out appropriate punishment. Honora scolded and Will spanked. The boys just grinned.

Bucky, who had attended Long Valley school and been separated from his cousins, joined Pat and Spud on weekend visits and during the summer. They'd been working together since they were old enough to haul water or tend header on the harvester, or ride a horse, and in their off-hours mischief was tripled. They hadn't been convicted of all the pranks for which they were the prime suspects, but two in particular earned them a valley-wide reputation.

One incident had occurred about seven years earlier. The boys were intrigued by the goings-on inside The Mint saloon in San Lucas, particularly after Spud and Pat's father, Will

Cleary, stepped into the middle of a gunfight. They noticed that some of the patrons occasionally had trouble with their equilibrium when they left the premises, and that others had a tendency to slump down onto one of the benches along the San Lucas boardwalks, situated to accommodate weary pedestrians. It was Spud who suggested that The Mint would be an appropriate place in which to release a skunk. Pat and Bucky agreed with the merit of this suggestion. But none of the three were all that enthusiastic about catching a skunk, and after several odor-producing tries, the plan was altered thanks to Pat Cleary's most recent adventure.

Pat had shot a female bobcat and captured a kitten. Careful nurturing created an animal that, while not a cuddly pet, was at least amenable to handling. The bobcat and The Mint seemed a natural combination to Spud, and again, the conspirators agreed. They sneaked around behind the building when it was devoid of customers on a quiet Sunday afternoon, found an unlatched door, and released the bobcat.

Those lined up at the bar the next evening were startled to hear a hissing sound ringing in their ears. Those who realized they hadn't, as yet, had that much to drink, located the source of the hissing. It was coming from an overhead rafter. Suddenly, the cat bounded to the floor, under the feet of a relaxed Mint regular asleep at a table, shocking him into a state of unaccustomed sobriety.

"What? What? What the hell is that?" he yelled, running for the back door and escaping into the alleyway.

"A devil, that's what it is! He'll get us for sure," cried another inebriate, diving under the table.

The bobcat jumped on top of the cash register, where it sat and spit, growled and hissed. Those who tried to grab it got scratched and clawed. They chased it along the bar. "Grab it, Tito," one patron yelled. "You grab it," the bartender responded. And back went the bobcat into the rafters. It was three days later that Tito Domingos finally captured the animal and put it in a cage, where it became another claim to fame for the

105

already infamous Mint. Some claimed the incident was nearly equal to the spot on the floor where Brisco had dropped Romero in the Wild West's last shoot-out.

When they heard about the bobcat in The Mint, the terrible trio smiled. And when Will accused them of being the perpetrators, they continued to smile. Evidence was circumstantial. The bobcat was missing from the Cleary place and they were seen in San Lucas that particular Sunday.

"Pat, Spud, Come here." Will called his two sons before him. "That bobcat you fellows had in a cage, what happened to it?"

Pat and Spud looked at each other, then back to their father. There was a long silence. Then Spud spoke up. "It got loose, sir."

"Loose, huh?" Will said, looking his son directly in the eye. "Any idea how a bobcat might have wound up in The Mint?"

"In the Mint, sir? That's unusual," Spud said. "You any idea, Pat?"

"Nope! Not me," Pat replied with a shrug. "Maybe they left the door open. Anything could wander in."

"Yep," Spud agreed.

Punishment was a longer shift on the harvester, but they didn't mind that. So it didn't discourage them from acting on Spud's next suggestion. This time the pranksters had come across a cave of bats down by the Salinas River. They were easy to catch, just hanging around upside down all over the cave. In short order three sacks full of bats were transported to King City, surreptitiously, when the Clearys, en masse, were in attendance at Goetz's Novelty Theatre, next door to the Vendome Hotel. They'd been attracted by an ad in *The Settler*, which claimed moving pictures, *with real plots to their acts by film companies such as Pathe, Vitagraph and Star Films, not the usual namby-pamby plotless, lollygagging exhibitions.*

Shortly after the family was settled in their seats, and the house lights dimmed, the bat sacks came out from under the coats of three young gentlemen, and the furry little fliers attacked the lit projection screen. They swooped and dipped across the silent motion picture, casting terrifying shadows as they soared. The Novelty Theatre fairly rocked with screams and cries as the bats landed on patrons' shoulders and, horror of horrors, got tangled in ladies' hair. This prompted a stampede to the entrance as the house lights came on, and the bats disappeared into the darkness of the overhead rafters. It took old man Goetz four days to roust out and eliminate the bats. There were numerous reports, although unconfirmed, that he even resorted to shooting them with his shotgun, which blew a hole in his movie screen. It took longer than four days for the trio of miscreants to clean up the bat guano from the theater. And when they were finished, old man Goetz banished them for life from the Novelty, a sentence which many women who'd been in the theater that fateful night didn't think was severe enough.

The last time they'd been to a Tully Hall dance they'd arrived late and noticed that most of the younger children had already been bedded down in the wagons and buggies, and in the back seats of the cars. It was quiet outside with everyone inside busily enjoying the midnight supper. The full moon shone into the vehicles, illuminating the soundly-sleeping children.

Spud rode up alongside a buckboard and looked down at two little heads tucked into the blankets. He chuckled as an idea came to him. He motioned to his cohorts to come over and whispered to them. They laughed and nodded.

Within seconds each had stepped down from his horse and quietly led their animals off to the hitching rack.

Spud tiptoed back and picked up one sleeping child from a buggy and transferred it to a wagon. Bucky lifted a slumbering youngster from a Model-T and placed it into a buggy. Pat switched another from a wagon to a car. In a few moments the terrible trio had swapped sleeping children all across the parking yard. They looked around and, satisfied with their work, nodded and entered the hall just as the band was tuning up again. In the time that was left they devoted themselves to serious dancing.

The Buckners noticed it first. They were nearly home in Lonoak when a querulous child's voice asked, "Mama?" And a blond head poked up from the blankets. Mrs. Buckner was horrified. None of hers were blond. "Oh, my God!" she exclaimed. "Who are you?"

"Karl Jorgensen, ma'am," the sleepy boy answered.

Charlie Buckner stopped the wagon and they checked. The other two sleeping forms were there own, all right. But where was Billy? "You put him in the wrong wagon, Charlie," Mrs. Buckner accused. "I told you not to drink so much."

"I did not. Hell and damnation!"

He turned the team around and they were retracing their way toward Bitterwater when they met the Jorgensens coming the other way. Sven Jorgensen was fuming. "Whose kids do you have?" he asked.

"One of yours," Buckner answered. "Do you have our Billy?"

"No, goddammit. I've got three of the Rist kids. I think they have Billy," Jorgensen called out as he put his Model-T in gear and drove off with a lurch that nearly knocked Mrs. Jorgensen to the floorboard.

The terrible trio managed to maintain straight faces whenever they heard the story repeated and embellished as time went on. But in this instance, the prank was blamed on some Peach Tree cowboys and the true culprits went undetected.

Now as they sat their horses outside Tully Hall, Spud Cleary spotted another opportunity. An old, white cow from the neighboring pasture had wandered into the enclosure and was nibbling grass amid the vehicles, obviously in forbidden territory. Spud took down his grass rope, formed a loop and, with just enough light escaping from the hall to help his aim, floated it over the cow's horns. Pat deftly added the hind feet to his score, and they stretched her out while Bucky, at the suggestion of Spud, picked up a couple of rusty coal oil cans from amid several similar relics adrift in the yard. These he quickly affixed to the cow's tail. Then they turned her loose, hazed her toward the dance hall, and drifted into the shadows.

The poor, frantic cow ran around the dance hall, trying to kick at the cans or to hook them, and every time she turned the cans made more of a racket. She swung around to get at the cans and they would disappear. She swung back the other way and they would still be behind her.

People began running out of the hall, but were unable to see in the dark after being in the brightly-lit interior, and couldn't make out the cow, which was going around and around the hall, weaving in and out among the buggies and cars. When they did catch a glimpse of the animal they thought it was a ghost. Horses were neighing and fidgeting when the cow, now on the prod for sure, started bawling and made for the lighted doorway of the hall.

Just at that moment, as the cow was practically inside on the dance floor scattering dancers, a rope whipped out of the night through the open door and settled on her horns. Spud Cleary took his turns and rode away, dragging the animal out of the doorway, through the yard, and back to her pasture, where another cowboy appeared out of the dark to dab a rope on the cow's hind feet while a third cut loose the tin cans.

"Wow, Spud, you got here just time," one dancer praised him.

"Sure did, Spud," said another, "she would have made a mess of the place if she'd got inside."

"Wonder what got into that old cow?" another young man asked.

"Dunno," Spud responded. "She seemed to be plumb loco."

"Thanks, Spud."

All he did was grin, say "Yep," and put up his horse. Bucky and Pat did the same. They took off their spurs and they went to dancing.

Millie hadn't seen Spud for several years, not since he'd left high school. But he looked as handsome as ever, and he was still laughing.

But he didn't ask her to dance.

CHAPTER SIXTEEN

Joins the Silent Majority, read the headline in *The Salinas Valley Settler* for February 4, 1911. *Jeremiah Cleary, Rancher, Capitalist and Pioneer, Died Wednesday. With sons and daughters at his bedside, at the ripe age of 85, Mr. Cleary passed peacefully and painlessly into that slumber which hath no awakening. Death came in the family home in Long Valley after a period of time during which Mr. Cleary had been gradually, and imperceptibly, growing weaker and weaker, a general wearing out of all the organs together, but suffering no sickness nor pain since he began to fail.*

Fred and Sarah were back at the newspaper office discussing the funeral, which they'd just attended in St. John's Catholic Church. Father Grauman, the new priest who'd replaced their friend, Father Garriga, had concelebrated the Requiem Mass with Father Dan Cleary, Jeremiah's son, and delivered a short eulogy.

"I personally didn't know the man, but I know a great deal about him from many of you. He was a man admired by his neighbors, and his family has reason to be proud of his achievements since coming to this country from his native Ireland. A progressive farmer, cattleman, and breeder of fine horses, a bank director, and public-spirited American, Mister Cleary accomplished much in the temporal world. But he should best be remembered for his kindness, his fairness, his willingness to help others and his absolute honesty. It isn't by his worldly deeds that we should judge a man, but how he treats his fellow men. Jeremiah Cleary leaves such a legacy."

"Well, old Jeremiah sure left some big shoes to fill, but it looks like Will is up to it all right," Fred attested. "He left a bundle to his family, I heard."

Sarah nodded. "All that land, and cattle and horses must come to quite a fortune," Sarah agreed. She was putting on her smock, getting ready to set some headlines from the California job case. "How did he do it, coming here from Ireland without a dime?"

"Little by little, Sarah," Fred said. He sat down at the rolltop and commenced to thumb through the subscription card index file. "Jeremiah homesteaded, bought out neighbors who gave up and left. Just stuck with it, dry years and wet. That must have been pretty tough, Long Valley in those early days."

"And what must it have been like for that poor little Irish girl who got killed, his first wife? Coming from that green country to hot, dry Long Valley. I can imagine what she went through," Sarah said, shaking her head wonderingly.

"Well, they certainly have an operation there now. I understand the ownership is split up among the seven children, but Will is in charge. And he's keeping his lease on the Trescony, too," Fred explained.

Again Sarah shook her head. "Don't know how he manages to do all that and still be county supervisor." She paused. "What about the other brother? Can't he help? The one that went to the gold fields?"

"Timothy? I don't know. Never see him," Fred answered. "I hear he just stays on his little place in Coyote Canyon. Drinks, they say."

"Oh," Sarah responded, but she'd lost interest in the Clearys and was thinking of something else. "Fred — " Sarah had that tentative tone in her voice, the one that indicated she was about to change the subject to something unpleasant. She put down her type stick and walked up beside his desk. Fred braced himself.

"Fred, what are we going to do about Millie's education? She'll be through high school next year and I don't want her going right into the newspaper to work."

"Well, why not? She's good at it, writes well, and she can set type. That'll hold her until some man comes along," Fred responded with a grin. Then a frown replaced the grin. "Holy Jehoshaphat, sometimes I wish she was the boy. That Bobby has no interest in the newspaper at all."

111

"Now, Fred." Sarah gave him the familiar look that said she didn't want to hear any more of that old complaint. "We're not talking about Bobby. If we had the money we could send Millie to teacher's college. Two years and she'd have something she could always fall back on."

"Fall back on?" Fred's irritation was starting to show in a crimson flush on his face. "For God's sakes, Sarah, she can fall back on *The Settler!* It's going to do better, soon as the town grows a little more." He held up a stack of cards indicating delinquent subscribers. "Look at these. Soon as they all pay up it'll be a whole lot better."

Sarah gave her derisive sniff. "Better? When? We haven't the money to send her to school now. Every loose bit of coin goes into the paper. What do you intend to do about your daughter?"

"I can pay her to set type."

"Fred, that's something she does anyhow. And for nothing. That and every other chore around the shop." Sarah's aggravation was matching her husband's.

"Just a minute, Sarah. Give me a chance, dammit." Every time Sarah started talking about money he felt like a bug getting stuck with a pin. "I was going to have to hire a typesetter, anyhow. Whatever I pay Millie would be less than I'd have to pay a professional, and it would soon add up to enough for college."

Sarah sighed and backed off. She knew how much Fred loved Millie and would always do the best for his daughter. "All right, Fred. If Millie wants to, give it a try. But don't forget, we have that payment coming due next year to Cosgrove," Sarah said over her shoulder as she picked up her typestick and went back to the case.

Cosgrove! How could Fred forget Cosgrove? The city had finally incorporated, after all those years that he'd editorialized and pushed for incorporation, and the taxes to pay for improvements to the town. Now you'd think it had all been Cosgrove's idea. That wily old bastard had even gotten himself elected to the town council, and brought in a lawyer to open an

112

office in King City, and serve part-time as city attorney. Cosgrove was pretty tight with him, Milton Osgood. Seemed like an oily sort, a smoothy like Cosgrove. Fred didn't like the man too much, but he didn't care for lawyers anyhow.

Well, at least, Fred liked Al Carlson, who'd been elected mayor, and thought the other council members were all good men. Fred was encouraged because they'd voted to move quickly on creating a sewer system for King City. It was long overdue. Lack of proper sanitary facilities had held the town back, Fred had insisted in his editorials and at public meetings called on the subject. In the past, Cosgrove had continually claimed the time was not quite right. "Premature, Fred," was the way he'd always put it. But now that he was on the town council, he was all for it.

Fred puzzled over this the next day as he walked to the office. He wondered why the change of heart. But he forgot about it as he worked through a heavy morning schedule so he could spend the afternoon with the family. They were to attend the Saturday afternoon performance of Kit Carson's Wild West Show. The advertisement in *The Settler* had the entire countryside in a fever of anticipation. *Straight from Kit Carson's buffalo ranch,* it cried in seventy two point Cooper, black letters about two inches high. *Recreation of Battle of Wounded Knee,* it claimed in only slightly smaller type, *Russian Cossacks to perform, See Fearless Cowboys Head Off Buffalo Stampede, Watch Soldiers and Indians Battle — all right here in King City. Plus, Kit Carson will pay $25 to anyone who brings in a mule or horse that our cowboys can't ride.*

Spud Cleary had taken one look at that same advertisement, showed it to his brother and his cousin and, without a word, the terrible trio caught up the old, gray work mare. Tinkerbelle was pretty long in the tooth, but that hadn't shut down any of her meanness when somebody tried to ride her. The terrible trio trailed the mare into town to the intersection of Vanderhurst and Broadway. There the Wild West show was set up on the vacant lot, which took the entire block. An arena had been constructed and temporary bleachers thrown up. Tents, wagons and horses were everywhere, and corralled in a corner were five mangy, shaggy, runty buffalo.

Quick costume changes between acts kept the Russian Cossacks from looking exactly like the fearless cowboys, and the blue-clad soldiers from being dead ringers for some of the near-naked Indians. But it was a good show and the trio enthusiastically applauded, even whooped and hollered at the appropriate times.

When they called for any bucking horses to test the performers, the boys brought up the old gray mare. One cowboy, still wiping off his Indian greasepaint, stepped forward, confident that an old skate like Tinkerbelle wouldn't be much challenge.

Tinkerbelle disabused him of his opinion immediately. Then she dumped an Indian in two jumps, and several Cossacks in less time than that. Each time Bucky, Pat or Spud would catch her as she waited patiently for them to come up to her. They'd ear ol' Tink down, just for show, as the next rider got settled, and then step back. The mare would do the rest. She'd bunch her feet under her and buck straight up, kicking out her hind legs at the apex of her leap, corkscrew her entire hindquarters, and return to earth with all four feet back under her. If the corkscrew didn't loosen up the riders, her sudden collision with the ground did. After seven of his best bronc riders had picked themselves up, brushing off King City dirt from the seats of their pants, the famous Kit Carson, or his impersonator, decided they'd call it a day and paid out the twenty-five bucks.

The terrible trio led the old gray mare from the arena to the wild applause of the crowd. King City spectators were content. They'd seen a good show and one of their own had triumphed.

Millie Godfrey clapped longer and harder than most.

CHAPTER SEVENTEEN

CONNIE BAXTER AND HER HUSBAND, Christopher, had just returned from a week in King City, where they had attended the funeral of Connie's uncle, Jeremiah Cleary, the man who had raised her after her mother had died and her father, Jeremiah's black sheep brother Matthew, had abandoned his only child to go back to the gold mines.

It had been an emotional time for Connie, visiting in Long Valley, being with her cousins and their families, seeing all the children, always made her envious of her female cousins. She'd wanted babies of her own for as long as she could remember, but never had any. There was "nothing wrong" with her, the doctors had said, but still, she and Christopher remained childless. The trip to Long Valley only served as a sad reminder of what she didn't have. But what the Baxters lacked in family life they more than made up for in material wealth and the trappings of the rich. When they arrived back home in San Francisco, Connie quickly settled back in the comforts of their mansion on Nob Hill, which had been refurbished and returned to its former glory after surviving the San Francisco earthquake five years earlier.

A few days later Christopher announced at dinner that he had to leave for Colorado and invited Connie to go with him. She often accompanied her husband on his numerous business travels, mainly because she hated being alone in the house with only the servants for company. But this time, because the trip to Long Valley had been so draining, Connie wasn't in the mood for travel again so soon.

"I'm just too tired, dear," she told Christopher. "But why are you going to Colorado?"

"That's where my client is—you know the Fabray Iron Works and mining interests. You met the Fabray girl once. Remember? Clara?"

"Oh, yes," Connie said somewhat absently, as she sipped her glass of white wine and delicately chewed a piece of poached salmon. "You handled her aunt's estate." Christopher nodded. "She inherited quite a fortune, didn't she?"

"That she did," Christopher said, helping himself to more wine, and another portion of scalloped potatoes. "And before that it was a little ranch down in your part of the country, near San Lucas, that she got when her grandparents died. Now she's going to inherit even more, which is why I'm off to Colorado. We just received a telegram that Clara's father died suddenly out there. Heart attack or something and he was only about fifty."

"Oh, what a shame!" Connie exclaimed, looking down the long expanse of the mahogany dining room table at her husband. A serving girl had just entered with dessert and coffee and the butler placed a box of Christopher's favorite Cuban cigars next to his coffee cup. When the servants had gathered the dishes and left the room, Connie asked, "Is there a Missus Fabray?"

"Somewhere," Christopher replied taking out a cigar from the box and clipping the end. "Amy Fabray ran off years ago, when Clara was around four. Big scandal at the time." Christopher puffed as he applied a match to his cigar and admired the glowing tip. "Just about broke Vincent Fabray's heart. No one seems to know if she's dead or alive."

"How terrible!" Connie looked appalled. "How could a mother run away and leave her child. What sort of person could do that?" But then, the memory of her own father momentarily stabbed again with that old hurt. Strange how it never completely went away, not even after all these years.

"Indeed, how could she have done that," Christopher agreed. "Fabray was crazy about his daughter, but he left her in the care of her aunt, that Missus Whitney. He couldn't stand to live here with the scandal still fresh in people's minds. Spent most of his time at the company mines in Colorado and Nevada. Had a home in Virginia City, I think. He was transacting some busi-

ness at the Fabray Colorado mines and just keeled over. I'm to
go there and to finish it up."

"How old is Clara now?"

"Let me see — " Christopher thought a moment and then
answered, "Clara Fabray is just twenty."

"Well," Connie said as she left her place at the table, "she's a
very wealthy young woman. I wonder what she's like?"

"You'll probably meet her again," Christopher said. "I'd like
you to attend the funeral. I won't be here and I'd appreciate
having you standing in for me. Oh, there'll be others from the
firm there, Fabray is one of our most important clients. But it
would be nice if you would go. If you don't mind, Connie?" He
smiled across the table at his wife, who silently wished she
didn't have to go to another funeral, but was grateful it would
not be taking a personal toll on her. "Of course, dear, I'll go for
you." Connie smiled back at Christopher.

* * * * *

Connie wrote all about it to her cousin, Annie Phillips in
Bitterwater. *It was a huge funeral and Grace Cathedral was
packed. I'd never been to an Episcopal service, but it's a lot like
ours. Clara Fabray is a beautiful young girl, even dressed in
mourning black. She's blond and stately and was very com-
posed. They say her father was mesmerized by her, she looked
so much like her mother who ran away with some other man
when Clara was only four. Her mother is that Amy Barnes, the
one who made a wreck of Tim's life. Can you imagine me actually knowing her daughter? And she's just as beautiful as Amy
was. Anyhow, Fabray left the raising and education of Clara
to her aunt, Mrs. Whitney, who died some years ago. Mrs.
Whitney left a fortune to Clara and now she'll inherit Fabray
Iron Works and those gold and silver mines in Nevada and
Colorado. She already owns the Barnes place in Pine Valley. I
visited with her after the funeral service and she's very nice.
Christopher handles all their affairs, so I'll probably see her*

again. Small world, like they say, isn't it, Annie? But please don't tell Tim about this. He doesn't need to know and be hurt any more. How are the children? I was amazed seeing them all so grown up at Uncle Jeremiah's funeral. My goodness, it is hard to believe that your oldest boy is twenty. You'll be a grandmother one of these days. Write soon. Hello to Charlie. Love, Connie.

* * * * *

Connie came down the stairs to meet her husband, home from another busy day at his law offices on Montgomery Street. Christopher Baxter slipped off his coat, loosened his tie and put on the smoking jacket held by the butler. "Thank you, Ralph," he nodded to the old retainer, who'd been with the Baxter family since the house was built. "I'll have my usual."

"How'd your day go, Chris?" Connie greeted her husband with a light kiss and seated herself beside him on a divan in the reception room off the great hall, which they both liked because it was smaller and more intimate than any of the other rooms on the ground floor.

"You'll never believe what happened today, darling." Christopher took her hand and held it for a moment, then laughed, incredulously. "Amy Fabray turned up."

"What?" Connie was puzzled. "What do you mean, Amy Fabray?"

"The long lost Missus Michael Vincent Fabray," Christopher explained. "She missed her poor, dear daughter so much that she's come back to comfort her in her bereavement."

"Chris! You must be joshing me. Why that woman's been gone for sixteen years. She doesn't care about Clara. Why on earth would she come back now?"

"Connie, Connie," her husband said. "You're a big girl. Think about it. Think about five million dollars, maybe more. A lot more. Darling Amy wants her share."

"Oh, but Chris, certainly she's not entitled to anything?"

"Of course not." Christopher said. "But she'll make a case. Fabray never legally divorced her, even though she was gone long past the legal time to be declared dead. He could have. But he never did. So it could be sticky."

"What a wicked woman," Connie said.

"Yeah, but Clara's falling for her soft soap. She's letting Amy stay with her, for godssakes. Clara invited me over there to Green Street this afternoon to meet her mother." Christopher shook his head in disbelief. "Amy is playing the distraught widow and the grieving, loving mother. Claims her absence was just a misunderstanding with Fabray and that she's been in touch with him all these years. And Clara wants to believe her. I could see it in her eyes."

"What are you going to do, Chris?"

"Try to convince Clara of her mother's true intentions," he said. "Amy took me aside, wanted to speak privately with me. She dropped all pretense and put it to me straight. Said flat out that she wants Fabray Iron Works and the mines. Clara can keep the Whitney fortune and the Pine Valley ranch. Otherwise, the sweet little Missus Fabray says she'll sue and take it all."

"And that's the woman our Tim lost his heart over." Connie said sadly.

"Oh, she's a looker, all right," Christopher said. "When I walked into Clara's drawing room and saw them both standing there, I thought they were sisters. She must be nearly fifty, but she looks half that age. It would be hard to pick out which is the most beautiful."

"The better to attract another man to run off with as soon as she gets what she came back after," Connie said with more sarcasm in her voice than Christopher had ever heard before.

* * * * *

"Sarah, look at this." Fred Godfrey was going over the San Francisco Examiner, checking for stories of interest to *Settler*

119

readers. Sarah walked over to his rolltop desk, where the paper was spread out and read over his shoulder. *Lawsuit Settled Out of Court,* was the headline. *A lawsuit filed in San Francisco superior court was settled yesterday before going to a trial that threatened to cause a great stir in the city's social circles. The considerable fortune of the late Michael Vincent Fabray III, owner of Fabray Iron Works and gold and silver mines in Colorado and Nevada, was claimed by a woman who insisted she is Fabray's widow and rightful heir. The fortune, estimated at more than six million dollars, was left to Fabray's daughter, the beautiful and socially prominent Clara Fabray, the only child of the mining tycoon who died suddenly of a heart attack six months ago.*

The woman attesting to be Fabray's legal wife, and Clara's mother, the former Amy Barnes, presented herself after an absence of 16 years to the law firm of Christopher Baxter of this city to claim her legacy. When she was refused, she filed a court action claiming, in addition to the Fabray estate, the considerable property of the late Mrs. Elbert Whitney, who had made Clara Fabray her heir, as well as a small ranch in Pine Valley near San Lucas in Monterey County, also the property of Miss Fabray. Baxter said that an undisclosed sum was settled on the woman with the understanding that she leave San Francisco, thus avoiding a revival of an old scandal.

"Holy Jehoshaphat, Sarah!" Fred exclaimed. "That must be the old Barnes place in Pine Valley. Wasn't that the Barnes girl that jilted Tim Cleary and went away to the city? We saw them together once at the harvest ball."

"Humph," Sarah said with a sniff. "Yes. And I remember telling you at the time that the girl was nothing but a flirt."

Fred picked up a pencil and began re-writing the story. "Do we have to print that, Fred?" Sarah asked.

"Well, it involves a ranch in Pine Valley. If we don't, people who hear about this'll wonder why they didn't read it in *The Settler.*" Fred said. "It's news."

Sarah gave a little sigh of resignation and set her typestick to two columns wide and went to the type case, taking out the letters for a 24-point headline. Then she sat down in front of the Simplex and began to put the story into type.

* * * * *

It was a week later when Tim Cleary rode into San Lucas to pick up his mail. Several back issues of *The Settler* were in his box. That night in his cabin in Coyote Canyon, after fixing supper, eating and carefully washing his few dishes, Tim started methodically reading each issue, taking sips from a bottle of Old Overholt as he turned the pages of the paper. It was late in the evening when he found the article on a back page. He read it several times. Then Tim finished off the bottle and went outside to stand in the dark night and look up at the stars.

CHAPTER EIGHTEEN

T HE LITTLE MEETING ROOM AT CITY HALL was jam-packed, "filled to the rafters," someone remarked. It had been the school house before incorporation, but now that the grammar school had a new building of its own, King City's founders had appropriated it. It sat in the center of a vacant half block, formerly the school playground, on Vanderhurst Avenue just a block off Broadway. Every one of the town's fifteen hundred citizens had crowded into the room, or, at least, it seemed so to Fred Godfrey.

He sat in the front row, notebook in hand, ready to record the events of the meeting, which was called to consider the bids for construction of King City's sewer system. It had been a long, hard campaign to finally get this matter to a vote. Fred thought of all the editorials he'd written over the past ten years, and all the arguments he'd had, before the city had finally incorporated, and now the townspeople could look forward to "more civilized living", as several ladies of Sarah Godfrey's social club had remarked.

The Settler had proclaimed the news in its largest type, "*Sewer Vote Favors Bonds.*" Tonight the city council would open bids, select the low bidder, and vote to issue revenue bonds. Anticipated cost, according to the design engineer, was fifteen thousand, six hundred ninety-nine dollars and ninety cents, safely under the limit of the city's bonding capacity. Fred fervently hoped nothing would go wrong now.

Mayor Al Carlson, with the city attorney Milton Osgood by his side at the council table, called the meeting to order. After the usual routine business, he cited the next item on the agenda, bid openings for the sewer project. Osgood, who also served as acting city clerk, opened the first of three envelopes.

Ace Sanitary Systems of San Jose bid fifteen thousand, three hundred sixty dollars. Then Associated Construction of San

Francisco bid fourteen thousand, nine ninety; and Brighton Brothers of San Mateo bid seventeen thousand six fifty.

Fred made a note of each bid as it was called out. Two of them under the estimated cost. He thought it looked as if the San Francisco firm had it.

In the general hubbub that followed the bid openings, Godfrey missed the looks that passed between Councilman Cosgrove and his friend, City Attorney Milton Osgood, acting clerk. But, if he'd seen them, he'd not have been surprised. The pair always had their heads together. On Cosgrove's part the look was one of concern. But Osgood merely winked back at him.

Mayor Carlson banged his gavel for quiet, and when the room was semi-still, he said, "I call for a motion to accept the low bid."

Councilman Stan Hill started to make the appropriate motion, but was cut off by the city attorney. "Excuse me, Stan, but we can't move so fast," Osgood intoned. "I must first review each of the bids to ascertain that there are no improprieties."

"Oh!" Carlson was surprised. "I thought we'd award the bid tonight and approve the bonds."

"Well," the lawyer patiently explained, "the city's bonding capacity is twenty thousand dollars. All three submissions are safely below that amount. You may take action tonight to authorize the revenue bonds up to the city's limit. Then, I suggest, that the council approve a motion to accept the lowest bid submitted in compliance with the specifications. In that manner, after I review each bid form, and ascertain which are in accord, the project may immediately proceed."

"Huh?" the mayor wondered.

"What's all that mean?" Hill questioned. Pete Morasci was asking the same of his fellow councilman, George Henry. The room was abuzz with the hum of conversation. Councilman Cosgrove sat quietly and watched.

The city attorney explained it again, patiently outlining the steps that the council could take. Finally, they seemed to understand and followed his advice. Both motions passed unanimously.

Fred was pleased. The town would have its sewer system at last, and step into the ranks of real cities, complete with what he considered the major attribute: Sanitation. This would eliminate the danger of an epidemic from a disease such as typhoid—a very real concern in areas without proper sewage disposal. Each property owner would now be required to pay his share of the bond cost in taxes, according to benefit. There were to be five main sewer laterals with twelve-inch pipe, running down Broadway, Lynn Street, Bassett and Pearl. There'd be branch lines on Third, Ellis and Second with smaller pipe, all specified in the call for bids. Pipe would be "vitrified, salt-glazed ironstone sewer pipe," all laid at specified depths, the project to be inspected by a city inspector each step of excavation and construction.

Fred had seen the notice to bidders. In fact, it had run three times in *The Settler* as a legal notice, taking up a great deal of space and subjecting him to some kidding at Himmah's barber shop. "No wonder you been pushing for a sewer, Fred," the barber kidded, "all that advertising in *The Settler* is going to make you fat."

"It's about time I got paid for some space," he retorted, "after all the paper I've wasted over the years trying to convince you dummies to get rid of your privies and septic tanks."

They'd all laughed and the conversation moved on. Fred didn't mind being kidded. But sometimes he wondered if any of them understood that their local newspaper was a business, dammit, the way he made his living.

But now, as the council meeting broke up, Fred was puzzled. What could be wrong with the bids that prevented Osgood from picking one right now? Fred could tell by the buzz of conversation as the people left the hall that others were as puzzled as he was by Milton Osgood. He approached the council table and looked directly at the lawyer.

"Say, Milt, mind if I take a look at those bids?"

"Oh, I'm sorry, Godfrey. Not possible right now. Not until I have time to go over them," Osgood replied politely but firmly. "Give 'em to you in a day or so, soon as we can make an announcement of the winning bidder."

Fred didn't push it. But he left city hall wondering what the hell was going on? When he arrived home he told Sarah about the meeting. "Those construction bids are public information, Sarah. Those two are up to something."

"Which two?"

"Cosgrove and Osgood — "

"Hah! I'm not surprised," Sarah said, sniffing her contempt for both men. "Who was the low bidder?" she asked. "Don't they have to give it to that one?"

"Not if there are discrepancies in a bid," Fred explained. "Oh well, two of the bids were under the estimate. Only Brighton Brothers was over it. By quite a bit, in fact."

"Brighton?" Millie, who'd been listening to her parents conversation, spoke up. "I set a news item for next week's paper, something about Betty Cosgrove being in San Mateo to visit her cousin, Nancy Brighton — "

Fred looked at his daughter wide-eyed. "Holy Jehoshaphat! That's it. But they can't be that blatant, to give it to the high bidder who happens to be a relative. I have to look into this."

"Now, Fred, wait a minute," Sarah said anxiously. "Do you have to? We still owe Cosgrove a lot of money."

"To hell with that, Sarah. If there's collusion between Osgood and Cosgrove to profit at the expense of the public, it's *The Settler's* responsibility to get at the facts. I just can't believe they'd be stupid enough to think they could get away with this."

"Go slow, Freddie," Sarah pleaded. "You don't really know that's what's happening. At least wait until you're sure."

Fred hated it when she called him Freddie that way. Like she was dealing with an impetuous, little boy. *I'll do what I have to do. But I wish I'd paid him off last year. It would have strapped us, but I'd have done it somehow.* It was Cosgrove's own idea that Fred re-finance the note, extend it for two years with interest payments only and the principle on demand. But right now he *was* strapped. Business hadn't been good lately. He couldn't pay Cosgrove off today, Fred realized, if his life depended on it.

Millie, who had graduated from King City High, had postponed college for a year so that she could help her father at the paper and earn some extra money. Bobby was about to finish high school and wanted to go right to work for Joe Carrigan at his automobile garage. But Fred and Sarah insisted he go to business school first, at least for a year. They knew Bobby never was interested in working on the newspaper, but they had higher hopes for him than to be a grease monkey for the rest his life. Where was all this money going to come from? Fred wondered as he spent a long sleepless night.

He waited until after nine the next morning before going to the office of Attorney Milton Osgood on the second floor of the Kirk Building, just a few doors down from the Vendome Hotel where he and Sarah had once lived. As he started walking up the stairs he felt a knot of anxiety gripping his stomach. He hated these confrontations. Just before he opened the door to Osgood's office, Fred took a deep breath to calm himself. He made up his mind to treat his visit simply as routine and to carefully watch the lawyer's reaction.

"Well, how's it look, Milt?" Fred asked as he sat in a chair across from Osgood's desk.

Osgood swung around in his swivel chair and looked out the back window, over the vacant lot, at the trash cans and the weeds, which were another target for *Settler* editorials. The view can't be that great, Fred thought, but Osgood seemed enthralled by it. Finally, he swung back to face the editor, took off his glasses and began to polish them with a white handkerchief. "Too soon to tell," he said, replacing his glasses and then adjusting them while Fred waited. "Haven't had time yet this morning for a proper review."

Fred could feel the heat rising in his face, but he kept his voice steady. "Now listen, Milt. I have to know so I can get it in type," Fred said, taking out a pad of paper and a pencil from his coat pocket. "*The Settler* comes out tomorrow and this news better be in it or people are going to wonder what the hell's going on."

"Going on? Just what do you mean, going on?" The attorney was indignant.

Fred chose his words carefully. "I don't know what I mean by that. Perhaps, if you tell me who gets the bid, I'll understand."

Milton Osgood calmed down himself and spoke in a soothing voice. "Well, I'll tell you, Fred, since you insist, but you have to keep it under your hat until the paper comes out. By that time it will be official. But it appears that we'll have to throw out two of the bids for neglecting the specifications. We're awarding the job to Brighton."

"Brighton, huh? Wasn't that one about two thousand bucks over the estimate? What's wrong with the lower bids?"

Osgood sighed deeply as if to say that laymen just didn't understand the complexities of legal matters. His patronizing smile only served to further irritate the newspaper editor. "I'll explain it all at the next council meeting, Fred. You be there."

"Now just a minute, Milt! You have to tell me." Godfrey's face was glowing red and he jabbed his pencil at the lawyer. "It's public business and the public has a right to know!"

"All you have to know is that there were errors in two of the bids and we're giving it to the only legal bidder." The city attorney was emphatic. "Now, if you'll excuse me, I have work to do." With that he swung his swivel chair to the window and his back to Fred Godfrey.

Fred stood there, seething. He was frustrated, but kept silent, considering his options. There weren't any, short of punching Osgood in the nose. Fred was tempted. He was capable of it, but he swallowed his pride, fought back his temper, and made a retreat down the stairs onto Broadway.

Back at *The Settler office* he walked into the shop, hung up his coat and had just turned to Millie, who was operating the typesetter, to tell her what had happened when the phone rang. Fred picked it up, receiver in one hand and mouthpiece in the other. *"Settler,"* he growled.

"Ah, Fred. George Cosgrove here." Fred shook his head, thinking that these guys don't waste any time. "I just wondered if you were in. Got something I'd like to talk over with you."

"Sure, George. Come on over," Fred answered. He put the receiver back on the hook and stood at his desk, wondering if Cosgrove was going to pressure him. Would he demand his loan be immediately paid off. Fred didn't have the money. What would he do?

Fred settled himself at his desk, moved a pile of papers and uncovered his humidor. He took out a panatela, bit off the end and lit it, feeling more fortified, in command at the big roll top desk, cigar smoke billowing out.

"Hi there, George — " Fred called out as the businessman, now turned city councilman, entered the office. He waved Cosgrove into a chair by his desk.

"Well, well. Good morning, Fred. How's everything today?"

"George, you didn't come in here to inquire about my health." Fred puffed his cigar, looked at the glowing tip and took the initiative. "What's on your mind?"

Cosgrove blinked, but didn't let the frontal attack jar him out of his usual methodical, unctuous manner. "Fred, you know I have a lot of confidence in you and I value the importance of your newspaper in this community."

"Yes, George, and I appreciate it." Sarah was right, he thought, you never trust a man like Cosgrove.

"The Settler has been very effective in arousing public support for many civic improvements over the years, Fred, and you've earned the respect of your readers," he continued, a smooth smile spreading over his jowly face. He leaned forward in his chair and gave Godfrey his most sincere look. "I'd cer-

tainly hate to see you do anything to harm that reputation, Fred."

"Well, I sure try to always do what's right, George. I'd hate to harm my reputation, too." The rising tide of blood was turning Fred's face crimson. "Just what the hell are you getting at?"

"Now, Fred. Take it easy. No reason to get upset. I know that a good newspaper can function much easier when there aren't any money problems. Write what you want without fear of upsetting anybody, or having subscriptions canceled, losing ads, things like that. Right, Fred?"

Fred's eyes locked on Cosgrove's. "I always print the truth, George. My paper is published in the best interests of the people of King City and the area. You know that." He waved the cigar to emphasize his point.

"Sure, I believe that, Fred," Cosgrove answered. "That's why I insist my department store have that half page ad in your paper every week. No reason to upset that, is there?"

"I don't see any reason!" Fred's voice climbed up a few octaves.

"Well now," Cosgrove said in his most placating tones, "this little misunderstanding that took place this morning with Mister Osgood. Can't we just forget that, Fred?"

"What do you mean, forget it? And there was no misunderstanding. I wanted to know the low bidder on the sewer project so I can print it in tomorrow's paper. He told me he'd thrown out two lower bids on technicalities and would have the city award it to Brighton, the highest bidder," Fred said, never taking his eyes off Cosgrove. "Some relative of yours, right, George?"

Fred felt better now that it was out. He let a sigh escape him. But Cosgrove had suddenly lost his oily, condescending manner. He shed his kid gloves and showed his claws.

"All right, Godfrey. I'll lay it on the line." He didn't shout, but his voice got lower and was laced with venom. He shook his finger in Fred's face. Millie, who had been intently listening, got up from her seat at the Simplex and moved to her father's side.

"If there's one damn word in your paper tomorrow that I don't think should be there," Cosgrove said, "I'm calling your note immediately. And canceling my ad."

Fred threw down his cigar and came out of his chair in a rush as Millie, wide-eyed, jumped out of his way. He took the bigger man by the neck and the seat of his pants, and swung him around. He propelled the surprised Cosgrove to the front door, and swung it open as he lifted his foot. Fred's shoe hit Cosgrove in the seat of the pants. Not hard, but hard enough to make the councilman lose his balance and fall to the side-walk in front of *The Settler* office.

Several passers-by jumped back, startled. As they looked in amazement at the sputtering man on the sidewalk, they saw the editor shaking his fist, and heard him yell in a voice that carried the length and breadth of the town, "Go to hell, Cosgrove! You don't own me! No man owns me! My writing and my paper aren't for sale."

Some heard Cosgrove's reply. He rose from his inglorious position, shook his fist in return, right under Godfrey's nose. "You'll rue this day, damn you, Godfrey!" he shouted. Then his voice dropped and again took on the sinister power of a hissing snake. His eyes narrowed. "Hear me, and hear me well. You'll make that payment immediately or lose this sorry rag."

With that Cosgrove brushed himself off, gathered what dignity he could muster, and marched off down Broadway. Fred stood in *The Settler* doorway, shaking with anger. But then a cold fear started in his belly and flowed through his veins. My God, what had he done?

CHAPTER NINETEEN

"**I**DIDN'T TRUST THAT OILY SLIME FROM THE FIRST," Sarah said to Fred, pouring them each a cup of coffee and sitting down at the kitchen table. "So how are we going to pay him off?"

Sometimes she surprised him, still, after twenty-five years of marriage. She was as indignant as he was. But instead of recriminations, she was ready to consider their options. Fred had gone straight home after kicking Cosgrove out of the office and told Sarah what had happened.

"Its not just that, Sarah. My God, how will we survive without his advertising?" Fred held his head in his hands.

"Just how much do we still owe?" she asked.

"Well, it amounts to fifteen hundred plus a little interest up to date." Fred did some quick, mental calculations. "We could raise maybe a thousand with a mortgage on the house. That shouldn't be hard with Monterey County bank, now that they've finally put a branch here. I wish they'd been located here when I needed the money. Maybe I could raise a little on my equity in the printing equipment."

"Fred, we are not going to mortgage this house." Sarah was adamant.

"Well, if I can't pay him off, he'll take the business and we'll have to go somewhere else. Start up again." Fred sorrowfully shook his head. "In that case we'd have to sell the house, anyway."

"We aren't going to let a skunk like Cosgrove drive us out of this town," Sarah insisted. "There'll be some way and we'll find it. Now you better get back down to *The Settler* office and get to work. Everybody in town will know Cosgrove threatened you and called your note. Get the paper out with that story *in it*. You'll show them. Something good will happen, Fred."

Godfrey hurried back to the office, his spirits lifted by Sarah's support and her encouragement. Holy Jehoshaphat! Fred marveled, what a backbone that woman had.

Fred sat at his desk and began to write, his soft lead pencil flying across the paper. He handed a sheaf of copy to Millie, who immediately sat down at the typesetter and started her fingers flying over the keyboard. The hum and clang of the Simplex as the letters dropped into line was suddenly interrupted by Millie's low whistle. "Wow, Dad!" she exclaimed as she realized what he'd written.

That night at the supper table Millie described for Bobby the incredible confrontation that he'd missed. "And then Dad grabbed Cosgrove by the coat and pants and kicked him out of the office," she told an admiring Bobby, who was, for once, genuinely interested in what had happened at the newspaper office. "Atta boy, Dad," Bobby said proudly.

"Hmmm," Sarah sniffed. "All well and good for your father to stand up for himself. But now what are we going to do?"

They all sat silently, looking at each other. Fred shrugged.

"Yes, well," Sarah said, "Nothing we can do about it tonight. Except pray. I'll do that. And Fred, it wouldn't hurt you to do some praying, too. We'll see what tomorrow brings."

The next day the argument between Fred Godfrey and George Cosgrove was the talk of the town. There were as many versions as there were speakers, but they all agreed that Cosgrove was going to try to put *The Settler* out of business. But nobody seemed to understand just what was behind it. Those who got their copy of *The Settler* in the mail that afternoon quickly figured it out.

A simple news story reported the council meeting and the fact that the city authorized the bonds and agreed to award the contract to the lowest, legitimate bidder, whoever that was in the opinion of the city attorney. But alongside the news story ran an editorial, signed by Fred Godfrey, that asked a number of pertinent, and some would say, impertinent, questions.

Does the city attorney, Milton Osgood, intend to disqualify, on technicalities, both of the lower bidders in order to award the contract to the highest bidder?

132

There is a gap of almost $2,300 between the low bid and the high bid. Does it make sense for the city to pay $2,300 more because of some minor technicality? Do any such technicalities really exist? The editor was not privileged to see the bids.

What relationship is there between the attorney Osgood and Councilman Cosgrove? Is there a business relationship?

We believe that principals of Brighton Brothers, the high bidder, which the city attorney claims is the only legitimate bidder, have a personal relationship to Councilman George Cosgrove. Does a conflict of interest exist?

After this issue of *The Settler* had been circulated, it became the topic of every conversation in every parlor, and around every family table. Shoppers and clerks discussed it, and men gathered on every street corner to talk about it. By noon the next day, the city council, feeling the heat, but not sure just what was wrong, called a special meeting. Again the chambers were filled.

Mayor Carlson asked the city attorney, acting as city clerk, for a report on his evaluation of the bids.

"Ah, ahem," Osgood cleared his throat, adjusted his glasses and pompously declared, "I find no irregularities and recommend that the City of King accept the low bid of Associated Construction of San Francisco in the amount of fourteen thousand nine hundred and ninety-nine dollars."

The room erupted with surprised reactions and raised voices. For a moment, the din was deafening. Then it died down and ninety-six pairs of eyes, representing all the citizens who could crowd into the room, turned toward Fred Godfrey. By their incredulous looks, it was apparent that they didn't know what had happened. Had he gone off half-cocked? Or did his editorial make an impact, change some minds?

Fred was relieved. The project would go ahead, even though he might not be around to see it. He felt as if he'd won a battle, but lost the war. He stayed close to home all week end and fretted.

133

On Monday morning at his office, Fred was served with two citations. One was the demand for payment of one thousand six hundred and twenty dollars within three days of that date. The other was notice of a libel suit being filed in Monterey County court on behalf of George Cosgrove and Milton Osgood. Both documents were the meticulous legal work of the city attorney.

Fred showed them to Millie and then phoned Sarah to tell her the news. When he got off the phone, he slumped into his chair, head in his hands, and let discouragement and despair wash over him. *I'm in a helluva fix. Damned if I see any way out. Those two finagled me into that editorial and all I have is my own word against Osgood's that he planned to award that contract to Cosgrove's brother-in-law, or whatever the hell he is. My editorial made them come up honest, but I'm dead in a court of law. It won't make much difference, though, Cosgrove has me nailed.*

Fred couldn't get on with his day's work. He suffered from the usual day-after-publication lethargy on top of his seemingly insurmountable troubles. He looked up as the door opened, half expecting to see another stick of dynamite coming at him. But it was Charlie Beyers from American Type, who sold type, leads and slugs and other printing supplies.

Fred was in no mood for small talk from the friendly, joshing, effervescent Charlie, a man he had always welcomed, even when he had no order for him. "Hello, Charlie," he managed.

"Hey, Fred, ol' buddy. What's the matter? Your subscriber die?" Charlie roared at his own joke as he always did, and usually his audience laughed with him. Not this time.

"No more orders from me," Fred said.

"Aw, c'mon, the joke wasn't that bad, was it?"

Fred tried a smile, a rueful one. "No, 'course not, Charlie. It's just that I won't be here much longer." And then he told Charlie Beyers the entire story.

A sobered Charlie listened without interruption, nodding sympathetically. When Fred was through, Charlie wrinkled his brow in thought for a moment and then said, "Fred, I have a idea. It might not work out. But my company considers you a good customer. You've always been fair and square with us. Paid something on your bill even when things were hardest. Always told us what to expect, always stuck to your word. You have a good reputation in the newspaper field, Fred. I don't think my company would want you to go down the chute over some lousy deal like this. Let me talk to the top guys. Maybe yes, maybe no. Can't promise, but I'll get back to you."

When Charlie left, Fred felt slightly better. It was nice to know he was appreciated, even on his death bed. He was about to leave the office to go home and tell Sarah about this possible reprieve, when the door opened again. It was Supervisor Will Cleary. Fred didn't feel much like discussing county politics, but he was always glad to see Cleary. He walked to the counter.

"Fred, I've something to discuss with you. May I?" Cleary pointed toward Fred's desk and the extra chair.

"Oh, sure, Will. Forgive me. Come in, come in."

Fred retreated to his desk and Will sat beside it. "Fred, I'll come right to the point. I was in town last evening and heard about what took place over your sewer thing. I may not have the straight of it, but what I hear is that Cosgrove called your note. Going to run you out of town, the way I heard it. Right?"

"That's about the size of it, Will."

"Now, perhaps I'm out of line, and you've got the money to pay him off, and get him out of your hair. I don't know. But, I do know this. You have a lot of friends around these parts who wouldn't want to see you leave." Fred started to offer his thanks for the sentiment, but Will waved him off. "No, just a minute, Fred. Hear me out. I think I can get a group together that would put up the money you need. How much is it?"

"Holy Jehoshaphat!" Fred was stunned. No wonder, he thought, Will Cleary is a successful man, in his business ventures and in politics. Fred was embarrassed to have to admit he was so short of cash, especially now. But there really was no choice. He decided to meet Cleary right up front.

"I need sixteen twenty," he said to Will Cleary.

"Is that all?" was the supervisor's surprised reaction.

"Yep. Cosgrove has me by the short hairs and I can't even raise that much." Fred felt somewhat ashamed that his newspaper business, after more than twenty-six years, was still such a marginal enterprise. But it was a shirt-tail operation and he may as well admit it to this friend who came to help him.

"All right," Will Cleary declared. "What's your deadline?"

"I have three banking days from today. That makes it noon, day after tomorrow."

"Fred, I'll be back by tomorrow afternoon. Wait here for me. I'll have your money and you can meet the deadline," Cleary promised in his no-nonsense style.

That night Fred told Sarah about Will's visit. "He's a good man," she proclaimed. "We can be proud to have his backing. You've earned it, Fred. Cleary is the kind of man who appreciates what you've been doing with the paper. You're building this community and you speak out. Our paper stands up for the south county."

Fred nodded. Sarah sometimes complained if his editorials caused the loss of revenue, but in a crisis, she was right there at his side. For that he was grateful. But it was discouraging, after more than two decades, to be pinching pennies and counting every nickel just to stay in business.

Will Cleary was back the next day with his signed bank draft for sixteen hundred and twenty dollars made out to Fred Godfrey. As he handed it to Fred, he said, "We set up a bank account at Monterey County Bank. We didn't want to embarrass you, so it's simply called the Cleary Fund. Here's the list of men who have subscribed to it." He handed Fred a sheet of paper that the editor quickly scanned. On it were the signatures of eleven of the leading ranchers and business men in the area, including Supervisors Paul Talbot and Will Cleary.

"I could have had a hundred men, if there were time," Cleary claimed. "You have a lot of friends with respect for what you are trying to do with *The Settler*. We want to keep you on the job."

Fred had tears in his eyes. He didn't know how to thank this big, bluff, generous man. But this was a business deal, and he had to emphasize that point. "How do we arrange this, Will? Some kind of company? What?"

"Well, Fred, how about if we make this a stock company? *The Settler* can incorporate and issue stock. Each of these men will have stock to represent his investment. You buy the stock back as soon as you're able."

"Sounds fine to me," Fred agreed.

Will Cleary smiled. "When the dust settles on this we'll have a meeting. How about a barbecue down at my place?" he suggested. "We'll get the structure set up and that will be that."

"Fine," Fred said. "But one other thing, Will. I must insist on it. Everyone has to know that there'll be no strings attached. I have to write what I believe is right. I'm my own man."

Will Cleary looked Fred Godfrey straight in the eye. "Fred, if we didn't know that, I wouldn't be here."

CHAPTER TWENTY

F RED ENTERED THE NEWSPAPER OFFICE and set the stack of mail on his desk.

"Anything there for me?" Sarah asked. She'd learned to operate the Simplex typesetting machine and was helping out in the shop part-time now that Millie was off at teachers college. Since Bobby was away, too, taking courses at Healds Business College, where both his parents were hoping he'd stay more than a year, Sarah was checking daily through each stack of mail for letters from her offspring. Bobby's short notes were infrequent, but Millie's newsy letters arrived often.

Although she wrote at length about her school work and her friends, boys were too frequently mentioned to suit Sarah. "Men," Millie called them, and Sarah sniffed at the reference. "Good grief," she'd said to Fred. "Men! Those college boys can't be old enough to shave."

"Millie is twenty," Fred reminded her. "Those boys are about the same age. You were an old, married woman by that age."

"Well, it's different now. Times have changed. I do hope Millie isn't serious about any of those boys. She does mention this Lloyd Weible a lot, and there's a Jordy something in her letters, and some others."

Sarah needn't have worried. Millie was a good student and she was enjoying college life. Her group of San Jose Normal girls had become friends with some Stanford students, so much of Millie's social life was with them. Lloyd was captain of the Stanford track team and nice enough. But he did take himself rather seriously, even though he could run faster and jump further than most. Jordy Johnson knew all the latest dance steps and had taught Millie to rag. She could do the turkey trot, the bunny hug and the tango, but she didn't dare demonstrate the steps when she came home for visits. Ragging was outlawed in King City. No matter, Millie had all the fun she could handle, going to fraternity parties and dances at

Stanford, taking in the picture shows, or the whole gang heading to the country, bouncing along in flivers, singing and
laughing, for Sunday picnics.

"Tell you the truth, Sarah, I'll be glad when she's through up
there," Fred said, as he handed a letter back to his wife. "If she
starts teaching she can support herself. But I'm not so sure we
won't need her right here."

Fred had just completed his rounds of the town, calling on
advertisers up and down Broadway. But he didn't have much
ad copy in his pocket. This next issue of *The Settler* would be a
meager one. "Everywhere I go, it's the same story," Fred
explained with a sigh. "Business is bad. With the drought last
year, farmers just aren't spending any money. Merchants say
it's no use advertising because nobody is buying anyhow. It'll
be better when this year's crops are harvested."

The Settler's immediate financial problems had been solved
by Will Cleary and his group of investors. Fred was able to
refuse with thanks the offer of help from Charlie Beyers of
American Type, but he was proud that they'd thought enough
of him to make the offer. And he was relieved when the libel
suit against the newspaper was dropped by Osgood and
Cosgrove. Sarah wondered why. "They must have something
else up their sleeves," she insisted. "That Cosgrove is slippery
as an eel. Watch your back, Fred."

But right now he was much more concerned with the big hole
on the back page. "Losing that half page ad each week is tough.
No matter how much I hustle Broadway, I can't make up for it.
But if we can just get a little rain things will perk up," he said
to Sarah, but with little faith that the rain would come.

Less than five inches of rain had fallen on southern
Monterey County in that year of 1913. Feed was so scarce in
the hills that cattle starved, and crops were short, mostly cut
for hay to feed the stock. Cleary Ranches had driven most of its
Long Valley herd to pasture, which Will had rented in the San
Joaquin Valley. Bucky, Pat and Spud, with Buck O'Keefe in
charge, had trailed the cattle over to Peachtree, up into Priest

Valley, down through Warthan Canyon, and out into the valley beyond Coalinga. The boys were kept busy the rest of that summer moving the other Cleary cattle from Will's Trescony lease onto stubble, which Will rented wherever he could find it from farmers between San Lucas and King City.

What little time that they weren't in the saddle was spent harvesting the fields for the few farmers who managed to make crops, and cutting and hauling hay. Will had also purchased several rail carloads of hay from the San Joaquin Valley, and it had to be unloaded from the boxcars at San Lucas, loaded onto wagons, and hauled to the ranch.

After weeks of anxiously watching the skies, farmers and townspeople alike were finally rewarded. Dark clouds floated over on a south wind and opened up, changing the landscape from brown to green and changing the frowns of worry to smiles on faces everywhere.

When the grass had a good start, the Cleary boys and Bucky were back in the saddle again, bringing the cattle home from the San Joaquin. The terrible trio hadn't had much time for their social life and usual pranks and were bemoaning that fact as they rode along through Warthan Canyon, pushing two-year-old steers and mother cows with young calves by their sides. It was slow work, especially in the driving rainstorm.

"Look at this country," Bucky complained, as the water dripped down from the brim of his hat and poured off his yellow slicker. "This was the hottest, driest, most miserable, rattlesnake infested canyon on God's earth when we drove through here last June. You couldn't even find a drink of water for ten miles around. Even the jack rabbits carried canteens. Now every gulch is a river."

"Quit your bitching," Spud called to him. His slicker leaked and his Levis were wet clear through to his skin despite his chaps. "We asked for rain. We got it." He splashed his horse through a gully and brought back a cow, which had strayed off to put her tail to the storm and try some of the young grass.

The wind whistled and whirled around them and it was hard to talk, but they tried.

"Yeah, but I can dream," his cousin shouted back. "I'd rather be up there in San Francisco at the Palace Hotel, all nice and dry, and warm. I'd just be tossing off a shot of good bourbon, and I'd have a big steak in front of me."

"To hell with the city. I could do with some little blond to keep me warm," Spud said.

"Any blond in particular?" Pat asked as he wrung out his bandanna and tied it back around his neck. It was wet and cold, but it kept the rain from sloshing down his collar. "You thinking about that one in King City? Or the one in the city, or the one in Salinas?"

"Nope. They're all good." Spud laughed despite his miseries. He was riding hunched forward in his saddle, leaning against the slashing rain. His horse, head down, kept slogging along. It was hard to push the cattle against the wind and the rain, but they had to keep going until they reached the old Burden corrals in Priest Valley, where they could hold the herd overnight, if there was any fence left.

It was after dark when they checked the fences, got the cattle settled, and put up their horses in what shelter the old barn offered. The storm had slackened by the time they found wood dry enough to get a fire going in the fireplace in the old shack. Bedrolls were wet clear through, despite the canvas coverings, and what food came out of the saddle bags was soggy and unpalatable. Buck had some coffee brewed, and he added a healthy gurgle to each tin cup from a bottle of bourbon he dug from his outfit.

"This'll help warm you fellows," he told them. They sat around the fire, drying themselves as their saddle blankets and bedrolls steamed. Buck O'Keefe felt good about these young men, his son and both nephews, and enjoyed being with them. His brother-in-law, Seamus, had remained at the ranch to do the chores and help his sister, Kitty.

"Now how could you have it any better than this?" he asked. He grinned at them as they began to warm up and relax. Buck brought out the fixings, which he'd somehow managed to keep dry. With one hand he held the cigarette paper, formed a little trough, and with the other he tipped a thin stream of tobacco from his Bull Durham sack. Catching the string in his teeth, he pulled the sack shut and returned it to his shirt pocket, licked the paper and rolled it, twisted the ends and lit up with a burning sliver of wood from the fire.

Bucky held out his hand and his dad tossed over the tobacco sack for him to repeat the process. Pat passed and Spud also waved it off. "You're not a real cowboy," Spud told them, "until you can roll your own at a full gallop in the rain against the wind. I know I could never do that, so I'm not even gonna try."

Buck flicked his cigarette ash into the cuff of his Levis and unscrewed the top of his Cyrus Noble bottle. He poured another little shot into the cups. Buck didn't worry about these boys drinking. They had a reputation for hell raising, but it wasn't with liquor. All three drank socially and in moderation.

It wasn't that they couldn't afford it. They were accustomed to all the best places in San Francisco and Salinas, and had an unlimited charge account wherever they went. The boys weren't paid a salary for their work on the ranch, but they had credit for whatever they needed. "Charge it to Cleary Ranches," were the magic words. So they were always broke, but never wanted for anything. Buck didn't care much for the system himself. But it had been Jeremiah's system, and now that his son Will was in charge, things hadn't changed. In good years profits were divided among the owners, Will's brothers and sisters. Buck and Kitty banked their share, but meanwhile, Cleary Ranches paid all the bills.

Spud held out his cup for more coffee, but waved off another shot of whiskey. He looked at Bucky and asked, "Say, Cuz, how's your love affair?" He and Pat had been kidding Bucky about Lilly Martin for years now, ever since she'd let him kiss her when they were in high school and he'd made the mistake of telling them about it. Lilly was now away at college. Her parents had sent her to a girl's school in the east, but Bucky saw a lot of her when she was home on vacations. He'd stopped sharing information with his cousins, but they hadn't stopped asking.

"Yep," Pat kidded, "Ol' Bucky here will be tying the knot one of these days. No more chasing around. We'll have to handle all the school marms on our own, Spud. Bucky's in love."

"Aw, you guys lay off," Bucky muttered. "I'm not in love. Anyhow, she's probably gonna marry some city swell."

"Better not let her get away," Pat advised. "Just as easy to fall for a rich girl as a poor one."

They all laughed at Bucky's discomfort, Buck included. He did wonder, though, if his son wasn't really seriously thinking about Lilly Martin. Nothing wrong with that. Her parents and aunt and uncle were long-time friends of the O'Keefes. Good people, Buck knew. And, among their many interests, they had a large cattle ranch on the San Antonio River.

There wasn't a cloud in the sky, and it was bitter cold as they saddled up at dawn. Late that night they turned the herd into the Cleary field just off the county road in Long Valley and after feeding their weary mounts, they ate a hearty supper and bedded down for a much deserved sleep in comfortable beds.

* * * * *

Will Cleary opened the gate off the Pine Valley road and drove his Model-T Ford onto the rutted trail that crossed the Cleary Ranch in Coyote Canyon. He was driving up to visit his brother, a trip he frequently made these days. If Tim wouldn't come to him, he'd go to Tim.

Tim Cleary rarely left the one-room cabin on his homestead near the spring in the midst of the Cleary property. He spent his time puttering around a little vegetable garden, or sitting on his stoop and brooding, it seemed to Will. Too often Will found him with a whiskey bottle at hand and in no mood for friendly conversation. But occasionally he'd find his brother working with a colt, and he had to admit that Tim was still a good hand gentling a young horse and putting it in the bridle. Tim had been in charge of custom harvesting for his father, Jeremiah, with the stationery machine until he'd gone off prospecting for gold in the Yukon. Will had taken over, and now, each of the eight years since Tim had returned, Will had invited him to take charge of a machine. And each time Tim had refused.

Will found Tim just finishing with a bay horse, one he'd been working in double reins. The four-year-old was carrying a spade bit, but wore a rawhide hackamore on its nose and Tim controlled it with hair rope reins. He loped a series of figure eights on the animal, to the right and then to the left, the bay changing leads, and then brought him to a sliding stop in front of Will.

"Not bad, Brother. Not bad." Will admired the horse. "Whose horse?"

"I'm finishing this one for Wes Wexler," Tim answered. "There are some folks around here who still have confidence in me."

Will let it slide. He hadn't come to preach, just to ask, once again, for help with the harvesting. The wet year had produced some outstanding crops and all three of his machines were contracted to be busy from June into September.

"I could sure use you this year, Tim." Will said. "Take over one of the harvesters, work this side of the river. How about it?"

But the answer was the same as it had been every other year. "Nope. Out of practice. Wouldn't know what to do. Besides, no time. Have to keep up with my chores right here."

"Oh, Tim, for godsakes," Will retorted, letting his anger and frustration take hold. "There's nothing to keep you here but that damn bottle!"

Tim didn't respond. He just led his horse away and unsaddled it by the shed. He turned the horse into his little corral and checked the water in the wooden trough. He threw a fork-ful of hay into the pen and, ignoring Will, walked up to his doorway. Tim stood there, looking down at his brother, who was still sitting at the wheel of his Model-T. "I'd invite you in to have a drink, but I can't stand you hooting at me," Tim said, then turned and went inside, shutting the door.

Will stared at the closed door for a long while. Then he got out of the car, took out his crank, hooked it up, and took several turns before the engine came to life. Will climbed back in, and, with a sigh and a look backward, started the drive down out of Coyote Canyon. What a shame. What a waste, Will thought. How could he ever change his brother?

Will was remembering his father's brother Matthew, Will's fun-loving uncle, who'd spent his life either searching for gold or in the saloons. He'd been a terrible burden and disappoint-ment to Will's father, Jeremiah, who'd tried everything to help him, even raised his child. And then Matthew had just disap-peared. Was history repeating itself? Will wondered if his brother was turning out just like his uncle.

Will drove on into King City. He had several errands to do there, but mostly he wanted to find out who was available for his harvest crews. He had his usual hands, the reliable ones who'd worked for him every year, although the other custom harvesters tried to hire them away. Especially Dan Loggins, the best separator man in the state, even if he was getting old. There were the three boys, Bucky, Pat and Spud, of course, all experienced, even if they were young. He could put each of them in charge of a harvester. Will made the turn off First Street onto Broadway and wondered what was going on. There was a crowd gathered at the railroad depot.

Bobby Godfrey had also seen the crowd beginning to form where several men were unloading a freight car. Bobby, whose tall lanky frame was topped by an unruly cowlick of rusty, red hair, was home on summer vacation and working for Joe Carrigan at the garage across the street. He unwound his length from under a car, wiped the grease from his hands onto his pants, and strolled across First Street to see what was going on.

Bobby watched the unloading for a few moments when realization struck him. He hurried to *The Settler* office and called out to his father as he entered the front door. Fred looked up from his desk, where he was trying to master the new typewriting machine, one finger at a time. He was startled by Bobby's agitation. "Easy now, Son. What is it?"

"They're unloading a printing press down at the S.P. depot!" Bobby gasped out the words. "And some other stuff. I saw a job press and some type cases."

"A printing press? Are you sure? What kind?" Fred was surprised and puzzled. "Who is it for?"

"I don't know, Dad. But it's a press, something like ours."

"Well, let's go see," Fred said, trying to hide the anxious feelings that were creeping over him. He and his son hurried up the street. But a block before they reached the depot Fred got his answer. Slim Smith's dray wagon had pulled up to the vacant building belonging to George Cosgrove on the south side of Broadway near Second Street. Bystanders were watching as the men moved the equipment inside.

"Oh, hello there, Fred," Mayor Al Carlson greeted him. "I see we're going to have another newspaper in town."

"Yeah," Slim Smith agreed. "Osgood is gonna put it out. Says he's gonna call it *The Banner, The King City Banner.*"

Fred Godfrey felt his heart hit bottom. Another newspaper? There wasn't enough business in that end of the county for one paper, let alone two. Holy Jehoshaphat, how in the hell would he be able to survive now? Osgood, huh? And in Cosgrove's building. It easily added up. This was their way of getting back at him.

"What do you think of this deal, Fred?" Carlson asked.

"Yeah, Fred. Looks like you got yourself some competition, huh?" One of the bystanders remarked. Several others had comments for him.

Fred smiled back. "Well, boys," he said, "competition is good for everybody. That's what makes this country work so well. I guess we'll just have to see who puts out the better newspaper."

Big words, he thought, as he and Bobby walked back to *The Settler* office. In truth, Fred Godfrey didn't know what in the world he was going to do? Things were better now that crops were plentiful and cattle were fat, but even in the best of times the newspaper business was touch and go. With Bobby and Millie both in school for another year, Sarah was helping at the shop, but he didn't want her to have to do that indefinitely. When he told her the terrible news, Sarah was her usual practical, matter-of-fact self in the face of adversity.

"Fred, it's a spite thing," Sarah responded calmly. "That slimy Cosgrove. And Osgood is no better. Those are petty, vengeful men and nothing based on such spite can succeed for long. The people know how you've fought for this town. We'll just continue to do our best. They'll be gone in a year."

That evening after supper the Godfrey family gathered in the music room, which was Fred's name for the front parlor. He hoped they could play a few pieces together and get his mind off what he was certain was impending doom. They'd often done this when the children were young. But Sarah had just about stopped playing the mandolin since their orchestra had now been disbanded. These days people wanted to dance to the blaring sounds of saxophones, cornets, trombones and trumpets. Millie had a good ear for music and a sweet voice, and she'd learned to play the banjo and could really make the instrument jump when she was in practice. But Bobby was practically a lost cause. He had what Fred called a "tin ear" when it came to music and his sense of time was atrocious. Fred had given the boy mandolin lessons ever since he was seven years old, but Bobby just never could get the hang of it.

Nevertheless, they were all playing Souza's "Washington Post March," on this less than happy evening. Fred's guitar kept time with the bass notes, Millie added the frills with the

147

banjo, while Sarah and Bobby played the mandolin parts. Fred had to continually increase the beat to stay with Bobby's lead, and the tempo of the march went faster and faster until an exasperated, red-faced Fred abruptly stopped playing and bellowed at his son, "Holy Jehoshaphat, Bobby! It's a march, not a race."

That ended the music for the evening. But it didn't serve to assuage Fred's worry. He lay awake long after Sarah had drifted off to sleep. He ran over and over in his mind the things Cosgrove and Osgood had been saying around town. He tossed and turned in worry. Those two had sworn to run him out of business. The first light of dawn was creeping into the bedroom when Fred decided. "Well, by God," he muttered, "they're going to have a fight."

CHAPTER TWENTY-ONE

IN THE SUMMER OF 1914 the barley crop was nearly three feet tall, thick, heavy-headed and a steady flow of rich, yellow grain poured into the sacks. Shanty Malone, the jigger, was shaking down the grain at a furious pace, turning the well-filled sacks for Clay Dalton, one of the fastest sack sewers around, to take his thirteen stitches, tie up the corners and tip the sack into the chute. High above the harvester, out over the wheelers, sat Spud Cleary driving twenty-six horses, six up in rows of four with two leaders. The team was pulling well, answering to his firm hands on the lines as he hauled on the brake to clamp the inside wheel and skid the big combine around the turn. The header tender, Red Mansfield, kept the cutting blade level, clipping a twenty-foot-wide swath of barley at about a foot off the ground.

This was one of Will Cleary's outfits custom harvesting for a farmer on the Trescony lease, a three hundred acre field adjacent to the Cleary place. Pat Cleary was the separator man, in charge of the machine, and feeling good about the work this July morning. The sweating men were in rhythm with the rolling machine, ground driven off the right wheel with a system of whizzing chains, revolving sprockets and grinding gears, all of which it was Pat's job to keep well-oiled. The rattle and screech of the chains, the dust and chaff, the noise of the machinery, Spud's shouted directions to the team of straining horses, and the moving knife blade of the header, created a cacophony of raucous sound and whirling motion.

Oil can in hand, Pat climbed down the ladder on the side of the moving machine, leaned in to reach the lower fan chain, and gave it a squirt of oil from the long-necked can. Pat was poised on the ladder, hanging by one hand, just inches away from the speeding cylinder chain, reaching in with his oil can when it happened.

The harvester suddenly lurched as the left wheel fell into a hidden badger hole. Pat's right foot slipped from the ladder. As he stretched his leg, feeling with his toe to regain his footing, the harvester swayed back to the right. The flying cylinder chain licked at his Levis, caught and snagged. The huge links snarled in his pants, pulled his leg into the chain, drew his boot directly into the sprocket.

Pat's scream pierced through all other sound!

Spud brought the straining team to a quick halt. He could hear the shouts of the other men, but he had to stay in his high seat, controlling the restless horses, thus, he couldn't see what had happened. But he knew from the voices that something terrible had happened to Pat. Adrenaline, born of fear for his brother, coursed through Spud.

Dalton, Malone and Mansfield jumped to the ground and rushed to Pat's side. He was conscious, but shock had dulled the pain. His right leg could be seen, mangled in the chain, the boot torn off by the sprocket, his foot imprisoned in the cruel links. Blood began to well up from the wounds as the men worked frantically to free him.

No matter how still Spud tried to hold the horses, every movement of the harvester slid the right wheel and moved the chain, grinding deeper into Pat's torn flesh. "Get that link sprung," Malone yelled, as Dalton pried with a huge screw driver. Slick with blood, it kept slipping off. Pat was moaning now and crying out in agonizing pain. Malone pulled out his knife and carefully cut away the pants material, freeing it from clogging the chain links. Dalton finally pried apart a connector. The chain sprang off the sprocket and the men gingerly lifted out Pat's mutilated leg and then they carefully lifted him down from the ladder. That was when he passed out. Gently they laid him on the ground in the shade alongside the harvester.

Spud tied up his lines, jumped down from the high seat and took a quick look at his unconscious brother. He ran to the front of the team and unhitched a leader. He swung up on the work horse and kicking it into a lumbering gallop, headed for the ranch house a half mile away. Oh God, he prayed, let Dad be there with the auto.

He raced across the field as fast as the big horse could go. When Spud reached the yard, hollering at the top of his lungs, Will Cleary stepped onto the front porch. Thank you, Lord, Spud thought.

"Dad — ! There's been an accident. Pat's hurt. Get the car!"

Will Cleary instantly ran to the Ford touring car, parked in the back of the house. He had it cranked to life by the time Spud had jumped off the horse and left it loose in the yard. Spud threw himself into the seat next to his father and they sped out of the yard and across the field, Will driving faster than he ever had before, following the path of the morning's cut to the harvester.

Will pulled to a stop beside his unconscious son. Malone was kneeling over Pat, tightening a tourniquet around his upper thigh. "He's bleeding bad," Malone said, looking up at Will, "I can't stop it."

"Quick — ! Get him in the car," Will ordered, opening the rear door. They laid Pat on the back seat and Spud climbed in to hold his brother. Will slammed through the gears and was in high before he hit the county road. He took the San Lucas bridge at better than fifty miles an hour and raced toward King City. Spud held his moaning brother in his arms and prayed that Doc Brumwell would be in town. "Easy, Pat. It won't be long. Doc will fix you up. It'll be okay." Spud's murmured encouragement did little to ease Pat's excruciating pain. He groaned and grimaced, clenched his teeth and tried desperately to bear it. Then he blacked out again.

Will made the turn onto Broadway and hit the horn, scattering teams, riders, autos and pedestrians as he tore down the main street and braked to a stop in front of the doctor's office. Will jumped out of the auto and ran to the door of the office, nearly colliding with Dr. Brumwell. "My son — !" Will gasped, but Doc had taken one look at the man in the Ford and was already back in his surgery room, readying the table.

Spud and Will lifted the groaning, writhing Pat and carried him inside. They laid him on the table. Dr. Brumwell had washed up and was already preparing an anesthetic. In a few moments Pat Cleary was quiet and the doctor examined the damaged leg and broken foot. Besides the deep cuts and torn flesh, Doc Brumwell judged, the leg had snapped in three places. Pat's foot was crushed and two toes had also been severed.

Will felt his son's pain as if it were his own. His body cringed at the sight of this young man with the gaping wounds and the splintered bone piercing through the skin. He asked the inevitable question. "Doc, will you have to take his leg off?"

Dr. Brumwell looked squarely at the distraught father. "I don't know, Will. I may. It's probable. But first I'm going to try to save it. You two will have to help."

Will looked across at his youngest son and Spud nodded. Together they held Pat still, assisting Dr. Brumwell with the ether cone held over Pat's nose, as he cleaned and separated the torn flesh, reduced the compound fractures and aligned the bones. They clamped down on the upper leg with all their strength as the doctor directed. He pulled and manipulated, and maneuvered the bones into place. It seemed to take forever. Even under the anesthetic, Pat's pain was felt acutely as he twisted and convulsed so that they could hardly hold him steady.

Several hours went by as the doctor worked and they sweltered in the afternoon heat of the small, cramped office. Will wiped his son's face with cool water. Spud replaced the cone as Dr. Brumwell dripped in more ether to keep Pat under. Will studied his son's pale face, anguish in his own. Spud was as white as his brother, who finally lay again quietly, as if dead, while Dr. Brumwell sewed up the stubs of the two amputated toes, finally finished dressing the leg, and applied splints.

"This will have to do for a while," he said. "We'll cast it later on, after the danger of infection has passed. I'll keep him here a few days and watch him. If we save that leg, I'm sorry to say, he'll have a limp."

"A limp? Good God, Doc! What's a limp? You've saved my boy's life," Will cried gratefully, "and maybe his leg. How can I thank you, Doc?"

"Just being able to do it is enough for me," Dr. Brumwell replied. "When I see him walking again, I'll be paid a thousand times over."

A week later, the doctor made the happy announcement that the immediate danger of infection was over, assured Will that his son's wounds were healing nicely, and moved Pat into a room at the Vendome Hotel, next door to his office, where Doc Brumwell usually kept his recovering patients.

Patrick Cleary lay on his back in his room on the second floor of the Vendome Hotel. His crippled leg was extended and held rigid by heavy splints from hip to toe. It was suspended above the bed by a series of pulleys and weights. He was immobile, except for his arms, and the debilitating pain came in waves despite the laudanum powders Doc Brumwell gave him.

Spud and Bucky had been in to visit every chance they had, and, with their silly antics, had tried to cheer him up. But it was forced. They all knew it. Honora and Will were there every day, his mother sitting silently for long hours by the side of her son, holding and stroking his hand, bathing his face. Other times she quietly read to him as he stared at the ceiling. Will kept asking, "Anything I can get you, Son?" But there was nothing. Pat just lay there.

He was alone just now. Doc Brumwell had arranged for Martha Gates to nurse and watch over him, but she'd gone downstairs into the hotel dining room for her noon meal. It was stifling hot in the room at midday in July. Pat lay there, staring at the ceiling, his eyes glazed, enduring the heat, the medicine barely keeping the pain at bay.

They told him that his leg would heal. In time, they said. But Pat wondered. And fretted. Would he ever be able to work again? Could he ever again ride a horse? How the hell could he stand in his boots with those toes missing?

He had just drifted off into a heat-induced sleep, more like a stupor, when awareness that something was wrong in the hotel came over him. He vaguely heard the shouts downstairs and outside in the street. Gradually the loud voices forced their way into his drugged brain. What was it? What was going on? Then he noticed the smell.

Smoke!

It curled in under the door and filtered around the door frame. It wafted into the room and hung in a cloud above his bed. Fire! My God, the building was on fire.

Pat was helpless. He couldn't move. He heard the flames crackling and sizzling in the hallway outside his room. Dear God, he thought, have they forgotten me?

He began to yell for help. "Get me out of here!" he yelled with every ounce of strength he could muster. "Help! Somebody hear me! Up here. Get me out!" He felt the panic rising from his belly and fought against the restraints. There was just no way to get free. He beat his fists against the bed in frustration and fear, and screamed at the top of his lungs, but no one came.

Gus Bahm, the owner of the Vendome Hotel, had been in the backyard when he saw smoke issuing from under the eaves of the building. He shouted, "Fire — !" and raced inside, grabbed the telephone crank and frantically turned. "Vendome Hotel," he breathlessly reported to Central. In moments the fire bell was clanging.

Martha Gates finished lunch, walked down the street to Oscar Branstetter's store and was at the pharmacy counter when she heard the fire bell. She sure hoped it wasn't the hotel, not with Pat up there helpless. But it was an idle thought as she paid for her prescription and stepped out on Broadway. She looked toward the Vendome, but didn't see anything unusual.

A number of the people in the hotel rushed to the kitchen, but found no fire there. Nor was it located anywhere downstairs, or in the hallways upstairs. They were beginning to wonder if it had been a false alarm when voices from in front, on Broadway, shouted, "There it is! Flames under the eaves. Look! There!"

All those still inside the Vendome came rushing outside. They stood in front of the building, looking up at the roof. First they saw tendrils of gray, and then suddenly black smoke billowed out and fierce orange-red flames followed. The crowd gasped and stepped back. Martha, too, saw the flames and began running up the street. She made for the front door, but was stopped by Mayor Al Carlson just as the city's hose and ladder brigade came running onto the scene. "Martha, you can't go in there. Everybody's been ordered out. Fire everywhere," the mayor said. He had taken charge because King City's fire chief was out of town.

"But the Cleary boy — " Martha's eyes pleaded as she tugged at his sleeve. "Mister Carlson, there's a patient of mine up — "

"Not now, miss — !" Carlson began ordering several men to hurry into position with the ladders and to drag hoses up to the water main. They swung open the valve and carried the nozzle up the extended ladder. Three men, lower on the ladder, held the pulsating hose, as another directed a stream against the blaze. But the fire kept spreading.

Pat's nurse was frantically trying to get somebody's attention. But firemen just brushed past her, and she was jostled aside by the crowd of onlookers in the street. She couldn't make herself heard above the din of shouted orders, the crackling flames, the water running, the hiss of steam. Finally she clutched Billy Wasson's arm as he was rushing past her and clung to it until he stopped.

"What — ?" he shouted the question. "Where?"

Martha screamed into his ear.

"Somebody's up there," Billy yelled to the other firemen.

"Who? Where?"

"Room seven," Martha cried. "Doc's patient."

"Oh, my God! That's the Cleary boy! He's helpless."

The firemen reacted. Wasson and two others took the hose from the men on the ladder and, directing the stream of water ahead of them, entered the Vendome's burning lobby. They wet down the smoldering stairway and sprayed into the hallway above. Heinie Branstetter and Buster McBride, coughing, choking in the smoke, their eyes streaming, crawled up the stairs and stumbled toward room seven. The door was burning and they smashed it open with their axes.

Pat Cleary was howling in pain and terror as the flames raced along the floor toward his bed. Buster hacked at the cords holding up the splinted leg, and Heinie draped the thrashing body across his shoulder. Pat shrieked as his injured leg struck the floor. He passed out as they half carried, half dragged him down the stairs, where two other firemen pulled him through the flaming lobby to safety.

The hotel was completely ablaze, and the firemen, with the help of many townspeople, turned their attention toward saving the cigar factory, which was adjacent to the Vendome on the east side, and Dr. Brumwell's office on the other side. Fred and Sarah Godfrey, along with Millie and Bobby, watched in horror as the intense heat from the fire reached across the street to the plate glass window of *The Settler* office. The glass cracked, then shattered and fell.

Sparks and flying cinders from the blazing inferno carried to the shed behind *The Settler* building, and to other sheds, privies and stables, which clogged the back yards along the main street, setting fires as far as two blocks away. But the volunteer fireman were everywhere and Fred joined them, helping to douse the flames and all structures were saved.

Except for the Vendome Hotel. In less than an hour King City's landmark was consumed, a jumble of blackened debris, smoking and steaming in the warm afternoon sun.

Pat Cleary had been placed in a wagon bed out of harm's way. Sarah and Millie walked over to Martha Gates, who was doing her best to ease and comfort him. "I don't know quite what to do," Martha told them. "Doc's way out in San Benito on a call and won't be back until tomorrow."

"Take him to our house," Sarah immediately suggested. "We can care for him until Doc comes back."

They had many helping hands to carry Pat in the wagon bed to San Lorenzo street and gently lift him into the house on a makeshift stretcher. He was settled into Bobby's room, which Sarah and Millie hastily put into order. "Bobby, ask if you can stay next door for a few days," Sarah ordered.

When Fred arrived home after cleaning up the glass and debris around the newspaper office, she explained. "I thought it best for the poor man. And it's the least we can do for Will Cleary." Fred agreed wholeheartedly.

Will and Honora hurried to town as soon as they heard about the fire and Pat's close call. Will was profuse in his praise and sought out each of the volunteers to thank them personally for helping to save Pat's life, and Honora was tearfully grateful to the Godfrey family for taking him in.

Doc Brumwell came by the next evening and cut off Pat's bandages, checked the healing, reset the splints, and claimed that the fire had left the young man no worse for wear. "But it will be a month or more before it's safe to put on a cast," he explained. "I'd like to keep him nearby until then." Sarah said she and Millie would gladly take care of Pat Cleary.

Spud and Bucky came over that first night and stood by the bed, looking down at the wounded member of the terrible trio. Pat was dazed with pain, but attempted a grin.

"What do you think of my nurse?" His eyes indicated Millie, who was fluffing up a pillow.

"Why you lucky devil," Spud said with a wink. "Nothing to do but lay there and be waited on by a pretty girl. Now you'll never heal up and get back to work."

Millie's eyes sparkled as she glanced at Spud, who was appraising her as if he'd never seen her before. He doesn't even remember me, she thought.

But Spud remembered. This was the newspaperman's kid. She'd grown into a beautiful woman. Spud took in the full bosom and narrow waist, accented, rather than hidden, by her long, loose dress. She smiled at him and he noted the even, white teeth, and the warmth in her large brown eyes. He saw the golden-brown hair, caught up in a blue ribbon at the nape of her neck, hanging softly down the whole length of her back, long enough to sit upon.

Sure now, Spud told himself in his grandfather Jeremiah's famous brogue, and isn't this is a matter that needs looking into?

CHAPTER TWENTY-TWO

MILLIE GODFREY WAS IN A QUANDARY. She'd be finishing school soon, having earned a teaching credential and the new California State School for the Blind in Oakland had offered her a job. She wanted to take it. Millie had spent months training herself to read Braille and this opportunity was too good to pass up.

On the other hand, was she needed at home? Her father was facing the competition of Cosgrove's new newspaper in King City, and she thought she should be there to help out, to write news stories and set type. Or would it be more help to the family to take the job? She could earn more money that way.

But Fred Godfrey had told his daughter, "Millie, you do what you want to do. Your mother and I can handle things here. Don't base your decision on *The Settler*. The paper will always be here."

Millie wasn't so sure. The rivalry with Milton Osgood's *Banner* was bitter. And she could tell, as she browsed through the weekly issues of *The Settler,* that there weren't as many advertisements as there used to be. King City just wasn't big enough to support two newspapers. Millie changed her mind every day about what she was going to do.

And then there was Spud.

She knew that she was really attracted to him. Actually, she admitted to herself, he'd been there in the back of her mind since she was a girl, that time she'd seen him ride the bucking horse, and she'd picked up his hat. His laughing eyes and crooked grin were in front of her now as she thought about him. He teased her and was full of fun, yes, but he was also strong and capable. He worked hard and had serious thoughts. She thought about the wonderful conversations she'd shared with Spud. No wonder Floyd Weible, Jordy Johnson, and the rest of the boys she knew, couldn't hold her interest.

Millie was also certain that Spud was more than mildly attracted to her. She knew it was going to happen, right from that first night he'd shown up when they'd taken in poor, broken Patrick after the Vendome fire. The way he looked at her, she knew it was just a matter of time.

"Millie," he finally said, after his third or fourth visit to see Pat, "There's a new picture show at the Novelty. Would you care to see it with me?"

"Yes, Spud, I would," Millie replied, and then she grinned mischievously. "But it seems to me I heard somewhere that you'd been banned from the Novelty Theatre."

Spud responded with a sheepish smile. "Aw, that was long ago. Time heals all wounds. Goetz will let me in."

"So, you fellows really did turn all those bats loose in there?"

"Well, let's just say we were convicted on circumstantial evidence." He looked at her with a broad grin. She smiled back and that started it.

The rest of the summer had passed swiftly for Millie. She worked at *The Settler* and helped Martha Gates, Dr. Brumwell's nurse, take care of Pat Cleary until his leg was finally put in a cast and he could go home. And she dated Spud on weekends.

When she returned to school, they wrote to each other. His letters were about events on the Cleary ranch and Pat's slow, painful progress learning to walk with crutches, hers were about her studies and her friends, but not about the boys who were always around. She looked forward to the next summer vacation, and Spud was there to meet the train and escort her home.

On weekends Spud would borrow his father's big Ford touring car and he and Millie would double date with Bucky O'Keefe and the girl he'd been smitten with for so long, Lilly Martin. The foursome would whiz off to the country dances, go bowling at Hable's new bowling alley, see a play at the opera house, or drive up Pine Canyon for a picnic.

Several times Spud saddled a gentle horse and took Millie riding, teaching her in a quiet way. Twice she went along when Bucky and Spud played baseball. They were on the San Ardo team, and she cheered when Spud hit the home run to beat King City.

One time she and Lilly traveled to San Ardo for a rodeo. They parked their car along with the others to form a circle, heading in so that the front bumpers created the arena in which the cowboys rode the bucking broncs and roped the steers. Spud stayed with old Pirate, the champion bronc of south county, a bald-faced, wall-eyed bay that had all the local punchers about half-scared.

Millie whooped with the rest of the crowd as Spud rode through a series of twisting, jolting jumps, striking the bronc with his spurs, and fanning him with his hat. Then she gasped in dismay as Pirate threw himself over backward. Millie grabbed Lilly's hand, but then, through the dust, she could see Spud safely on the ground and she sighed with relief. When the bronc rose, Spud was back in the saddle. Pirate seemed surprised his rider was still with him. After several dispirited crow hops, he stopped pitching all together and trotted around the arena as Spud grinned and waved his hat.

A bull's head had been cooking in the ground and the San Ardo people had prepared salads and cakes. After the rodeo everyone had gathered for the meal and to talk it over. Spud was congratulated on every side. "Old Juan Bravo couldn't have forked him any better," they said. He was invited by this group and that one to join them for a "little snort to celebrate." Millie noticed that he took just enough to be sociable, but quickly returned to her side.

These happy times were occasionally intruded upon when the war news from Europe reached them. They were appalled by the stories of atrocities in Belgium, and discussed with shocked sympathy the twelve hundred people who drowned when the German U-boat sank the Lusitania off the coast of

Ireland. But, for the most part in that summer of 1915 that war was taking place in a different world.

Millie wrote to Spud, telling him she was planning to teach at the blind school, and was strangely disappointed when he responded with enthusiasm for her opportunity. Damn, she bit her lip and thought, maybe he doesn't care. Deep down she knew that she'd been hoping he'd object, ask her to come home and—and what, Millie Godfrey?

Marriage? Nobody had mentioned marriage. They had fun together. They shared common interests, had great conversations. Sure, they seemed attracted to each other. Their parents were friends and obviously approved of Millie and Spud as a couple. What else? she asked herself. The few times they'd kissed had been wonderful, but Spud always stopped. There was a point beyond which he wouldn't venture and Millie felt so safe. *All right, all right, Millie, admit it. You're in love with Spud Cleary.* But if she turned down this job and went home now, wouldn't it look as if she was chasing after him?

Millie took her teaching credential, packed her bags and stepped aboard the train for Oakland.

* * * * *

"Holy Jehoshaphat, Sarah, it's not like I want to spend the money. I have to."

"That's all well and good, but where are you going to get it?"

They were arguing over Fred's decision to buy an automobile. His trips around the countryside were still being made in a rented rig with a buggy horse from Blackhawk Livery Stable. "I just can't cover the territory. I'm missing out. And that damn Osgood is showing up everywhere in his Model T." Fred sighed with exasperation.

Joe Carrigan was selling black Model-T Ford runabouts for four hundred fifty dollars and offering a sixty-dollar discount for cash. Fred had to have an automobile to keep *The Settler* competitive, but the three ninety price tag would wipe out what little savings they had. "Look at it like another piece of printing equipment, Sarah. We have to get it to stay in business."

"Well," she complained, "we spent more than we should on that exposition trip. But I suppose that was something else that had to be done."

The Godfreys had joined a hundred twenty residents of King City and other south county people, on a special excursion train to San Francisco for the Pan-American International Exposition. Les Hables, one of King City's leading businessman, had organized the trip, and, although it had seriously taxed the Godfrey purse, they'd felt obliged to participate. Supervisor Will Cleary had been aboard the train with his entire family and would be staying at the Palace Hotel. Sarah and Fred had spent the night in the Manx Hotel, where they had a trade account, trading accommodations for advertising.

The exposition had proven well worthwhile and Fred wrote glowingly in *The Settler* about the trip and the extraordinary sights. He was particularly enthralled by the reproduction of the Panama Canal Zone, laid out on five acres, to represent the typography of two oceans, land and lakes, locks and canals, all viewed from a moving platform in a half hour ride. He also wrote of the re-enactment of the Battle of Gettysburg, of the Irish Village, the South Seas, Days of Forty-Nine, Egypt, and a dive in a submarine. People of the entire countryside, even those who hadn't gone to San Francisco, talked of the exposition for weeks. It was something Fred had to cover. But it certainly had knocked a hole in the budget, leaving little reserve for the much-needed vehicle.

The Banner was just completing its first year of publishing, and, although it was much smaller than *The Settler,* had only a handful of paid subscribers, and was given away free in many places, it was drawing off some advertising revenue. It seemed to Fred and Sarah, and to the many local residents who had commented to them, that the sole purpose in life of Editor Milton Osgood was to destroy *The Settler*. His every issue contained a dig of some kind against Godfrey and the older newspaper.

Do you take a newspaper just because it is more than twenty-five years old, even though it has outlived its usefulness, or do you subscribe to a better, up and coming paper? — How easy it is for the other rag in town to fill newspaper columns with poster type, and boilerplate, and a few dead ads, instead of publishing good live news. — Readers recognize the value of a newspaper which is not gotten out poster style with ads spread all over it and no room for reading matter.

The Banner also seemed to be against everything *The Settler* stood for. It practically chortled with typographical glee when Editor Godfrey was by-passed by county supervisors for delegate to the irrigation conference, but neglected to mention later when Fred was appointed by Governor Hiram Johnson. It spoofed Godfrey's editorials on street trees, suggesting the city didn't have enough dogs to water all the trees already in existence. It pretended to wonder if *The Settler* had delusions of grandeur, which required more space, because Godfrey continually urged the construction of a new high school to replace the school rooms above the newspaper office.

But when Fred heard that Osgood's press had broken down and that he couldn't publish that week's issue, he offered to print *The Banner* on his own press, an offer that was accepted. "I'll beat the son-of-a-bitch," was Fred's answer to those who wondered why he'd extended the courtesy, "but it won't be that way."

"I'd never have done it, if it had been up to me!" Sarah declared.

He was sitting at his desk laying out the ad he'd run for his new circulation campaign. *Three Dolly Dimple Dolls with each one year subscription to The Settler.* He muttered aloud as he wrote the copy, "Holy Jehoshaphat, dolls to sell newspapers." *This life-like doll, 26 inches tall, may be dressed in real baby clothes. Your daughters will love them. And for you, your choice of any of these magazines: Today's Magazine for Women, Women's World, Farm Life, or Farm and Home.*

Dammit, he thought, it costs more to get the subscriptions with these damn campaigns than he'd make. But it had to be done to keep ahead of *The Banner,* which was mostly given away free.

Sarah walked in. She'd been doing some grocery shopping at Lon Sing's and the meat market. "I hope you don't mind corned beef again, Fred. It was only ten cents a pound at Nelson's. Here's Osgood's offering for today." She laid the latest *Banner* on his desk.

Fred thought later that he should have been wise to what was coming from the article in that issue. He thought it was just one shot fired, but it proved to be the first of a barrage, a fusillade that would rattle around his ears for months to come.

The Settler had recently published, in magazine format on slick paper, a special Colonist and Homeseekers' Edition, describing the advantages of farming and living in Southern Monterey County, an edition to advertise the county and attract new people to the area. The board of supervisors had ordered twenty-five hundred copies to be distributed in other states. But, under a bold headline, the *Banner* said, *This should be held up. We are informed by reliable authority that the board of supervisors has agreed to take a large number of copies of a certain newspaper of which two of the members are said to be stockholders. That certain newspaper editor soaked the county for $250 and a warrant for payment has been issued by the board. This warrant should be voided because of the obvious conflict of interest.*

"Holy Jehoshaphat," Fred exploded. "Look at this!" He handed the paper to Sarah. "What's that slimy worm going to do next? That's a legitimate charge for valuable merchandise. Ten cents apiece? My God, Sarah, it cost us more than that to put it out."

Fred flushed crimson. He was ready to go over to Osgood's office and call him out. But his wife calmed him down. "I feel like doing that myself," she said. "But it won't solve anything. Ride it out, Fred."

The following week the news in *The Banner* was even worse. It took Fred completely by surprise. *SUPERVISOR CLEARY TO BE RECALLED,* the newspaper screamed in headline type twice the poster size for which it had criticized *The Settler.* Subheadings yelled, *Citizens want accounting for road fund. Ask where are promised bridges? Supervisor has daughter on county payroll.* The story beneath informed readers that a petition for the recall of Supervisor Will Cleary was being circulated in the Fourth Supervisorial District and that no difficulty was anticipated in achieving the required number of signatures to mandate an election. It asked a series of questions, such as what happened to the sixty-four thousand dollar road fund? Why is there no new bridge in San Lucas? Why is the Parkfield road full of chuck holes? Is Miss Mary Cleary being paid an exorbitant salary to perform as Monterey County's hostess at the Pan-American Exposition? Has a man who has held office for twenty-five years outlasted his worth?

Sarah had never seen her husband so livid. Nor heard his more colorful language. "Now what the hell? Does that sonofabitch think he's getting at me by attacking Cleary's reputation? Or is he after Cleary because he knows Will helped bail me out? Damn, damn, damn his miserable hide." For once, Sarah didn't complain about Fred's vocabulary. This time she was thinking the same thoughts.

Fred wanted to refute Osgood's charges, but he hadn't seen Will Cleary since the malicious questions were circulated by *The Banner.* However, he had absolute confidence in Will's integrity, so he couldn't restrain himself from comment in his next edition. *A diagnosis of Editor Osgood's malady, which resulted in his rantings against the chairman of the board of supervisors last week, brings a conclusion that bitterness against the public for declining to assist in his verbally announced effort to run Godfrey out of town within a year, has set up a nervous condition which has affected his intestinal process of eliminating toxins. Why else would he attack Will Cleary, a man of unimpeachable integrity? A liberal dose of blue mass is indicated.*

Shortly after *The Settler* was circulated, Will Cleary dropped by the office. "Fred," he said. "I sincerely thank you."

Godfrey waved away the thanks, "Not necessary, Will. But what's it all about?"

"Near as I can tell it's the work of Bradford's family and friends down in Parkfield," Will reasoned. "You'll recall that I took the seat from him back in ninety? Old grudges die hard."

"You'll have to make a statement, Will. Let the folks know the truth of this business," Fred suggested, pencil poised to take notes.

"Nope. I've lived here all my life," Cleary answered. "Fifty-six years of it so far. And I've represented these people at the courthouse for the last twenty-five years. If they don't know me by now, nothing I say will make any difference."

Fred nodded reluctantly. "All right, Will. But I'll have to print something. How about I put out a statement for you telling the people you won't dignify the charges or your detractors with a reply?"

"Oh?" Will looked at Fred thoughtfully, his broad, open face furrowed with a frown. "Tell you what, Fred. You print that, just like you said it, and add that I think these charges are just plain silly."

The two men shook hands somberly, united in their mutual respect and a new commitment not to let Osgood get away with any more malicious lies and accusations.

CHAPTER TWENTY-THREE

F RED RELUCTANTLY PUSHED ASIDE HIS PLATE. He'd just finished a second helping of Sarah's lamb stew. Even the knot in his stomach over the current issue of *The Banner* was soothed by that stew. Fred sat back and again picked up the rival paper.

"Listen to this," he said to Sarah, who stopped clearing the table to listen. *The rag down the street, owned by Supervisors Talbott and Cleary, did the expected last week. It attempted to defend Will Cleary and the defense was willy-nilly weak. Of course, the supervisor won't dignify the charges with an honest reply. The simple reason is that he can't.*

Sarah came back to the table and sat down. She looked across at her husband and said, "You know, Fred, it's time you straightened things out on that ownership business. If I can't remember, how do you expect the public to?"

"Holy Jehoshaphat, Sarah. It's published every year in the post office statement. Stockholders of *The Settler* Publishing Company are a matter of record." Fred's face was red and he pounded the table. "By God, I'll print it right on the front page this time!"

"Take it easy, dear." Sarah reached out and took Fred's hand, patting it. "Just how much does Will own?"

"Ten shares, for godsakes. There are six hundred shares total," Fred explained. "We own three hundred. Paul has twenty-five, Will only has ten. There are sixty-four unsold and they're not for sale. That leaves a hundred and one divided among twelve other stockholders."

"What's this business about Will's daughter?" Sarah asked. "Is she really getting a big salary to work at the Pan American Exposition?"

"That's where it really gets silly. Mary Cleary is teaching primary grades in a San Francisco school. She's an unpaid volunteer, working in the Monterey County booth on weekends."

Sarah laughed. "You'd think they'd check things out, wouldn't you?"

The next day Fred was making his rounds on Broadway when he met up with Mayor Al Carlson. "How's it going, Fred? That lawyer-turned-editor of ours, he in your hair pretty bad?"

"Old sour face, you mean, Al?" Godfrey chuckled. "He doesn't care much for Will Cleary, either."

"He sure doesn't," Carlson agreed. "What is the trouble with that Parkfield Good Roads bunch? Weren't they around when we had those floods last winter?"

The winter of 1914-15 had been a particularly soggy one with nearly seventeen inches of rain in the gauge at S.P. Milling Company. Bridges and roads all around the county had washed out. The approach to the King City bridge over the Salinas had fallen in and gone down the river in February and the city had brought back the "flying duck," a box hanging from a cable, the same contraption used in 1910 to carry people and supplies across the wide gap. The bridge approach at King City had been quickly and easily repaired, but the county had over-spent its road fund rebuilding other bridges and roads.

"Maybe we should be complaining about our bridge like those folks down south," the mayor said. "At least it didn't wash out. We have bridges, even if they are old. It'll be a long time before this county can afford any new ones. With all the big problems around the county, what are a few chuck holes in the Parkfield road, huh?"

"Al, I think the only chance we have for a new bridge will come with a state highway through here," Fred stated. "I've been talking with Will and Paul about this, and they're working on it with the state highway people. It'll be awhile, but it'll come."

"Hope Will can stay in there and get the job done," the mayor said. "Think he'll beat this recall thing?"

"Sure, I do. He's the best man on that county board. They know it, too. That's why they made him chairman. And the

169

people down there in the fourth district know it." Fred sounded a great deal more confident than he was.

In truth, he was quite concerned about his friend, Will Cleary, as he made his way back to *The Settler* office. This recall election law was a strange one. Voters could cast their vote either yes, for the recall, or no, against it. But at the same time, they also voted for candidates for supervisor to replace the incumbent if the recall was successful. The incumbent had to poll more votes than all others combined, or the seat went to the top vote getter among the challengers.

Fred had seen the list of seven candidates who were being proposed against Will Cleary. Each was from a different area of the 4th District. Fred knew them to be decent men, and each was bound to have a nucleus of friends who would vote for them. But he didn't think any of them were outstanding, not one of them was even in the same league with Will Cleary.

Fred set the last space into the line of type, and placed it into the chase, which was a page-size metal frame, and added the wooden blocks or "furniture" to space it out. He placed the quoins at the side and bottom to expand against the chase and tightened them with his quoin key so he could lift and carry the form to his little Chandler and Price job press. He changed the paper in the packing to exactly the right height so the envelopes would just kiss the type for a perfect impression. He opened a can and with an ink knife placed a measured amount of black ink on the ink disc. Then Fred reached down a box of number ten envelopes from the shelf, and prepared to feed the clapper, so called because it brought the type against the paper just as a person would clap his hands together. He hated to hand feed this damn press, but Oscar Branstetter needed these envelopes to get out the bills for his drugstore by tomorrow. Fred sighed, rolled up his sleeves and went to work.

He got into the rhythm of the press, his left hand removing the printed envelope as the press came open and the right hand inserting an envelope into the guides just before the press closed up. Fred's pace had to exactly match the speed of the press or he could lose a finger, but it was repetitive, monotonous.

He had time to think and his thoughts went back to the Cleary recall. He could see their strategy. They figured on getting as many candidates as they could talk into running. Fred wondered how they got those fellows to agree? Did Will have that many enemies, or did they just appeal to their egos? They'll all take a few votes away from Will and then it'll be damn hard for him to beat their combined total. They'll have him. Fred sadly shook his head. It was a damned unfair system.

When he got Branstetter's envelopes off the press, he wrote an editorial. *Don't Change Cleary, Change the System,* was the headline. In it he explained the voting process and urged fair-minded citizens to remember Will Cleary's record and refuse to sign the petition.

But the petition circulators, five of them racing around the district in their Model-T Fords, Oldsmobiles and Overlands, continued to report success. They needed twenty percent of the electorate. There were eight hundred and sixty-one voters in the 4th District, from just south of King City to the San Luis Obispo county line. Therefore, one hundred seventy-three signatures were required.

"Just sign it," they told people. "Put it to a vote of the citizens. This isn't saying you're against Will. Just that you want to give the people a chance to vote. If Cleary wins, it'll show that the people are with him."

Their strategy worked and many of the people in the area, even some of Will's friends, accepted and signed the petition. The day before the deadline, the Parkfield Good Road's League claimed its quota. *The Banner* blared, *Cleary Must Face Voters*.

Godfrey's editorial in *The Settler* called for *Fair Play for Cleary*. He wrote, *Sometimes this newspaper has occasion to criticize public officials. When such times do arise, the strictures are made in these editorial columns, fearlessly, and contain our honest beliefs. No man nor organization ever had* money enough to buy our space for use in an attempt to besmirch character.

The other paper in this town, however, is a different sort of a paper. Its columns are for sale for mudslinging, and last week's issue shows that money can buy any dirty stuff imaginable. The Banner openly acknowledges that Parkfield Good Roads League paid for the slanderous attack on Supervisor Cleary and his daughter. At that, it was a wisely-written sham, a fine Blackstonian hand being discernible in its get-up.

We have no brief to defend Supervisor Cleary. Nor does he need any defense from these trivial, misleading charges, put in question form, with no substance except the legal-editor's imaginings. This scurrilous screed is a well-known trick of tinhorn lawyers seeking to impugn the character and reputation of one about whom they know no fact of dubious deeds.

But we do urge all honest voters to give Will Cleary a full measure of confidence by voting a resounding No when this recall measure comes to the polls."

But Fred didn't have much faith that his editorial would make an appreciable difference. Will was right. He'd have to stand on his reputation.

* * * * *

Millie didn't know what to think. She'd been reading the paper sent to her each week, but she had no opportunity to read *The Banner,* so the references were sometimes confusing. But she definitely knew that her father was mad as a wet hen at Editor Osgood and pulling hard for Will Cleary. The election was set for Tuesday, October 20, and it just happened that Cleary's annual Harvest Ball in San Lucas would be that Saturday. Millie was taking the early morning train home that day to attend the dance with Spud Cleary. If Will isn't the winner, that Harvest Ball will be a sad affair, she thought.

Fred had asked Will about that when he came into the office to put the annual invitation into the paper. "If I win," Will answered, "It will be a celebration. If I don't, I'll still spend a fine evening with friends. After all, it's a thank-you to God and the community for a good harvest. This one has been a whopper."

"He's a fine man," Sarah remarked when Fred reported the conversation that night at the dinner table. "It's a good family. I wonder how serious Millie is with Spud."

"I thought you'd have some idea of that," Fred said. "Don't daughters share their secrets with their mothers?"

"Well, yes .... some," Sarah admitted. "I think there's always been something there, ever since she was a little girl. I remember that branding we went to at Cleary's. Millie went with her hair in pigtails. Then she saw Spud and came home all grown up with her hair in a big, thick braid."

Fred laughed. "I never noticed that."

"Oh, you fathers," Sarah sniffed. "You never notice anything."

"Well, I sure hope Will wins. Wish I could vote in that district. We have a good man here in Talbott, too. He's pretty disgusted by this thing against Will. But he admitted to me the other day that he can't venture a guess how the election will go."

Sarah was worried as her husband. "What do you hear on the street?"

"Not much," he replied. "Sometimes when I walk up to join a group they clam right up or change the subject. Lots of folks, though, they say 'Bully for you, Fred. We're all for Cleary, too.' But most of those people can't vote in that district."

"I saw Missus Braydon in Brunetti's store the other day," Sarah said. "She told me the recall is the talk of the countryside. She said that she'll certainly vote for Will, but she didn't say who George was for. I'd think he'd be strong for Will. Didn't Spud say that Will had sent him and Bucky over there to put in their crop when George was down with the pleurisy?"

"You know, Sarah, if everybody who Will's befriended over the years were for him, there'd have been nobody left to sign that petition. People are damn funny."

"You mean men are funny," Sarah chided. "Good thing women can vote now. Maybe there'll be some common sense in this thing you call the political process. Women realize what a good man Will is and won't believe any of that trash that's been spread."

Thanks to the reforms of Governor Hiram Johnson, whom *The Settler* had strongly supported in 1911, women's suffrage had been granted after a close state-wide vote. Of course, it had lost by a large majority in King City, and throughout south county, and Fred had taken an unmerciful drubbing when his editorial had come out.

Give Women the Right to Vote, had been his headline. *Woman's life, her heart and hope are in the home. Every statute and ordinance, national, state and local, affects the home financially, physically and morally. Woman is needed in the political arena as man is too engrossed in business affairs to properly consider the needs of home and children. Woman's judgment, put into law, will correct many evils of omission and commission that now exist.*

"Hey, Fred. Sarah write that one for you?" was the first question put to him when he entered Tom Himmah's barber shop. The men were all laughing, so he smiled, too.

"Don't blame Fred," Heinie Branstetter said. "Hell, he wouldn't dare go home if he didn't support that proposal."

"It don't make no difference, anyhow." Slim Smith unwrapped his face from under a hot towel. "That damn thing doesn't have a chance."

But it did. The women's suffrage proposal, along with railroad reforms and the right for Californians to initiate laws through the initiative process, were part of the reform package of the new Johnson administration. Fred was delighted because he'd supported them all, though there was considerable grumbling along Broadway. "Damn women'll be running everything" — "Bad enough, they rule the roost at home. Now they'll be sticking their noses into politics" — "Fault of those damn city slickers. They voted it in. We sure as hell didn't." Such comments were made in the city's saloons and on the streets, but, carefully, not in the homes.

Fred stayed late in the office the night of the election. Polls closed at seven and he'd arranged for election officials at each precinct to call him after the votes were counted. It wouldn't take long. But by the time eight o'clock had rolled around, he was waiting nervously for the phone to ring. When it finally did, the loud jangle made him jump and he nearly dropped the receiver.

"*Settler* office," he answered.

Fred listened a moment, wrote down some numbers, said, "Yes, thank you." Not a good sign, he thought as he stared at his pad. Cleary 21, Haskins 7, Fortino 10, Gallito 2. No on the recall 21, and in favor 19. That was Pleyto. He thought they'd go stronger there for Will. Did this mean Will was beaten?

The phone rang again. It was from Gorda on the coast. The count was 36 for Will, 12 for Gallito, 4 to Haskins and 4 to Flint. With 36 to 20 against the recall, that was a little better, Fred figured.

"*Settler* office," he answered. This time it was the Parkfield precinct reporting and Will got trounced there. Valleton phoned in next and that was about the same. Results were similar from Indian Valley and Fred totaled what he had as he waited for the next phone call.

It was 103 favoring the recall and only 34 votes for Will. Not so good, Fred thought, but these are the smaller precincts, the first to finish counting, the home territory of the Parkfield Good Roads bunch. Maybe it'll change, he hoped.

It did! Peach Tree checked in with a 35 to 12 margin favoring Will. Next was San Lucas reporting 97 no votes on the recall and only 39 for it. Fred started to smile when he thanked Romona Duck for phoning in the Jolon totals.

He was downright cheerful when he answered the phone for Mrs. Heinsen calling from Lockwood. "How many? More than double, isn't it? Yes, Will is running well ahead everywhere except way down south. Looks like he'll make it. Thanks for your call." He was looking at the totals when Oasis reported 39-15, and then San Ardo was on the line. Fred let out a loud whoop as he wrote No 166 and Yes 46.

Final totals were 508 against the recall and for Will Cleary, and 280 for the recall, which was the combined total for his seven opponents. Of the 861 voters registered in the 4th District, 788 had gone to the polls. That was the heaviest turnout ever, 91 percent.

The first thing Fred did was telephone Will. He got the exchange in Bunte's store, and the operator cranked out the two longs and a short for the Cleary ranch. The phone was picked up on the first rings. "Will Cleary speaking. Well, hello Fred. What's the bad news?"

"No bad news, Will. You whipped 'em! I just got all the totals in. Five hundred and eight against the recall and all those votes were for you. The others only had two hundred eighty all together. Congratulations, Will."

"Now that's good news. Thank you, Fred." He turned aside from the phone and called out, "Honora. It's all counted. I won." Fred could hear Will's wife give a glad cry in the background. "Oh, I'm so relieved," he heard her say.

Then Will came back on the phone. "Your support did it, Fred. Thanks. Your paper helped me a lot. I'll sure sleep better tonight. Say, Fred, put a nice thank you ad in the paper next week, tell them I appreciate the voters' confidence in me."

"Sure, but you can thank them yourself at the Harvest Ball, Will."

"I'll do that, too. See you there?"

"You bet. Sarah and I wouldn't miss it. So long." Fred rang off.

He clicked the receiver and gave central his home number. "One oh three, please."

When Sarah picked up the phone, Fred asked, "Wake you up?"

"No, I can't sleep. What happened?"

"Will stomped 'em," Fred declared and gave Sarah the totals.

"Now I'll sleep," she said. He knew Sarah had a broad smile on her face.

Fred had no sooner returned the receiver to its hook than the bell clanged. Mayor Al Carlson wanted to know the result. And then the phone rang again and it was Johnny Tompkins of the Blackhawk Livery Stable. Bob Irwin, Heinie Branstetter, Billy Wasson and some others called in. Fred was there until after midnight answering the phone and announcing the totals. He didn't mind.

CHAPTER TWENTY-FOUR

MILLIE'S FIRST QUESTION WHEN SHE STEPPED OFF the train was, "How did the election go?" She beamed when her father told her about Will's substantial victory. Her second question was about Patrick Cleary. "He's doing fine, last I heard," Fred said. "He's still confined at home, of course."

Actually, Pat wasn't doing well at all despite the fact that his leg was healing. Doc Brumwell had checked it, and put on a new cast the day before the election, and that allowed Pat to go with his parents into San Lucas to vote. Pat Cleary was damned tired of laying on a bed, or dragging himself around the house on crutches. He was irritable and unhappy most of the time. He'd turned down the offer of a ride to the Harvest Ball because he couldn't see himself being a wallflower while everyone else danced. It was even an effort for Pat to maintain the usual banter with his brother as he watched Spud get ready to go to the dance.

"Getting all spoofed up, huh, brother? I can smell you clear from here. You'll have every dog in San Lucas following you."

Spud laughed. "It's not your opinion that matters, Patrick, my lad, it's the favor of young Miss Millie Godfrey I seek," Spud said. "I don't give a hoot what your nose thinks if this stuff makes Millie's twitch."

"Twitch?" Pat scoffed. "It'll make her snort. She'll cough and choke, probably throw a fit before you get to the dance."

"Don't you worry about us, dear brother. Just handle those crutches. If you hadn't been so damned clumsy you wouldn't be in that fix." Spud tossed the last remark over his shoulder as he went outside to crank up the ranch truck, a 1912 International Harvester half ton, the use of which he'd appropriated for the evening. His father and mother had left for San Lucas sometime earlier in the Ford touring car so that they'd be on hand at Bunte's dance hall above the store in time to greet arriving guests.

Spud wore a suit, high-collared white shirt and string tie, though his feet were encased in his accustomed footwear, boots. But these were his dancing boots, as he referred to the highly-polished, intricately tooled, custom-made cowboy boots. Spud removed his wide-brimmed Stetson as Fred Godfrey opened the front door.

He nodded politely to Fred and Sarah. "Good evening, Mister Godfrey, Missus Godfrey. How are you folks this evening?" Spud asked. "Going to the dance?"

"We'll be along. Wouldn't miss it," Fred replied. "Want to personally congratulate your father. Quite a victory."

"Wasn't it!" Spud agreed. "Things are a little easier on the ranch now. Dad tried to act as if he wasn't worried, but he was. We could tell because every time he heard a bad rumor he'd come home and find more work for us to do."

"Hi." Millie came into the front room, looking fresh and pretty in a yellow frock, her long hair piled in coils atop her head. She handed her coat to Spud and he held it for her. "Ready to go?"

Spud was staring at Millie in admiration and it took him a second to nod his head. Sarah saw the look and realized that this young man was definitely in love with her daughter. "See you at the dance," Spud told the Godfreys as he and Millie walked out the door, hand in hand.

"Sorry about this," Spud said, pointing to the old International Truck. "Only contraption left on the ranch tonight." Millie laughed, happily dismissing his apology, when she saw they'd be sitting in the open air cab. She tied her shawl tightly over her head, and settled into the seat. Spud hit the crank and they chugged down San Lorenzo Avenue and turned on Division Street. He changed into high gear as they came onto the highway and headed for San Lucas.

Usually glib, Spud was shy for the first time with this girl. What's come over me? he wondered. So he hadn't seen her for a couple of months, so what?

Millie felt the same way. She couldn't think of a thing to say, so she sat quietly and enjoyed the sensation of the wind blowing in her face as they sped along at a forty-mile-an-hour clip. A fleeting regret over the damage to her carefully arranged hair was forgotten in the excitement of being with Spud.

It wasn't until they pulled into the parking space beside Bunte's store, and Spud cut the engine, that they turned to each other and started to speak, both at the same instant. They laughed and Spud said, "You first."

Millie asked about Pat and Spud said, "Doc thinks it will be a year or so before he can really get around on that leg. He's lucky to have it. So tell me about your new job, do you like it?"

"Oh yes, I love it." She told Spud about some of the wonderful things the blind children could do with a little encouragement, about the satisfaction she got from teaching them Braille, some of whom had never read before.

"But there are funny things, too," she told him. "Once we were singing *'Onward Christian Soldiers'* and it didn't sound quite right. I listened closely and finally made it out. They were singing *'with the cross-eyed Jesus marching on before'* instead of *'cross of Jesus.'* Cross-eyed made more sense to these children than cross of." Millie smiled softly.

"Cold out here. Maybe we should get into the dance or people might talk about us," Spud said."

"Let them. I don't care." Spud was pleased by Millie's response. She took his arm and he escorted her up the stairs. They could hear the musicians tuning up above the babble of voices and Spud was excited about the evening. But he was uncomfortable, too, an uncertainty nagged in the corner of his mind. Millie seemed to be enjoying her work, appeared so dedicated to it, loving the children and feeling useful. Would she ever want to give that up to be a rancher's wife?

They danced, with each other and with others. Millie's cheeks were flushed and she hardly had time to catch her breath before each new partner claimed her. Spud roamed the hall and took his turns around the floor with various girls, but always kept an eye on Millie. The McReynolds family orchestra from King City played at a furious clip. Just before the intermission, a caller announced an old-fashioned quadrille and Spud and Millie were the first couple on the floor, offering encouragement to Will Cleary, who had the arm of Sarah Godfrey, and to Fred and Honora. They advanced and retreated, bowed and curtsied, whirled around and around, and promenaded down the hall.

When the music ended, many of the couples went outside, over to the Pleasant View for a snack, courtesy of Will Cleary. Some chose to continue their celebrating by accepting the invitation to "have a snort" from bottles cached in the autos. Others acted on the suggestion, "Let's wet our whistles over at The Mint." A few couples sneaked off into the shadows behind the blacksmith shop. Spud and Millie picked up cups of punch and sat in a quiet corner of the hall.

"Spud," Millie asked, "whatever happened to your Uncle Timothy?"

"Oh, he still lives up there on his little squat in Coyote Canyon. He doesn't come out very often, sort of a recluse."

"That's too bad," Millie said, and then she smiled at an old memory. "He was so nice to me at your branding one time. He let me ride his horse."

"Yeah," Spud said, looking mischievously at her. "I remember. Thanks again for saving my hat."

Millie laughed. "I'd hoped you'd forgotten. I felt like such a silly, little girl. I couldn't even get back on my horse. You had to help me, give me a boost."

"I sure remember that part," Spud gave her his teasing grin. He was surprised to see Millie blushing. She never did that. Spud changed the subject. "I heard a story about Uncle Tim the other day."

"What was that?" Millie asked just as anxious to change the subject as Spud was.

"Tim was in San Lucas and one of those fellows with the petition against Dad came along. I guess he didn't know Tim, hadn't seen him that much. Anyhow, the fellow asked him to sign the petition.

" 'What's it all about?' asks Tim.

" 'This is to get rid of our no-good supervisor, that Will Cleary,' says the fellow.

"Bam! Tim knocks him to the ground with one punch. No words, no nothing. Just wham. Then Uncle Tim stands there, over him, points down at him and tells him, 'Will Cleary is a better man than you'll ever be, a better man than any of us.' With that he gets on his horse and trots out of town. He didn't come back until election day, but he was in San Lucas to vote. They say he didn't speak to a soul, just voted and left again."

"Good for Uncle Tim!" Millie exclaimed. Then she paused, pensive for a moment. "But the poor man, he must be so lonesome. Does he show up for any of your family things?"

"Christmas and Easter, maybe a branding once in a while."

"Why do you suppose he stays up there all by himself?"

"Something about a girl a long time ago. Dad says Tim gave his heart, but only got rejection in return," Spud told her. "The girl didn't amount to much, according to my dad."

181

"Poor Tim. We should go see him someday."

Spud gave her a quick look. What did she mean by that? Probably nothing. She'd be getting on the evening train in a day or so, headed back to Oakland, and who knew when he'd see her again? He didn't know what to say. Suddenly, from behind, a hand clapped him on the shoulder. He was grateful he didn't have to pursue Millie's last remark.

"Come on you two. We've got something to tell you."

It was Bucky O'Keefe with his arm around Lilly Martin. She was clinging to Bucky and looking up at him bright-eyed, waiting for him to speak. Spud and Millie stood up and gave their full attention to the other two.

"Well, go ahead," Spud prompted. "Quit giggling and tell us."

"We're going to get married," Bucky announced.

"He just proposed, outside by the Ford. And I said yes," Lilly told them.

"Congratulations," Spud said, slapping his cousin on the back and then giving him a good, firm handshake.

"I'm so happy for you." Millie smiled and gave her friend a hug. "When?"

"Next spring," Bucky proudly proclaimed.

"You better wait until after we get the cattle gathered, and branded," Spud warned.

"To hell with you, Cleary!" Bucky laughed and gave Spud a playful tap on the chest. "You sound just like your dad."

That night on the ride home Millie sat close to Spud. Neither said much, but their thoughts were on their friends and the coming marriage. When they kissed goodnight, they hardly touched, but Millie lifted her face and looked intently at Spud, almost questioningly. She parted her lips, and her kiss was soft and tender. Spud felt it was something special. But what?

CHAPTER TWENTY-FIVE

"IF YOU PUT COVERINGS ON THE CHAINS and clutter up the machine with safety devices, you can't use the damn harvester," Will Cleary complained.

"Same way with printing presses," Fred Godfrey agreed. "Put guards on the belts and flywheels and you can't feed the press. Damn printers take them off anyhow."

Fred Godfrey and Will Cleary were off in a corner of the Peerless Saloon, sipping Old Joe steam beer and helping themselves to the free lunch. Fred was making notes about Cleary's new harvester, the first of its kind in the area. Fred wrote, "Gas motor, four cylinder, 40 horse power, 42 1/2-inch separator, 44-inch draper, 20-foot cut." He asked, "How much, Will? Mind saying?"

"Well, I'll tell you, Fred. It was three thousand eight hundred and fifty. But don't print that. Looks like I'm showing off."

"Course not, Will, if you don't want it. But the story is important. Shows the way to other farmers and makes folks aware of the opportunities here in south county," Fred said. "Your success is a good example, yours and a few other live ones I could name."

Again Will Cleary was in the forefront of farming practices. He'd invested in one of Ben Holt's Caterpillar tractors and then purchased a Harris Upland Gas Harvester from Stockton. But he wasn't too happy about it. "I guess I'm too much of a teamster at heart," he admitted. "Just like my dad. I don't really trust these new machines and I'm not sure they're any safer." He'd retired the old Fairbanks-Morse stationary machine in a shed on the Long Valley place, but he still had the horse-drawn Holts and his custom harvesting operation kept them busy all summer. He paused and a sad, worried look came over his face. "Safety's been my main concern since Pat's accident." Fred nodded sympathetically. "Tried a lot of things, but I don't seem to be meeting with much success," Will said.

The two men sat silently for a few moments, then Fred put his notebook away and tossed off his beer. "Something else I want to discuss with you, Will." He sat back in his chair and studied Cleary for a moment. Then he leaned forward and said, "I'd like to start buying back your *Settler* stock within the next week or so, unless you have an objection. It'll take me a while. Pay you when I can, if you'll take my note. I've already bought out Paul Talbott."

"Well, no, Fred, no objection." Will was surprised. "What brings this about?"

"I just feel that any ownership of the paper on your part, you and Paul, even that little bit, can prove an embarrassment," Fred responded. "That election you just went through was a good example. If I support you they say it's because of your ownership position."

"Hell, Fred. We both know that's not true." Will shook his head and smiled at the editor. "You've criticized the board more than a few times, strongly, and me, in particular, when you thought it necessary. Damned if I agreed with you," Will said with a laugh. "You were wrong every time. But I recognized that in your misguided, misinformed way, you thought you were right."

Fred laughed, too. "Will, you saved my bacon and I'm eternally grateful. I'll be sending you a check for the first installment early next week."

"Well, in that case, I guess I can afford to buy us another round." Will motioned to the bartender to draw two more drafts of Old Joe.

"Thanks, Will," Fred said as a foaming, frosty glass was set in front of him. Then he asked, "How about the election? I know where you stand, but who do you think will win?"

They'd had their arguments on this score. Fred Godfrey had been a solid booster for Teddy Roosevelt and was disappointed when the Bull Moose party failed in 1912. Will Cleary was a steadfast Democrat, as his father had been before him. "Registered Democratic," old Jeremiah used to say. "All the

Irish did. But I voted for Lincoln, my first vote, right after I got my citizenship papers. Never regretted it. But that was the end of it. I've voted Democratic ever since."

A leader in the county Democratic party, Will Cleary was for Woodrow Wilson. He had to be. But he wasn't happy about it, either. "This neutrality has me bothered. How many American lives are going to be lost to those German U-boats before Wilson falls off the fence?"

"That's just it, Will," Fred said as he took a drink of his steam beer and wiped the froth from his lips. "Holy Jehoshaphat, I just don't trust Wilson. Claims he kept us out of the war. But the Kaiser is pushing us around and laughing in our face. Four more years of Woodrow and we'll all be eating sauerkraut. People should be listening to Teddy Roosevelt."

Roosevelt had been going around the country stumping for Charles Evans Hughes, the Republican presidential candidate, and Fred had commended him in an editorial entitled, *Bully for Teddy*. But Sarah hadn't liked it. And Fred knew Will wasn't sold on the man, either.

"Fred, Roosevelt is past his time," Will chided. He reached for another hard-boiled egg and peeled off the shell. "And you can't blame Wilson. The country doesn't want war."

Cleary finished chewing his egg, drained his beer glass and stood up. "Guess, I'll never convince you, Fred. Looks like you'll be bullheaded all your life." He laughed and started for the door. "See you after the election. Remember, Wilson's the man."

Fred grinned and waved goodbye. But he'd had the same argument with his wife. Sarah was going to vote for Wilson, sure as hell, no matter how persuasively Fred argued. So would Millie, who felt the same as her mother. "I don't want my brother going off to war," Millie said. But she was thinking more of Spud Cleary than her brother, Bobby. And Bobby, Fred knew, was all for leaving his job at Carrigan's Garage and going after the Huns right now.

When election results were in, Wilson had narrowly defeated Hughes. But to Fred the big news was the county district attorney race. Milton Osgood had moved his law practice to Salinas, declared himself a candidate for district attorney and, much to Fred's barely contained delight, had been soundly thrashed, particularly in south county. But, best of all, as far as Fred was concerned, was that before Osgood closed his law office upstairs in the Kirk Building on Broadway, he had sold his interest in *The Banner*.

The new editor introduced himself in a front page editorial in the newspaper. He claimed to be an experienced journalist, having served on the staff of a number of metropolitan dailies, though he didn't specify which ones. He had moved to King City because he wanted the small town lifestyle and the peace of a pastoral countryside. He promised to *provide the necessary leadership, which the community had obviously lacked, and would fill the void of editorial comment needed to assure the progress of the city and the prosperity of the area.*

Fred turned red with anger when he saw *The Banner's* front page. "Provide leadership? Fill an editorial void? Holy Jehoshaphat, who does this guy think he is?" Fred slammed the paper down on his desk and looked over at his wife, who was working that day, helping to gather the pages and bind the new catalogue for Wideman and Co, the department store. Sarah sniffed derisively. "He doesn't sound any better than Osgood!"

Sarah picked up her folding bone and returned to her work of creasing the pages when the front door of *The Settler* office opened and a man of medium size and indeterminate age entered the office. He wore thick glasses perched on a bulbous red nose, and a derby hat from which gray hair hung limply to the shoulders of an old-fashioned frock coat buttoned over a waistcoat of varied colors. His scrawny neck stuck up from a shirt collar several sizes too large and served as a track for an Adams apple, which bobbed up and down as he spoke.

He introduced himself as Horace Bissell, "Lately of the mid-west and now making my abode in this fair city." He waved his hand to majestically encompass Broadway and its environs.

Fred turned to his wife. "Sarah, meet the new *Banner* man."

"How do you do, my fair lady," Bissell greeted her, sweeping off his derby with a flourish and a bow. He tried to kiss her hand, but Sarah's fists were tightly closed, clutched around a stack of Wideman's catalogue pages.

"How nice to meet you, my dear. I should like you to know that I will do my utmost to assist your husband in every way to improve his newspaper, provide guidance and counsel, and direct him in the best path for the progress of our town. Both papers, pulling together for a common good." Sarah immediately thought the man a pompous ass, but chose to be polite and cool. She let him babble on. "My experience and expertise are at your command, sir," Bissell said to Fred. "Together we shall raise this little community to metropolitan heights. You have my word on it." He turned back to Sarah. "And to you, madam, it's always a pleasure to find members of the fairer sex toiling beside their men, true helpmates."

Sarah frowned, trying to control her real feelings while Fred visibly struggled to fight off an attack of apoplexy. When Bissell excused himself, "to attend to my multitude of duties in the service of the people," Fred let out the breath he'd been holding. Later he admitted that the only reason he'd kept his mouth shut was because "I was speechless." And Sarah wondered aloud, "Was that man drunk?"

The answer wasn't long in coming. It was a matter of conjecture around King City for a month or so, but then it became irrefutably evident that Mr. Bissell had a weakness for what he himself referred to in frequent editorials as "Demon Rum." Visitors to his office swore there was a bottle of Cyrus Noble beside his typewriter. This was discounted as an unconfirmed rumor until the December 10, 1916 edition of *The Banner*.

A man had been found dead under the King City bridge. The coroner's verdict was "death from a self-inflicted gunshot wound." Bissell was in a frenzy of determination to get that news onto the street before *The Settler*. He frantically grabbed a typestick and pulled out his case of eighty-four point wood type, the largest he had. His fingers flew over the tray as he set, *Man Shot Self to Death*. He swiftly placed the head over the front page story, hurriedly locked up the form and hand cranked his little drum press. He carried the papers, with the ink still wet, to the post office and to the stores. He rang up the paper boys and hurried them to *The Banner* office for their street sale copies. He easily beat out *The Settler* with the news.

But it didn't take the citizens of King City very long to realize that they had in their hands a collector's item—something that would make newspaper history for many years to come. Horace Bissell, in an excited hurry to print the story, and with his hand guided, perhaps, by a mischievous spirit from the demon rum, had picked an "i" from the case instead of an "o." The headline read, *Man Shit Self to Death*. The entire edition of *The Banner* sold out within the hour. It was the only time in Fred Godfrey's career that he didn't mind being scooped by a rival newspaper.

CHAPTER TWENTY-SIX

IT WAS ONE OF THOSE BEAUTIFULLY clear, crisp, bright days in early January that made Millie feel so wonderfully alive. Rain had fallen heavily over Christmas so the grass was growing green and lush in the fields. And now the sun had been shining for several days so that the dirt road, although dotted here and there by puddles through which the auto splashed and splattered, was dry enough to travel. Spud guided the Ford past Jolon and onto the Indians Road. They were quiet, these two, a comfortable silence between them. But Millie's mind was busy.

She'd spent Christmas vacation with her parents in King City, and although it was a wonderful visit, she felt frustrated and unsatisfied. A nagging something was wrong and Millie knew it was Spud. They'd seen each other several times over the holidays and had shared an especially romantic evening at the New Year's Eve dance at the El Camino Real Hotel. The Spanish Room was festooned with red, white and blue bunting and the patriotic motif was everywhere. Conversations, no matter how they started, always turned to the threat of war. But Spud would divert the talk to cattle or crops, to the college football games, or tell a funny story and then whisk Millie off for another dance.

He held her close as they danced and she flowed into him, feeling their bodies join as they moved to the music. Her head rested on his chest and when she'd break away to look up at him she'd see that his eyes were warm, brimming with love. Tonight he'll say it, she thought. He'll tell me that he loves me and we'll set a wedding date. Tonight!

But the evening passed and Spud said nothing. Millie fretted. She'd be getting on the train again for Oakland in two days to go back to her classroom full of blind children. Millie loved those children, she was proud of them and reveled in their achievements. But now she wanted children of her own;

above all she ached for Spud Cleary. And she was sure Spud felt the same way for her. So why hadn't he said anything? Was it shyness? Surely, this gregarious, self-confident, very capable man wasn't too shy to tell his girl he loved her? It must be something else, Millie decided. But she couldn't figure out what.

Spud turned off the Indians Road onto the lane into the Hidalgo ranch, which Bucky O'Keefe now managed for his in-laws. He and Lilly lived in the majestic old adobe on the banks of the San Antonio River. They'd gotten married last year and both Millie and Spud had been in the wedding party. Now they had a baby girl and Millie wanted to see her before she went back to Oakland.

She was cradling the child in her arms, cooing to it and rocking. Bucky was in the kitchen mixing drinks for their get-together celebration. Lilly had gone in search of some "darling baby clothes" to show Millie. Spud and Millie were alone in the living room. Millie's attention was all on the baby. Spud stood there, watching her.

"Millie, will you marry me?" His voice came from halfway across the room.

Startled, Millie's eyes opened wide as she looked at Spud. She took a step back and tightened her grip on the baby, who was as startled as Millie and began to cry. Lilly hurried back into the room. Bucky entered, his hands full of glasses. Spud, oblivious to the others, his eyes intent on Millie, leaned slightly forward, waiting for her to answer. Lilly took the baby. Bucky set down the glasses. No one spoke. The silence grew until it completely surrounded them.

Millie looked down at her cradled arms, surprised she no longer held the baby, then her eyes shifted back to Spud. She stood still, but gasped, "Yes." The word was barely audible. Then she threw open her arms and ran across the room into his.

"Yes, Spud. Yes."

He kissed her, gently. And he kissed away her tears that had started to flow, and when she tried to speak he shushed her, and gently kissed her again, and again, while Bucky and Lilly quietly watched, and even the sounds of the crying baby faded to whimpers and then to silence.

Spud looked up from Millie and seemed bewildered that they weren't alone in the world. He grinned sheepishly. "We're going to be married," he explained.

Bucky let out a whoop and Lilly a cry of joy. Bucky grabbed Spud's hand and began pumping it while Lilly hugged Millie. The baby, squeezed between them, started to cry again. Lilly, handing her baby to Millie, gave Spud a hug and a kiss. Bucky leaned down to brush Millie's cheek with his lips, patting her shoulder.

Bucky poured the drinks and, when all four of them had glasses, he raised his and proposed a toast, but it was actually a comment. "It's about time!" he chortled.

Spud and Millie made plans on the ride back to King City that afternoon. Millie would have to finish out the school year so they couldn't get married until late June. "After we brand and ship cattle and just before harvest," Spud said. And she'd have Lilly in the wedding party, of course, but she also wanted her childhood friend, Teddy Irwin. And Spud wanted his brother, Pat, and Bucky, of course. They'd have Dad's brother, Father Dan Cleary, perform the ceremony at St. John's Catholic Church in King City, with just the family and a few close friends in attendance.

Spud wondered, "What'll your folks say?"

Millie laughed. "Just what Bucky said. About time. What'll Will and Honora say?"

"About time." The two again burst into laughter.

"Oh, Spud. I almost gave up on you," Millie teased.

"Well, Millie," Spud said, growing serious. He took his eyes from the road for a second to look down at her, close to him on the seat, curled in the crook of his arm. "I knew I wanted to marry you that first summer, when Pat got hurt. But you were

191

going away to teacher's college and you had to finish that. Then you got that great job and seemed so happy and content with those children. I didn't know if you'd want to be a rancher's wife, married to a clod-hopping cowboy."

Millie smiled at him. "I love that clod-hopping cowboy. And I'll love being a rancher's wife." She let her hand wander up to the back of his neck and caressed it as he drove. "I've always known that deep down, I guess, since I was a little girl. I had to grow up first for you to notice me."

"Aw, I noticed you, all right." Spud gave her a squeeze.

They both laughed, and then Millie looked at Spud with curiosity. "That was certainly a unique proposal, Spud Cleary. How did you happen to wait all these years and suddenly propose to me when you did—right there in Bucky and Lilly's living room?"

"I've come so close so many times, Millie." Spud's voice was filled with emotion. "The words just wouldn't come. But when I saw you with that baby in your arms, they just jumped out of my mouth. I was as surprised as you."

He looked down lovingly at this wonderful young woman beside him, with whom he was planning a future. He'd have to get her an engagement ring. And talk to his father about which Cleary place, the one on the Trescony or the ranch in Long Valley, would be Spud and Millie's new home. But there was a cloud over all of it. Spud tried to push it away, to ignore it, to change the subject. But every day it came closer. There would be war for America. And he'd be in it.

* * * * *

On February 3, 1917, President Woodrow Wilson dismissed the German ambassador from Washington D.C.

Two months later Wilson went before Congress and formally requested a Declaration of War against Germany. A woefully unprepared America began to mobilize troops and war machines that were so desperately needed by the Allies. *Over*

There was the song on everyone's lips and Uncle Sam looked down from thousands of posters plastered on billboards and buildings, pointing his finger ominously and declaring "Uncle Sam Wants You!"

Advance notice of a U.S. Army recruiting party in south county appeared in *The Settler* and it brought a crowd of young men to the King City depot on the morning of April 13, 1917. Among the first in line was twenty-one-year-old Bobby Godfrey. That afternoon the recruiter was at the San Lucas post office where Matthew "Spud" Cleary signed up.

"I have to, Dad," Spud explained to his father. "Of the three of us, I'm the only one who can serve. Pat's out of it with that bad leg, but he can help you here. And Bucky has his hands full with Lilly and the baby."

"I'm proud of you, Son," Will Cleary said. "And your grandfather would be proud of you. Patriotism and public service are important to this family. But what about Millie? What will she say? Couldn't you wait for the draft?"

"Millie will understand," Spud reassured his father. But as he drove to San Lucas he wondered how he'd tell her, would she understand, would she wait for him?

"Occupation?" The recruiter, resplendent in Army dress blues with a row of medals across his chest, looked up from the enlistment papers.

"Rancher," Spud replied and the recruiter wrote, "Farmer."

"Skills?" he asked. And Spud replied, "I'm a good hand with horses. I'd like to get into the cavalry, something with horses."

"Well, good, sure, sure," the recruiter said as he wrote down the word: "Infantry."

He shook Spud's hand, welcomed him into the Army of the United States, and gave him orders to report to the Presidio of San Francisco on May 1, 1917. Spud would have only two weeks to settle his affairs and make his good-byes. It was over the Easter holidays that he told his fiancee that he'd enlisted.

"But Spud — ! Our wedding plans. How could you!" Millie was shocked at his news. She fought back tears and tried to understand. "Why do you have to be the first? There's going to be a draft. You could wait to be called."

"I just couldn't, Millie." He tried to make light of it. "One of the terrible trio has to go. It's up to me. We can't let the Kaiser off that easy."

"Well, let's make the best of it," Millie said as she squared her jaw and straightened her shoulders. "We'll get married next weekend and go to my place in Oakland for a honeymoon before you report. Father Grauman will understand, the war and all. You go see him tomorrow and I'll take the late train home Friday. I can keep my job while your gone and — "

"Millie, Millie — ! Slow down, sweetheart." Spud interrupted. He shook his head and drew her into his arms. "I can't marry you like that and then go off to war. It's not fair to you." He didn't say, "I might get killed and I don't want to leave a twenty-three-year-old widow." He held her close and murmured into her hair, "Wait for me, darling. When I come back we'll do it right. Please wait for me, Millie."

They argued about it all that day. They talked to Fred and Sarah, who agreed with Spud. And with Will and Honora, who agreed with Spud. Finally, Millie gave up.

"Of course, I'll wait for you, you fool." Millie was sobbing against his chest. "I've waited all my life for you. But I'd rather marry you this minute. Oh, Spud, I'll worry so about you and write you every day." He held her close against him and buried his face in her thick hair. When he kissed her, his tears mingled with hers.

She took the ferry boat from Oakland across the bay and met Spud in San Francisco. She was with him to say goodbye when he reported at the Presidio. And when she returned to her little apartment in Oakland, she'd never been so sad and lonely in her life. Even her pupils noticed it. In their blindness they weren't so blind—they sensed her unhappiness and she got extra hugs, and special favors as they tried to cheer her up.

Spud was put on a train for Fort Lewis in Washington and assigned to Company F of the 162nd Infantry, many of whom were old soldiers who'd been chasing Pancho Villa on the Mexican border. They drilled the raw recruits, whipping them into soldiers as swiftly as possible. Spud drilled in the rain and fired his Springfield. He crawled in the mud and learned how to cross a tangle of barbed wire. He learned to salute and say, "Yes, Sir," and marched for miles with a full pack. He was strong and hard, in good shape from a youth filled with ranch work. He thrived, but he never even saw a horse and couldn't understand why the Army wasn't making the best use of his skills.

Spud's outfit finally left Fort Lewis and spent two monotonous weeks on a troop train creeping toward the east coast, spending much of the time shuttled off onto sidings where they exercised and drilled beside the tracks. In New Jersey they encamped for more, long, hot, humid, tedious days of drilling and long marches, mock maneuvers and hours on the firing range. Spud was a crack shot from his deer hunting days and soon made marksman. His twenty-six years, which made him slightly older than other recruits, and his leadership ability, put stripes on his arm. By the time they stood to on the dock at Hoboken to board the SS Tuscania for France, Spud Cleary was a buck sergeant.

The former luxury liner, converted into a troop ship, finally docked at Le Havre, France in late October. Spud had a knot in his stomach as they marched along the roads of France. He knew they were headed for the front. He'd be in battle soon. How would he hold up?

Are you a coward, Spud Cleary? he asked himself. Will you be brave under fire? Spud looked about him, at the eager young boys in his squad, so cocky, so confident as they marched along, singing the songs they'd picked up. *"Mademoiselle from Armenteer, parley-vous — hasn't been kissed in forty years, inky dinky parley vous."* Will we be so cocky with the Germans shooting at us? he wondered.

He wrote to his parents about the French countryside, about the crops he saw growing, and the young boys and old men in the fields with the women, working with donkeys and oxen, and a few teams of horses. *Not many tractors here,* he wrote his father. *Farming seems old fashioned compared to what we're used to. All the young Frenchmen are at the front. The country is good, looks like fine farm land except for the ruins. They've been fighting back and forth through here for years and it shows. We'll get at them soon and send the Huns packing back to Germany. That'll put an end to it.*

He wrote to Millie telling her about the beauty of the French landscape, about the people he saw, the French townspeople who lined up on the streets and cheered them as they marched through. *We're going to pull the fat out of the fire for them,* he wrote, *and they appreciate us.* He told Millie how much he missed her— *I think of you all the time, Millie dear, and plan for the day we'll be together again*—how much he loved her— *I'm going to spend my life making you happy*— But he didn't mention his belief that they'd soon be in battle.

Spud needn't have worried. His outfit marched to Le Mans in the interior of France for more training. And with winter came the rains. French mud was worse than the mud in Washington state and they lived in it, ate in it, slept in it, trained in it. They were camped on the outskirts of the city with only a rare pass to see the sights. Winter turned into spring and still they trained. By now the troops were grumbling, raring to go. They had heard about battles, such as the good showing the U.S. Marines made in Belleau Woods, and they wanted their crack at the Huns. But still they waited.

Finally Spud's outfit shouldered their packs and marched on the road to Paris. They skirted the city and camped outside with thousands of other American troops. They were going into the line, an offensive at last. Again Spud wondered how he would react under fire?

And again, he needn't have been concerned. Sergeant Cleary's squad was marched front and center, and the six-footers were counted out, three steps to the front, the same as several other squads. "March these men off, sergeant," a major

196

ordered. They stood at attention before the headquarters tent until a captain came outside. Spud saluted him and the salute was returned.

"You men are now Military Police Company Two Hundred and Eighty. You're detached from the One Sixty Second. Take those trucks and report to Military Police Headquarters in Paris."

Spud's infantry outfit marched through Verdun and finally into the assault on St. Mihiel, and then more action in the dense forest of the Argonne, while Spud policed Paris. He'd seen enough wounded men, seen the destruction of war, to know he was well off. But he couldn't help telling himself, "This is a helluva way to fight a war, Spud Cleary."

CHAPTER TWENTY-SEVEN

"WAR IS HERE," CRIED *THE SETTLER'S* HEADLINE in April and Fred Godfrey wrote an editorial noting that Americans were changing their terminology. *German toast is now French toast and we are urged to call sauerkraut 'liberty cabbage.' But with all of this we should remember to treat fairly those among us of German extraction, whom we know to be good citizens and neighbors. Their German dialect does not interfere with their Americanism. It was natural that their sympathies were with their Fatherland up to now, while Germany was fighting other nations. But now that Germany is fighting America, their adopted nation, their sympathies and efforts are all with us, even against Germany. Remember, many of their sons are in uniforms of The United States. Be fair.*

But Fred had other worries on his mind besides the demonstrations against the good German folk of Lockwood and those elsewhere in the Salinas Valley. Fred's immediate problem was money. He'd installed a Model Fourteen Linotype, complete with extra magazines filled with a variety of fonts and sizes of type, just before the war started. It was secondhand, of course, but at seventeen hundred and fifty dollars, paying for it in monthly installments had become harder and harder as the delinquent subscription list and overdue ad accounts continued to grow.

"Dammit, Sarah," he said one afternoon as he sat at his desk holding a handful of bills and thumbing through them in frustration. "There's one thousand two hundred and sixty-eight dollars past due on subscriptions. If they'd pungle up, we'd be in the clear. But those Liberty Bonds are sucking up all the loose money around."

Fred had run a list of bond contributions and pledges in *The Settler*. He'd put in a hundred himself, but he noted Will Cleary had contributed a thousand. The southern part of the county had gone way over its quota in the first bond drive.

Sarah was sitting in the only comfortable chair in the office. It was a small, cushioned chair that she had insisted Fred buy for her since she was spending long hours working at the paper. Now and then she stopped for a cup of tea and she wanted to drink it in the comfort of a chair that was, well, a bit more like home. This day Sarah only half listened to her husband. She was sympathetic, but she'd heard all this before. She was going through a stack of mail and had pulled out a letter from Bobby which she hastily opened.

She unfolded the letter and interrupted her husband. "Fred, it's from Bobby." She quickly scanned the pages. Her son was writing from Fort Lewis that he'd been placed in a motor supply outfit. "Listen to this," she said. *I was surprised to wind up here. I'd told them I was a mechanic, but sure didn't expect them to pay any attention. The Army has a way of placing men where they seem to least fit. I know a guy in this outfit who had been a cook and he thought he'd be in a mess hall somewhere, but he's under a truck with a wrench in his hand just like me. I guess the horseshoers are in the kitchen from the way the chow tastes.*

"Well, at least he's all right," Sarah said with a relieved sigh. She had fretted ever since Bobby went off to war. Fred assured her that if their son was driving a supply truck he wouldn't be in the front lines. They'd seen the film *The Western Front,* at the Novelty Theatre and it had upset Sarah. Then, after they'd heard a speaker on *The Kulture of the Beast of Berlin,* Sarah had difficulty sleeping for several weeks.

Fred was equally grateful that their son was fine, but at this particular moment he was incensed by "that unctuous bastard down the street." The latest edition of *The Banner* had taken him to task for *getting the populace unnecessarily riled by publishing erroneous, untrue reports of fantasy.*

Editor Bissell seemed to emerge from his bottle with regularity each press day and managed to put another edition of *The Banner* on the street. Although his exaggerated, courtly demeanor and pomposity had King City residents snickering behind his back, he was able to enthrall just enough subscribers, readers and merchants to take a small measure of business from *The Settler.* Fred had remarked to several friends at the barbershop one day, "As Bissell himself would put it, he's a festering pustule on the posterior."

In contention on this occasion was the new King City bridge, or, more practically, the promise of a new bridge across the Salinas River at King City. When the river had last gone on its rampage and washed out the approach in the winter of 1916, temporary repairs had been made. County supervisors, led by Talbott and Cleary, had voted to replace the bridge provided the State of California would construct a highway. Highway commissioners had voted approval of a stretch between Thompson's Gulch, a few miles north of King City, to San Lucas, nine miles south. But approval hinged on the county financing the bridge.

Fred had been tipped by Will Cleary that there was opposition developing among the three supervisors from Salinas, Monterey and north county. They didn't want to put out the forty thousand dollars for the bridge in the south when the money was wanted in the more populated northern end of the county. So Fred Godfrey jumped back into the fray. He wrote an editorial warning south county citizens that the highway might be constructed across the river on the west side, bypassing King City completely, if the supervisors didn't restate their agreement to build the bridge.

The chamber of commerce was about to appoint a delegation to call on the county board when *The Banner* hit the street. Bissell suggested that *the editor of The Settler was trying to shoot from the hip with a gun that is half cocked. Citizens of this community may rest assured, despite the rantings of that misguided, but perhaps well-intentioned so-called newspaper in this fair city, that the state, in its wisdom, has no intent to build a highway down the west side of our river. The enterprising editor of The Banner has ascertained this information directly from the highway department and had it verified by night letter this date. Relax, King City, and pay no further attention to the unfounded prattlings of that other so-nervous editor and his uncertain trigger finger.*

When Fred read that, he was so furious he could hardly explain to Sarah where he was going as he hurriedly threw some extra clothing into a suitcase. "To Sacramento. I'll get it direct from the highway commission," he finally sputtered. He was on the northbound that evening.

The next issue of *The Settler* set things straight. The headline simply read, *Banner Bushwa*. The editorial followed. *A personal interview, being much more satisfactory than a night letter, even one printed in heavy, black type, this editor presented himself in the offices of the state highway commission Tuesday, last, to definitely ask the question, 'Does the state intend to build the new highway across the river and through King City to San Lucas on the east side?'*

The answer was, 'Yes.' But in the explanatory statement from Mr. Harrison Torgensen, commission secretary, lies the crux of the matter. 'We have an agreement with the County of Monterey, which will build the bridge. Should the county decide not to build the bridge, it will be more economical to locate the new highway on the west side of the river. But, of course, we have no intention of doing that because of our agreement.'

Thus, the situation stands as The Settler claimed. It hinges on the bridge. It behooves local residents to petition the board of supervisors to live up to their agreement or the highway will leave this city high and dry on the other side of the river.

This editor must point out to the gentleman up the street that it is, of course, more costly to travel to Sacramento for a face-to-face interview than it is to send a night letter with an ambiguously-worded question. But The Settler has never been cheap in its endeavors to serve the public with the correct information.

Is it necessary to point out to readers that most of what appears in The Banner is bushwa? And we all know what that is.

Two months later a delegation from King City heard the board of supervisors, led by Cleary and Talbott, re-affirm their agreement to build the King City bridge. The next month *The Settler* reported that *Will Cleary, chairman of the county board, returned from Sacramento with a copy of the signed agreement to start construction of a paved highway from Thompson Gulch through King City to San Lucas at a cost of $146,000, including a new 21-foot-wide bridge, to be paid for by the county.*

At the next meeting of the Chamber of Commerce, A.B. McReynolds proposed a resolution of appreciation to *The Settler* "for its efforts to encourage the supervisors to build the King City bridge and thus assure this community its place on the new state highway. *The Settler* kept things moving and splendid work and cooperation by all have had the desired result." It passed unanimously. However, one member abstained. Fred later said it was because "Horace Bissell had excused himself to go confer with Cyrus Noble."

That winter a letter from Corporal Bobby Godfrey was proudly published in one of his father's columns. *Cpl. Godfrey writes to us from England: Well, here we are, ready to go across*

*the pond. Kaiser Bill is in for it for sure when we land. The
English cheer us in every town we pass through. It's a good feeling and when we sing together they gather around and call out,
'More, more.' They must be hearing the other guys. You know
the kind of voice I've got. We see airplanes flying over us all the
time. Makes me wonder what it would be like to work on those
engines. You tell the folks at home that we are ready for a whack
at the Kaiser.*

Bobby's outfit, Motor Truck Company 324, saw its new
Liberty trucks lifted aboard the USS Santa Teresa at
Portsmouth, England and unloaded at Le Havre two days
later. Bobby and his men hauled supplies to the French Army
battling near Compeigne, but came under no fire, and always
claimed it was their presence that broke the back of the
German offensive and turned the tide of the war.

Stationed near Paris in July, Bobby drove his five-ton truck,
loaded with buddies on pass into the great French metropolis
to watch the Bastille Day parade. There were soldiers of every
allied nation, led by French Chasseurers in sporty berets, and
the Scots in their kilts marching to their mournful bagpipes,
Italians in plumed hats, Portuguese in dishpan helmets. There
were Poles and Slavs, Bohemians, Montenegrins, Romanians,
Greeks, and anti-Bolshevik Cossacks on spirited horses. Each
of these nations aligned against Germany was preceded by a
band playing its national anthem.

When Bobby saw the American troops, fresh-faced, mostly
untested, but confident and eager, marching under the Arc de
Triomphe to the strains of the *Star Spangled Banner,* and
heard the cheers and shouts of the crowd, he started his engine
and pulled his Liberty truck right in behind them. His buddies
jumped into the back and they all blew kisses to the crowd.
"Vivent les Americains," was the cry as the 324th joined the
parade marching to the Place de la Concorde.

Somebody produced a bottle of cognac and, with that to stimulate their vocal chords, Bobby and his buddies drove around
Paris helping the French celebrate Bastille Day, singing at the

top of their lungs every war song they'd learned from the British. *"The bells of hell go ting-a-ling-a-ling...."* and *"I wore a tunic, a dirty khaki tunic, and you wore civilian clothes, you were with the wenches, while I was in the trenches —"* The vigorous singing, the flourished cognac bottle, and the enthusiastic beckoning of Bobby and the boys soon enticed several of the bolder French 'wenches' into the truck. *"Wash me in the water that you washed the colonel's daughter — "* they roared out the verses, all one hundred eight of them, hugged and kissed the girls, stayed just ahead of the military police, and acted as if they'd already won the war.

He wrote to his parents about his visit to Paris, *After viewing all the French beauties, I maintain the girls of the states have them all beaten.* That was for home consumption, but the truth was that Bobby Godfrey, a shy boy back in King City, found his big, wide smile and unruly red hair to be great assets with the French girls. One *mademoiselle* in particular, a little brunette with large, brown eyes and other attributes to match, had captivated him. He was trying to figure a way to wrap her up and ship her home after the war when the 324th was ordered away from Paris.

They joined the rest of Motor Supply Train 406 that was moving ammunition and other supplies for the American 1st Army attacking St. Mihiel. They unloaded their trucks at the front and returned carrying the wounded. At first these trips were uneventful, although Bobby found it was sobering to drive through the devastated countryside, past the remains of broken buildings, seeing the occasional dead soldier by the road, and the walking wounded trudging to the rear. The worst sight for Bobby were the piles of dead horses bloating by the wayside, the fog-like stench lingering in the open cab of his truck.

Bobby wrote to his sister, Millie, *I have just returned from another trip up the line. I had charge of a convoy of three trucks and we got through just fine. We travel at night and can't use our lights. I can't tell you where, but these French roads are like a spider web and they are terrible, especially when it's wet. And it seems to always be raining.*

To combat the mud, Bobby's outfit received a few of the new FWD trucks with four-wheel drive, and with the gas tank right behind the cab, rather than on the floor next to the driver. Some comfort, Bobby thought. Well, at least, he wasn't staring at it all the time, waiting for a shell to hit it. But with a truck bed full of ammunition, what difference did it make?

The rain had turned into a deluge and Bob Godfrey was wheeling his rig along a rutted path, fighting to see in the blackness against the downpour. He was carrying a desperately-needed load of shells to a battery near the front. Just often enough he could make out the edges of the road by the flash of an exploding bomb or the glare of phosphorous shells. The boom and thump of the big German guns ahead sent a lump into his throat.

He swallowed hard, loosened his grip on the wheel, and wiped his sweaty hands on his pants. He stared intently at the road ahead, bumping and bouncing in his seat as his truck slithered and slid through the mud. Then the blackness turned to a yellow gray and he realized the road was lit by the glow from the woods to his right, blazing into flame from the gun fire barrage.

Is this the right road? he wondered. Is it a road? He wasn't even sure where he was supposed to be. There should be trucks ahead of him. He strained to see the road in front, but he couldn't make out any trucks. He stopped his vehicle, and craned his neck around to look behind, but he couldn't see, or hear, any sign of others with the noise of rain splashing down, and the rumble of the guns.

Fear began to grow a knot in his gut. What was he driving into? The question gripped him, nearly paralyzing him, but he fought to keep his hands on the wheel, somehow meshed the gears, and pushed his foot against the gas pedal. He prayed aloud, "Lord Almighty, please don't let me be stuck here." The big truck swayed and lurched forward.

A shell struck in the road just ahead of him. Dirty water and mud cascaded over the hood of the truck, into the open cab and drenched him. He swerved and skirted the edge of the crater. Bobby didn't know if his other trucks were following. Were they hit? Now he had no time to look back. Couldn't see in the blackness anyhow. But this was no place to stop, so he fought the steering wheel and kept his bounding truck in the tracks. Bombs exploded on each side. The German gunners seemed to have straddled the road. Bobby thought of the load of ammunition in the bed of his truck. "Oh God, please," he cried out, "get me through this!"

It wasn't a direct hit. The shell struck the bank beside the road. It burrowed into the mud before exploding. The concussion blasted the truck. Bobby's body sailed through the blackness and landed with a soft thud in the wet field. The rolling truck, in a series of explosions, burst into flames, which illuminated the area for a hundred yards around. There were no other trucks on the road. And as the fire burned out, the red light of flames flickered over the crumpled figure of Corporal Bob Godfrey.

* * * * *

Back in his office in King City, Fred was sitting at his roll top desk, writing an editorial to be set by his linotype operator, Chester Simpson, whom Fred had hired part-time to give Sarah some rest. It worked out just right because, as Fred explained, Chester was also a part-time drunk who went on a bender every few weeks. About the time Sarah got tired, or when work piled up, Fred would find Chester in his room at the El Camino Hotel, sober him up and sit him in front of the typesetter where smoke from his ever-present cigarette curled up in front of his eyes and his hands played the keyboard like a concert pianist. Drunk or sober, Chester could "hang the elevator," a phrase that meant he could set clean type faster than the machine could operate.

"When you get to this, Chester, put it in ten point two column," Fred said as he spiked the copy on the hook. *While our boys are facing the guns on the western front today, we must do our part to support them and make them as proud of us as we are of them. We can do this by buying Liberty Bonds.*

Show your patriotism. Back our boys. Attend the Red Cross dance and card tournament at the high school gym, and don't miss the big bond drive in San Lucas this week end.

The Settler enthusiastically reported the San Lucas festivities. The unheard of total of eight thousand, five hundred dollars was pledged for Liberty Bonds and several thousand south county citizens watched the parade, horse races and roping events, the barbecue dinner, and the dance which followed to the music of Al Feldt's orchestra. Cowboys from all the ranches, including some top hands from the Peachtree ranch competed in the rodeo events, but old Juan Bravo topped the bronc riding. Seamus Cleary won the horse race riding Ghost, his gray gelding. Julius Trescony, son of the prosperous land owner, in his Navy uniform, made a patriotic speech for the bond sale and proudly led the parade on his palomino. Three beeves slowly turned over a huge fire pit, sending delicious aromas to entice the diners. J.A. Trescony, W.C. Eade, W.R. Barbree and Will Cleary had contributed the beeves, and Mrs. Will Cleary was chairman of the food committee. All those who sat down to the loaded tables agreed she did an excellent service. Following the barbecue the Red Cross sponsored a dance in Bunte's Hall and Pat Cleary served as floor manager.

But soon after the happy, social and patriotic success of the bond rally, San Lucas suffered another of its tragic fires. *The Pleasant View Hotel burned to the ground last night, The Settler reported. King City Hose Co. No. 1, was meeting at the time that word of the fire reached King City. The men jumped into cars and sped to the scene to do what they could to help. But the blaze had taken too strong a hold on the old hotel and they turned their attentions to saving nearby buildings. Heroic work by all the fire fighters and the fortuitous placement of an adobe firewall saved Bunte's Store and the hall upstairs, where all of our Harvest Balls are held. But the old caravansary, a San Lucas landmark and famous since the town was started, is no more.*

Sarah had been reading the paper. She looked over at Fred, relaxing in his easy chair. "Why did you have to print this?" she asked. She leaned forward and held out the paper to him. He looked where her finger pointed out the item. It was a report of an American victory near St. Mihiel. *Colonel George Patton,* it read, *wounded early in the battle, remarked, 'No one ever won a war by dying for his country, but only by making some other poor son of a — — — die for his.'*

"That was copied from one of the city papers," Fred replied. "It's to show how tough our soldiers are, I suppose."

"Well, I don't think he's a very nice man," Sarah declared. Her thoughts turned to her own son somewhere in France. "I wonder how Bobby is doing?"

"We'll be hearing from him soon, dear," Fred said reassuringly.

"Fred, don't *you* worry about him being over there?"

Fred tried to make light of it. "Sarah honey, you worry enough for both of us."

CHAPTER TWENTY-EIGHT

CORPORAL BOB GODFREY LAY ON HIS BACK, unable to move, partially enfolded by the mud of the field below the road, his left arm flung wide, the right crumpled underneath him, his eyes open and staring at the bright red dawn breaking through the clouds. But he couldn't see the beauty of the early morning sky, the brightness of it was only a kaleidoscope of changing color, mostly orange, like a shield of gauze over his eyes. He had no thoughts. Only the occasional blinking of his eyes, reacting when the climbing sun penetrated the streaming morning mist, gave him any sign of life.

A truck slowly moved up the road, winding among the craters now filled with mud and water. The low, hoarse roar of its rumbling engine changed to a whine as it climbed, and then reverted to a groaning moan as it started downhill. The clash of gears as the driver shifted, and the motor noises, made it impossible for the men it carried to even hear each other speak.

Slowly a far-off humming penetrated Bobby Godfrey's damaged eardrums. Linking the hum to the sound of a laboring truck motor was a slow process. He finally made the connection between the familiar sound and a moving truck. Bobby began to blink away the gauze of many colors shrouding his eyes and struggled to focus. But the sky swam above him. He tried to move, but he was immobile. The ability to think trickled back, bit by bit, into his brain. And suddenly, fear returned.

What truck was coming? Whose—was it German or American? How badly am I hurt? I can't seem to move. Am I all alone out here behind the lines? Whose? If it's German I'm best being still. They'll think I'm dead and pass on. But if it's American I want to be seen. Am I going to live? I must need care. I want to live. God, dear God, please save me.

Bobby lay perfectly still in the muddy field as the vehicle pulled alongside the gutted ruins of his truck. It stopped and he could hear the motor idling. The soldiers yelled to each other to be heard over the rumbling. Bobby strained to make out the words. My God, what language were they speaking? The truck sputtered and died. In the sudden lull, Bobby could hear the soldiers talking.

"That one sure took a hit, Dan. Must've been an ammo truck. Blown sky high."

"Yeah. Nothing to be saved here. No sign of a driver."

"Hell, Ski, nobody could have ridden that out. Guy must be in pieces. May as well get going."

American voices. A surge of relief swarmed through Bobby's body. Thank you, Lord! He was going to get out of this. But he heard the engine cough and catch. The driver levered it into gear. They were leaving. Bobby's heart dropped, a sob escaped him. But then the truck lurched and died.

Bobby tried to call out, but no sounds came from his crushed larynx. He tried to wave, but he couldn't lift his left hand out of the mud. Something seemed to be wrong with his right arm. "Don't leave me," he shouted. "I'm right over here." But his voice came out in a low whisper.

The driver was trying to restart the truck. It growled and spluttered. He could hear the driver cursing it. "These god-damned Liberties! I should never have turned the damn thing off."

"Hey, Dan. Hold it," called one of the men in the rear of the truck. "What's that over there?"

"Where?"

He pointed toward the field. "There. See?"

"Ah, hell. Another stiff. Leave him for the graves registration guys. Let's get outa here."

"Aw, just a minute. I'm gonna check it out. Hang on a minute, Dan."

"Suit yourself, Ski. You're gonna drown in all that mud."

Bobby Godfrey blessed Ski, whoever he was. In moments a big, hulking American soldier stood over him, his metal helmet at an angle, a cigarette dangling from his lips. Bobby tried to speak. His lips moved, but no sound came out. He let his eyes spill out their gratitude.

"Hey, Dan — ! This guy's alive! Come help me get him outa here."

"Well, I'll be a son of a bitch. Nobody could live through that blast." Dan came slogging quickly through the mud, almost falling several times, and when he got to where Ski was standing he looked down at Bobby and leaned over to say, "Hang on, buddy. We're gonna get you out of here!"

They rushed Bobby Godfrey to an aid station near Bar-le-Duc. He whispered his thanks and asked for their names so they wrote them on a scrap of paper, Dan Kelly from Red Bank, Montana and Stanley Weisniewski of Winthrop, Massachusetts—two names Bob Godfrey would never forget. He was transferred that afternoon to a field hospital near Reims where the doctors assessed Bobby's injuries. He had a severe concussion, broken shoulder, broken right wrist, lacerations and contusions to his left arm, superficial chest wounds, and a damaged larynx.

With his bandages and plaster casts, Bobby was no threat to the pretty, young Red Cross nurse. Nor could he say much—it was still too painful to talk and it hurt to swallow his food. So he teased her with his smile, and his eyes let her know things would be different once he got back into action. The doctors said his healing would be slow, but his hearing had returned, and his voice would, too. The lacerations were mending, but the broken bones would take much longer. So the Red Cross nurse wrote the letter for him.

Dear Mom and Pop; I'm just laying around and taking it easy for a while. I'm so lazy I'm letting this good-looking Red Cross gal do my writing for me. Took a header out of the truck and landed on my noggin, and you know what a hard head I have. They can't hurt me that way. Busted up my writing arm a bit, though. Looks like they had to send to Paris for an extra load of their plaster to fix it up, but I'll be on my way home soon good as new. Say hello to my sis and everybody at home. Love, Bobby.

He reached for the girl with his good hand, but she laughingly evaded him, so he whispered his thanks. She left smiling and promising to return with a bottle of cognac "one of these days." These boys, she thought, what spirit. Nothing gets them down for long.

Sarah and Fred Godfrey puzzled over their son's letter for several days. Was he wounded in action? Bobby made it sound as if he were fooling around and fell out of the truck. How bad was it? Sarah had started to cry when Fred took her in his arms and said, "If Bobby can joke about it, it must not be too bad." But then again, he thought to himself, with Bobby, who knew?

Finally the telegram arrived notifying them that their son, Robert Frederick Godfrey, Corporal, USAR, Serial Number 8870781, had been wounded in battle, but was recovering and would be returned to the United States for convalescent leave.

Millie arrived on the train the same day as the telegram. Her visit was completely unexpected and she explained to her parents, "We've closed the blind school because of a flu epidemic. None of the children have any symptoms, so this was just a preventative measure. They'll call me back when they re-open."

Fred showed her the item in that week's *Settler*. *Both King City schools are closed because Spanish influenza, or whatever sort of flu it is, seems to have gotten a foothold in this area. So far as we can tell, this is just the same old la grippe with which we are all familiar, but precautions and preventions make good sense considering the alarming reports from many other localities all about the country.*

But it wasn't the same old "la grippe" with which everyone was familiar. This was different. A stronger, more virulent and deadly influenza soon was sweeping the entire nation. The November 8 issue of *The Settler* reported that fifty-two cases had sprung up in the King City area alone. Dr. Brumwell was exhausted trying to keep up with the burgeoning outbreak. Some people were cared for at home and the twelve beds were filled in the little hospital established above *The Settler* offices when the high school had moved to its new building.

Each day new cases of influenza were reported. Sudden fever, headaches, and muscular pains invaded what were perfectly healthy bodies only hours before. Victims throats would become dry and inflamed, then turn raw, red and sore. A cough would appear on about the third day and then drenching sweats would follow. The weaker ones, the sick, the elderly, children, would catch pneumonia, and an appalling number died.

By the second week of the epidemic one hundred sixty cases were reported in King City and in the countryside nearby. The high school principal offered the school buildings as a hospital, and the Red Cross immediately accepted. The auditorium was set up as a ward for women and children, and the library became the wing for men. Care was free and generous donations made it possible. *The Settler* thanked Spreckels Sugar, Wideman's Store, El Camino Hotel, King City Mercantile Co., Supervisors Will Cleary and Paul Talbot, W.C. Eade, Will Copley and J.A. Trescony. With each edition of the paper the list of donors grew.

One of the town's most prominent citizens organized a nursing corps and many of the town's leaders became male nurses including Mayor Carlson, A.B. McReynolds and Les Hables, who had the bowling alley.

The women donned Red Cross uniforms, the long, white, cotton dresses with the red cross on the arm and the headbands emblazoned with the same emblem of mercy. They were under the direction of Mrs. Brunetti, a local resident who happened to be a registered nurse, and they took turns caring for the women and children. *The Settler's* report naming the nurses read like the guest list of an important King City social event. Sarah Godfrey worked in the kitchen and tirelessly helped prepare meals for the sick, and then assisted in feeding them.

The disease seemed to strike the younger women more quickly than the older ones, so in order to limit their exposure, the younger volunteers were assigned to make masks out of gauze, which were worn by the entire population.

"I'm going to volunteer as a nurse," Millie told her mother.

"Oh, Millie, you shouldn't." Sarah became distraught. "You mustn't expose yourself."

"Now, Mom, please don't worry. I'm strong," Millie said reassuringly. "If I haven't gotten it yet, I'm not going to catch it. Beside we all wear masks."

* * * * *

Tom Pettitt's hearse was pulling into the high school grounds when Millie appeared for her morning shift. She stopped out front on the sidewalk and watched, her hand to her throat. "Oh, dear, another death," she thought as she saw the hearse drive up to the back door of the auditorium. That meant another woman or a child had died. Millie's eyes teared up as she crossed herself and prayed, "Dear Lord, we commend this soul to Your mercy, whoever it is." She hurried on into the school.

There'd been too many deaths. This was the thirty-second day of operation for the high school hospital and there'd been thirty-five deaths, an average of more than one a day. Fear and a constant, desperate worry filled the community as parents watched their children closely, and kept them from contact with other youngsters. Stores were closed. Hables' bowling ally and the Novelty Theatre had been shut down since the schools had closed nearly a month before. But still the influenza epidemic raged.

Millie worked alongside her friend, Teddy Irwin, in the womens ward, bathing the fevered bodies, cleaning those who had fouled themselves, spooning broth to those able to swallow it, changing sheets and pillows. It was hard, back-breaking work, she wasn't getting much sleep and she was bone tired after only a week of it. But Millie was rewarded by the grateful smiles, especially from those who finally became well enough to get up from their cots and go home. She'd take heart, but just when she thought that perhaps the epidemic was on the wane, she'd see her father and Slim Smith or some other team of stretcher bearers carrying in another woman or child to take the bed just vacated. And then the whole business would start all over again.

Millie worked for several hours straight before she even stopped long enough to stretch and ease her back. It seemed as if her whole body ached this particular morning. She wiped the perspiration from her forehead. It was November, but still hot in here, she thought. Millie went to the kitchen for another bucket of cool water to bath poor Mrs. Chambers. Sarah looked up at her daughter from a sink full of dishes. Was Millie looking flushed? Still, she seemed all right. Sarah frowned but said nothing, then went back to her chores.

But Millie wasn't all right. And soon even she had to admit it. The headache struck as she reached Mrs. Chambers' cot. Was she really catching it? she wondered. She tried to swallow, but suddenly she couldn't. Her throat throbbed in pain. She put down the bucket and looked around the room. Dr. Brumwell was just coming in to start on his rounds. She stood by Mrs. Chamber's bed, waiting for him, but then the room started to spin, and as Millie clutched the edge of the cot her strength gave way and she sank to the floor.

Dr. Brumwell rushed to her side, at the same time calling to one of the volunteers, "Missus Ulrey. Over here, please, Missus Ulrey — We must get this young lady to bed."

Millie lay back on the cot, too sick to move. She felt terrible, awful. But it felt good to let somebody take care of her. She dropped off to sleep, thanks to something Doc had given her. When she awoke, a cool cloth was being placed on her forehead. "There, there, dear. You'll be fine. Just fine." It was her mother's voice. Sarah sat beside her daughter, sponging her off. She wanted to tell her mother not to worry. *I'll be fine, Mom. I'm just tired. I'll rest a bit and then I'll get back to work. Rest a minute.*

But Millie coughed, a racking, hurting cough. With her raw, aching throat making it nearly impossible to swallow, and her continual coughing spells, she hardly took any of the hot soup her mother tried to spoon into her mouth.

Millie's fever raged, making her weaker and weaker. Her father came to sit by her side and hold her hand. Sarah was exhausted as she tried to nurse her daughter and still keep up with her duties in the kitchen. She didn't leave the school hospital except to go home for a bath and change of clothing.

But despite his concern for Millie and his volunteer duties as a stretcher bearer, Fred had to get the paper out. Old Chester Simpson, the linotype operator, had been one of the first to die of the influenza, so *The Settler* had become a one-man operation. For several issues Fred struggled to print four pages, most of it boiler plate using the filler material he bought already in type from Western Newspaper Union. There were no ads as the town was practically shut down. Obituaries took up most of the front page and there was very little other local news that didn't have to do with the influenza.

Fred Godfrey ate very little and slept less, some days just catnapping in his office with his head on the rolltop desk. He was exhausted with worry over Millie and his schedule at the hospital, in addition to putting out a paper, such as it was. But the news he had to print for the issue of November 12, 1918 gave him a new burst of energy.

Fred pulled out the drawer of wood type with letters three inches high and happily set a headline to proclaim: *WAR ENDS*. Germany had been forced to surrender and an armistice had been signed at 5 a.m. the day before. Fred cranked enough copies of *The Settler* off the press to make the mails and a few street sales. He hurried to the schoolhouse hospital with copies for Sarah and the other volunteers.

They stood in small groups and smiled, wan, weary smiles, relieved that the war was over and that their sons and husbands, fathers and brothers would soon be coming home. But they still had their own war to fight.

215

That was the day that Millie was drenched in sweat as her fever broke, but her chest was tight and she could barely speak. Her cough had become hard and dry, and it hurt more than ever. She tried to describe it to her mother. But talking took too much effort and she fell back on the cot. Fred held a copy of *The Settler* and wanted to show her the good news, but Millie was in no condition to understand. He took Sarah's hand and the two of them stood looking down on their daughter, a prayer on their lips.

Through her daze, Millie knew that Dr. Brumwell had come to check on her. He took her pulse, thumped on her chest, and shook his head when he read the thermometer. "Bronchopneumonia," he said sadly to Sarah and Fred. "We'll do everything we can, but I must tell you, this looks bad."

The Godfreys prayed. They continued to help with the other patients—Fred in the men's ward, Sarah in the kitchen—but they returned at every opportunity to the auditorium to sit by Millie who sometimes was frighteningly still on the narrow cot and sometimes thrashed and moaned. And every time Tom Pettitt drove onto the school grounds they held their breath.

"I don't know why it hits the younger ones so hard," Doc Brumwell said. He stroked his beard, which itched under his mask, for even he had decided it would be best to wear one. He took Sarah and Fred aside. "Millie's nearing a crisis. We'll know tomorrow."

Sarah and Fred stayed awake all night, alternating praying, tending the sick and sitting beside their daughter's bed.

It was five in the morning—Sarah remembered hearing a distant clock chiming—when Millie opened her eyes and asked in a weak, but normal voice, without that terrible rasp, "Did we win the war?"

Sarah's eyes welled up as she stroked Millie's forehead and smiled down at her daughter.

"Yes, dear," she answered. "We won the war."

Three days later, when Millie was finally able to sit up and even walk around a bit, and she'd eaten a few meals, Sarah and Fred brought their daughter home. That same afternoon Fred came home from the office with the mail and Sarah took it in to Millie, whom she had insisted stay in bed for a few more days. "It's from Spud — !"

Millie grabbed it and eagerly ripped it open. She read aloud. *Dearest Millie, The war is over and as soon as I finish up a few things here, such as keeping Wilson and Pershing, and the rest of them on the right path, I'll be along home. We sent the Kaiser packing and I think he's hiding in Holland, or somewhere, but he'll trouble the world no longer. I seem to remember some unfinished business between you and me. Can we be getting back to that soon?*

Millie stopped reading long enough to hug her mother. Joy and relief had suddenly brought the color back to her cheeks and revived the strength that had been so drained out of her over the last two weeks. She went back to Spud's letter, reading the rest of it quickly to herself and then looked up at her parents and said, "This part is...." She didn't want to say the word "private" but they understood and nodded. Smiling at each other, Sarah and Fred left the bedroom as Millie snuggled down into her blankets and read the last two paragraphs over and over.

CHAPTER TWENTY-NINE

THE TWO FAMILIES WERE GATHERED in the big front room of the Cleary home on the Trescony lease where Honora and Will had arranged a gala homecoming for their soldiers. Their Chinese cook, Lin Toy, had outdone himself. The long table was laden with a huge turkey, stuffed with Honora's special recipe, which Spud loved and called "Ma's stuffin'," and there was an equally large honey-glazed ham, mashed potatoes with gravy, salads, dishes of vegetables and every delicacy imaginable. Although the Clearys outnumbered the Godfreys, they were all one big family. The guests of honor were the former corporal, Bobby Godfrey, his arm still in a sling, but otherwise as mischievous as ever, and ex-Sergeant Matthew "Spud" Cleary, fit and ready for civilian life.

Even Tim Cleary showed up to pay tribute to the returning soldiers, riding horseback out of Coyote Canyon and sober for one of his infrequent social appearances. Buck and Kitty O'Keefe were there, and Seamus, and Annie and Charlie Phillips from Bitterwater. Bucky and Lilly, pregnant again, were there with their two-year-old "enfant terrible" as Honora called her. Spud's Aunt Peggy and her husband, Joe Carrigan, who told Bobby to hurry and get well as he was needed at Carrigan's Ford garage, were also there. Pat Cleary, finally recovered from his terrible accident, but carrying the limp that would be with him for the rest of his life, helped his father pour the drinks. Father Dan Cleary said the grace and Will Cleary stood up and proposed the toast.

"This occasion marks, not only the homecoming of our favorite soldiers," he said proudly, gesturing with his glass toward Spud, then Bobby, "but the formal engagement of Millicent Virginia, the daughter of our good friends, the Godfreys," and here he bowed to Fred and Sarah, "and our son, Matthew Jeremiah Cleary. Honora joins me in declaring that nothing gives us more pleasure than this forthcoming union."

Spud, his arm around Millie, leaned over and kissed his bride-to-be. Millie's face flushed and everyone in the room cheered. Someone called for "war stories" from the soldier boys and, although everyone was stuffed from the scrumptious meal, they were all still eager to hear of the adventures in France.

Bobby just grinned sheepishly and told them how glad he was to be home. "I drove my truck into a pile of trouble," he said. "Got myself blown up, but I hit on my head so I was okay." Everyone laughed and Pat suggested Bobby give them more details of the action he'd seen, particularly of the day he was hit, but Bobby shook his head, not wanting to talk about it.

"Maybe he'll tell me sometime," Fred said, "and then you can read about it in *The Settler.*"

Everyone laughed again, but Bobby said, "Not for publication, Dad."

Spud insisted, that compared to Bobby's, his own adventure was "pretty darn boring." But he told them about the funny incidents of patrolling the streets of Paris, and about how proud he was to have been chosen to serve as a member of President Wilson's honor guard when he visited Versailles to meet with Lloyd George of England and Clemenceau of France. Their conferences on the peace treaty were held in the Hall of Mirrors at the Palace. Each morning, Spud recalled, the 280th Military Police Company lined up as an honor guard in front of Wilson's quarters. Rigidly at attention, they stood as the President and his entourage, sometimes including General George Pershing, passed between their ranks to settle into their cars.

"When the vehicles had departed," Spud said with a laugh, "we had to trail arms and run like hell along the back pathways, through the gardens, and line up at the Palace gates in two files. We'd get there out of breath and just in time to stand rigidly at attention as the President and his escorts stepped from the cars. They'd pass between our two lines to enter the Palace of Versailles. I often wondered if Wilson just thought all his soldiers looked alike, or if he even noticed us."

"Tell them the other story, Son," Will urged, "the one you told me about going to Ireland."

"Ireland?" Fred Godfrey wondered. "How did you ever get to Ireland?"

Spud smiled broadly. "Well, that's a strange one, all right. I haven't said much about it because it involves such a coincidence you'll find it hard to believe."

"I'll believe you, Spud," Millie injected. "You wouldn't lie in front of your future wife."

Spud threw up his hands and gave her such a protesting look of innocence that it made everyone laugh. When the room settled down, Spud cleared his throat and began. "After the war was over they pulled my old infantry outfit out of the lines and sent them to England. They were in barracks near Portsmouth and so our M.P. company was shipped across the channel to join them. We were supposed to catch a ship from there for New York. But then one day the captain calls me in—me and another fellow, an Irishman named Casey.

" 'They're holding a deserter from the one sixty-second in Ireland,' he says. 'You're to go get him.' " As Spud spoke the room had grown still, everyone listened attentively, even the children were quiet. "Fellow's name was Frankie Hanrahan and he was in the custody of the Royal Irish Constabulary in Cork. I guess the captain figured it was good politics to send a couple of guys with Irish names to go after an Irishman in Ireland. And let me tell you, we welcomed the assignment. It was getting pretty boring hanging around the barracks just waiting for a ship.

"So we took a ferry from Fishguard across to someplace near Wexford in Ireland and caught a bus to Cork. It was late when we found the R.I.C. headquarters and the deserter was delivered to us in leg chains and cuffs. We signed for him and then wondered, 'Now what the hell do we do with him?' It was too late to start back and we didn't have any place to stay.

"We were hungry and wanted to go into some eating house, but not with our side arms and not with a guy in leg chains and cuffs. 'You gonna run off,' I asked him? 'Hell no,' he promised. So I took out the key and let him loose. While we had a beer and ate a sandwich, he told us his story.

"Seems he was born in Boston, but his folks were from Ireland. They'd left an older brother with some uncles and aunts when they emigrated and he wanted to see them. 'I knew I'd never get any closer to Ireland than I was right then, so I took off. I was just going to pay a visit and then come back and be on the ship when it headed home. But they picked me up coming through Cork. Here I am. I almost made it.'

"'Where were you headed?' I asked. 'Skibbereen,' he says. Well, I'd sure heard of Skibbereen, but damned if I had any idea where it was. 'How far?' I asked. He said it was maybe fifty miles or so.

"Casey and I looked at each other and I guess the idea hit both of us at the same time. We had four days to get back and we'd only used up one. Why not? We'd never get back to Ireland again, so why not see the country?

"'Wait here,' I said. And I went back to the R.I.C. headquarters, hoping my sergeant stripes would carry some weight. Luckily I got a sympathetic mick on the desk and I explained Hanrahan's story, told him ours and how much time we had, and asked for a car. Damned if he didn't give me one, checked it out for two days. 'Our bit for international cooperation, Yank,' he says, 'hands across the sea and all that.'

"So we drove to Skibbereen. Must have found his relatives about ten o'clock at night. But you never saw such a welcome. They insisted on feeding us and kept our glasses full while they rounded up more relatives. Pretty soon the little house was packed with people all talking at once, and there was singing and dancing, and hugging and kissing going on all around. Casey and I couldn't take it any more. We told Hanrahan we'd see him the next day and we sneaked out to find a room somewhere.

"But first we stopped in a pub to get directions. I still remember the name of the place—Beehive, 'cause it sure was. Full of people. We were having one more shot of Jamison's that we didn't really need when I heard somebody shout, 'Hey, Cleary. Ha'r ya?'

"I spun around to see who was calling me. But nobody was looking at me. A tall, young fellow stood up from one of the tables in the back and was greeting the newcomer, a guy who was clapping him on the back and saying, 'Ah, Matt, Matt, my boy. It's just grand to be seeing you.'

"I watched them for a bit and my curiosity got the better of me. I wanted to meet this guy with the same name as mine. So I walked over to their table and when they noticed me, I asked, 'Your name Matthew Cleary?' "

At this point the Cleary parlor was so quiet and everyone's attention so rapt, you could hear a pin drop. Spud took a sip of his coffee and all eyes were on him as they waited for him to continue.

"When I asked 'Is your name Matthew Cleary?' he jumped up like he was ready to fight.

" 'And if it is, Yank, what of it?' he answered.

" 'Just that my name is Matthew Cleary, too,' I said. He looked me up and down and I could see the belligerency fade out of him. 'Sit yourself down, Yank, and call your partner over here.' He motioned to Casey standing by the bar. When we were seated my namesake called for another round and introduced me to his friend, a fellow who'd just been discharged from the Royal Munster Fusiliers of the British Army. That's where they'd last seen each other, both in the British Army although they lived right there in Skibbereen.

" 'But you now, Yank,' the other Matt Cleary says, 'you wouldn't be from California, now would you?'

"I said yes, and he asks me, 'Would you ever be hearing of a place called San Lucas?' You could have dropped me with your little finger when he asked that.

" 'My hometown,' I said and he grabbed me and gave me such a bear hug I thought he was going to kill me. 'Well now,' he whoops, 'and it's my very own cousin you are!'

"When I got my breath back, I asked him what the hell he was talking about. He said his father's name was Patrick and they lived on a little farm near Skibbereen. He said his grandfather's name was Liam, and that his grandfather had often told stories about a brother in California who had sent money back home to feed the family during the famine and to pay the rents."

" 'Yep,' I said. 'That must have been my grandfather, Jeremiah.' And then he talked about his father remembering a cousin from California named Jeremiah, Jr. who'd visited the farm at Skibbereen one time—he'd been in Ireland with Parnell— and then gone off and gotten himself killed in a Land League skirmish of some sort. Said it so terribly grieved a beautiful, young girl who'd only met him that one night, that somebody made up a song about it and they still talk of that young Jerry Cleary around there to this day, he said.

Spud looked over at his father and noticed Will's eyes had tears in them. "This Matt Cleary tells me he'd been named after another of his grandfather's brothers who had gone off to America to prospect for gold."

"What was this young fellow doing now that the war was over?" Tim Cleary asked his nephew.

Spud looked at his uncle whose curiosity had grown with the first mention of his father, Jeremiah. "I got the idea that he and his friends were in some kind of rebel army, drilling recruits, and planning to fight the British. 'Bloody Brits,' they called them. I asked if they hadn't just been in the British Army fighting Germans and they said they had. But they hated the Brits.

" 'Sure, and didn't they promise us that if we'd help them whip the Huns to free small nations, they'd give us Irish home rule when the war was over?' Matt explained, 'Wasn't it my own brother who gave his life for it? But when it ended the lying bastards didn't give us crap. Their dirty repression is worse than ever. It's off to gaol, or they're after executing anybody who speaks out.' He spoke softly, though, and looked

223

about, like he was making sure he was among friends, and then laughed and said, 'Stick around, cousin, and we'll be making a rebel out of you.'

"I wanted to go and meet his dad and grandfather," Spud continued, "but he told me they were long dead, and that his own brother, Tim, had been killed in the war. There was just him now and he didn't know if he'd go back to farming or not.

"He took Casey and me home with him. We drove in our car, and he laughed and laughed when we told him it was borrowed from the Royal Irish Constabulary. We went to some little cottage up the hill and we spent the night, or what was left of it. We talked all the next morning and I told him all about life in California, and our ranches, and he told me about Ireland, about his family, and the Hurleys, but he said there weren't any of them around anymore, either.

"We said we'd keep in touch and Matt promised to visit California someday. But then he said a strange thing. 'I'll be out there one day — that is — if I muddle through.' I got the idea he meant to put his life on the line. So we said goodbye.

"That afternoon we picked up Hanrahan and headed back. Just before we got off the ferry we shackled poor old Frankie, and cuffed him up, strapped on our side arms, and slipped on our military police armbands, and delivered him to the captain."

Spud's eyes turned to his father and he saw that Will had a thoughtful, far-off look. Memories of his long-dead brother Jerry, scenes of their youth together, he and Jerry and Tim, with their father, working cattle, riding in the wagon, farming, branding calves, playing games with their mother, Molly, her sudden, horrible death when she was gored by the great Hereford bull, the love of their Aunt Cauth, their mother's sister who came to care for them and married their father, Jerry's music, the terrible news that he'd been killed in Ireland—they all came floating back, tumbling and drifting, one memory triggering another.

Will glanced at his brother Tim, who had quietly listened to the whole story with an expression that was hard to read. Tim looked at Will and nodded. "Well, I'll be damned," was all he said.

Will and Tim were silent for a moment, absorbing Spud's story and the fact of a nephew in Ireland. The other family members began commenting to each other and asking Spud for more details. All were curious about this Irish relative. What was this Matthew Cleary like? Would they ever get to know him?

CHAPTER THIRTY

THE WEDDING NIGHT OF MR. AND MRS. Matthew "Spud" Cleary was a disaster. Spud was humiliated, but Millie wasn't disappointed. She loved her husband all the more because of it. They'd spent the night at El Camino Real Hotel, and now were aboard the morning train, headed north for a honeymoon week in San Francisco. Millie settled back against the plush, red upholstery of her window seat in the first class car and glanced at Spud. He looked so much like a shepherd pup expecting a spanking that Millie nearly laughed. But she swallowed her smile and took his hand in hers and squeezed, then turned to watch the Salinas Valley roll past.

They had been married by Spud's uncle, Father Dan Cleary, in an afternoon ceremony at St. John's Catholic Church. Sarah Godfrey and her daughter had wanted a nuptial Mass, but Father Dan had parish duties in San Mateo, which he couldn't disregard, so, because everyone wanted him to perform the ceremony, the wedding had to be held at four in the afternoon.

When Spud stood at the altar and watched Millie come down the aisle on the arm of her father, his heart quickened with joy and pride and the lump in his throat made it hard for him to breathe. She seemed to sparkle, although her gown was a simple one, satin with a lace overlay and a wide satin sash tied to emphasize her small waist. A delicate wreath of lily of the valley flowers sat atop her head and held her long lace veil in place. Around her neck was a gift from her mother, a lovely pearl choker that had once belonged to Sarah's mother.

Millie's graceful, gliding steps as she moved toward him presented a vision of vibrancy and beauty and to Spud she looked like a princess wearing a crown of flowers. When they drew close, Fred Godfrey took his daughter's hand and placed it in Spud's, who looked into his bride's shining eyes and saw her happy smile beneath her veil. He swallowed the lump in his throat and grinned down at her.

Spud tried to concentrate as Father Dan performed the ceremony, but his thoughts were focused on Millie, on the love he'd had for her for so long, how he cherished her and wanted to care for her, but also how fiercely much he wanted to possess her. And now, this very night, all his fantasies of the wedding night would come true. He struggled to clear his mind of the images and nearly missed his cue to say, "I do!"

Afterwards the family and guests gathered in the Spanish Room of the hotel, where Pat Cleary, Spud's best man, proposed a toast for the bride and groom. "Health and long life to you," he said to Millie and Spud as everyone raised their champagne glasses. Then Pat recited an old Irish toast that had been handed down in the family from Jeremiah's time. "May the hand of a friend always be near you — May God fill your hearts with gladness to cheer you — May there always be work for your hands to do — And may your purse always hold a coin or two."

All the Clearys were there, even Uncle Tim, and Millie, somehow, felt particularly honored by that. His loneliness and the story of his lost love had always touched her, so she had a special fondness for Spud's uncle. Several of Mama's brothers and sisters, and some of Millie's cousins, from San Leandro had come for the wedding. Also present was Spud's wealthy cousin, Connie, and her husband, Christopher Baxter, a state senator and head of San Francisco's leading law firm, who

invited the newlyweds to visit them while in San Francisco—
"If you're not going to be too busy honeymooning to put up with
relatives."

A wedding supper was served in the Spanish Room, which
had been beautifully decorated by friends of Millie's mother,
and then came a huge, double-tiered cake for the couple to cut.
Both bride and groom were too excited to eat much, going hand
in hand to visit at the different tables. After the supper clutter
was cleared away, the tables were pushed back to form a dance
floor, and A.B. McReynolds and two of his children, provided
an abbreviated version of the family orchestra, just right for
the occasion.

Millie and Spud had the first dance, their eyes locked on
each other as Spud whirled them around the room to the
strains of *Tales from the Vienna Woods*. Then Millie waltzed
with Will Cleary as Spud danced with Sarah. Then Spud
waltzed with his mother while Millie circled the floor with her
father. The wedding attendants danced together, Bucky and
Lilly and Teddy Irwin with Pat, who made a game effort to
move around on his bad leg. After that everybody danced and
Millie was soon being partnered with every man and boy in the
room. It was a giddy whirl and she hardly saw Spud, but she
laughed and made conversation, and felt her excitement growing deep inside.

About midnight Sarah gave Millie a hug, and she found herself and Spud being escorted up the stairs, with much laughter and a few bawdy remarks. They were stopped on the second floor landing when somebody called, "Millie, your bouquet
— Throw your bouquet!" There was a flurry to find it, and she
tossed it so Teddy Irwin would catch it, and then they clamored
for the garter. Spud got all red in the face, but finally fumbled
it off Millie's leg. Spud flung it, there was a mad scramble and
Bobby Godfrey retrieved it and held it high. "You're next,
Bobby," someone shouted. He just grinned.

The hotel owner had set them up in the best room in the
house, second floor, corner, overlooking Broadway and First

Street. They were finally alone. And there was the bed, a huge double bed, and atop it were Spud's pajamas and Millie's nightgown, carefully laid out by their friends. Spud looked at the garments, and the bed, and turned beet red. But he folded Millie in his arms and gave her a long, urgent kiss. She moved from his arms and picked up her nightgown. She said softly, "I'll only be a moment, dear," and went into the bathroom.

She wasn't long, only as long as it took to slip out of her wedding dress and into the rose-colored nightgown, but when she pulled the switch on the bathroom light and came back into the bedroom, it was dark. Black dark. Millie couldn't see a thing. She stumbled and fell against the bed.

"Where are you?" she asked. Spud mumbled something and Millie crawled into bed beside him. His hands found her and he kissed her. "Oh, Millie, I love you so and I've wanted you for so long." Spud's hands roamed her body.

There came a sudden pounding on the door and a series of loud voices calling: "Hey, Spud. How ya doing?" "Anything going on in there yet?" There were scuffling noises and loud giggling in the hall. They were singing and talking and calling advice, some of it slurred. "Need any help, Spud, old pal?" came the voice of Bucky O'Keefe.

"Be real quiet and they'll go away," Spud whispered to Millie.

No sooner had the hallway commotion quieted down than Millie felt Spud awkwardly fumbling with her nightgown. Just as quickly, he was pressing down on her, moving urgently against her. Spud shuddered and Millie felt a sudden, hot wetness. Spud slumped on top of her and she couldn't move. "Spud? Spud? What's wrong?"

He didn't answer. Then he got up and she heard him mutter, "Damn." He stood for a moment in the darkness. Millie rose and felt her way into the bathroom. She turned on the light and cleaned herself. She was puzzled, not sure what had happened. But it certainly hadn't been the rapture that Lilly O'Keefe had described. And Spud was upset. With her? No, she didn't think so. She hadn't done anything wrong. In fact, she'd hardly had time to do anything, or feel anything.

Millie returned to the bed and placed her head on Spud's shoulder. He lay on his back and, finally, his arm went around her. All he said was, "I'm sorry, Millie." She leaned over, softly kissed him, and said, "I love you."

"It'll be better next time, Millie," Spud said. "I promise you."

So, thought Millie, whatever the problem was, Spud felt it was his fault. He wasn't the experienced man-of-the-world that he'd seemed to be. This self-assured, mature, twenty-eight-year-old man she had loved and admired for so long, wasn't an experienced lover, after all. Millie had wondered about that. Spud, who always appeared as much at home in a drawing room as on a bucking horse, her confident Spud, who always knew what to say, or do, for every occasion, whom she once thought had his pick of girls, hadn't known how to act on his wedding night.

But at the same time Millie was thrilled. She needed no other proof that Spud was her man, and hers alone. She'd had no experience either, but her mother had prepared her, not as a Victorian, which would be expected of prim and proper Sarah, but as a loving wife who had learned what true marriage could be. And Lilly had confided more, perhaps, than she should have, about the secrets of love and marriage.

Sometime in the night Spud moved against her and she felt his hardness. "Tomorrow night," she said. "Tomorrow night, at The Palace."

They checked into the Palace Hotel and Spud was greeted personally by an assistant manager who bowed them to their suite. "It's so nice to have you back, Mister Cleary, and for such a happy reason. Our best wishes, Missus Cleary. Please accept the congratulations of The Palace Hotel." He pointed to the magnum of champagne cooling in an ice bucket and a bouquet of red roses on the round teakwood table.

"Spud," Millie said as she glanced about the room. "How extravagant! Can we afford all this?"

"Huh?" Spud asked, surprised at the question. "Oh, sure. Dad arranged it. Anything we want. Just charge it to Cleary Ranches."

Will had given them their choice, a cruise to Hawaii on one of the President Line ships, if they'd wait until after harvest, or this week in San Francisco. Millie had picked the week in San Francisco. "I don't want to wait. Let's go now, Spud. That will be wonderful."

Spud would be farming the Baxley place in Long Valley. Will had leased the twelve hundred acres so the young couple would have a ranch of their own, and the house was being fixed up and painted for them. "Don't you worry about a thing, Millie," Will had told her when he announced the arrangement. "When you two get back from San Francisco, you'll find all your things moved in, all ready for you."

Millie asked Spud about furniture, and linens and dishes. "We'll get some of that kind of stuff for wedding gifts and I guess Ma will pick out whatever else we need, and Dad will have somebody get it all set up."

"Oh," Millie said, quickly suppressing the disappointment that she wouldn't be the one to make these decisions. There'll be a time for that she told herself. Spud's family only wants to make things easy for us. They're just generous, not trying to run our lives.

Their first night in San Francisco, the honeymooners had a romantic dinner by candlelight in the Garden Court. After they'd danced twice Millie whispered, "I'm going up to the room, Spud. You wait down here a while. Give me about fifteen minutes, and then come on up."

Millie quickly changed into her nightgown, took down her long, wavy hair, and left on the bathroom light. It cast a golden glow into the room when Spud entered. Millie lay on the bed, propped up by some pillows, her hair falling loosely over one shoulder. Spud stopped short and stared. He shut the door behind him without taking his eyes from Millie's. "You're so beautiful," he said, catching his breath. Spud stood there, loving her with his eyes.

Then he entered the bathroom and emerged just a few moments later, clad only in his boxer shorts. "Leave the light on," Millie said. Spud slid under the sheets beside Millie and reached for her with a groan of pleasure. He kissed her, gently at first and then fiercely. He began to caress her, urgently, harshly. But then he stopped himself and looked at Millie, her eyes wide as she waited and wondered. Spud took a deep breath and slowly, gently kissed her lips, her eyes, her neck and then his mouth found her breasts. Millie threw her arms around him, pulled him to her and this time, as he'd promised, it was better. Much, much better.

The week in San Francisco went quickly. There were cable car rides, lunches at Fisherman's Wharf, where they ate clams and oysters and sourdough bread, walks through Chinatown, dinners at the Cliff House, dancing at the Palace and the St. Francis Hotel. There were ferry boat trips across the bay, a theatrical play at the Orpheum, and Spud bought Millie a spray of rosebuds to pin on her suit from a Podesta Baldocchi streetside flower cart.

One evening they accepted the invitation to dine with the Baxters and took a cab ride up Nob Hill. Neither Spud nor Millie had ever seen the mansion where Spud's Aunt Connie lived and they were overwhelmed by the opulence. But both Connie and Senator Baxter were warm and cordial and soon set their guests at ease. Afterwards, as a cab returned them to The Palace Hotel, Spud remarked, "Quite a layout, huh?"

"Hard to imagine such luxury," Millie agreed. "But it's more than I could take."

"Good thing, Millie. Great place to visit. Connie and Chris sure were nice. But that lifestyle's not for me. Not this clod-hopping cowpoke."

The final two days of their honeymoon, Millie went shopping. She found she had charge accounts at the White House, City of Paris, Gumps and anywhere else she wanted to shop. But mostly she looked, and bought very little. Millie didn't think she needed much. She had everything.

CHAPTER THIRTY-ONE

MILLIE STOOD BY THE CORRAL FENCE, flung her arms wide and took a breath so deep it raised her onto her tiptoes. She loved their ranch, especially at the beginning of an April day such as this one in 1921. She inhaled the morning, filled herself with the sweet blossom-scented air, accented by the fragrant blue lupines beginning to poke up among the clover, the wild oats, and filaree on the hillside. On her cheek she felt the slight breeze, which was gently waving the barley, just heading out. Her eyes drank in the beauty of the green hills, dotted here and there by splashes of color—the red Indian paint brushes, white daisies, golden poppies, and yellow buttercups raised their heads to the morning sun. And in her ears was the morning music, a symphony of the sad, plaintive sounds of the mourning dove, the meadowlarks' sweet, melodious warbling, the quail calling their warning from the chemise brush, and the discordant shrieks of the crows arguing overhead.

"Come, pig, sooo-ee, sooo-ee, come pig, pig, pig!" That sound echoing out across the yard shattered Millie's mood. It was Fortunado Arbelloa, the hired man, calling the sows in for their morning slops. Millie had named them all. There was Minnie, Maggie, Myrtle, Mamie and Mabel and each had her own little herd of piglets trotting behind her.

Only it wasn't a herd of piglets, Millie reminded herself. It was a litter of shoats. Millie still couldn't get used to the ranch terminology, despite two years of instruction from Spud. One time when her father-in-law, Will Cleary, had stopped by, she excitedly told him the good news. "Spud's heifer just had a girl colt, the cutest little thing, all legs." Her husband and his father roared with laughter. Millie looked indignantly from one to the other while they tried to control themselves. Will took out his bandanna and wiped the tears from his eyes. Finally, Spud explained that she should have said, "The mare had a filly. Heifers are young cows, honey."

Millie had always thought cows were cows, just as she'd accepted that pigs were pigs. But she listened and learned that there were all sorts of pigs. There were the mammas, or sows, and the daddies, the boars, and there were babies called shoats, and the gilts were young females, and the barrows were castrated males, and that sows and gilts had litters.

Millie stopped to look in the pig pen where the sows were rooting and grunting and sloshing in the slops, obviously enjoying their breakfast and oblivious to their offspring. One slipped into the trough, squealing, slipping and slithering as it frantically tried to get out. No wonder they're called pigs, she thought, wrinkling her nose in distaste, but grinning in spite of herself. They don't place much emphasis on etiquette.

Millie opened the door to the granary and filled a small pail with grain. The chickens came clucking and pecking and followed her as she scattered handfulls around the yard. Millie looked about her domain—at the cattle grazing in the tall grass, the work horses and two saddle horses in the corral munching their morning hay from the rack, her shepherd pup, Stuffy, sniffing around the saddle room looking for the cat to devil.

The sheep were following the bell wether, the soft clang of the clapper another ranch sound Millie had come to love. They were trailing out to pasture from their pen by the barn, their overnight protection from the coyotes that roamed the hills. That was another whole litany, Millie thought as she watched them file past—ewes and bucks, or rams, and wethers and lambs. Fortunado stood by the gate, checking them through.

He smiled at her when he saw Millie watching, a shy, sweet smile that crinkled the parchment skin of his weathered face. He was a gentlemanly old bachelor, with a thousand tiny wrinkles at the corners of his kindly, brown eyes. Fortunado Arbelloa had been one of the Basque sheepherders on the Trescony ranch, long before Will Cleary had leased a part of it. He'd stayed on to work for Will. Now he lived in the old adobe bunkhouse on the home place up Long Valley, working for Buck and Kitty, and helping out part time for Spud, who always arranged for Fortunado to stay over when he was gone overnight.

Millie regretfully left the yard and returned to her duties in the kitchen. Fortunado had nearly finished with his morning chores and he'd be coming in for breakfast soon. It was just the two of them that day as Spud was off driving cattle from the Laguna Ranch with the Eade boys. Millie had mixed the hotcake batter before going out to enjoy her morning commune with her world. Now she tested the griddle with a drop of water. She couldn't bring herself to spit on as she'd seen some camp cooks do.

While she worked, her mind was practicing her litany of ranch jargon. Let's see now, Millie recited to herself, cattle come in herds, or bunches, and there are cows and bulls, and young cows are heifers until they have calves and then they become cows, unless they are called first calf heifers. Castrated calves are steers.

She deftly ladled the batter into the pan, and as she watched it mold itself into perfectly round cakes and start to bubble, she turned to the terminology regarding horses. Mares have colts, and the castrated males are called geldings—no wonder Spud and his father had laughed so hard that day—and females are fillies until they've had a colt, then they are called mares. Horses run in herds, unless a particular cowboy has his own string. What else? Millie wondered. Oh, yes, there are cow horses and work horses, and the big horses work in teams.

234

She flipped the hot cakes and was satisfied by their golden brown color and pleased with her growing accomplishments in the kitchen. It always amazed Millie how this old wood stove could produce just the right amount of heat.

Now, what is it about mules? They are something else again. Let's see, they're part horse and part donkey, unless they're jennets, which are part donkey and part horse, and a female mule is a jenny, and they work in spans —

"Missus Cleary — oh, Missus Cleary —."

Millie's reverie was interrupted by Fortunado's calling. She went to the kitchen door and looked out. He was at the sheep pen, beckoning her. "Missus Cleary, I need help here. Could you please come?"

She pulled the griddle off the stove and hurried outside, running across the yard to the corrals. "What's the matter, Fortunado?"

The old man was straddling a sheep, which was struggling against his hold. "This young ewe," he said. "She's having a late lamb and it's a big one. She needs help. But I can't hold her and help her at the same time. Perhaps you could hold her for me?"

"What do I do?" Millie asked, entering the pen.

"Kneel over here by her neck and hold her down," Fortunado instructed as the ewe tried to get up. "See, come around here, get a grip like this." The old sheepherder demonstrated and then moved away, leaving the apprehensive Millie atop the straining animal.

Fortunado lifted a hind leg and Millie could see a tiny foot protruding from the ewe's opening. "One foot is coming out, but the other must be doubled back inside." Fortunado tried to work his hand inside the ewe. Millie could hear him muttering, "Too tight, too tight." He looked up at her in frustration just as the ewe broke loose from her hold and squirmed away.

"I can't hold her, Fortunado. She's too strong."

"And my hands are too big."

"What will we do?" Millie was anxious for the ewe, which now stood against the side of the pen, panting, in obvious distress.

"I will hold her and you must reach inside and turn the leg," Fortunado said.

"Me?" Millie was appalled. "I've never done anything like that. I don't know how."

"There is no one else."

Millie was reluctant, afraid to attempt the unknown. She studied the ewe with apprehension, her brow wrinkled with indecision as Fortunado watched her. The poor animal. Somebody had to help her. At least she could make an attempt. Millie took a deep breath and nodded. "I'll try."

"First," Fortunado instructed her, "we'll need some soapy water and a rag." Millie rushed back to the house and returned with a bucket, dropping a bar of Ivory soap into the water while Fortunado captured the ewe in his strong hands and laid it on its side. "Now lather your hands good so they will slip," he said.

Millie knelt behind the ewe, which was laying quietly, exhausted, breathing in short gasps. She looked at Fortunado, waiting instructions. "Work your hand in alongside that leg sticking out. Feel for the other leg."

Millie forced herself to place her soapy fingers in the opening, but she was stopped by Fortunado. "Your ring, Missus Cleary."

Millie retrieved her hand and looked at her ring finger. Her engagement and wedding rings, would they hurt the ewe? "You might lose them," Fortunado explained. Millie easily slipped the rings from her finger, placed them carefully in her pocket and again approached the opening. She worked her hand in alongside the little foot and followed the leg. It was tight inside and hard work, the ewe was pushing against her hand.

"Easy, *muchacha*, easy, little girl." The old Basque was making soothing sounds to the ewe. Millie caught Fortunado's eye with a question in hers. "Wait until she stops pushing and don't be afraid," he reassured her. She found the other leg and traced it with her fingers. "It's doubled up."

"Straighten it out and pull it alongside the first."

Millie waited out another contraction and slowly pulled the tiny leg into the opening. Again she looked at Fortunado. He smiled at her success and nodded encouragement. "Now reach in again and find the lamb's head. See if it is doubled back."

Millie's exploring fingers searched and located the little neck and felt around the head. "Yes," she said. "I think it is bent backward."

"Try to straighten it, move it down toward the feet." Millie manipulated the head into position and removed her hand. It was nearly numb from being clamped by the ewe's contractions.

"Now hold the feet and when she pushes, you pull."

At the next contraction a great rush of blood and water splashed out from the ewe, practically in Millie's lap, and a tiny bloody, wet bundle fell to the ground. Millie's dress was drenched, but she hardly noticed as she felt a great surge of relief. She stood up as Fortunado released the ewe and rose also, arching his back and stretching himself. Millie looked at the lamb by her feet. It didn't move.

"Oh, Fortunado. It's dead. After all that, the poor thing is dead." Millie felt terrible. She was about to cry.

But Fortunado just smiled at her and said, "Watch."

The ewe had struggled to her feet and was making soft mothering noises. She nosed the lamb and began to lick it. The little thing twitched, a leg moved, its skin quivered and, while Millie watched in amazement, it came to life under its mother's ministering tongue.

Fortunado washed up in the bucket and wiped his hands on the rag. "I must now finish the milking," he said.

"And I'd better see what happened to your hot cakes." But Millie couldn't pull herself away from the sheep pen where the ewe was cleaning her baby and soon had it spic and span and bleating as it moved on wobbly legs to search out an udder.

Millie watched with a wonderful glow of satisfaction. She'd done it, she'd saved that baby's life, and probably the ewe's, too. When she left it was greedily sucking. It was exciting to be part of the miracle of life.

She was singing as she built up the fire, washed herself again, replaced her rings and put on a fresh house dress. Stuffy got the burned pancakes and Millie had a new stack ready for Fortunado when he came in, stamping his feet on the steps. He set the pail of milk on the shelf, where Millie would later run it through the separator to take off the cream. She could hear him washing up in the basin on the porch and when he stepped into the kitchen he wore a wide grin. Millie returned it with one of her own.

Fortunado thanked her for breakfast and hurried off to catch up his horse for the ride back to the Cleary place up the valley. He had chores to do there, too. So Millie was alone as she did the dishes. Then she went back outside to gather the eggs. It was like an Easter egg hunt every day to find where the nesting hens hid them and she had time to let her thoughts run. Spud had only been gone one night, but she missed him. The bed was cold without his warmth, and she let ideas come into her mind that she'd never have dreamed before she was married. Millie smiled to herself. Lilly needn't be so superior with her about married life anymore. She and Spud could show them a thing or two. Then she scolded herself at the idea of ever sharing such a private, wonderful thing.

She returned to the kitchen, poured herself another cup of coffee and sat at the table with her warm thoughts of Spud. *But where's my baby? I'm twenty-seven and still no baby.* Millie fretted when she thought about her married friends, some with several children, and they looked at her as though she were some kind of a freak. Mother Cleary never said a word, but Millie knew her mother-in-law wondered if she and Spud were having trouble. Dad Cleary just smiled and patted her on the back, but she was sure he craved a grandson. Especially since it didn't seem likely that Pat would ever get married.

Spud said his brother hadn't even gone out with a girl since the accident. And Will's two daughters had moved away, Mary to teach school in San Francisco and Norah to marry a railroad man in the other valley. *So it's up to me.*

Spud just kidded her about it. "Let's just keep trying," he would joke. "How about right now?" And he'd pick up Millie, all hot and sweaty from cooking over that wood stove, and carry her into the bedroom where they'd make love in the middle of the afternoon.

Damn those busybodies, Millie thought, biting her lip. She recalled the woman who'd looked her up and down, and wondered aloud, "No baby yet, Millie?" Or those who asked, "And when are you going to start your family?"

Other than her nagging concern about getting pregnant, Millie did enjoy her married life even though living on the ranch still had its primitive side. There was no electricity in the valley, so they still used kerosene lamps, and Millie had to heat water in the pipes that ran through the big, iron, wood-burning stove, or in buckets on the stove top if she had a big washing to do. At least the house had plumbing and Dad Cleary had put in a real bathroom for them. Millie tended her vegetable garden and just keeping the rabbits and squirrels, and all the birds, away from her plants was a never-ending job. Millie had tried milking with Spud showing her how to squirt milk across the corral to the waiting cat, which just opened its mouth as a target, and then mewed until Spud did it again. But Millie could hardly get any in the bucket, let alone hit the cat in the mouth, so she gave up milking.

Millie decided to have a third cup of coffee. There wasn't much left in the big, black pot, but she drained it. She deserved it, she told herself. After all, she'd already saved a life today. She couldn't wait to tell Spud about it.

Spud was great fun, often taking her with him horseback when he could, sometimes to gather cattle with Buck and Kitty, who still rode beautifully. Sometimes they'd jump into Lizzie, the Model T Ford coupe Dad Cleary had given them,

and motor in to King City for the picture show, to buy groceries, or visit Sarah and Fred. Once in a while they'd go all
the way to Salinas on business for a stay at the Jeffery Hotel.
And on special occasions, such as after harvest season, they'd
travel to San Francisco for another fling in the city.
Everywhere they went, it seemed, they had a charge account.
Most of the time the clerks didn't even ask, they just took it for
granted that the bill would go on the Cleary Ranch account.

Millie wondered about that. Spud didn't seem to have any
salary, no money of his own, just a few dollars in his pocket
now and then. But they could buy anything they wanted just
about anywhere. "Everything goes into the ranch account,"
Spud explained, "and we all just take out what we need. It's
always been that way, Millie."

"But, Spud, how are we to get ahead?" Millie protested. "How
can I budget or manage the house without knowing how much
you make? How will we ever save or have anything of our
own?"

"Honey, you can have anything you want. Just name it."
Spud didn't seem to understand. But he was wonderful in
every other way.

Spud sometimes tried to sing along with her when she
plucked her banjo in the evening, or sometimes they played
cards, and she'd learned cut-throat pedro and gin rummy well
enough to sometimes beat him. They went to brandings and
barbecues, dances in King City, or at Tully hall, and, of course,
to Cleary's annual Harvest Ball in San Lucas. Once they'd
picked up Spud's brother Pat, and driven Lizzie to the banks of
the San Antonio River to visit Bucky and Lilly, and all laughed
over the wild pranks and scrapes the terrible trio had gotten
themselves into "back in the old days."

Millie loved the Sunday dinners with all the Clearys on the
Trescony, or up in Long Valley at the home place. Once Millie
and Spud had thrown a barbecue for all of them at their own
ranch. The Godfreys had come out from King City and Millie's
brother Bobby had brought a girl named Barbara Putnam,

whose father managed the King City Mercantile Company. When Bobby introduced her to the family everyone wondered if this meant he was finally serious about a girl. But Millie knew that no one, not even she, could tell when Bobby was serious. If he could joke about nearly getting killed in France he could joke about anything, Millie thought.

When Uncle Tim didn't show up at any of the Sunday gatherings, Millie filled up a picnic basket, baked an apple pie because she knew it was his favorite, and Spud maneuvered Lizzie up Long Valley, past where Buck and Kitty lived on the home place, and wound up the grade into the head of Pine Valley, and then down to the Coyote Canyon road, still no more than wheel tracks across the rolling hills leading to Tim's homestead. Tim Cleary seemed fine and Millie was pleased to note he was nearly sober and glad to see them. He showed them the colt he was breaking and then all three picnicked right alongside the Coyote spring. When it was time to leave he held Millie's hand and invited her to "be sure to come back again sometime."

She often thought about Timothy Cleary over there all by himself. Millie took a last sip of coffee, rose from the kitchen table and started her housework. As she swept, she was thinking, damn that long-ago girl who broke his heart, whoever she was.

CHAPTER THIRTY-TWO

"TIM, YOUR GIRLFRIEND IS BACK IN PINE VALLEY." Tim Cleary raised a quizzical eyebrow at his younger brother and wondered what nonsense Seamus was talking about now. Sometimes it was hard to follow the thought process of this fifty-year-old man with the ten-year-old mind. Some sort of fantasy, Tim decided. The entire family was gathered for Easter at the home ranch in Long Valley after Mass in San Lucas and had just sat down to dinner when Seamus suddenly blurted out this bit of information.

Tim looked over at Buck, sitting across the table from him. Buck shook his head. "I think Seamus means he saw a girl there at the old Barnes place who looks a lot like Amy Barnes did. That's all."

"No, siree, Buck. I remember that girl." Seamus insisted. "She sure was pretty. It was the same girl."

It was suddenly quiet around the table. Everyone stopped eating and heads turned toward Tim, who was studying the slice of ham he'd just placed on his plate. No one could think of anything to say. Finally, Will Cleary remarked, "Don't see many squirrels around the place, Buck. That new poison must be working, huh?"

"Well, yeah, but it's so expensive," Buck replied. "Can't afford to use enough of it. Millie, could you please pass the ham?"

Buck helped himself to a slice, handed the platter to Spud, and took the potato bowl in exchange. Conversation again was flowing and plates were being filled. Pat was telling Dan Carrigan that there were still quite a few coyotes coming out of the river bottom and Annie was explaining to Peggy that a little bit of green pepper was the ingredient that made her scalloped potatoes so different when Seamus again interrupted in a loud voice, "I sure do like yellow hair!"

Silence settled on the room again. Forks stopped halfway to mouths and eyes dropped down to the plates in front of them, all avoiding a look in Tim's direction. Buck tried to pass it off. "Yeah, you're right, Seamus. I sure do like yellow hair, too."

Kitty gave a nervous laugh and touched her graying red-gold locks. "You'd better," she teased her husband.

"Naw," Seamus blithely said. "Your hair's nice, Kitty. But I mean real yellow like that Amy."

Tim pushed back his chair, got up and walked out onto the porch. Buck shrugged and sighed. He left the table and went out to where Tim was staring off at the mountain. Buck could see how upset he was. "Seamus was helping Wexler's cowboys gather cattle on the old Barnes place and he stopped in the yard to water his horse," Buck explained. "He told me there was a woman there sitting in a big car giving orders to some men. She waved to Seamus and he's convinced it was Amy Barnes. Obviously, that's impossible. But you know Seamus. He doesn't mean any harm, Tim."

Tim nodded. But he didn't reply. He stood there a few moments and Buck, not knowing what else to say, went back into the house and sat down at the table. When Tim didn't return to the Easter dinner, Buck asked his son to go look for him.

Bucky hurried out just in time to see Tim riding off horseback. "He's gone. Headed back up the Coyote Canyon trail," Bucky reported to the family seated around the dinner table. They ate the rest of the meal in saddened silence, trying to make small talk now and again, but lapsing back into their own private thoughts of Tim.

* * * * *

Tim Cleary tried not to think about it. He knew it couldn't be Amy. For godsakes he hadn't seen her in thirty years, hadn't heard anything about her, except for that story in *The Settler* and that was at least nine years ago. But the night of the

243

earthquake in San Francisco, when her aunt had told him that Amy had run off with another man, leaving her husband and baby daughter behind, still throbbed in his mind.

Wherever she was, she'd be almost as old as he was, nearly sixty, he figured, an old lady. Not even Seamus would be confused enough to think he'd seen a young girl if it were Amy. But who was it?

He pondered over it for several days, but couldn't shake it. Finally he decided it was time he rode into San Lucas to check his mail and pick up a few groceries. He saddled up and headed for town, but this trip he took the Pine Valley road instead of his usual route.

When he reached the old Barnes place, Tim pulled up his horse and watched the activity. The old two-story house was being completely redone. Three carpenters were framing in a new wing and a wide porch had been added with a sloped roof held up by carved columns. Tim recognized Mike Hoalton unrolling a sheaf of blueprints and rode over to him. "Hello, Mike. Looks like quite a project you got going here," Tim said.

"Yep," Hoalton said. "Fanciest building I've done since way back when I built your home place for Jeremiah. Won't know the old Barnes place when we finish. Lady wants a regular Victorian mansion right here."

"Lady?" Tim was almost afraid to ask. "What lady?"

"Name's Missus Joshua Mertens. Widow lady," Hoalton said. "Owns this place now. Says Mort and Ida Barnes were her grandparents. They died and left it to her a long time ago."

Tim thought that must be Clara, the young girl he'd seen with Amy's aunt, the one he'd read about. Amy's daughter back in Pine Valley? And she looked enough like Amy to confuse Seamus? Why was she going to live here?

Hoalton continued to talk about the young woman, but his words didn't seem to register with Tim, who nodded to the builder, mumbled, "See you later," and quickly rode out of the yard.

It wasn't until he had hit the main road and turned his horse north toward San Lucas, that Tim actually grasped what Hoalton had said. That Clara Mertens was a wealthy young widow from San Francisco, that her husband had been killed over in France during the war. Hoalton had said he was sending all his bills to some iron works up in San Francisco, but that the lady didn't want to live in the city any more, that she planned to move to Pine Valley as soon as the house was finished. "Real nice young woman," Hoalton said, "very pretty, even wearing all that black."

Clara, Tim thought. *Clara Fabray. Fabray Iron Works. Must have inherited it all and then won that lawsuit brought by her mother, Amy. And looks just like her. What's she like? She couldn't be anything like Amy if she wants to live down here, in Pine Valley, for godsakes. I don't ever want to see her.*

Tim rode home the other way, up the Long Valley road and over the hill. He didn't want to go past the old Barnes place. Not ever again.

CHAPTER THIRTY-THREE

THE FREIGHT TRAIN SLOWED as it came into San Lucas and the door to a boxcar slid open. Matthew Cleary of Skibbereen, Ireland, sat on the floor of the car in the open doorway and jumped off as the train ground to a halt. He walked across the tracks and stopped in the middle of San Lucas' hot, dusty main street, and looked up and down.

Not much of a village was his verdict. He was disappointed. He'd heard about this place all his life and expected more of his cousins' hometown. There were a few buildings across from the railroad tracks, but they looked empty or burned out. To his right were the cattle corrals, a huge granary and a church with a cross on the steeple, probably Catholic, Matthew judged. On the slope of the hill behind the single street he could see a few dwellings, but immediately in front of him was a store, Bunte Brothers, General Merchandise, read the sign, and there was a small American flag flying in front of a tiny post office building. So this is San Lucas, the place the American branch of the Cleary family called home. Well it would have to be his home for a while, too, now that he was on the run. It had happened just a few short weeks ago and the memory was fresh in his mind.

* * * * *

It had been a mild afternoon, the street still slick from the morning rain, as Matthew Cleary peddled his bicycle down the narrow, crooked lane between the tiny houses. He saw the small sign, "Duggan's," hanging over the door of the two-story building at the end of the lane. It didn't need a big sign. Everyone knew Duggan's as the most popular pub in that part of Ireland. Everyone except Matthew Cleary. He'd never been there before. But it had been described to him. Carefully!

He leaned his cycle against the wall of the building, took the clips from his trousers and placed them in his pocket and then unstrapped the bundle from behind the seat of the bike. Matthew stretched. It had been a long ride. He looked intently up and down the empty street.

He tucked the bundle under his arm and stepped into the pub. Matthew stood by the door, letting his eyes become accustomed to the dim interior, and then surveyed the room. There was certainly nothing elegant about it to account for its popularity. It was a dark room, a well-used room, permeated by a century of tobacco smoke and stale beer. But it was cozy, friendly and Matthew saw that the handful of customers there that warm afternoon were settled in. Three men were in a quiet conversation at a corner table. Several others were gathered at the end of the bar where a woman worked the ornate brass beer pull to top off the heads on their tankards of Guinness. They glanced up, but not recognizing him, turned back to their conversations. No one seemed interested in him except an ancient sitting by himself against the far wall.

The old man nodded to Matthew Cleary and rolled his eyes in the direction of the stairway to the right of the bar. Matthew settled his wool cap firmly on his head and quietly moved to the stairs. After a quick glance over his shoulder assured him that no one was paying any attention to him he quickly ran up the stairs and into the corridor that extended the length of the building. Matthew counted two doors and stopped before the third one on the right.

He took a deep breath and pushed the door open. He saw a heavy-set man, whom Matthew judged to be middle aged, sound asleep on the bed. Matthew stood above him for a moment, watching his jowls expand and contract as air softly whistled in and out of his widely gaping mouth. Matthew nudged him.

"What — ? Huh — Who — ?" The big man came slowly awake, blinking his eyes, looking puzzled at the intruder in his bedroom.

"Are you Michael Duggan?" Matthew asked.

"I am," he answered, sitting up, yawning, stretching, trying to focus on his visitor. "Who the hell are you?"

Matthew ignored the question, but asked another of his own. "Are you the Michael Duggan who is proprietor of this pub?"

"I am," Duggan replied. "What the hell's it to you?" He started to stand, but Matthew Cleary placed a firm hand on his chest and pushed him back onto the bed.

"Michael Duggan, you've been tried and judged guilty by the provisional court of Ireland." Matthew reached his free hand into the bundle he carried and pushed the wadded cloth against Duggan's forehead as he said, "You've been sentenced to die as an informer — " He pulled the trigger and the big revolver bucked inside the muffling bundle— "under the authority of the Irish Republican Army."

Duggan flopped back against the bed, a neat hole in his forehead midway between his wide open eyes, the surprise in them fading as they glazed over. Matthew stood for a second, looking at the blood and gore spreading from the back of Duggan's head to the mattress beneath it. He swallowed hard and looked away. He re-wrapped the bundle with the gun inside, tucked it under his arm and left the room.

Downstairs in the pub all was as he'd left it. The woman was talking with the customers at the end of the bar. The group around the table were quietly conversing and the old man still sat with his chair against the wall. Matthew caught his eye and nodded.

Outside, he tied his bundle behind the cycle seat and fastened his clips to protect his trousers from the bike chains. He gave his cap a tug, righted the bicycle, stepped on it and slowly pedaled away.

Much later that night Matthew Cleary sat across the table from Daniel Boyle in a back room of the Beehive, a public house in Skibbereen. Each held a hot cup of tea against the damp chill.

"You're sure now, are you, that you were clean away?"

Daniel Boyle's eyes behind the thick glasses bored into Matthew Cleary's. He took them off and polished them, blinking blindly in the harsh light of the lamp, looking more like an owl than the rebel leader Matthew knew him to be. And he was to be called Daniel, never Dan or Danny, always Daniel.

"Aye, no one noticed me except the old man," he answered, returning Boyle's cold stare. Then Cleary's eyes dropped. He sipped his tea, then looked around the room. Most of it was in shadow, the light flickering over kegs of beer, gleaming off the bottles of porter and Jameson's lining the shelves. It was late at night and the barroom had been closed for hours.

"What's bothering you, Matt?"

The direct question startled him. He'd been thinking about the woman. He began to explain to Boyle. "His missus — "

"She's better off," Boyle said, his deep, harsh voice at odds with his professorial appearance. "She can have the custom of that pub and support herself without caring for his lazy arse."

"Sure now, I suppose so, but — " Matthew let his voice trail off and returned his attention to his mug of tea.

Boyle studied him. He liked this young man, had recruited him from the ranks of Tom Barry's brigade and kept him by his side for several operations. Boyle had checked him out thoroughly. A Skibbereen farmer, who'd served in the British Army in France and lost a brother in the war, Cleary's fervor for the republican cause and the audacious way he carried out his assignments had impressed Boyle. Word of Matthew Cleary had gone all the way up to Mick Collins himself.

Both men sat quietly, silently as Boyle thought, watching Cleary over the brim of his mug. He was remembering that first time, in Cork, with the Royal Irish Constabulary sergeant who had gained a reputation for his skill with pinchers and the electric wires, trying to turn the farm boys and the storekeepers' sons into informers. They'd caught up to the sergeant on the street as he left the constables' barracks and Cleary had tapped him on the shoulder. Surprised, the sergeant had turned around and Cleary had shot him full in the face. Then he fired a second shot into the man's skull before running back to join Boyle.

It was Cleary who'd boarded the train at Athenry, located the British colonel in civilian clothing and followed him to the restroom, leaving him dead, seated there on the toilet, and jumped from the train before it reached Galway. Boyle had a number of other young men to carry out assignments handed down from Dublin, but none with the cold nerve of Matt Cleary.

But now, what was it? Was Cleary losing that nerve?

"That had to be, Matt. Duggan named every one of those men who'd met in his pub," Boyle said in measured tones, describing it again as if he were giving a lecture in his history class. "Their homes were visited by the Black and Tans. Burned out, they were, and some shot. Some are in British jails, their women brutalized. The whole village was terrorized."

"I know, I know," Matthew muttered. "But it's a helluva way to fight a war."

"It's the only way we have," Boyle insisted. "We can't go charging off against the British Army like they did in France, like you did against the Germans, Matt. We don't have the weapons. But for ambushes, for hit and run operations, we have the men — " Boyle's voice, although he spoke quietly, started to resonate with the emotion of his passion — "men like yourself, thousands of them — hundreds of thousands of them, all over Ireland — all wanting Ireland free, after eight hundred years of British domination, Matt, fighting to bring about the republic, and the women, too, every way they can, to fulfill the dream of those who lost their lives in the Easter Rising."

He stopped and looked around the little room, as if expecting to see a crowd of hundreds. He nodded to himself, blinked behind his glasses and again focused his piercing eyes on Matthew Cleary.

"I think you'd better be on the run, Matt," he said.

"What?" Matthew was surprised. "Me?"

"Aye, they know you. We've found your name on a list from Dublin Castle. We have our own informers, you know. They may not know all about you, where to find you. Not yet. But they know of you."

"Where do I go? The cabin in the Derrynasaggarts?"

"America."

Matthew Cleary rose up from the table. "America! How the hell am I getting there? Swim?"

"Toby Smyth," Boyle said. "You find him on the waterfront at Cobh at the sign of the Turtle. He'll find you a seaman's berth. Get seasick?"

"And won't I be finding out!" Matthew Cleary said.

"When you're settled, get in touch. I'll be in County Galway. Write me in care of general delivery, Clifden."

Matthew drew on his coat and took his cap from the pocket. He pulled it low over his eyes and gave Boyle a jaunty wave as he left.

* * * * *

Matthew crossed San Lucas' dusty main street, stepped up onto the board sidewalk and pushed open the door into Bunte Brother's store.

It was a huge store by Matthew's standards and he could see by the variety of merchandise visible on the shelves that they sold just about everything. A portly man wearing a clerk's apron came from a back room and met him at the counter. "Hello there, how may I help you?" Sam Bunte politely inquired.

"H'ar ya," Matthew greeted him with a nod. "Just looking for directions."

"Sure," Sam said. "Who you looking for? Know just about everybody here."

"Cleary?" Matthew asked.

"Which one?" Bunte wondered. "There's Will and his family over on the Trescony grant across the river. And there's Spud

251

in Long Valley on the Baxley place. Just got married, Spud did, nicest little wife. And there's the home place further up the valley, Jeremiah's old place. That's where Buck and Kitty O'Keefe live. She was a Cleary, you know. And then there's old Tim. He lives way up in Coyote Canyon. Who you looking for?"

"Spud," Matthew declared.

"Well, you take the Long Valley road just south of town. You go east up about five miles. Place is on your left, not far off the road. You afoot? Just get off that freight?"

Matthew didn't answer. He just stared hard at Bunte, who noted the cold blue eyes. "Long hot walk in this weather," the storekeeper called out as Matthew mumbled, "Thanks," waved and left the store. He stepped back into the hot July street and started walking toward Long Valley. Bunte followed him out the door and watched him stride off, his long legs quickly putting him out of sight, except for puffs of dust.

Bunte returned to the back of his store. "Strange fellow out there," he told his wife. "Didn't say much, but he seemed to have an Irish accent. Looking for Spud Cleary. About Spud's age. Wonder who he is?"

It was late afternoon when Millie Cleary heard a sharp rap on the front door. She was cautious answering it as Spud had warned her about tramps who occasionally came up the road. This fellow certainly looked like one in his worn clothing, with a wool cap pushed back on his head revealing an unruly mop of black hair. He also looked hot and dusty. Millie kept the screen door shut between them.

"H'ar ya, missus," the man said. "This where Spud Cleary lives?"

"Well, yes it is," Millie replied, recognizing the Irish accent and thinking there was something familiar about the man.

"I'm Matthew Cleary from Skibbereen," he said and stood waiting for Millie to speak. She slowly came to realize who he was, Spud's cousin, the one he'd spoken about. No wonder the man looked familiar.

"Well, hello, Matthew!" Millie cried out. "Spud has told us so much about you. Come in, come in." Millie threw open the screen door and Matthew followed her into the living room. Millie studied him for a moment. Same size as Spud, black hair, but blue eyes, not brown, the same nose and chin with the chiseled look and the slight dimple. He was a Cleary, all right, but a much more serious type than her Spud.

"Spud is just off up the canyon horseback. Checking on some cows. He'll be back any minute," Millie said. "Sit down." She indicated the sofa. "Shall I make us some tea?"

Matthew sat in a straight back chair, twisting his cap in his hands, quiet until the tea arrived. He accepted the cup, but didn't seem to know quite what to do with his cap, so Millie took it from him and placed it on the table. They sipped the hot tea and Millie tried to make polite conversation, but Matthew didn't have much to say. Millie was relieved when she saw Spud through the window riding into the yard.

She went through the kitchen to the back door and called out, "Spud — ! Look who's here."

Spud Cleary, unsaddling his horse, squinted against the sun setting behind the house and couldn't make out the tall fellow walking toward him. Suddenly, it hit him. Matt Cleary, by God! Spud dropped the saddle on the ground and reached for Matthew's hand, pumping it and clapping his cousin on the shoulder. "By God, Matt, you really did come to California!"

"I did!" Matthew agreed.

"Great, but how come? What brings you here?"

"Let's just say I'm traveling for my health," Matthew said with a wry grin. "The climate in Ireland doesn't agree with me right now."

"Well, whatever, I'm sure glad to see you," Spud said, leading his horse into the corral. "Give me a minute while I put up this skate and then we can go in and have a snort or two to celebrate." Spud put up his saddle and bridle and forked out some hay.

"Your wife kindly gave me tea," Matthew told him.

253

"Well, we can do better than that!" Spud laughed as he put his arm around his cousin and propelled him toward the house.

They were still at supper, around the kitchen table, when they heard the familiar sound of Will's Ford pulling into the yard. Will Cleary had just been up the valley looking in on Buck and Kitty and stopped by to visit Spud and Millie on his way back home. He was surprised by the sudden arrival of his nephew from Ireland, but gave the young man a hearty welcome and joined them for coffee.

"Well, by God, Matthew, it is sure good to meet you. You're a Cleary, all right. You look like you could be one of my own sons," Will boomed.

"Dad, Matt here is going to be around a while and he says he needs a job," Spud explained. "I told him he's welcome to visit as long as he likes, but he's a bull-headed Irishman and wants to work. Do you suppose we can find a place for him on one of the harvesting crews?"

"Why sure we can," Will said.

"I'm not knowing about harvesting machines, Uncle Will," Matthew said.

"Nothing to know," Spud injected. "Look at me. Doesn't take brains, just a strong back."

"Sure now, and I've got that," Matthew said.

Will took his nephew home with him that night so he could stay at Will's place where there was more room and start working right away.

"Your cousin is awfully quiet," Millie remarked to Spud as they stood in the yard and watched Will's Ford drive out the lane and turn into the county road.

"Yeah, I noticed," Spud agreed. "And he hardly smiled. He wasn't that way when I met him in Ireland. He was full of talk and we laughed together at everything. I wonder what's happened to him?"

Spud and Millie walked back into their house arm in arm.

* * * * *

Harvest season was just about over and Matt Cleary had a day off from bucking sacks. He'd finally written the letter he'd promised to Daniel Boyle and addressed it to general delivery, Clifden, County Galway, Ireland. Matt paid for the stamps at the San Lucas post office, dropped the letter in the slot and stepped next door into Bunte's Store. Will had ordered some items for him to carry back to the Cleary ranch.

Matthew couldn't help but notice the beautiful, fashionably-dressed young woman talking to Sam Bunte. "I'm in need of a handyman," she told the storekeeper. "The fences at the Barnes place are in such disrepair, I'm going to have to re-fence the entire property. And the corrals and barn need work. Do you know of anyone?"

"Well, let's see now, Missus Mertens, there should be some young fellows around who don't think that they're cowboys and above such work," Bunte said with a smile. "And harvest will be over soon and there'll be some hands available."

"Perhaps you could put this help wanted notice on your bulletin board, Mister Bunte," Clara Mertens said, handing Bunte a neatly-written ad.

"No need to do that, ma'am," Matthew Cleary said as he walked up to the counter and tipped his wool cap at Clara. "I'd be happy for such work."

"This is Matt Cleary from Ireland, Missus Mertens, cousin to the Cleary boys."

"How do you do," Clara said, smiling as she looked carefully at the tall, lean, rugged, young Irishman. But he didn't smile in return. He looked straight at her, waiting for her answer. He looked quite serious and strong.

"Do you know the Barnes place on the Pine Valley road, Mister Cleary?"

"I can find it, ma'am."

"How soon can you start?" she asked.

"How soon do you need me?"

Clara laughed and turned to Bunte. "I think we can forget posting this notice, Mister Bunte." He smiled back and nodded. "Is next Monday all right?" she asked Matthew.

He agreed. Matthew knew that, although harvesting would be over, the Clearys could find some other job for him. But he liked the idea of being independent.

"Good. Then I'll show you the work to be done and we can agree on your wages."

Three days later, Will Cleary, on his way up the Pine Valley Road to visit Tim in Coyote Canyon, dropped his nephew off at the Barnes place. "Good luck," he called as he watched Matthew walk toward the large Victorian house that looked so out of place in it's surroundings.

Matthew's first task was repairing the roof of the bunkhouse, into which he moved his meager possessions. He was to take his meals in the kitchen with the housekeeper and Chinese cook, Mar Lin.

That night he lay starting at the ceiling of the bunkhouse. Even after the hard day's work, sleep was elusive. He lay there pondering the recent changes in his life and feeling oddly displaced.

CHAPTER THIRTY-FOUR

"I DON'T GET IT, FRED," THE SOUTHERN PACIFIC station agent looked up from writing out a receipt for sixty-five dollars. "How come you're paying the freight bill for *The Banner's* paper?"

"Beats the hell out of me," Fred Godfrey said. He'd heard on the street that Bissell's shipment of newsprint was sitting on the S.P. dock, so Fred had gone down and made the C.O.D. payment so Bissell could pick up the paper and print another issue of *The Banner*. "I guess it's the fraternity of the newspaper business," Fred told him. "You know, show must go on, that sort of stuff."

"Godfrey, kind sir, your magnanimous spirit is a thing of magnificent proportions. My gratitude is eternal," Bissell said when he heard his impounded paper was released. He appeared at *The Settler* office with his bow and flourish. "My only desire is that one day I shall have the exquisite pleasure of an opportunity to reciprocate."

Bissell hurried off to his shop to get his paper out and the headline read, *Settler Editor Wants Higher Taxes*.

"Holy Jehoshaphat, Sarah," Fred exclaimed when she showed him the paper. "If that's the way he expresses gratitude, I'd hate to have his enmity."

The previous week, Fred had editorialized in favor of a new water system. *Our suggestion of bonding for a city-wide water system meets with general approval. All believe we would get better drinking water as well as softer water for washing than we do from the present system of individual wells. A municipal water works would make money for the city and the savings alone for homeowners on fire insurance would go a long way toward paying off the bonds. It took us five or more years to get a sewer. Let us hope that we can have a water works in far less time.*

So Bissell used his new shipment of newsprint to print: *The Settler editor must not realize that bonds, even those for his pet projects, have to be paid off. That means money and money means taxes. Is our city ready for higher taxes?*

Fred wadded up *The Banner* and threw it across the room. "It seems every time I pull that damn Bissell's chestnuts out of the fire, he takes another potshot at me with some snide remark or other."

"You keep turning the other cheek, Fred." Sarah laughed at her husband's discomfort. "For the life of me I don't know why you keep him in business. You pay for his newsprint. You go up there and set type for him. You send Bobby over there to fix his little cockamainy press, you even printed *The Banner* yourself when he was broken down. Wise up."

Fred grinned ruefully. "I was trained that newspaper people help each other. Good clean competition is fine. But Bissell doesn't play that way." He nodded. Sarah was right.

One of Fred's editorials dealt with shopping at home. *Ten years ago a certain farmer put his initials on a $1 bill and spent it with a local merchant. Four times in six years that $1 came back to him and he heard of it at least three times being in the pocket of a neighbor. Then he sent it to a mail order house and has never seen that $1 bill again. That $1 will never do him any good again, never pay for schools for his children, never pay a local road tax, never help build nor brighten local homes. He sent it out entirely from its circle of usefulness to himself and his neighbors.*

The next week one of the items in Bissell's column, or as Fred referred to them, Bissellettes, asked, *How can a certain editor, who advocates that we keep all of our dollars working for us here at home, fill the inside pages of his newspaper with mail order items?*

In Fred's Chat column he frequently mentioned things that were topics on the street. One such read that, *Horsemen are talking about the handsome Belgian stallion purchased by a combine of area ranchers, Bill Copley, Will Cleary, Wes Eade, and H.C Brown. A rich bay in color, he weighs a ton and stands 17 hands high, one of the finest horses ever shipped into the county. He'll be standing at stud at the Cleary ranch in Long Valley, and Buck O'Keefe will put up any mares whose owners want to improve their strain of work horses.*

The Bissellette for the week noted the item about the stallion. *I see it is now the practice of a certain editor to include stud horse ads in his column. Oh well, he keeps it all in the family.*

But Bissell shot himself in the foot next week. Charlie Phillips from Bitterwater was in town and let slip the story of a huge herd of wild horses, led by a great gray stallion, which had been spotted drinking from the lake. Bissell dug into his copy of Brittanica and came up with all the dope about wild horses. He ran a front page story about the herd and sat back to accept congratulations on his big scoop over *The Settler.*

Fred's next Chat column said, *Hold your horses, Mr. Editor. That gray stallion with his herd of wild mustangs is galloping through your dreams. There haven't been any wild horses in these parts for more than 25 years. Ask any rancher. Except, of course, that wag who pulled your leg.*

Bissell did. He asked the boys in the back room of the Peerless Soda Fountain. When the country voted in prohibition, it had been converted to soft drinks, with the exception of this hideout, known to all but the revenue agents. "Why sure, Horace," they agreed. "There are wild horses all over the place." Slim Smith spun a quarter on the bar. "Give old Horace here another snort. He wants to see more wild horses."

"The poor man," Sarah said when Fred told her the aftermath. "He must be lonely." This time it was Fred who sniffed. "Holy Jehoshaphat, Sarah. He lives in his shop, cooks on the Linotype pot, sleeps on the paper stacks like a damn rat. He has no family to support. Doesn't spend any money except on his bootleg whiskey. No wonder he can undersell us. If we didn't have to buck him we could earn a decent living. Makes some nasty remark about *The Settler,* or me, every issue. I'm through helping him and I don't give a damn if he is lonely."

But Fred had problems of his own that day. He'd locked up the page forms and carried them to his press, but when he turned on the old Brower all he got was a groan. He quickly shut it off and stood there scratching his head. He had just three hours to get his run off and make the mails. He went out to his desk, picked up the phone and called Bobby.

"That should do it, Pop." Bobby Godfrey wiped his hands on a rag and put up the wrench. Fred had been helping his son fix the press, handing him tools, fetching parts. Fred often marveled at Bobby's mechanical ability. He sure hadn't inherited that from him, Fred knew. Bobby'd managed to get the old Brower drum press to print again. Fred had purchased it in 1907 and it must have been ten or twelve years old then. Bobby had been called in a number of times this past year or so to fix the clutch or install bearings. "Can't keep it running much longer, though," he said. "You're gonna have to think about replacing it one of these days."

That was the last thing Fred wanted to think about. He'd finally paid off Millie's wedding party at the El Camino and was barely making payroll for his printer and news reporter. Good thing Bobby was an excellent mechanic. He loved to fix things, presses as well as automobiles. Joe Carrigan relied upon him more and more, called him the manager, and Bobby's time at Heald's Business School was also being put to good use. Fred suffered a secret pang every time he thought of Bobby up there at the Ford Garage when he could be here at *The Settler*. But Bobby's heart was in the automobile business. He loved grease, not ink. Still, he'd drop everything to keep his father's equipment running.

"Gotta get back to the garage now, Pop. Will Cleary's new Ford came in and he's gonna pick it up this afternoon. Gotta tune it up."

Fred watched Bobby head at a trot up Broadway and then returned to his press. He licked his fingers and flipped a sheet of paper, threw the lever and started feeding the sheets into the cylinder. The press hummed and clanked along now as it should. Fred was proud of his son, of course. Bobby was supervising the construction of an expansion of Carrigan's garage, extending it across the vacant lot between the original two-story building to the El Camino Hotel. A fifteen thousand square foot addition would make it the largest garage in three counties. Bobby had drawn up the plans for the mechanic bays, offices, new show and sales room, and Joe was letting him buy into the business. But, Holy Jehoshaphat, it would have been nice to put all that ability and energy into the newspaper.

* * * * *

Will Cleary changed gears, dropping his Ford into low to climb up the Pine Valley grade. He liked the sound and feel of his new car. That young Godfrey sure had this beauty tuned up. Joe Carrigan had just made him a deal on his old 1913 Model T touring car and Will was pleased. This new four-door sedan, first of its kind on the market, had a base price of seven hundred and fifteen dollars. But Will had received the family discount from his brother-in-law. "You advertise it for me, Will. As much as you get around, folks will see it. Any problems, give us a call and Bobby will come down and fix it."

Will had just stopped at a farmhouse, where he'd delivered some papers he'd picked up at the court house in Salinas. Will's day had started with the chickens as he made his rounds. First into San Ardo with funds so a storekeeper could cash checks, then out to a ranch just out of town with some tractor parts, and now he was on his way to visit his brother, Timothy, in Coyote Canyon. It was now approaching noon and he was feeling the heat as he stopped for the gate in the fence marking Cleary property. He got out of his car and struggled with the tight wire gap. Will settled back in the car seat and wiped his sweaty face. Damn, he thought, why does Tim insist on living up here?

Will made this trip regularly every month, except those few times when heavy rainfall made the road impassable, and that didn't happen often in this country. Will occasionally brought a few groceries with him, or something he'd come across that he thought might make his brother's life a little easier. And he'd always bring anything that Tim had mentioned he needed. But Tim didn't seem to care much. Nor did he appear especially grateful, a fact Will ignored.

Will bounced over the ruts and climbed up the slope to the cabin. He parked the Ford beneath a tall eucalyptus tree. Tim had planted several of them years ago, along with a couple of pepper trees at the back of the house, shading the privy, and had faithfully watered them until they were growing on their own. Will noted there were some hollyhocks alongside the cabin and wild roses bloomed down the hill below the boxed-in spring. Still, the place was bleak as hell. There were the unpainted, weathered redwood boards of the one-room cabin, a black stove pipe poking up from the tin roof, which covered the original shakes, a small window in one wall with tiny panes, and glass so thick it distorted the view.

Tim was just putting up the horse he'd been working that morning. He turned it into the little pole corral and carried his saddle to the shed he used as a barn and tackroom. Tim walked up to the car as Will killed the engine. "Morning, Will. Out doing your missionary work, I see," Tim greeted, waving at the packages in the rear seat.

"Stuff you wanted there," Will responded. "Tea kettle and the thirty-thirty shells. I picked up a breast strap to replace that old thing you're holding together with twine, and there's a couple of cans of peaches."

"Yeah? How much I owe you?"

"Nothing. Can't a man give his brother something now and then?"

"I pay my way." Tim's voice was flat, hard. "How much?"

Will sighed. This wasn't going well. It never did. "Well, let's see then. The Concord breast strap was a buck seventy-five and the shells were seventy-five cents. The damn tea kettle was about three dollars. I'll throw in the peaches."

Tim studied him a moment, then nodded. "All right, Will. I like peaches. Thanks." He knew Will would make an accounting and deduct the five fifty next time he made a distribution of the ranch profits. Tim owned a share of the ranch and his occasional payments were enough to meet his needs. He didn't take charity.

"Any coffee on?" Will asked.

"Put some on in a minute. Come on in," Tim invited.

This didn't happen often. Will realized Timothy was sober and in a good mood as he followed his brother into the cabin. Will was always impressed with how neat and clean Tim kept the little place. The board floor was freshly swept, a piece of clean linoleum in the kitchen area, dishes washed and stacked on the counter top, cooking pots hanging by the stove. And in the corner, but so large it dominated the little room, was a huge, four poster bed, its ornate carvings and richly-finished headboard in sharp contrast to the otherwise spartan furnishings. Will knew that had been Tim's bed at the ranch, carried in sections by pack mule over the hill when Tim furnished his cabin. Covering the bed was a colorful patchwork quilt, a loving gift from Aunt Cauth many years ago. Beside the bed was an apple box on end, serving as a night stand, and on it was a coal oil lamp and a small tin box, which, Will guessed, held Tim's personal treasures.

Tim dipped water from the bucket, threw in a handful of coffee from the red Hills Brothers can and stoked up the fire, which had been smoldering in the big iron stove. Tim sat down in one of the two chairs at the little table facing his brother. "So what's doing in this county of yours, Will?" he asked, making conversation while the coffee boiled.

"Same things, Tim. Everyone complaining about the roads and not enough money to fix them. Paul and I getting outvoted by the city fellows on everything that comes along." Will shrugged. "We can't seem to get our way on anything for south county."

"Why do you stick with it, Will? You've had that job for — what? — twenty-five years?"

"Damned if I know," his brother said with a laugh. "Seems like something I just have to do. I think this'll be my last term, though. Don't intend to stand for election again."

"Good!" Tim got up to take the pot off the stove. He added a bit of cold water and let the grounds settle before pouring two cups of coffee. Tim came back to the table with a small bottle and motioned with it over Will's cup. His brother waved off the offer as Tim added a splash to his own. "Where you headed from here?" he asked.

"Oh, I'll stop at the ranch and check on Buck and Kitty, and go to the Baxley and see how Spud and Millie are getting along — the usual rounds."

"Old Will! Has to check up on everybody." Tim shook his head and gave his older brother a lopsided grin. "Will, you'll never change. You always have to take care of the whole damn family. Been doing it ever since we were kids. Well, I don't need to be taken care of. Better drive over to Bitterwater and see if Annie needs anything and go on into King City and find out how Carrigan is treating Peggy. Call the bishop and make sure he's fair to Dan."

Will just smiled, a strained smile. He didn't want to start anything with his brother, not today. Let's just see if we can't get through a visit without a blow up, he reminded himself. But his eyes narrowed as he saw Tim fill his cup from the bottle, not even bothering with more coffee. He lowered his eyes, but not before Tim caught the look.

"Dammit, Will. If you don't like my habits, why the hell do you come around? I don't need your sanctimonious looks."

Will tried to hold his temper, but his frustration got the better of him. "God dammit, Tim! It just kills me to see you wasting your life like this."

"It's my life."

"Yeah, but you don't have to live like this. You could have a room at my place. Or you could be living down at the ranch. Hell, you're only sixty years old. You could be enjoying life."

"Who says I don't?" Tim glared at his brother and poured himself another shot. "I live the way I want to live. I don't need much. And I don't need anybody. If you don't like my place, what the hell do you come up here for?"

Will said nothing, just sadly shook his head and walked out of the cabin. He put the Ford into gear and started down the hill, waving over his shoulder as he left, slowly to keep the dust down. Tim stared after his brother for a long while, until the car disappeared behind the hill, and the cloud of dust had settled. Then he stepped back into his cabin and poured another drink.

It wasn't bad stuff, about the best he could find since prohibition. This came from some still in Lockwood and Tim picked it up from Jose Alvarado in San Ardo. Not the usual rot gut that was around, not that it really mattered. As long as it eased the hurt he had carried deep inside for so very long.

He sat on his bed and opened the little tin box. Inside were five letters, each still in an envelope postmarked San Francisco more than thirty years before. He read each letter slowly and then returned it to its envelope. Finally, he carefully unfolded a newspaper clipping, its edges frayed, the paper yellowed by the years. He smoothed it in his hands, and stared at the image of a beautiful young girl in her wedding gown, her veil pulled back, her head tilted up toward the groom, as she waited to be kissed.

CHAPTER THIRTY-FIVE

MATTHEW CLEARY WAS STRIPPED to the waist and the sweat dripped off him as he adjusted the stretcher and clamped it down around the barbed wire. He pulled on the rope and the length of wire tightened across the span between posts. With three quick strokes of his hammer he seated a big staple and stepped back, rubbing the back of his hand across his forehead, brushing the sweat and the unruly mop of back hair from his eyes. He readjusted his hat against the warm September sun and was reaching for the next strand of wire when he noted the cloud of dust.

The Dodge Brothers sedan was bumping across the old furrows of a field that hadn't been farmed in ten years, taking the ruts at a speed which showed the driver had little concern for its chassis and springs. Matthew could hear Clara Mertens' laughter above the roar of the engine as she braked to a sudden stop beside the fence, simultaneously turning off the engine.

"Driving a motor car is such fun, don't you think, Matthew?" she said breathlessly as she jumped to the ground.

"Wouldn't know, ma'am," he replied. "Never drove one."

"Well, it is," she said. "I brought out more fence staples for you, but I thought maybe you'd like to ride back with me and have lunch."

"I'm fine, Missus Mertens."

"Matthew, I wish you'd call me Clara. Missus Mertens makes me sound like I'm older than you, such an old lady. And I'm not!"

"Yes, ma'am — I mean, no ma'am." Matthew's hot face grew even redder. This woman never failed to fluster him. She was a wealthy, elegant lady who did the strangest things, he thought. Like driving out to where he was building fence at any hour of the day. Sure, she sometimes brought supplies he needed, but often just to visit, or to bring him a cold drink. One noon she'd brought lunch and spread out a cloth in the shade of an oak tree where she insisted they eat together. She was so pretty, young and fresh looking, so pert and pleasant, so quick to laugh. He was puzzled. She was gentry.

"Come on," she ordered.

Matthew shrugged. She was, after all, the boss. Suddenly conscious of his sweaty body, he picked up his shirt and put in one arm, but the cloth stuck to his wet back. He felt Clara Mertens' soft, small hands pull it down and smooth it over his shoulders. He sucked in a deep breath as her fingers fastened the buttons across his chest.

She stepped up into the car and started the ignition as he slid into the seat beside her, careful not to get too close. He stared straight ahead as the car bumped across the ruts. Again she laughed as the Dodge bounced them so high they hit their heads on the roof. But Matthew was quiet. Something was happening between them that Matthew didn't understand.

Clara didn't understand it, either. This was a penniless, unlettered foreigner, an Irish laboring man, the kind that dug ditches and carried bricks and fought the fires and kept the peace in San Francisco. Definitely not the type of young man who would be welcome in her circle of friends. Clara smiled at the thought of Matthew Cleary in the drawing room of her Green Street home.

But she'd left San Francisco and all that it stood for to begin a new life in the country. There were different values here. Things were more real. And Matt Cleary was a real man. She could feel herself blush with that thought.

There'd been no one since Josh had gone overseas. More than four years had passed since she'd pinned the second lieutenant bars on his shoulder at the Presidio ceremony and said good-bye. They didn't know it was forever. But now she could hardly remember what Josh looked like, except that he seemed so young, such a boy—compared to this Irishman

They had lunch together in the big dining room and, if Mar Lin thought this strange, he didn't show it. Neither did the housekeeper. But Matthew was uncomfortable sitting at the huge table, being waited on. He was embarrassed and kept his head down and his eyes on his plate. He hardly answered as Clara attempted conversation. When he did look up she'd see his clear blue eyes questioning her and she'd fall silent. When they finished lunch she drove him back to his fencing job. But they were both silent.

This happened several times as summer wore on and gave away to fall. The fences were finished and Matthew was at work fixing corrals and repairing sheds. He welcomed her visits, they broke up his work day and her cheerful manner brightened his life. But he was bothered.

It was near dark one night as Matthew shrugged out of his heavy wool coat, hung it on the peg with his cap and pushed open the kitchen door. It had been a long, hard day working on the new corrals and he was hungry. But Mar Lin wasn't there at the stove. The housekeeper wasn't in the kitchen. There was a roaring fire in the wood cookstove, but the room was empty. Matthew stood there, uncertain, wondering at this change of routine when the dining room door opened.

"Oh, there you are, Matt. I have a surprise for you. I'm your cook tonight."

Clara Mertens, her long blond hair tied at the nape of her neck with a red ribbon, a gaily colored apron across her sleeveless blue dress, took down a frying pan from its hook on the wall and placed it on the stove. "It's the housekeeper's day off and Mar was called to Salinas — family matters," she said over her shoulder. "It's just you and I, so we'll have supper right here. I'm so tired of eating by myself in the dining room."

She scooped lard from the bucket and it was quickly sputtering and spattering in the hot pan. Matthew watched her in astonishment as she dropped pieces of chicken into the hot grease and leaned over the pan to sprinkle them with salt.

"Oh!" she exclaimed, jumping back from the stove as the hot grease spit out of the pan and the fire flared up. Matthew swiftly moved to the stove and removed the frying pan of hot grease from the fire.

Clara was staring at the raw, red burn on her forearm. Tears, more from frustration than pain, had gathered in the corners of her eyes. Matthew quickly reached into the lard bucket and gently took her arm, smearing the grease on the small burn.

"Sure now, that'll be helping some," he said.

He dropped her arm, but she stood still, close to him, her head down as she murmured, "Thank you, Matt."

Then she raised her head and looked up at him, her blue eyes still shining with tears. Her hands were on his chest and their eyes locked together. Then her fingers slowly climbed up his chest in gentle, caressing motions, to his shoulders and behind his neck. Matthew's hands, against his will, moved around her slight figure to lock behind her back. He looked wonderingly at her and lowered his lips to meet hers.

As he pulled her fiercely against him, he knew it had never been like this. He'd kissed girls, furtive stolen kisses, but never had he kissed a woman and known that the kiss held the promise of all she could give.

It was Matthew who stopped. "No," he cried, but it was hardly aloud, a word wrenched from the depths of his being. He still held her tightly against him. "No! My God, I can't." He choked out the words as he took her shoulders in his hands and firmly pushed her away from him.

Matthew Cleary had dreamed about this woman, anguished over her. There were so many reasons he couldn't have her. She was gentry and he was a peasant and centuries of cruel tradition couldn't be overcome, even in America. She was wealthy and he was poor. She was Protestant and he was Catholic. She was educated and he could barely read and write.

But her eyes told him that none of that mattered. Sure now, didn't it, though. Maybe! Yes, her eyes, the trust in them, the tenderness, might convince him. But there was something else she didn't know.

"No," he said again. "I'm not the man for you, Clara. There are things about me that you aren't knowing. I've had to do things — !" He didn't want to tell her about the dark side of his soul. He couldn't. "My life's not my own! Its gone too far —" He stopped, knowing there were no words to explain.

Matthew gently turned her away, not being able to bear those eyes any longer, and held out a chair for her at the kitchen table. They didn't speak, but Clara watched his every move as he spread out the fire in the stove, let it cool down, then poured off some of the grease from the pan and began to fry the chicken. The torrent of emotion in Matthew's chest ebbed and finally he spoke.

"You've not cooked much, I'm thinking, Clara." He turned from the stove and smiled at her with a crooked grin.

She admitted that she never had. "I know so very little that's practical, Matt. The skills they teach girls like me aren't much use in Pine Valley." Clara dabbed her eyes with her handkerchief and attempted a smile. "But I can learn, Matt."

"Aye, I'm sure you could. And you will Clara. You will."

"For you, Matthew! I could for you. Our differences wouldn't matter. Oh, maybe in the city, but not here in the country. We could live here in Pine Valley and raise purebred Herefords. I've read all about it. This place would be ideal. And I'll learn how to please you." There she'd said it. She held her breath waiting for his reply.

Matthew turned back to the stove and tried to concentrate on frying the chicken. But his thoughts were filled with her. In his mind he was taking her in his arms, giving up to that ripe, tender mouth, burying himself in her sweetness, washing his soul in her love. He wrenched such dreams from his mind and turned to face her.

"The plates?" he asked. "And would you be knowing where they're kept?"

When he saw the hurt in her eyes, he almost relented. Instead he found the plates himself and served the chicken. They sat facing each other, trying to eat, but neither could swallow. She spoke past the lump of hurt in her throat.

"How did you learn to cook?" she asked him.

"Well now, for a while it was just me and my brother, Pat, there in the house on our farm, and we took turns with the food," Matthew told her. "After the war, Pat didn't come back — he was killed in France — so there was just me. Later on I cooked here and there — for a few of the lads — " he let his voice trail off.

"You wouldn't have to cook here," Clara said. "We could keep Mar Lin. We'd have plenty of money. You could do anything you wanted."

"Money?" Matthew said the word quizzically. "Money! I'm just wondering now, what it's like for a person to have all the money you ever need for anything?"

Clara thought about it for a second. "I guess I don't really know, Matt. I've always taken money for granted. It's always there. My attorney, Christopher Baxter, manages my affairs. I just got tired of all the worthless things I was doing, the social affairs, making inane conversation with people I didn't really care about, going to all the right places, shopping in the right stores to buy the fashionable things. After Josh was killed it was all so meaningless. That's why I moved here."

Matthew stared at her, his whole body filled with longing. "You're a lovely woman, Clara. Sure and you're beautiful. And you're — you're —" Matthew searched for a word. "Nice, Clara. You're a very nice person. You must have had many men around to court you."

"Oh, I suppose so. But there's been no one of interest to me until —"

The unfinished sentence hung between them. Matthew started to clear the table, but suddenly stopped. Looking back at Clara, his resolve melted. He sat down again and took her hands in his. He held them clasped against his bowed fore-

271

head. "Clara, Clara, you tempt me more than I can stand. Any man would be crazy not to want you. But it just can't be!"

Matthew rose from the table and carried the plates to the sink. He prepared to do the dishes but Clara insisted that she wash. "At least I can do this," she said. They finished the dishes in silence.

Then Matthew turned quickly and left. She looked after him as he walked into the dark bunkhouse and kept watching long after his lantern had been turned out.

For the next two days he worked diligently setting redwood posts and hammering corral boards. He stayed away from the house except for meals and made sure only Mar Lin was there in the kitchen. But on the third day he knocked at the front door, his small carpetbag in hand. The housekeeper let him in and he was standing in the parlor, twisting his wool cap in his hands, when Clara entered.

"Clara, I've been putting off telling you this, but now is the right time," Matthew said. "I've finished the corral and leaving. I'm off for Ireland."

"Oh, no!" Clara's voice was almost a whimper. "Why must you go? Please stay, Matt, if it's only to work."

"I can't be staying," he said, his hand straying to the letter in his pocket. "I'm needed in Ireland."

The letter had come to the San Lucas post office the week before. It was from Daniel Boyle. *You'll be safe here now, Matt. The British have released all the lads from the prisons and there's a truce. But it's not over. They're negotiating away all we've fought for. Even Mick Collins has given up our republic and Ulster. He says it has to be a compromise, something called Irish Free State under Britain. DeValera is for fighting on for the republic. Come back. You're needed.*

"I've been thinking," he said. "When my job is finished in Ireland, I'll be coming back — if I can — and you might be needing help."

"Oh, yes, Matt! Yes!" Clara cried and reached out toward him.

But Matthew Cleary turned away, picked up his bag and was gone.

* * * * *

August 22, 1922 was a grand day in Skibbereen. The town had just been retaken from the Irish Republican Army by the Free Staters. The local population, sick of war, had turned out to hail Michael Collins, a West Cork lad, one of their very own they called the "Big Fella," now head of the executive council of the young, but troubled, Irish Free State. His convoy, led by a lieutenant on a motorcycle, consisting of a Crossley tender for the riflemen and machine gunners, the big, yellow touring car for Collins and General Emmet Dalton, and the Rolls Royce armored car, was parked on the street in front of the Eldon Hotel.

Matthew Cleary sneaked back into town and was mingling with the crowd around the Eldon Hotel when Collins came out, handsome and resplendent in his green uniform with a Sam Browne belt across his chest. Matthew pretended to join in the applause and the wild cheering as Collins and another general waved as the motorcade pulled away, but on his face was a frown.

By that afternoon the people of Skibbereen had the news. Michael Collins' convoy had been ambushed not far from town. The "Big Fella" was shot and killed.

* * * * *

It was just before Christmas when the letter reached Clara Mertens in San Lucas, California. Clara gasped with joy when she saw the envelope had an Irish postmark. She excitedly tore it open, her heart beating fast as she read. *We were on the run together when he told me about you and that he would return to you when our fight was over,* wrote Daniel Boyle. *So I thought it best that I let you know. I am sorry to tell you that he*

273

won't be going back there. He was caught by Free State soldiers and executed.

Clara Mertens was standing on the wide front porch of her Victorian mansion as she read the letter. Her hands began to tremble and her legs gave way so she sank into one of the white wicker chairs. Tears slowly welled up in her eyes and gathered on her cheeks to fall on the piece of paper in her lap. Soon the words of Daniel Boyle were a watery blur.

CHAPTER THIRTY-SIX

"FUNNY, ISN'T IT, SARAH, HOW YOU GO ALONG and go along and nothing much seems to happen. Then all of a sudden, bingo! Everything happens." Fred Godfrey was delivering his wife to Millie and Spud's place in Long Valley, where Sarah would spend several weeks helping her daughter with the new baby. Timmy Cleary had been a long time coming—Millie and Spud had been married four years—and it was a difficult, tenuous pregnancy. Millie had to spend a great deal of the time in bed and Timmy's birth had been hard on her and the baby was rather frail.

Doc Brumwell had explained to the new parents that both mother and son would need a lot of care, so Millie and Timmy had remained in King City with Sarah and Fred for two weeks before the doctor would allow them to go home. Spud had bundled them into Lizzie that morning and they were being settled in at the ranch as Sarah and Fred drove out to Long Valley.

"I don't see why Millie and the baby couldn't have stayed in town where Doc could look in on them," Sarah complained as they jolted up the dirt road. Fred slowed as they approached a chuck hole, geared down with a clash, and the car lurched forward. "What are you trying to do, Fred? Jump over the hole? Slow down, for goodness sakes." Fred had never really learned to drive an automobile. He'd tell himself that the damn things came along too late in life for him, but he'd never admit it to Sarah.

"Holy Jehoshaphat, Sarah, hang on to your hat! We'll get there."

The road evened out for a while and Sarah changed the subject back to her first grandchild. "He seems so peaked and thin," she complained. "I'd never say it in front of Millie, but with that mop of black hair and yellow skin, I'd think he belonged to a Chinaman. If he hadn't been born right in our own house, I'd declare he'd been switched with another."

275

"Now, Sarah, he'll be just fine and so will Millie. Doc says it's just a little jaundice. I just hope I'm not too decrepit to take him hunting and fishing by the time he's old enough to go. I wonder how long it's going to be before Bobby and Barbara start having children."

"Good grief, Fred. They're not even married yet!"

"Well, at least, they're finally engaged." Fred shook his head and let his smile grow, "That sure was some production."

The whole town had talked about it. Bobby Godfrey commandeered King City's brand new, blazing red fire engine and came roaring up to Barbara Putnam's house on Ellis Street, siren screaming and bells clanging. The volunteers answered the call. They came running, riding, and driving to the scene of the supposed fire and found Bobby helping the laughing, but embarrassed, Barbara into the front seat of the big, red La France fire truck.

"Climb on, you guys!" Bobby called out. He'd been elected engineer and driver as soon as he joined the fire company. So off he and Barbara went for a tour of the town, the siren, the bells and the laughing firemen attracting spectators on every street.

Above the noise no one could hear what Bobby was saying to his passenger. But Barbara heard and nodded her head. Bobby hit the siren again and when the wail died down, he stopped the motor, turned to the members of King City Fire Department hanging on to the truck and announced, "She said yes! We're going to be married!"

Fire Chief Bob Irwin was a bit annoyed with Bob Godfrey for appropriating the fire engine for his romantic escapade, and the city council officially frowned, but privately laughed. After all, Bob Godfrey was an authentic, wounded, war hero. Besides he was the only one who could expertly maintain the new vehicle and drive it properly. And they all thought it was about time he asked Barbara Putnam to marry him, anyhow.

Since this little escapade coincided with the birth of his grandson, no wonder Fred Godfrey thought everything happened at once.

He delivered Sarah, visited his daughter and the baby, who looked a little better now than Sarah's last assessment of him, shook hands with his beaming son-in-law—Spud was the proudest father Fred had ever seen— and then headed back to King City, thinking the whole way what a perfect world it would be if it weren't for that damn Bissell and his damn *Banner*.

Fred was now publishing twice a week. He didn't want to. There certainly wasn't enough business for a semi-weekly. But he had to. Bissell had started coming out on Tuesday as well as Friday. Four dinky, skimpy, little six-column pages each time. There wasn't enough business in those measly pages to pay for the paper, except for that damn half page ad from George Cosgrove's store. It was keeping Bissell in business.

The unctuous bastard, Fred thought. Bissell had even tried again to take the official King City legal business from *The Settler*, too. But now that Cosgrove was off the council, there wasn't any support for that maneuver, but Fred found it a damn nuisance to have to fight all the time. Fred had the same problem with the county's legal notices. And there were damn few of those, anyway. When a legal matter pertained to San Ardo, or some other south county area, the supervisors ran the public notice in the *Salinas Index*, even though *The Settler's* subscription list in south county was ten to one over *The Index*. Where was service to the public in that? Fred thought angrily. But Supervisors Will Cleary and Paul Talbot couldn't change it, not with the board dominated by the urban area. It was just another of those three to two votes.

For Fred, publishing twice a week did not increase revenue, but it did increase his operating costs. And it created more work for him and the crew, a part-time printer and an office girl who helped him with the writing. Meeting payroll was a weekly problem and Fred spent long hours scratching his head and adding up totals.

"By God, if I can't pay my bills I'll get out of business," he told himself and anyone else who'd listen. But it was a source of embarrassment to Fred Godfrey that his newspaper enterprise was so marginal he still had to scrimp and save after nearly thirty-five years in the business. He was particularly embarrassed when he was around the Clearys. Millie had married into a highly-successful family. They worked hard, but took their wealth for granted. Anything they wanted, it was just there. Millie was fortunate, he thought. But he knew it still bothered her, charging everything to Cleary Ranches, Spud not having a salary of his own, he and Millie not having their own bank account. She had once confided this to her father, but she also emphasized that, although she and Spud had discussed it many times, she didn't want to make an issue of it. Will and Honora Cleary were so good to her, she didn't want to hurt their feelings, either.

Millie enjoyed the comforts, especially now as she lay back on the pillows her mother had fluffed up for her. She wore a crocheted bed jacket and her long hair was caught in back with a red ribbon. Her color had returned, but she knew she looked much better than she felt. She still ached all over and wasn't getting much sleep with the baby crying all the time. Spud leaned down and kissed her and returned to the kitchen to eat the supper Sarah had prepared.

"Hello, hello. Anybody home?"

It was the booming voice of Will Cleary. He knocked on the kitchen door and came in. Timmy's squalling was so loud, they hadn't even heard him drive into the yard. "I had to come up and have another look at that grandson of mine," he said to Spud. "Millie," he called out toward the bedroom, "mind if I come in?"

"Come on in, Dad Cleary," Millie answered. Will entered the bedroom, greeted Sarah and bent over the crib. Timmy quieted down for a moment. Will put a big hand into the crib and slipped a finger into the tiny fist. Timmy gripped it. "Well, well," Will said. "He's kind of puny now, but he has a good grip. Shook hands right proper. May as well raise him, Millie. He might turn out all right."

Will patted his daughter-in-law on the shoulder. "Hope you're doing better now, my dear." He suddenly remembered something. "Oh, I forgot something in the car. Be right back."

He hurried out and returned with a small box, wrapped in white tissue, tied with blue ribbon. He set it on the bed beside Millie and she picked it up, shook it and looked questioningly at Will. "Something for the baby?"

"Sure is. Just what he needs." Will laughed as he watched Millie tear off the wrappings and open the box. She lifted out a tiny pair of high-heeled cowboy boots, black with an intricate pattern stitched in red and white. Millie and Sarah both laughed at the prospect of Timmy's little feet in even these tiny boots.

"Ordered them some time ago from the same outfit that makes my boots," Will explained. "They just came into the San Lucas post office today. He'll grow into them and when he outgrows them we'll get another pair."

"Now, Will, how on earth did you know it would be a boy?" Sarah asked.

"I didn't," he said with his hearty chuckle. "But girls need boots, too. Look at my sister, Kitty."

Sarah invited Will to stay for supper, but he'd already eaten earlier up the valley with Buck and Kitty. "I'd better be getting along home or Honora will be wondering what happened to me."

Will spent a few moments talking over ranch work with Spud and went out to his car. "Take care of that boy, Son. He'll do to ride with one day," he called as he fired up the Ford, turned on his headlights and drove out of the yard.

Will drove slowly. He didn't really feel well tonight, ever since supper. Not that Kitty was that bad a cook. He smiled to himself as he steered around another bend in the road just outside San Lucas. He'd always kidded Kitty that she'd rather be on a horse than in a kitchen. Maybe he'd just eaten too much, he decided. Take something for this damn gas before he went to bed.

Will's head lights illuminated the San Lucas bridge. He drove across and took the turn to the left toward the Trescony when the pain struck his chest again, sharper this time. He tried to belch to relieve the pressure, but it gripped him tighter. Sweat broke out on his forehead. Must get home and take something, he thought. Get home. He clasped the steering wheel in both hands and pressed down on the gas pedal. The Ford answered with a roar, sped down the lane and into the Cleary yard.

Now the pain clutched his chest in a vise. Will slumped over the steering wheel. He was weak, sweating and shaking. He could hardly breathe. He tried to shut down the engine, turn off the lights, but his hands weren't working right. Get into the house, he told himself. Get to Honora.

Will stepped out of the car on one foot. When it touched the ground, his leg folded under him. He sprawled and lay still, half in, half out of the car. Must get to the house. The pain in his chest consumed him. His head whirled and buzzed and he couldn't see. But he tried to move, struggled to move. Get to the house. Honora! Honora —

CHAPTER THIRTY-SEVEN

FRED GODFREY, WRITING IN *THE SETTLER*, described it as one of the most largely attended funeral services ever held in south county. Every pew in St. John's Catholic Church was filled with mourners who loved him, valued his friendship, respected him, or had been befriended by him. There were also dignitaries from state government, all the Monterey County supervisors and staff members from the courthouse, and leading civic and business leaders from Salinas and other valley towns. Those who couldn't fit into the church, lined the street outside, and stood in respectful silence when the body of William Declan Cleary was carried out to his grave.

Supervisor Cleary, read the obituary on page one, *was a very prominent citizen because of the many attributes possessed by him not common to the average man. He was extremely successful as a farmer, and his heart was so big that much of what he earned he gave again as hopeless loans or direct charity. Without turning a hand to enter politics, he was elected and re-elected time and again. He was more than a man to south county. At the age of just 64, he was an institution.*

Will was put to rest in the family plot with his father, Jeremiah, and Catherine Cleary, his beloved Aunt Cauth. Then the family, exhausted and emotionally spent by the rigors of the last three days since the shock of Will's sudden death, met friends for refreshments in the home of Will's sister and husband, Peggy and Joe Carrigan, in King City. It was late that night when each family returned to its own home.

Patrick Cleary, as the eldest son, was executor of the estate. That had been a surprise to Pat. He hadn't thought about it until Dan Parker, the Salinas attorney who had handled legal matters for Will Cleary, called him aside at the Carrigan home after the funeral. "You know our firm handled your father's will," Parker said. "He named you as executor."

"Oh? I didn't know. What is it I'm to do?"

"You'll oversee things, sign papers, make decisions for the estate, pay the bills, that sort of thing, for your mother. She inherits the estate," Parker explained. "Could you be in my office early next week?"

"Well, sure," Pat agreed. "What happens then?"

"Bring all your father's papers, any bills you have for payment, anything you run across that looks like unfinished business. There may be some accounts due to him that will be payable to the estate. And there must be insurance policies. We'll get it all set up. Say, Tuesday afternoon at two?"

Honora and her son spent several hours going through Will's desk. Pat located various bills from Wideman's store for Holt tractor parts, from Bunte's for groceries, from the Jeffery for hotel charges, bills from King City Mercantile, from Hales in Salinas and White House in San Francisco. There were stacks of them, and each indicated a recent payment had been made on the account, but sizable balances still remained. He showed them to Honora.

"Did you know we had all these unpaid bills, Ma?"

"Of course not, dear. There must be some mistake," Honora said innocently. Pat assumed his mother was right despite a growing concern that was beginning to creep into his thoughts.

"I'll check with the stores and get them all straightened out," Pat told Honora and then put his arms around his mother and held her. Grief over losing the man she loved so much, the one they all depended upon, the realization that she'd have to go on without him, had again overcome her.

The next day Patrick Cleary went to see the bookkeeper for King City Mercantile. "Oh, no problem, Pat," he said. "Your dad always paid, sometimes just part of the bill. But he always paid something. We never worried. Yes, that account is correct." It was the same response everywhere that Pat inquired about unpaid bills.

When he boarded the train in San Lucas on Tuesday morning, Pat had with him several boxes of bills, and a valise filled with mortgage papers, an insurance policy, and copies of notes owed to Will Cleary. He set them on Dan Parker's desk and the two men went through them together.

A fear began to grow deep in Pat's gut, just a nagging notion at first, but the more documents that Parker looked over and explained, the more the fear grew. There were mortgages to First National Bank on the Long Valley ranch, on the old Thompson place, Will's own homestead, and the Coyote Canyon property Jeremiah had purchased. Holt Tractor Company in Stockton held the note on the new gas-motor combined harvester.

"Don't worry, Patrick. I'm sure these are all in order," Parker said, but he didn't sound at all reassuring. "I'll check over at First National and find out where we stand. Let's see that insurance policy." He scanned the document and then gave Patrick a cautious smile. "Ah, that's quite a satisfactory amount. Your father carried fifty thousand on his life with your mother as beneficiary. I'll notify the company."

"But look, Dan," Pat said, showing the lawyer another sheaf of papers, "there are these grain receipts, and I don't see that we received any money for the steers we just shipped, either." True, he felt a bit better knowing there was a fifty-thousand-dollar life insurance policy, but Pat was still puzzled and worried about his father's accounts. "And these notes here, the ones due Dad, they add up to quite a bit. Some are bills for harvesting crops going back several years."

"Hmmm," Parker said, looking over the statements and frowning. "Yes, they do. There's another fifty thousand or so here. We'll call these in, Pat. Let's meet again same time next week."

Pat stayed over at the Jeffery Hotel, signed for the room charges as usual, and took the early train back to San Lucas. Sorrowing for his father and trying not to think about the financial problems, Pat set his mind to deciding how Will would have organized the ranch work. He could leave Long Valley in the hands of Buck and Spud, but he'd have to see to the Trescony himself, Pat thought. There'd be late calves to

brand, steers to ship, cows to be culled. And he'd have to get
the harvesters into working order with the season coming up.
He stopped in at the post office and picked up the mail. More
bills. They nearly matched the number of condolence letters
addressed to Honora.

Pat spent a busy week, sorting out the operation of the
ranches with Buck and Spud, trying to pick up the threads of
his father's former busy life, comforting his mother and coping
with his own sadness. When he stepped off the train in
Salinas, he was confident that Attorney Dan Parker would
have things well in hand. It was a long session in the lawyer's
office, and Pat was very tired afterwards. His bad leg ached
terribly and all he wanted to do was lie down. But Pat chose
not to stay overnight at the Jeffery Hotel. He took the night
train home, and very early next morning—he hadn't been to
sleep yet—he telephoned his brother.

Two longs and a short. The phone rang twice before Millie
could free her hands of breakfast dishes to take down the
receiver. "Morning, Millie. Did I catch Spud or has he already
gone?"

"Hi, Pat. No, he's right here, just finishing breakfast." She
held the receiver out to her husband and stepped back from
the wall phone.

"Spud. We have to call a family meeting," Pat said. "We have
trouble."

It took another day and a half to gather everyone and for
Dan Parker to come from Salinas. They were all together, seated in a circle in the front room at Buck and Kitty's old home in
Long Valley, Annie and her husband, Charlie Phillips, from
Bitterwater, Dan and Peggy Carrigan from King City, Spud
and Millie, Bucky and Lilly from San Antonio. Tim Cleary sat
in the back of the room with Seamus. Honora, all in black, but
straight and dry-eyed, sat next to Pat with a sheaf of documents in her hand. The only one missing was Father Dan, who
had officiated at his brother's funeral, but now had parish
duties that made it impossible for him to attend this meeting.

The family was listening attentively to Dan Parker, except for Seamus, who sat quietly, but didn't understand a word that was being said.

"The plain truth," Parker said, "and I know of no other way to tell you, but straight out, is that there aren't enough assets to cover the debts." Honora gasped, but said nothing. "All the property is encumbered and the bank advises me that only the interest has been paid for the past five years, nothing on principal." Parker's head slowly turned and his eyes met those of everyone in the room. "That last shipment of steers you mentioned, Pat, that was consigned to creditors in San Francisco. Your grain receipts are duplicates. The bank holds the originals so the grain belongs to them. Under the ordinary course of events they'd apply this credit to Mister Trescony for his share, and to your father's account, and that would keep the interest current. But I was told that the death of your father means the principal on each note must be brought current. As long as Will Cleary was alive they'd allow this practice. His reputation, his prestige — the respect they all had for him — held it all together. But now — " Parker took a deep breath and spoke as he exhaled, "I'm afraid they'll put a lien on the estate."

The family sat silent, stunned. Then the questions began. "What about that insurance policy made out to mother?" Pat asked.

The lawyer shook his head. "I'm sorry, but the company claims that the full amount was borrowed out of that policy six years ago," Parker stated sadly. "The remainder went to keep the payments current. It finally expired for non-payment."

Honora simply smiled. "But, Dan, look at these," she said hopefully, handing the attorney a small stack of papers. "You didn't know about these. These are stock certificates. Will had them hidden away. I just found them." Parker leafed through them.

"King City Brick and Enamel Works, five hundred shares issued in nineteen ten," he read aloud.

"Never heard of it!" Pat exclaimed.

"King City, Jolon and San Lucas Telephone Company, one hundred shares. And Martin Steam Conveyance Company of San Francisco, two hundred and fifty shares," Parker read.

"A phone company that doesn't exist anymore and a steam car?" Spud said derisively.

"Here's one for a thousand shares in Monterey Quicksilver Mining Company of New Idria," Parker announced, studying the gilt-edged certificate he held in his hand.

"That should be worth a lot," Honora said, refusing to be discouraged.

"Oh, Mother," Spud said. "Those mines have been closed for years."

"This one is for a thousand shares in the Pacific Coal, Clay and Oil Company."

"Hell," Charlie Phillips interjected. "That's the outfit that was wildcatting in Bitterwater. Nothing but dusters." His wife nodded in sad agreement.

Parker stopped sifting through the little bundle of worthless papers and handed them back to Honora. "I'm so sorry, Missus Cleary. It looks as if all you have here is memorabilia."

Parker looked directly at Pat. "I wrote letters for you to sign to all those who owed your father money, asking that it be paid. There's over fifty thousand in old debts due the estate. But, frankly, I doubt if you'll collect much. Some of them are quite old. I can think of several cases in which your father probably forgave the debts to widows. He was a most generous man." Honora's eyes had tears brimming in them as Parker spoke, but she continued to hold herself tall and straight in her chair.

"How did all this happen?" Kitty asked, shaking her head in disbelief at what her beloved brother had done.

"Well," Parker responded, "when your father, Jeremiah, died he left everything equally to his surviving children. There were seven of you. You all signed over power of attorney to Will to run the ranches. You'll recall I handled that for you. Will expanded the operation and continued to expand. He used the equity in one property to buy another, to purchase new equipment, to improve the breeding stock for the cattle and horses. Sometimes the ranches made a substantial profit and you all shared in it. Other times it didn't. But even then Will distributed funds among you from his own personal account so you thought everything was going well. No one questioned him. I'll bet not one of you ever asked for an accounting."

Millie glanced at Spud. He knew what she was thinking, all those times she had wanted them to be on their own financially, not blithely charging everything to Cleary Ranches. But it was all too late now, much too late. Spud gave his attention back to Dan Parker.

"The world thought Will Cleary was rich," Dan said, "and he kept up the pretense. Everyone with a wild scheme that needed financing went to him and everyone in trouble got his help."

The Clearys all nodded agreement.

"Will took care of us all, from the time we were children," Annie said. She dabbed her eyes with a cotton handkerchief and her voice choked. "We all looked to him for everything. And then he took on the responsibility for the whole south county. Poor Will, trying to carry such a load."

"If he'd had two or three bumper years in a row he'd probably have come out of it. But that didn't happen. Perhaps, if he'd lived he would have made it." Parker shook his head sadly.

"Don't we own anything?" Kitty questioned.

"The only property I find that is still free and clear," Parker said, "is that held in the name of Timothy Cleary." All eyes in the room turned to look at Tim, who had sat, grim-faced and silent, through the entire proceeding. "All the rest is heavily mortgaged, and you'll probably have to sell it to settle the loans, or the bank will take it anyhow."

"What can we do?" Pat asked.

"Right now, not much," Parker replied. "We'll see if we can't locate some cash to pay the current bills. Perhaps you can sell enough cattle to cover them. Then we'll see how things sort out with the bank. I'll keep you informed." Dan Parker paused. "I'm sorry. Will Cleary was my good friend, but his generous heart was his downfall."

Pat accompanied the lawyer out to his car and returned to the living room to find the family still sitting in stunned silence. He went to his mother and put his hand on her shoulder. "Don't you worry, Ma," he said. "We'll all see you never want for anything."

"You can come and live here," Kitty suggested. "There's plenty of room in this big, old house."

"Why would I ever want to leave my home on the Trescony?" Honora's puzzled look went from her son to her sister-in-law.

"Well, Ma, we may have to give up the Trescony lease," Pat explained. "We'll see how this all shakes out. But don't you worry."

Spud and Millie were the first to leave. They climbed into Lizzie for the trip down the valley. Millie was anxious to get home. Sarah had come to stay with the baby, but it was feeding time and Millie's breasts ached. Millie looked at her husband behind the wheel. She saw the perplexed look on his face as he studied the road ahead. "You're poor father, Spud. How he must have worried," Millie said, "trying to hold everything together. No wonder he had a heart attack."

"Hell," Spud muttered. "I wonder if this car is even paid for?"

CHAPTER THIRTY-EIGHT

Seamus wasn't surprised that they were gathering cattle. It was way past time to ship the big steers, but he was puzzled because Buck had told him to bring everything, cows, calves, steers, heifers, even the bulls. "Why're we doing that, Buck?"

"We're clearing off the whole ranch, Seamus. Bring all the cattle."

Seamus, Spud and Buck made their circles in the Coyote country, brought the herd right past his brother's place. Seamus saw Tim sitting on the stoop of his little cabin. Even though Seamus had waved, Tim didn't seem to pay any attention. They drove the cattle over the hill to join the rest of the Cleary herd, those gathered in Long Valley, and from Will's place, and off the old Thompson place. Buck said they'd keep back thirty pair and the best of the bulls. The rest would go on the road to San Lucas.

Seamus tried to understand as he rode along. He puzzled over it. Seamus, at fifty-four years of age, was still strong and healthy and could cowboy longer and harder than someone half his age, but his simple young boy's mind couldn't comprehend the changes taking place. Oh, Buck had explained. But it just didn't make sense that they had to sell all the cattle to pay bills. They'd never done that before, and he'd been on this ranch his whole life. So if it had happened, he'd know about it.

Buck had also explained to Seamus that he would be going to work for Wes Eade. "You'll keep your room here at the house, Seamus. That won't change," Buck said. "But we won't have enough cattle here, or horses, to keep you busy, and Mister Eade can use you. Understand?"

"Sure, Buck. I'll do it." Seamus always did everything Buck told him to do. "Will I still have Chappo?" he asked with a worried look. The gray gelding was the one he was riding, one he'd put in the bridle himself. "I want to keep Chappo."

"Yeah, I think so, Seamus. At least for now. You keep Chappo."

So Seamus brought Chappo in at a long lope to join up with Buck and Spud, who were putting cattle through the gate of the holding field. Pat sat on his horse by the gate, counting the animals as they moved them through onto the county road.

Buck held a few back and Pat closed the gate. "There's your herd, Pat," Buck called. "Goddamn, what a shame. Makes me want to cry." Seamus wanted to cry, too, if Buck did. But Buck said a guy fifty-four-years old shouldn't cry.

Buck wasn't worried about himself. Hell, he was sixty-two years old and pretty well set since his parents had died and left him and his brother some money from the sale of the O'Keefe's San Juan ranch. Buck and Kitty intended to stay on in Long Valley and Buck thought he might try his hand at buying and selling cattle, something like that.

But Pat Cleary had to give up the Trescony lease. He couldn't farm on so large a scale without equipment, work animals and some capital. And everything had been sold at auction. Even the harvesters. That had been the toughest part of it for Pat. At first he'd planned to keep one, so that he could stay in the custom harvesting business. It was harvest season and the machines were in demand. But the bank was against it, so the harvesters just sat there, useless, while the grain ripened all around. Finally the machines were sold for half their worth at auction, and the new owners put them right to work. When he and Spud watched their former machines cutting in neighboring fields, it really hurt. Pat and his mother had moved to Long Valley, into the big house with Buck and Kitty.

"Dad must be rolling over in his grave if he knows this is happening," Pat said as he rode up alongside Spud. They drove the Cleary herd on down the Long Valley road toward the Baxley place where Spud had some cattle in the holding field. "Yeah," Spud agreed. "I sure know he didn't mean to leave us in this fix, but he did. So we deal with it."

The Baxley lease had been terminated, too. Spud couldn't keep it without the money to buy cattle or equipment to work up the ground. So he and Millie and baby Timmy had moved to King City and rented a little house on Russ Street.

"Don't worry about us," Spud told Pat as they worked the cattle out of the field and into the herd on the road. "I've already been offered a job. Going to be hell to work for a living, but we'll make out fine." Spud made a joke of it, but Pat knew his brother's bravado concealed a multitude of worries. All of Spud's life had revolved around cattle and horses and farming. What kind of job would he now have to take?

It was Claude Markham, manager of farm implements for King City Mercantile Company, who had approached Spud on the day of the auction. Spud was hanging back on the fringes, hardly talking to anyone. Fact was, he was embarrassed as hell. All his neighbors, most of them friends since childhood, were there bidding on his possessions—the tractors, seeders, plows and rakes, particularly the harvesters that had been so much a part of the Cleary reputation. When the big work horses, superior because of their Percheron blood, had come under the gavel, Spud hid out on the other side of the barn. And the wagons and all the harness went, even Jeremiah's old freighter, what was left of it. They even sold the old ranch truck, the one Spud had courted Millie in, and Lizzie, and Will's Ford touring car. Spud couldn't bear to watch. But as hard as that was, it was worse to see the saddle horses being led off, most of them the grays that had become the Cleary trademark since his grandfather's day.

Markham had found Spud, though, and said, "I don't know what you're planning to do, but there's something I'd like you to consider."

"What's that, Claude?" Spud's eyes were brimming with tears and he didn't want to look straight at the man.

"Nobody knows Holt equipment like you do. You've been running it for years, the harvesters, our Caterpillar tractors. And you know farming," Markham said.

291

"Yeah," Spud agreed, wondering what he was leading up to.

"And you know everybody in the country. And they know you. You've got a good reputation, Spud. We'd like you to come to work for us."

"Huh? Work for you? What the hell could I do?"

"You could sell farm implements, Spud. Probably sell them like crazy. We'll pay you one fifty a month plus commissions, give you a car to use and some expense money."

Spud shook his head. "I don't know, Claude. Don't know if I can sell. Never tried it."

"With your personality, you'd be great. Everybody likes you. And you'd be one salesman who knows his stuff. Think about it, Spud. Come and see me."

"Okay, Claude. I'll think about it. And thanks."

Spud still hadn't made up his mind as they were pushing the cattle down the valley toward the railroad yard in San Lucas. He wondered what it would be like driving around the valley, visiting the ranches, calling on old friends, trying to sell them something. He'd probably show up when they were busy and they wouldn't have time to talk to him, he thought. Hell! Could he do that? Stick his nose into their business? Tell them what kind of equipment they needed? The idea bothered him. But he knew he had to do something, and soon.

Millie had offered to go to work. "I'll wean Timmy, and soon as I get him on the bottle my mother can take care of him. I could teach school or write for the paper." Millie sounded optimistic, but Spud couldn't be won over. He insisted she stay home with Timmy. "I don't want my wife working. I'll earn the living for this family, by God."

Spud touched his horse with his spurs and set off after a bunch of cows moving into a neighbor's farming field. Most of the Long Valley road was fenced on each side, but there was a gap and those damn cattle always found it. Spud cleared them out and followed them on down the dusty road.

Spud tried to imagine what it would it be like getting a salary, living on a regular income. Always had those charge accounts, never really knew what things cost, he realized. Charge it to Cleary Ranches had been the only way of life he'd every known. Now when he needed money he had to go to the bank. First National had given way to Bank of Italy, and Gene Rianda was a square guy, but it was "damn demeaning," Spud told Millie, "to have every check countersigned by the bank manager." In any case, the money set aside by the bank for living expenses was about to run out.

One thing, though. Spud sat up straighter in the saddle when he thought of it. The Clearys won't owe anybody a damn dime after they put wheels under these cattle. All the debts will be settled and the bank satisfied. Spud could, once again, look them all straight in the eye.

Well, almost all the debts. Spud glanced over at his brother, Pat, riding beside him on a Cleary gray that they'd been allowed to keep. Poor old Pat had a debt to settle. All the land had been sold, everything his grandfather and father had put together over so many years, was now in the hands of others. Except for the home place. Pat was able to keep twelve hundred acres. But it had a mortgage and he'd have to pay it off. Spud thought it made sense for Pat to be the one to try to save something. After all, he wasn't married, had no wife and kid to feed. But he did have Ma. That was a responsibility. Spud knew it would be hard for Pat to make the place pay off, growing grain, running cattle. He'd be farming with horses and the old equipment that hadn't been sold.

I could do it, if I had the chance, he told himself. But that's Pat's deal and I wish him well.

The only piece that came out clean was Uncle Tim's "little squat in Coyote" as the family referred to it. It was all Tim's, one hundred and sixty acres and the spring. But all the Cleary land around it would be sold off by the bank. Spud wondered what it would be like for Tim to cross somebody else's land to reach his place, to have neighbors. Cranky as he is, set in his ways, it's going to be tough, Spud thought. Then again Tim must have set something aside from his gold mining days. And he still earned a little bit by breaking a colt now and then. But he was getting too old for that. He never seemed to need money, though. Spud thought his Uncle Tim was a strange old codger.

Millie was the only one who seemed to really get along with him. They had some kind of a bond, Spud mused. She'd even insisted the baby be named after him. "Oh, Spud. The poor old man all alone up there in Coyote Canyon. Just think about how he must feel, thinks the world's against him. If we call the boy Timothy it will give him something to feel proud of."

"Millie, we've tried for years to bring Uncle Tim back into the human race. Dad did his best to stop him from sucking on the jug. We all did. No luck. But, if you think you can do it, go ahead. Timothy it is," Spud had said.

Spud and Pat, Buck and Seamus pushed the Cleary cattle into the stock corrals by the tracks in San Lucas. He turned his horse over to Pat. "Be nice if you can keep Skeeter around, too." Spud sadly gave the big horse a pat on the shoulder. "Maybe I can come out sometime and ride him, give you a hand with that big herd of yours." Spud tried to laugh, but it was hollow and his joke fell flat.

He hitched a ride on the train with the cattle as far as King City and then walked home from the depot. His mind was finally made up. He'd take that job. Had to. Of all the Clearys, Spud worried the most about the future and if it would be one he could live with. At least he wouldn't have to walk. Claude had said he'd have a company car.

CHAPTER THIRTY-NINE

"SARAH, SARAH!" FRED PRACTICALLY JUMPED UP the front steps despite his sixty-eight years, calling out to his wife, anxious to share some good news. She came out of the kitchen where she'd been preparing lunch. "What, Fred? What?"

"Cosgrove left town! Sold out and moved away! Can you believe it? I didn't even know a thing about it. Not a word around town beforehand."

"Well, that's interesting, but — "

Fred's face had turned the usual bright red with excitement. "Holy Jehoshaphat, Sarah! That's only the half of it. The new owner is a guy named Cyrus Maxwell, and he came into the office just now and laid copy on the counter for a half page, asked the rates and told me to save space for him every week. They have a bully new slogan for the store. 'We've got it, we'll get it, or it's not to be had.' Looks like this fellow's a live wire." Fred was out of breath and gratefully took the glass of cold water that Sarah handed him.

"Oh, Fred, that's wonderful news." Sarah hugged her husband. "That means Bissell has lost his main support. It'll make a big difference to us, won't it?"

"You bet it will! And now — " Fred stopped himself suddenly and Sarah could see the enthusiasm drain out of him. "Now that I've got that ad after all these years, I just hope to hell I can get a paper out." Fred slumped down into one of the kitchen chairs.

"Get a paper out? What do you mean?" Sarah put a bowl of soup and a ham sandwich in front of him and sat across from her husband. She began to spoon her own soup.

"A bearing in the Brower press is whining like it's about to give up and die," Fred explained. "Bobby says there isn't much he can do anymore and he told me today that he can't fix the melting pot on the Lino any more, either. I'll have to replace it."

Bob Godfrey had studied the Merganthaler Linotype, traced the electrical circuits in the typesetting machine's melting pot and taken it apart. "It was just last year he fixed it," Fred said. "Remember how he had asbestos all scattered out and parts all over the plant? I wondered if he'd ever get it back together. But, by God, he did. Said it was the throat heater. But now it's on the blink again, doesn't always heat up."

"Fred, eat your soup before it gets cold," Sarah said, but her husband ignored her, stared off into space and spoke as if he was thinking aloud. "I'd like to order a new pot and have it installed, but that'll run three hundred bucks. And that Babcock press I want will go two thousand. I don't even have enough cash for a down payment and they won't give me a dime on the old press." Fred sighed, picked up his sandwich and chewed a moment.

"Damn, Sarah, you got into a helluva mess, marrying me. I kept thinking this town would grow, that we'd have more advertisers, make enough money to put some aside. And then, when we did get a few more stores, that damn Bissell cut into them. We've been at this nearly forty years and what do we have to show for it? Some broken-down equipment and a lot of unpaid subscriptions."

Sarah listened sympathetically. But she was thinking, things couldn't be as bad as all that. Fred was usually an optimist, a man who saw possibilities in the impossible, sometimes a future in the impractical. But not today.

"And there's another thing," Fred was saying. "Millie stopped by the office yesterday. She's wondering if I have a job for her. She's a good writer and I sure could use her. I think they need the money. But how the hell am I going to pay her?"

He put down his half-eaten sandwich and pushed away from the table. Fred sighed. "Can't even afford to pay my own daughter what she's worth. Maybe I ought to just pack it in, sell out, if I can find a buyer."

Sarah was startled. She looked sharply at her husband, studied him a moment. He looked tired. She'd not noticed before just how worn and haggard he'd become. He suddenly looked every one of his sixty-eight years. He'd never seemed so low, so bleak and discouraged.

Sarah made a quick decision, one she'd never thought she'd make.

"Fred, buck up, for goodness sakes. Put a mortgage on the house. Buy the new press and fix the Linotype. With that new ad schedule you can pay off the mortgage in no time. Hire Millie and we'll have a better newspaper."

Fred stared in shock at his wife. "Sarah! You mean that?"

"Of course, I do."

Fred jumped up from the table, his eyes lit up again, his enthusiasm and confidence returning as swiftly as they had gone. "I'll talk to Wes McKinsey and Gene Rianda today. See which bank will make us the best deal." He grabbed his hat and was out the door in seconds, still putting on his coat, thinking, *That Sarah! I never in my wildest dreams thought she'd consider mortgaging the house. After all these years she's still full of surprises!*

Across town that same day. Bob Godfrey had also come to a difficult decision, but one he knew was necessary. The automobile business had never been so good. The new garage building was working out well and the repair work was booming. Since Ford had come out with its first style change since 1914, all the models were selling as fast as they could get them in from the factory. Bob could see the profits mounting and his share was up to twenty percent. And Bob Godfrey loved the work. But he also knew how badly his father needed him.

The old man was a great writer, a booster for the town, and nobody had more journalistic integrity than Fred Godfrey. But he was a damn lousy businessman. And he didn't know beans about keeping his equipment in shape.

And there was that drunken old coot Bissell who had no overhead and put out a crappy little sheet that he practically had to give away, but he took just enough business from *The Settler* to limit any chance of a decent profit. And every time

Dad goes on an editorial jag he loses a few more subscribers, Bobby thought. He needs help all right.

Bob sat across from Carrigan's old wooden desk. "Truth is, Joe, my dad is getting old and he really needs me. I just hate to give up this business, but I've got to help my father."

Joe Carrigan leaned back in his squeaky chair. "Well, Bob, I've seen it coming. No surprise to me. And I'm no spring chicken myself," Joe said. "I was figuring on turning it all over to you, but this changes things. I had an offer from Powell and Luckett to buy the agency. They wanted to include you in the deal, if I'd sell, but I turned it down. If you're sure about this, let me know. I can always get back to them."

Bob breathed a sigh of relief. Joe Carrigan had always been such a straight shooter. He'd talk it over with Barbara one more time. It meant losing his chance to own an auto agency, giving up his dream. But what else could he do? Bob shrugged, brushed the red hair out of his eyes, and smiled broadly. "Thanks, Joe. I'll let you know for sure in a day or so."

* * * * *

Matthew "Spud" Cleary was behind the wheel of the King City Mercantile's jitney, which had a small truckbed instead of a rumble seat so he could deliver spare parts on his rounds. He was driving down the Oasis road, wearing a coat and tie, a fedora instead of a cowboy hat, and his feet on the pedals were encased in shoes, not boots. Spud was dressing the part of a city salesman. No use pretending he was a rancher like some of the salesmen did, wearing their big hats, their feet crammed into boots that never stepped into a stirrup. How many times had he and Pat and Bucky poked fun at the city slickers all duded up in cowboy outfits getting in the way at the brandings? Damned if he was going to play that role.

Spud had just stopped to see Cleo Johnsen, a friend of many years, to leave off some parts. They'd talked crops and grain prices, mutual friends, the chance of spring rains, and the latest baseball scores. But Spud just couldn't get around to discussing Holt tractors. The way he figured it, Cleo knew he was a tractor salesman. If he needed a tractor, he'd mention it to Spud. When he didn't, Spud cranked up the little 1923 Ford roadster, and, as the motor roared to life, he jumped in and waved goodbye to Cleo.

That night Spud Cleary ate his supper in silence and then sat in his arm chair thumbing through Holt tractor brochures. He'd gone over the same damn one a dozen times. Timmy was asleep and Millie finished the dishes and hung up her apron. She entered the living room and sat across from Spud, determined to again try to make conversation. She knew Spud wasn't having any success selling tractors. He didn't say anything, but his paycheck remained the same each month, so there weren't any commissions.

"How did it go today, Spud?"

"Huh?" He looked up from the brochure with a frown.

"Who'd you see? Any prospects today?"

"Nope!"

"Well, there's always tomorrow," Millie said, giving Spud her brightest smile.

But he didn't answer. Ignoring Millie, he picked up the tractor brochure and flipped through the pages. Millie got up from her chair and stood watching him for a moment. *Spud is so quiet and serious all the time now,* she thought. *Everything used to be fun with Spud. He's not the same. He doesn't want to be around any of the ranchers or cowboys he knows. He won't make friends with the town folks. And he doesn't want to go out anywhere, not even to the picture show at the Reel Joy.*

Suddenly, he crumpled the brochure into a wad and threw it across the room. Millie was startled. "Spud, what's wrong?"

"Nothing! Leave me alone."

"But I'm worried about you. You work all day and come home late. You won't talk to me. You never seem to have any fun anymore."

"Life's not all fun, you know."

"Oh, Spud, of course not. I understand what you're going through," Millie said. She put her hand on his shoulder. "I know you miss the ranch. But you won't even go out horseback with your old friends when you have the chance."

Millie remembered a telephone conversation Spud had a week ago when he'd been invited to help the Eade brothers gather cattle. "Nope. Can't. Don't even have a horse." Then Spud listened for a moment and replied, "Thanks, but I don't even know where my saddle is. Besides, I'm a town dog now. Wouldn't know what I was doing." He listened again and then said, "Yeah. Well, thanks. See you around." He hung up the phone.

"Yeah, well damned if I'm gonna pretend I'm something that I'm not," Spud said, glaring at her. "I'm a tractor salesman. And a damn poor one, at that."

"But Spud, you said yourself that it takes time."

"Oh, hell, Millie." Spud sighed and looked up at her. "You know me. I couldn't sell a heater in Alaska. Just not cut out for it, I guess."

King City Mercantile had been very patient with Spud Cleary, but after nearly nine months with only three orders, Spud lost patience with himself. Claude Markham was sitting at his desk when Spud entered. "Got a minute, Claude?"

"Sure, Spud. What's on your mind?"

"My job here, Claude, that's what's on my mind. I'm doing a lousy job for you and I want to quit," Spud answered. "I can't sell a damn thing. Time for me to try something else where I can pull my weight."

"Well, I'll be damned!" Markham said, thinking Cleary was making it easy for him. He was just working up to a discussion with Spud, to tell him that he'd have to start bringing in some orders or the store couldn't carry him any longer. But he hated to do it. Markham knew Spud was a nice guy, that he made the calls, got around and saw everybody. But the word was out that Spud just couldn't close a deal. He seemed embarrassed trying to sell equipment to his friends.

"Tell you what, Spud. You hang in there for a couple of weeks more. We'll look for another outside salesman. What you planning to do?" he asked.

"Look for a job," Cleary answered. "Gotta eat."

"Try Standard Oil. I heard they need a driver. I'll sure give you a recommendation."

So Spud Cleary became the driver of the Zerolene truck, delivering oil to the ranches and service stations and sometimes he took out the Red Crown gas truck. Occasionally he worked in the station. The pay was all right, as much as he made trying to sell Holt equipment and at least he didn't have to embarrass himself. Millie even noticed that his attitude took a turn for the better. Except when she broached the idea of going to work as a reporter for her father. She needed something to do, something creative. She was feeling stifled in the little rented house—housework and Timmy didn't take all day. Beside, they certainly could use the money.

"Spud, we need a car. When you worked for the Mercantile at least we had a car," Millie argued. "And I don't want to live in a rented house all my life. We just barely get by on your pay. I can bring in enough to make a difference."

"No! Dammit! What would people think? That I can't support my family?" Spud was adamant. "Your place is here, taking care of Timmy."

"My mother will take Timmy in the mornings. I'll only be working part time, Spud," she explained. "I've got to do something. I'll go nuts cooped up here in this little house. We never go out. I don't know how long its been since we've even been to the ranch. Or visited Uncle Tim. Without a car, I'm stuck."

Millie stopped to catch her breath. She felt she was almost on the verge of hysteria. But she had to get through to Spud. "If we can't afford to go out, couldn't we have a party here? Invite some friends in? Have a dinner?"

"Yeah? Who?" Spud shot back. "I don't have any friends here. And damned if I want any of my old friends coming around here, feeling sorry for me. To hell with it!"

Millie brought up some of the old arguments, assuring him that they could make new friends and that his old friends weren't feeling sorry for him, that he had nothing to be ashamed of, that he should accept the invitations to borrow a horse and help gather cattle on Sundays, or go to the brandings when they were invited.

But Spud Cleary wasn't listening.

CHAPTER FORTY

THE OLD FLIVER RATTLED AND BANGED over the ruts as Spud started up the Coyote Canyon road. He and Millie and Timmy were bouncing along in the 1914 Model T Runabout, the one that Bob Godfrey had practically given to them before he officially left Carrigan's auto agency to take over as manager of his father's *Salinas Valley Settler*. "Sixty-five bucks is all she's worth," Bobby had insisted. "Pay ten dollars a month for seven months and that will cover the interest." Spud had been ready to turn the offer down. It sounded too much like charity, but the look on Millie's face changed his mind.

Bob had tuned her up so she ran pretty good, Spud thought, as he left the car idling while he opened the gap gate on the road and noted the sign, "No Trespassing. Keep Out. Violators will be Prosecuted to the Full Extent of the Law. Oscar Bauman Ranch." This was the third such gate he'd come to across the old road since he left Pine Valley. A bachelor named Bauman had purchased the Cleary land, built a little house just off the county road, and fenced the property with four-strands of barbed wire.

"I wonder how Uncle Tim likes going through all these barriers to get to his place?" Spud remarked with irritation as he climbed back into the fliver and dropped it into gear.

When they pulled up to Tim's homestead they found something else new. The yard was fenced off and there was another gate, a wooden one, and Tim, who'd heard the Ford coming for the last half hour, was there to open it. He greeted his nephew and Millie warmly and she was relieved that he seemed sober. But Millie knew you could never tell with Uncle Tim.

"Hello there, young feller," he called out to three-year-old Timmy, who climbed down from the car and ran to jump into his great uncle's arms. Tim swung the boy around and placed him back on his feet. "You've sure grown since the last time I saw you. Quite a boy there, Millie."

Spud handed Tim his mail, which he'd picked up in San Lucas. It wasn't much. A few back copies of *The Settler* and a couple of catalogs. Spud had been surprised to see that one envelope was a bank statement.

Millie brought out the picnic basket and Tim led the way into the house. She'd fried a chicken and put together a potato salad, which she placed on the table. Tim watched as she unfolded the cloth over the pie tin and shared a smile with her when the aroma of freshly-baked apple pie filled the room. Spud couldn't help but wonder at the miracle his wife had worked with Uncle Tim, just by naming the baby after him. In fact, the only time Spud had ever seen the old codger smile was when his namesake was around. They sat down at the small table and Millie began passing around plates of food.

"How you getting along with your new neighbor?" Spud asked his uncle.

Immediately Tim's face darkened and Spud wished he'd never asked the question. "Damn fool accused me of leaving one of his gates open," Tim said with a glare. "I've never left a gate open in my life. Anywhere. My dad always told us, 'Leave the gates as you find them.' He'd have skinned us if we'd found a gate shut and left it open."

"Yeah," Spud agreed.

"Bauman came up here in dove season and parked himself over there on the hill, just inside his fence, above the spring, and potted my doves as they came to water," Tim grumbled. "Climbed through my fence to pick 'em up. Got the wires all sagging. Had to tighten them up. I told him to stay the hell out of here. Oh, excuse me, Millie."

They tried to talk of other things, family, local events, deaths, marriages, but Tim didn't have much interest. Instead he started a game with Timmy, swinging his foot while the boy tried to ride it, squealing with laughter when he fell off. "Come on, Timmy, let's you and me go check the horses." Tim had a couple of horses in his little corral, colts he was putting in the bridle. He took the boy by the hand and off they went down the hill, Timmy's short, little legs running and skipping to keep up with Uncle Tim's long strides. Millie cleaned up the dishes and carefully put everything back exactly as Tim kept it.

On the ride home, Millie asked, "Doesn't he ever go to town?"

"Oh, sure," Spud replied. "He rides horseback into San Lucas for his mail and what groceries he can haul in his saddlebags. He used to drive a little buggy, but that fell apart long ago. Besides his buggy horse is dead. He rides over the hill to the ranch now and then, goes into San Lucas from there."

"He was looking over our car, Spud. Acted like he was thinking of buying one," Millie observed.

Spud glanced over at his wife in surprise. "Oh, my God. He doesn't even know how to drive! Wouldn't that be something? Tim, with his belly full of rot gut, wheeling a car down this road and trying to get through these gates. If there's hard feelings with his neighbor now, wait'll he knocks out a few of Bauman's fences."

When Spud and Millie and their little boy left, Tim sat on his stoop for a while, until the Ford was out of sight down the canyon. Then he sighed and went inside his cabin. He brought out a tin coffee cup and filled it from a Mason jar of jackass whiskey from Alvarado's. He set the cup on his bedside apple crate and opened the little tin box resting there. Carefully he took out the old letters, read them again as he'd done so many times, and unfolded the newspaper clipping to look at the faded photograph of the beautiful girl. Tim re-folded the papers and put them back in the box. He picked up his cup and took a long swallow. He carried the cup back to the table and lifted his thirty-thirty rifle from its rack on the wall. Tim got out his oil can and a rag and, between sips, carefully cleaned the rifle and hung it back on the wall. Out of meat, he thought, better take a gander around tomorrow morning, find a deer. When the cup was empty he refilled it from the Mason jar.

He took the mail Spud had brought him and glanced through the copies of *The Settler*. Then, almost as an afterthought, he picked up the envelope from the Monterey County Bank. Tim carefully slit it open with his pocket knife, took out the statement, and held it to the light of his single window. It showed a balance of $13,876.47. Amazing what a few thousand dollars will grow into if you leave them alone for twenty years. He nodded his head, remembering when he started this account with the few nuggets he had left in his money belt after the San Francisco earthquake. Tim hadn't spent much through the years, a few jugs of booze now and then to ease the pain of memory, coffee, tobacco, some canned goods, new pair of boots when the old ones wore out, or some Levis. He made a few bucks now and then breaking colts. His vegetable garden and some venison got him by.

But his joints ached more all the time and it was harder to get around. He thought that horseback ride over the hill and down to San Lucas seemed to get longer and longer. It was even further into San Ardo. And he hated riding past the old Barnes place, that fancy Victorian house now standing vacant and boarded up, all the buildings rotting away, the fences sagging and fields gone to grass. Some big shot San Francisco lawyer managed it, they said. Wouldn't even rent it out. Damn shame. At least that yellow-headed girl was gone! But Alvarado's jackass booze was the best, worth the trip. Damn prohibition!

Tim lifted his tin cup, took a swallow, and leaned back in his chair. Yep, he decided. He'd buy a car. There'll still be plenty of money left in the bank for Timmy.

CHAPTER FORTY-ONE

B OB GODFREY LOOSENED HIS TIE. He didn't care much for the damn things, hadn't needed one when he was sliding around under cars. Anyhow he was sitting at the kitchen table at his folks house, so he could relax. He'd come over for lunch to treat himself to his mother's lamb stew, and talk some business with his mother and father. It had only been six months since he'd become manager of *The Settler*, but he could see he had to do something. And soon. Or the paper would be in big trouble.

Fred had put up his home for collateral and bought the new Babcock press, fixed the Linotype and added some new type fonts without the hairlines, which had dirtied the printed pages so badly readers had been complaining. The half page ad each week from H-A-F Company improved *The Settler's* financial picture, but it wasn't enough. If Bob was going to take out a decent salary for himself, pay the mortgage, make the payroll, meet the monthly bills, and have anything left for his parents, *The Settler* simply had to get rid of the competition. The town just wasn't big enough for two newspapers. That's what Bob Godfrey had come to talk to Fred and Sarah about.

"Good stew, Mom," he said as Sarah started to rise from the table. "Let the dishes wait a minute. I've got an idea that needs some thought."

"What's that, Bobby?" Fred was tamping his pipe, getting ready to light up, but he put it down and settled his elbows on the table. Sarah gave her attention to her son.

"Plain and simple, we can't go on the way things are. The business is all right for the moment, but we're going to go further in the hole as time goes on. Pretty soon we won't be able to pay the mortgage"—Sarah's eyes widened in alarm— "unless we increase advertising and job work." Bob looked directly at each of his parents, emphasizing his concern.

"It can't be that bad, can it, Son?" Fred asked, noticing Sarah's concern.

"Yep, Pop, it is. We need at least an average of another three hundred a month to cover everything." Bob said it flatly, matter of factly, and let that figure hang there in the air.

"Holy Jehoshaphat!" Fred exclaimed. He hated hearing this news. "I've put my whole life into this paper and now you're telling me we can't make it?"

"Gotta face facts, Pop."

Fred's face began turning crimson and he started to sputter, but Sarah reached over and laid her hand on his arm. He looked at her and quieted down. They both looked at their son. "You said you had an idea, Bobby. What is it?" Sarah asked.

Bob brushed back the rebellious, red hair from his eyes and grinned. "Yeah, I've got an idea. Been thinking about this for quite a while." His parents eyes were riveted on him. Bob took a deep breath and exhaled.

"We're gonna buy out *The Banner*."

Fred and Sarah stared at their son in shock, which is exactly what Bobby expected them to do. "How the hell are we going to do that?" Fred asked. "You just told us we don't have any money."

"We've got fifty bucks."

"Fifty dollars? What good will that do?" wondered Sarah.

Bob grinned. He explained his plan. His parents chuckled. "Holy Jehoshaphat, Bobby!" Fred exclaimed. "If you can pull that off, I'll be a monkey's uncle!"

The next day Bob Godfrey was seen in the offices of each of the town's three real estate agents, and he was spotted visiting with Austin Hayes, the builder, and then with Bill Smart at Tynan Lumber. Two days later he paid out fifty dollars for an option on a vacant lot on Third Street that measured 50x150 feet.

"Yep," he told Thad Jenkins when he took the option on the lot, "We need more space. I don't know how my dad got along all these years without it. Business is so good, and we've so

307

many new contracts coming in, I'm going to have to expand. Buy more equipment and —" Bob stopped talking and looked around as if to make sure he wasn't being overheard. "Keep this under your hat for a while, Thad. I don't want *The Banner* getting wind of it."

That afternoon as Bob was under the face towel at Hot Shot Frazier's barber shop, Burt Jackson and Clem Manzoni came in. Not knowing who was under the towel, the two men continued the conversation they'd been having on the street. Jackson said, "The way I heard it from Thad Jenkins, *The Settler* has to expand, can't handle the business they're getting without more room."

"Guess that new press, and the other stuff old Fred just got, is paying off," Manzoni agreed. "Bob being in there makes a lot of difference, too."

"What're they gonna do?" a customer asked as he overheard the two men.

"Build a new building on Third Street," Jackson replied.

"Wow, they must be making money," the man said with a low whistle.

"Wonder what Bissell is gonna do?" Hot Shot asked.

"Probably have another drink," Manzoni said with a laugh. The others joined him and Bob Godfrey had to smile under his hot towel. The word was getting around. He knew he could count on Jenkins to spread it.

Two days later the phone rang in the newspaper office and Bob picked it up. *"Settler,"* he said. "Yeah. This is Bob Godfrey. Oh, hello, Mister Bissell. How are you today? — That's good...I'm just fine... What can I do for you?" Bob listened for a moment and then said, "Sure, come on over."

As he hung up the phone Bob heaved a big sigh of relief and spun around in the swivel chair. He grinned his happy, crooked grin, lit up a cigar, and sat back in his chair in anticipation.

Horace Bissell wasted no time in making his appearance at *The Settler* front door. Bob Godfrey pulled up a chair to his desk and invited the rival editor to sit down. "Well, well,"

Bissell began, smiling and rubbing his hands together. "What a pleasure this is, this opportunity to visit with you. Why I remember when you were just a tad over there at the auto garage. I'd watch you from my place across the street. What an industrious lad, I'd think. And here you are, doing such a wonderful job managing this nice little newspaper for your father. Please accept my congratulations, young man."

"Thank you, Mister Bissell."

"And how is that fine gentleman, your father, and your mother, that wonderful lady?"

"Just fine, Mister Bissell. Just fine," Bob replied, wondering when the old goat, "the unctuous bastard" as his father called him, was going to get down to business.

"And where is your father today?" Bissell asked and peered into the back shop.

"Oh, he's taking a few days off. Mother and Dad are planning an extensive trip." Bobby decided to lay it on thick. "Maybe a cruise on the President Jackson to Hawaii, now that they have the money."

Bissell's eyebrows arched. "Well, well, wonderful, wonderful. Hmmm — ah — you know, Robert, it's quite a coincidence, I've been thinking of something like that for myself. But it's so difficult to get the time off. Should relax more, take it easier. Know what I mean?"

Yeah, he knew what Bissell meant, the old reprobate, but he played along. "You really been thinking of that, Mister Bissell?"

"Certainly have, my boy, certainly have. I've been thinking for some time that I might accept one of the offers I've received for *The Banner*. Sell out, you know. Retire. Enjoy life!"

"That would be nice," Bob agreed, nodding, smiling, taking another puff on his cigar and examining the ash.

"But I'd never sell to a stranger," Bissell said, "not to some out of town interest. Of course, I'd offer it to you folks first. Common courtesy. Yes sir, common courtesy."

"That's very nice of you, Mister Bissell." Bob smiled and waited.

"Not that I have any intention of selling out just right now, of course. But if I ever did, I wondered if you folks would be interested." Bissell looked over at Bob, his eyebrows raised. "Hmmm?"

Bob's smile was replaced with a serious, studied look. "Oh, I don't know about that," he replied. "I'd have to ask my mother and father. Be up to them. I wouldn't want to commit them. Quite frankly, Mister Bissell, they might feel that they don't need your paper. You see, *The Settler* is doing so well right now, more advertising and job work than we can handle."

"Ah, yes." Bissell thought a minute and then his curiosity got the better of him. "Heard you might be putting up a new building over on Third Street?"

Bob pretended to be surprised. He removed his cigar from his mouth, looked at it for a moment and then back to Bissell. "Well, yes, that's true, Mister Bissell. But we'd prefer you treat that information with professional courtesy. Don't want it to get out until we're ready to announce it in our own paper. Hope you understand?"

"Of course, of course. Wouldn't dream of scooping you on your own story. But you will discuss this with your parents, find out if there is any interest in acquiring *The Banner*?" Bissell laughed. "Wouldn't mind one of those cruises myself, you know." Bissell rose from the chair. "Well, I won't keep you. I know how busy you are." As he headed for the door, he said, "I'm looking forward to hearing from you."

When the door shut behind *The Banner* editor, Bob chuckled and reached for the phone. "One-Oh-Three, he told central. "Hello, Pop. He took the bait. Yeah, he was just over here. Wants to know if he should ever decide to sell out if you would be interested. Yeah — very curious about our plans for a new building. Sure, see you this evening."

Bob waited two more days before contacting Horace Bissell. This time he made an appointment and went to *The Banner* office. Bob Godfrey was appalled at the chaos in the place. Paper scattered all over the floor, stacked on every work space, blankets in a corner, pied type spilled, ink running over the edges of opened cans, locked-up forms askew in the racks, metal from last week's paper heaped in a jumble on the composing stone, remnants of Bissell's most recent meal on the floor by his desk, and a half-filled Mason jar next to the Smith and Son's typewriter.

A smiling Bissell greeted him with a floor-sweeping bow. He is an unctuous bastard, Bob thought. "Come in, my boy, come in. You're most welcome, most welcome." With a flourish, Bissell showed Bob to a seat, which he first had to clear of a stack of old *Banners*. How this man ever managed to get out a newspaper was a mystery to Bob Godfrey, and for a moment he thought he should just let time take care of Bissell and his *Banner*. But then he reminded himself that Bissell was taking just enough business away from *The Settler* to make a difference and that he had come here to make a deal.

Bob settled himself in the dirty chair and spoke quickly and firmly. "I've talked it over with my parents and they agreed to take the newspaper off your hands, provided the deal is completed right away, so it won't interfere with their cruise plans."

Bissell smiled, a sly glint in his eye. "Fine, fine. Wonderful! Now my requirements are modest. Only twenty thousand will take it." Bissell stood up and leaned forward with his hand outstretched, but Bob didn't shake it.

"Nope, Mister Bissell," Bob shook his head and said with a frown, "Here's our offer, our only one. My folks are in a hurry. Take it or leave it. Ninety bucks a month for the rest of your life. That's it."

Bissell sat down, suddenly. All the air rushed out of him like a deflated balloon. He sat there, quietly, thinking. Bob Godfrey stood up, waiting. Bissell must be more than sixty years old, he figured, and the way he drank and abused himself, the old reprobate probably didn't have five years left in him. If he lasted ten years that would be only ten thousand, eight hundred dollars, more than a fair price for this pile of junk. And *The Settler* could make the ninety dollar a month payment. Would the old goat take it?

Bissell hemmed and hawed a bit, cleared his throat and scribbled numbers on a piece of soiled copy paper. Bob Godfrey just stood there, silent. Finally Bissell reached out his hand again and this time Bob shook it. The next morning Godfrey and Bissell drew up the papers at the Monterey County Bank, and Wes McKinsey witnessed them and had them notarized.

Without the competition nit picking away, *The Settler's* books almost immediately showed dramatic improvement, Bob Godfrey was satisfied. He had another lamb stew lunch at his parent's house and remarked, "Now I guess, in all fairness to the community, we'd better go ahead with the building. What the hell, we can use the space." Then he laughed. "But you'd better cancel that cruise to Hawaii."

Fred and Sarah chuckled over that, but Sarah sighed. "Ah, but it did sound wonderful."

Bobby continued explaining his new plans. "I'll sell most of Bissell's junk off the floor over there, no sense in moving it. But we can use that Model Eight Linotype. And there's a pedal-operated stapler, and his C&P press, maybe some other things." Fred nodded approvingly.

As soon as the new building on Third Street was ready, Bob rented a Mac truck with a flat bed, and cleared out *The Banner* shop. It took several trips to haul that equipment along with the Godfreys' own presses and Linotype to Third Street. Timmy Cleary rode in the truck, standing up in the back with his Uncle Bob, proudly waving to his friends, as they made the trips up and down Broadway.

Fred Godfrey was a happy man. The only thing he didn't like was the new name for the paper, *The Settler-Banner*. It just didn't sound right.

CHAPTER FORTY-TWO

MILLIE AND TIMMY HAD JUST RETURNED from Sunday Mass. Spud didn't go with them. He rarely did anymore, saying Sunday was his one day of rest and that the Lord would understand. "If He put in the hours I do, he wouldn't go to church either," Spud announced. Millie wished he wouldn't talk like that, even kidding, especially in front of Timmy. Back when they had lived on the ranch and it was so much more difficult to get to church, Spud would take Millie to Mass every chance he had.

Now what he did on Sunday was sit in his easy chair, read the papers, and then in the afternoon they'd drive out to Long Valley to see his mother, have Sunday dinner with the rest of the Cleary family. Honora did wonders on her huge iron, wood-burning stove, serving up grand dinners, just as she had in her kitchen on the Trescony when Will Cleary was alive, and she wouldn't let Kitty or Millie do much to help. Timmy loved going to the ranch. His grandmother fussed over him, and sometimes Uncle Pat put him up on a horse and led him around and Uncle Seamus would shoot marbles with him. But Millie wondered if it had to be every Sunday. She longed for some variety in her week ends. She asked Spud if they could do something different just once. Maybe go to a picture show at the Reel Joy or drive to Monterey to see the ocean. Spud invariably talked her out of such ideas and, with a sigh of resignation, Millie got herself and Timmy ready to go to the ranch.

Spud was reading *The Settler-Banner*. She had to be sure to save it for him each week, because he was usually too tired to look at it on week nights. And Spud read it cover-to-cover, particularly the personal items about the San Ardo and San Lucas people he knew. But he never wanted any news of himself, or his own family, to appear in the paper. The few times Millie had put items in her column, *Talk of the Countryside*, about any of the Clearys, she'd been told that they didn't approve of "our names being in the paper. What we do is our business." Spud had just muttered and grumped about it, but Honora Cleary had been adamant when she told Millie, nicely but firmly, "our name is not to be in the newspapers." But they sure did like to read about other people, Millie noted.

People liked her column of briefs. They called items in to the office and to her at home. Sometimes they dropped off news notes. A few times people had given written items to Spud to deliver to her. He hadn't liked it. She could tell he was embarrassed by it. But he did it.

Strange family she'd married into, Millie thought. When Will Cleary was alive their names and events were in the paper all the time because he was county supervisor and such a public person. And if her father, in one of his editorials, criticized the board or Supervisor Cleary in an editorial, the two men would go have a beer and talk it out.

Millie glanced at Spud where he was still reading and noticed his face tighten. His jaw set and a frown grew. She saw he was looking at her column on child raising. He never did approve of her column. He agreed with his mother, who once had said to Millie, "There are those who might resent it, dear, you telling people how to raise children, and you having only one of your own."

"But Mother Cleary," Millie protested, "that's all just information that I learned in courses on child development at teacher's college."

"Well, Millie, there are those who believe that practical experience is more important than what you might obtain from a book," Honora said. Millie bit her tongue and said nothing more.

But what was bothering Spud just now? Millie wondered. He'd flung the paper on the floor. She decided to take it head on. "What's the matter, Spud?"

"Nothing!"

"Come on, Spud. Out with it! I know something's wrong. Was it what I wrote?"

"What difference does it make? You never pay attention to anything I say, anyhow."

"That's not fair," she protested.

"Well, it sure seems that way to me. Look here." He leaned over, and picked up the paper, and turned to her column. "Just listen! Listen to this."

Spud read aloud, *I don't know much about Petey except that he is an only child, about five years old, and that his mother is dismayed because he refuses to sleep unless the light is left on.* Spud tossed the paper down again. "There. How do you think I feel having everyone in the countryside think my kid is afraid of the dark?"

"That isn't our kid. I didn't use his name. That's just an example," Millie claimed. ·

"Well, everyone is going to think it's about Timmy," Spud insisted. "You write about him all the time."

Millie was silent for a moment. She had to admit Spud had a point, although she hadn't thought of it that way. She had put Timmy's cute antics and sayings in her column from time to time. People enjoyed that. Their comments were always complimentary. "My Jimmy is exactly like that, Millie. You hit the nail on the head." And people called into the office with problems and questions for her to answer in the column.

"Well, I'm sorry, Spud. I didn't mean it to sound like Timmy. But what difference does it make? Lots of children are afraid of the dark. They get over it. Timmy did!"

Spud didn't answer. He just walked by her and went out the back door. She heard the screen door slam. Millie knew he was going to check on his project in the garage. Spud had been just like the other veterans about Prohibition. They were all angry, believing the temperance advocates had taken advantage of the boys still being in France when they turned the country dry. Spud didn't drink much. Millie was grateful for that.

315

But Spud was mad. It was a matter of principle, he said. By God, if he wanted to have a drink after a long day's work, he should be able to. He wasn't interested in joining the boys in the back of some soda fountain, where the liquor flowed as heavily as it had out front before Prohibition. Nor did he frequent the blind pigs and speakeasies in the city, not that he and Millie ever got to the city.

Spud just bought himself a five-gallon crock and filled it with near beer, Pabst Doppel Brau from Milwaukee. To this wort, he added a package of yeast and let the fermentation process take its course. Spud dipped a cup into his crock of home brew and tasted. Stuff wasn't half bad. Damn near ready. But it was a pain having to do this. The whole damn Volsted Act was a travesty, he thought. He hoped that New York Governor, Al Smith, would get elected president in 1924 and do something about it.

Spud was going to vote for Al Smith, but he didn't hold out much hope for him against Herbert Hoover. Al Smith was a Catholic and folks just didn't vote for Catholics. Millie said she was going to vote for Hoover because *The Settler-Banner* was for Hoover. But she felt a little guilty not voting for the Catholic. She looked for a convincing argument to override her father's editorials.

"Spud," she had asked him, "why are you voting for Al Smith?"

"Because he's a Democrat."

"Why are you a Democrat?"

"The Clearys have always been Democrats," Spud had explained with finality.

Millie went out to the garage, anxious to patch up this latest rift. "How's your beer doing?"

"Okay, I guess," he responded. Spud was willing to let it go for now. "Should be ready to drink by tomorrow night. Time to leave?"

The visit to the ranch went well. At least, for Timmy, it went well. As soon as the car stopped Timmy jumped out and ran straight for the equipment shed. He was enthralled by the plows and discs, the seeder and hayrake. Millie strolled after him to keep an eye on him, keep him from getting hurt, if she could, while he climbed up on the old stationary harvester stored there, the one his grandfather and his great grandfather had used, which had been too obsolete to sell at the auction when the Clearys lost everything. His next stop was the hayrake parked beside the shed, and Timmy sat in the seat, and gave orders to his pretend team of horses just as he'd heard Uncle Pat do when he'd ridden on the seeder box and picked up the terminology. "Ho there, Dolly — Get up, Dandy — " Timmy gave his imaginary reins a shake and called, "Move out there, Tigertooth, you miserable old son-of-a-bitch."

"Timothy Cleary." Millie spoke sharply. "You mustn't use such language."

"Uncle Pat does. He knows how to talk to horses." Timmy slipped off the hayrake seat and dashed up to the corral to pester his Uncle Pat to let him ride a horse.

Millie choked back her laugh and watched her son until he was safely in the custody of Pat, who lifted up his nephew and placed him astride Dandy, the huge, old, gentle, white work horse. Dandy stood in the shade of the pepper tree hanging out over the corral fence. Timmy's legs were so short, and Dandy's back so wide, that no matter how much the boy kicked his feet, Dandy could ignore them. Timmy cried, "Giddyup, giddyup." But Dandy didn't move. Pat, Spud and Buck leaned on the fence, talking, but all three were as impervious to Timmy's entreaties as Dandy was. Even after the sun invaded Dandy's shade, he wouldn't move. Pretty soon Timmy had enough hot sun and unmovable horse, and begged to be taken off.

He went in search of Uncle Seamus, who was always ready to share his sack of marbles. Soon old Seamus was down on his knees, despite his arthritis, showing Timmy the difference between a shooter and a lager. Although it hurt him, Seamus could always be counted on to play a game with Timmy.

They were all ready when the call came for dinner. Fried chicken, mashed potatoes, coleslaw and lemonade, in abundance, followed by what Spud called "Ma's apple pie," a certain perfection that Millie could never achieve. She helped Kitty and Honora with the dishes while the men went outside to walk around the corrals talking man talk, Timmy trailing along.

In the kitchen, as the women cleaned up, conversation was general until Honora said, "My boys were never afraid of the dark. Were Bucky or Julie?" She directed her gaze at Kitty, but Millic knew the question was for her benefit.

"No. I don't remember them ever being afraid," Kitty answered.

"Well, if any of them had been, I'd have just let them cry," Mother Cleary declared. "They'd get tired of that soon enough."

Millie refused to rise to the bait. But it stuck with her and she was a bit sulky on the ride back to town. She could have explained all the child development theories about building confidence in the youngster so he wouldn't be afraid, about how letting them cry was the worst thing you could do, about the things her professor had taught about child psychology. But she knew her views would be scorned. How can they be so nice and seem to love me, she wondered, but never give me credit for knowing anything?

CHAPTER FORTY-THREE

Tim Cleary slowly came awake to find himself sprawled across his big bed, his shirt draped over the ornate headboard, which was so incongruous in the little redwood shack. Tim rose, stretched, and reached for his shirt. Must have been hot. Took it off. When? Last night? Yesterday? Didn't matter. Sometimes the nights and days were all the same. He looked out the window and figured it to be about nine in the morning. He wondered when he'd eaten last.

But that reminded him. He'd better feed that colt. Tim stumbled outside, rubbing his eyes, walked to the privy and relieved himself. Then he forked some hay to the colt and checked the water. He noticed the horse tracks by the spring, and saw where they headed off up the trail toward Long Valley. Kitty and Millie had probably ridden over to see him. And he was in no shape to visit. He walked back to his cabin, sadly shaking his head, sorry to have missed them. Better eat.

Tim got the fire going in the wood stove, cut some bacon, checked to see if the beans were still good, and put some in the same pan with the bacon. He threw a handful of coffee into the pot and finished cooking while it boiled up. Tim poured a little cold water into the coffee pot, waited a minute for the grounds to settle, and poured a cupful. He took his time eating, looking around the cabin. Place needed a cleaning.

Tim built up the stove fire to boil water and began washing clothes. He hung them on a line behind his shack. Then he cut a new supply of firewood from some pine logs he'd hauled in and realized he'd developed a new thirst. But his Mason jars were all empty. That meant a trip to San Ardo.

It was mid-afternoon by the time Tim was cranking up the old Dodge Brothers coupe he'd bought. Tim had seen it in front of Bunte's Store in San Lucas with a "For Sale" sign on the cracked windshield. What the hell, he thought, save him a trip to King City. One car's as good as the next. When the owner showed up Tim made a deal. He paid a hundred fifty dollars for the car, one driving lesson and a five-gallon can of gas. Tim received a signed pink slip and the advice to get a driver's license. He drove the car with instructions from the previous owner, mashing the gears and lurching around San Lucas for half an hour. Then he started slowly down the highway toward the Pine Valley road, his wary, nervous saddle horse tied behind the vehicle. Somehow he'd made it home, much to the relief of the trailing horse, and parked the car. He hadn't driven it since.

Now it was working fine and by the time he drove onto the Pine Valley road, after stopping to open and close all those damn gates Bauman had put up, Tim had the hang of it. He wheeled onto the highway and headed for San Ardo at a heady thirty miles an hour. Tim managed to stop the car in front of Alvarado's.

The old man saw him coming and, without a word, went to the shed behind the store, lifted up the floor boards and brought out a dozen Mason jars, each filled with bootleg whiskey distilled somewhere in Lockwood. Nobody professed to know just where, nor how it arrived under the floorboards behind Alvarado's. But it was, to Tim's taste, the best jackass made in south county. He pulled over as soon as he turned onto the Pine Valley road and sampled the batch. Tim did that several more times, and it was beginning to get dark, before he reached the first fence on Bauman's property.

Bauman's land! That stuck in Tim Cleary's craw. This was Cleary land, God dammit. He couldn't get used to anyone else owning it. And all those cows should be packing Cleary's quarter circle triangle, not that stupid Box B brand. Tim opened the gate, drove through and got out to close it. And had another drink. Suddenly, unexpectedly, the damn Dodge died and no matter how hard he tried, he couldn't get it started. Had to crank it again. Finally, he put it into gear and lurched forward. Some damn cows on the road. Tim hit the horn and laughed when they scattered. Not Cleary cows. To hell with them!

Tim's wheels made new tracks up the canyon. He stopped for another gate and aimed his car through the center of it. He closed the gate and had another drink. There was one more gate up ahead. Tim took another swallow to fortify himself for the ordeal.

It was getting dark. Where the hell are the lights on this thing? Tim couldn't find them and muttered to himself, "Hell with 'em." The gate suddenly loomed ahead and Tim stomped on the brake. The car slid to a stop, and Tim fell forward, hitting his head on the windshield. He sat there staring at the gate and rubbing the lump that was growing on his forehead. Shouldn't be all these gates. This should be Cleary land, open range through here. Tim got out and tried to open the gate. This was a tight one. He had to put his arm around it and pull it to him to get it loose enough to slip the wire catch over the top of the post. When it finally gave, he nearly fell into it. Tim pulled the gap aside, got back into the car and reached for the Mason jar. He had to open a new one.

Tim carefully lined up the car in the center of the gate and slowly let out the clutch. But his foot slipped off the pedal. The car jumped forward. It hit the gate post a glancing blow, pushed it aside, and plunged into the stubble field. Tim spent the better part of an hour, in the dark, trying to straighten the post and close the gate. He finally did. Or thought he did. He'd come back in the morning and fix the damn thing right. The hell with it for now.

But Tim Cleary was still asleep in the morning when a loud voice woke him. There was a pounding on the door and somebody shouting, "Cleary! Cleary! God dammit! Wake up in there!"

Bleary-eyed, Tim stumbled from his bed, still fully clothed. He opened the door to face an angry Oscar Bauman, shaking his fist. "You wrecked my fence, you drunken sot! Knocked down my gate, by God! My cattle are all mixed up. What are you going to do about it?" Bauman fairly shook with rage.

321

Tim blinked. He tried to think. Gate? Then it came to him. Yes, he had driven into this man's gate. He planned to fix it first thing in the morning. Now he realized he'd overslept. Bauman was right. "Sorry," Tim said. There was sincerity in his voice. "My responsibility. I aim to go down there right now and fix it."

"You fix it?" Bauman laughed at him. "You're in no shape to fix anything, old man. I'll fix it myself. You just stay to hell off my land. Your right-of-way is revoked."

"You can't do that," Tim protested. "Clearys always had a right to that road. That's our road."

"Maybe it was your road, but by God, it's my road now. And you stay off of it." Bauman turned on his heel, strode to his car, jumped in and backed it around. He headed out in a cloud of dust as Tim stood on the stoop, looking after him.

Well, Cleary, Tim thought, you did it that time. Can't blame Bauman for being sore. But stop him from using the road? No way! He would have fixed his damn gate, fixed it good as new, if he'd given him a chance, the miserable sonofabitch. Now what was he gonna do?

Tim solved that one by reaching for the Mason jar.

* * * * *

Millie pulled off the Pine Valley road at Oscar Bauman's property and stepped out of the old jitney to open the gate. It was a pleasant afternoon and she had brought Timmy to visit his Uncle Tim. Millie was fighting the tight gate when a loud voice startled her. "You there — where do you think you're going?"

She looked toward the house and saw the man standing in the yard. He started walking quickly as Millie called out, "I'm Missus Matthew Cleary. My son and I are on our way up to visit Tim Cleary."

"Not over my land, you're not! Can't you read?" he said, pointing to the sign. "It says no trespassing, lady. That means you."

"But we've always used this road. I understood Tim Cleary has a right-of-way across here."

"Well, you're wrong, lady. He doesn't use this road anymore. And neither does anybody else," the man yelled. Millie just stood there, in the middle of the road, her hand on the gate. She didn't know what to do. The man approached the car. "My name's Oscar Bauman. I own this place."

"Yes, I know you do, Mister Bauman," Millie said as politely as she could, wondering how she was going to placate him. "But I didn't know that we'd been forbidden to go through here. I'm sorry if I upset you."

Bauman paused for a moment, studied the harmless woman and her little boy, then, somewhat reluctantly, reached over and opened the gate. "You can go through this time, Missus Cleary. But no more." He spoke quietly, but then his voice slowly rose to a shout, "Tell that old drunken uncle of yours he'll have to build a road in the other way. Nobody crosses my land after today. That's final!"

Millie was fuming inside, but she gathered up what dignity she could muster and stepped up into the Ford. "Thank you very much, Mister Bauman, for your so very kind courtesy." She put as much sarcasm in her voice as she dared and slipped the car into gear and slowly drove through the gate.

"What's the matter with that man, Mama?" five-year-old Timmy asked. "Why's he mad at us?"

"I'm not sure, Timmy, but I think he had a run-in with your uncle. We'll find out when we get to his place."

"He's not very polite, is he, Mama? I don't like him," Timmy said.

"Well, I'm not too fond of him, either." She felt sorry for Tim having to deal with the nasty new owner of the Cleary land. Millie made it through two more gates and was getting out to open the wooden one in front of Tim's place when she saw him emerge from the house.

"Hello, there — ! Good to see you," he greeted them. Millie was relieved—he seemed sober, as sober as he ever was. Most of the time, with Uncle Tim, it was hard to tell. Millie had brought a picnic basket and the three of them were eating the delicious cold chicken and slices of ham with potato salad when Tim suddenly stopped eating and said, "I've been cross-ways with that damn Bauman ever since he bought the place. Can't please him. Not my fault. He thinks he can keep me off his road, but I've got a legal right."

"Do you really, Uncle Tim?"

Tim nodded emphatically. "Sure do, Millie. Used to be Cleary land, all of it. And that was our road. Just because he bought the place doesn't take away our right to use the road. He bought it with my right-of-way in place. Bank saw to it when they first sold it. And I'm gonna drive on it any time I feel like it!"

"Now Tim, don't make any trouble," Millie pleaded. "I don't want any harm to come to you."

Tim had taken another bite out of his chicken leg and chewed as he spoke. "Won't be me that harm comes to," he muttered and swallowed. "Damn him! He comes up here sneaking onto my place to hunt deer, too. I caught him at it. That canyon up there," Tim gestured with the chicken leg in the direction of a deep gulch behind him. "Some old bucks hide out in there. They go down into Bauman's grain field so he thinks he has a right to them because he feeds them. But they water and live on my place. I ran him off."

Timmy interrupted his mother and uncle with an impatient plea to go horseback riding.

"All right, Timmy. Let's see if old Beauford wants to take you for a little ride," Tim said. They'd finished lunch and Millie was putting away the leftovers. As usual, she left them in the cabin so that Tim would have another meal or two. They walked over to the corral and Millie asked, "Are all your horses named Beauford? Seems I had my first horseback ride ever on a horse of yours named Beauford. And that was a long time ago."

"Oh, I guess so, Millie. I just don't bother to name each one so I call them all Beauford. Doesn't seem to matter to them." Tim put his saddle on the old gelding and lifted Timmy up. He led the horse around the yard until they all finally got tired, including Beauford. Timmy got off by himself, slipping down the leathers, hanging onto a saddle string, then to the stirrup and dropping to the ground. When Tim had put up the horse, Timmy was ready for another one of the rituals that accompanied a visit to Uncle Tim.

"Tell us about hunting for gold in the Yukon," Timmy said brightly. He loved the stories about the sled dogs and the snow, the frozen rivers and the midnight sun.

"Do better than that, Timmy. I'll show you how we found gold."

"You will? Wow! How you gonna do that here?"

"I can find gold anywhere. It's easy if you know how. Wait right here." Tim walked to the house and disappeared. He came out with a big, wide pan. "See, you do it like this." Millie and her wide-eyed son watched as Tim squatted down and put some dirt with little rocks into the pan. Then he added some water from the trough by the spring and swished the pan around. Timmy was fascinated.

"Look! See there." Tim held the pan so the boy could see inside. There in the middle was a speck of gold, a tiny nugget. "There's your gold, Timmy." He picked up the nugget and placed it in Timmy's palm. "You keep it. Now you try it. See if you can find another one."

Timmy handed his nugget to his mother. Then he put dirt and rocks into the pan, and Tim helped him add water. He clumsily made the same circular motion with the pan as his uncle had and slopped the water out. There in the bottom of the pan was another little nugget. Timmy let out a shrill squeal and proudly showed his mother. "See, Mama. See! I found gold!"

Millie grinned. "How about that? You're a lucky miner. Take those home and show your daddy how you struck gold in Coyote Canyon."

That night when Spud finally got home, Timmy climbed up into his father's lap and showed him the two tiny specks of gold. "Uncle Tim said these are real gold, Daddy, and I panned for them in Coyote Canyon. Did you know there was gold there?"

"That's great, Son. But don't count on getting rich panning for gold in Coyote Canyon. Or anywhere else, for that matter." Spud was tired and a little foolishness went a long way after a day such as he'd just put in. Timmy was disappointed by his father's lack of enthusiasm. Millie noticed her husband's irritability and rather grim mood. She took Timmy and put him to bed and she came back into the kitchen where Spud was pouring himself a cup of coffee.

"I've got a new job," he said, almost matter-of-factly. "Or I will have, if I want it. Pays more money. Maybe you can have that house you want one of these days." There was no particular promise or confidence in his tone. Millie would have to be optimistic for the both of them.

"What's the job, Spud?"

"Cy Haver wants me to drive the truck for Haver Farms."

"You mean be a milkman?" Millie asked innocently.

"No, no!" Spud was irritated again. "Not the delivery wagon around town. The big one, the reefer truck. I'd be going north as far as San Jose and down to Paso. Deliver ice cream and milk to the stores and big restaurants. The hours will be long, but the pay is pretty good. Cy offered one hundred sixty bucks a month. More later, if I learn refrigeration. I think I'll take it. Told him I wanted to talk to you first, though."

"Sure, Spud. Take it, if you want to." Millie did some quick calculating. "Do you think we could talk to Herb Pledger? I heard that he started building a house on Vanderhurst for somebody, and whoever it was ran out of money. Herb may have a deal on it."

Spud nodded, unsmiling. "I'll see him first chance I get."

Millie hugged her husband. She wished it hadn't been—still was—so hard for him to accept that he was no longer a rancher. He was still bitter and angry about the loss of the Cleary land and homes. Still resentful that he had to become an ordinary working man, not liking the jobs, not doing well at them, and, as he once confided to Millie, not setting a great example for Timmy.

Millie held Spud tightly. But he didn't return the embrace. She tried to encourage him. "It's going to be fine, Spud, just fine."

Spud took the Haver job, gave two weeks notice at Standard Oil, and then looked up Herb Pledger. When he got the price from the builder, he drove Millie over that next Sunday to see the house. It hadn't been finished yet, but Millie had already been all through it, planned some changes and picked out her own colors. But she let Spud surprise her. She liked the house very much. So he took an hour off from work on Monday morning and went into the Monterey County Bank. When he came out, Spud Cleary had a new house and a thirty-year mortgage. He didn't like being in debt. But maybe it would make Millie happy.

Within a month the house was finished and they moved in. Millie was happily decorating and Spud had to admit his wife knew how to make a place cozy and comfortable. He'd become a little more cheerful of late. He liked wheeling up the highway in Haver's big, new, two-ton, refrigerated truck. It was a Dodge, painted yellow with Haver's milk bottle logo on the side. It purred along Highway 101 and Spud liked driving it, except for the long hours. He left in the morning before daylight and didn't get home until after dark.

Spud was making friends along the route, and the store owners and restaurant managers looked forward to seeing him. What's more, Haver had sent him to refrigeration school for two weeks and he learned just enough about their freezers so that if somebody was having a problem, Spud invariably could fix it. This went a long way in restoring Spud's self esteem, but it didn't take the place of farming and ranching life. Spud missed the hills and being out horseback.

CHAPTER FORTY-FOUR

THERE WAS ONE EVENT, THOUGH, that got Spud's adrenaline pumping again. And Millie had noticed, made him happier than she'd seen him be in a long time. He was going to appear in a movie.

It had started with a telephone call from his brother Pat. "They're going to shoot some scenes for a cowboy movie out here in Peachtree and over on the Trescony," Pat said excitedly. "They asked me to round up some cowboys—extras, they call them. Pay is fifteen dollars per day for man and horse."

Spud thought it was the damnest thing he'd ever heard. Besides he was embarrassed to do it. "Ah, hell, Pat. I haven't been horseback for nearly five years. I'd fall off."

Pat laughed. "Yeah, sure. Listen, Julius is going to do it. The movie guys are staying at his place. Hoot Gibson and that crowd. And the Eades said they'd be in the movie. And some of the Peachtree guys you know. Maybe I can get Bucky to come over. Be like the old days." Pat was pleading.

Spud thought for a minute. Hell, why not? The money was very good and he sure could use it. He was saving for a new Ford, one of those Model A roadsters. And Millie wouldn't mind. She was so damn busy writing for the newspaper, she wouldn't even know he was gone. "Got a horse for me, Pat?"

Pat was elated. "Sure do, Brother. And your saddle's right here in the saddle room. All you have to do is show up early. We'll ride together."

"Well, I'll see if I can take the time off. I'm due for a vacation," Spud said.

"Great. I'll have your horse here all saddled and waiting."

"I can saddle my own horse," Spud said indignantly.

A few days later, Spud and his brother, along with Harold and Kenneth Eade, rode over to the Peachtree, where they joined up with some of the cowboys from ranch headquarters. The director, a short man who sported a beret and carried a megaphone in one hand, told the assembled cowboys that their job was to jump on their horses and race off in front of the cameras. They galloped back and forth, over and over again, as the funny little man with the Frenchie hat, shouted directions at them through his megaphone. Sometimes he'd have them chase a Buick touring car, top down, with a camera mounted behind the driver and a cameraman grinding away at them as they raced down the road at full gallop.

Spud actually enjoyed himself. He noticed that Pat was having a great time, too. Although, Pat still walked with a limp, it didn't bother him horseback. Bucky didn't show up, but a lot of Spud's old friends were there and they treated him the same as they always had. The kidding and fooling around was still the same, the camaraderie was still there. Spud realized how much he'd missed it. Especially being out in the country. And atop a horse!

But what they were doing in the movie Spud found rather silly. It was obvious that neither the director nor the crew, not even the main actors, knew anything about horses. These movie types didn't seem to think a horse ever walked. Or needed to be tied up. Or had to eat and drink. Or maybe even rest once in while. Old Hoot Gibson wasn't a bad guy, though. He could even ride a little bit, despite his huge hat and white boots. And the food was good. Gibson's movie company put out a spread under the oaks trees every day at noon that was hard to back away from. Spud stayed with Pat at the old home place each night. It was a vacation for him just to be horseback and again breathe the clean country air. God, how he missed it!

And how disappointed he was when the shooting was completed the following Tuesday. He still had another week before he had to go back to work at Haver's. But he didn't have any reason to hang around. And then the Eade boys suggested they all ride up to their Laguna Ranch and hunt bucks for a couple of days.

Spud didn't need any convincing. He jumped at the chance. It had been six years since he'd been hunting. He phoned Millie from the ranch and happily told her what he was going to do. "Sure, honey. Go ahead. Have a good time," she said, hiding her true feelings.

When Millie hung up the phone she slapped her hand on the table so hard it tingled for a few minutes. "Damn him," she said loudly. *He gets all that time off and he's going hunting when we could be taking a little trip somewhere. Something. Anything. But no, he's going hunting. And I'm the sweet little wife who stays home all the time.* Millie had a little cry and then give herself a talking to. *Come on, Millie Cleary, you wanted Spud to get back with his friends, get out horseback in the country. Maybe it will help him come alive again, so it's not all work, work, work. Life would be so much better around here if he were happy.*

But dammit, she swore to herself this time, if he's going to be gone having fun all week, then she was going to do something, too. Something outrageous, just for her. She swung around and her long, thick braid of honey-brown hair fell over her shoulder. She took it in her hand and looked in the mirror and started to smile.

* * * * *

Spud and Pat were up early the next morning, met Harold and Kenneth Eade on the Long Valley road, and the three started on the long ride up to Wes Eade's Laguna Ranch.

Spud had found his old two-fifty Savage there at the home place, and now had it in the scabbard tucked under his right leg. But when daylight came, Spud could see that Pat was carrying an ancient thirty-thirty. "What happened to your two-fifty?" he asked.

"Well, that's a story," Pat answered, as the two men rode side by side.

"Well, what isn't? Go ahead."

"I found a lion kill," Pat said, "over where our place corners in Pine Valley. Cougar got a newborn calf. Well, I'm no lion hunter. Neither is that shepherd pup I just got. But it must've just happened, sign was plumb fresh, 'cause that pup took off with his nose to the ground, which sure surprised me. Usually those dogs got no nose at all. So I jumped back on my horse and followed the dog at a good clip."

Pat paused. Spud looked over at his brother. "Yeah? Go on."

Pat continued, "We followed that cat trail up the hill, across that ledge with all the chalk rock, you know, and through those pines and out along the ridge. It gets pretty steep and the trail is narrow up there. Remember?"

Spud remembered. "Yeah. Go on," he repeated.

"Well, I came around a turn in the trail and there was that damn cat right in front of me. Crouched there in the middle of the trail, just whipping that big, long tail back and forth, snarling at the dog yapping at him. My horse tried to swap ends right there. Wasn't room to turn around, so he just went straight up. For a minute I thought we were going over backwards. I damn near fell out of the saddle. By the time I got my horse back to earth on all four feet, the lion had whirled and left the country."

Again they rode awhile in silence. Finally, Spud broke it. "Well, the rifle, what happened to the rifle?"

"Oh, yeah. Well, it fell out of the scabbard when the horse reared up. Hit in the rocks. Busted the stock all to hell. Haven't had a chance to get it fixed yet."

Clearys and the Eades had the ranch house at Laguna to themselves when they got up on top of the mountain that night. A can of tomatoes and some venison jerky served as sup-

per and Pat started some beans soaking for the next day. There
were enough old blankets on the bunks and they slept well.
Harold pulled some bacon and bread out of his saddlebags for
breakfast and they got an early start on their hunt.

Spud was riding down Horse Thief Canyon, working around
the big red rocks where he remembered the bucks liked to lay.
A nice forked horn jumped up and ran off, disappearing in
some pin oaks. Spud took his time, got down off his horse, and
kept the lead rope in his hand. He eased the rifle out of the
scabbard and knelt in front of his horse, levering in a shell. He
scanned the hillside where he thought the buck would come
out. Sure enough, there it was, sneaking out, about two hundred yards away. Just as Spud sighted in, the buck began to
run. Spud swung the sights out in front of the buck a foot or so
and squeezed the trigger. The buck dropped.

Spud's horse shied and reared up and tried to break away,
but he held onto the lead rope and the horse quickly settled
down. Spud waited a while, watched the place where the deer
had fallen and made sure it wasn't going to get up. Then he
mounted and rode over to it. Nice, fat forkie. Spud gutted the
buck, and drew his hunting knife around the leg joints, twisted and the legs came off. He punched slits in the skin, took two
piggin strings out of his saddlebag, and worked them through
the slits.

Now came the test. Spud didn't know if this horse would let
him load a deer onto it. But he'd soon find out. He took his red
bandanna and worked it through the headstall, making blinds.
Then he used the lead rope to fashion hobbles. The horse stood
still as Spud lifted the buck and eased it into the saddle, tying
the piggin strings to the cinch rings on each side. Then he
undid the makeshift hobbles and used the rope to tie the buck's
horns to the saddle horn, bringing the head around to balance
the carcass. When all was secure he took down the reins,
pulled out the bandanna, and carrying his rifle, led the horse
off by the reins. Not a bobble! Spud gave a sigh of relief.

It was a long walk back to the ranch house, but Spud was satisfied. He had camp meat and there'd be some he could take home to Millie, maybe a hind quarter. He hoped she'd like that. He knew she was partial to venison.

* * * * *

Spud Cleary was humming and whistling as he parked in his driveway and opened the trunk of his car to remove the haunch of venison wrapped in a flour sack. He carried it into the house and called, "Millie, Millie!"

But there was no answer. Spud looked at the clock on the kitchen wall. It was 4:30 p.m. Millie should have been home from work with Timmy at least an hour ago. He'd expected her to be home and he was brimming over with stories about his deer hunt and movie making. He couldn't wait to tell her and Timmy. His son would be wide-eyed hearing the stories. After two weeks away Spud realized how much he missed his family.

Spud placed the deer meat on the drainboard and found the cutting board and his meat saw. With a sharp knife he began dividing the venison into steaks and chops. Again he looked at the clock. It was nearly five. He saved out some chops for supper and put the rest into the new Frigidaire. Spud started peeling potatoes and wondered what else he could fix to surprise Millie when she got home.

He found a bottle of burgundy wine in the cupboard. They'd have a glass with the chops to celebrate his homecoming. He'd make it fun for Millie. God knows he'd been cranky as hell lately. He'd make it up to her. Spud was singing as he set the table. *"Jack of Diamonds, Jack of Diamonds, I know you of old, you robbed my poor pockets of silver and gold. You —"*

The front door opened and shut and Spud rushed into the living room to meet his wife and son. "Hello, honey," Millie greeted him and Timmy came running and jumped into his arms. Spud gave his son a big bear hug and then held him close as he heard Millie say, "I didn't expect you home today. We stopped to visit my mother after work. I'm so glad you're —"

"My God, Millie! What did you do to your hair."

Spud put Timmy on the floor and stared at his wife. She ran her fingers through her short hair, fluffed it up and it fell back in place. "Like it?" Millie asked.

"Like it? It's awful!" Spud could hardly get the words out. He was horrified. Millie's long, honey-brown hair was her glory. Spud loved it, liked to brag that his wife's hair was so long she could sit on it. Loved to run his hands through it, now look at her. "How could you do such a thing without even asking me?"

"Well, you were gone and I just wanted to do it."

"And you never even thought about what I like?"

"Well, it's my hair."

Spud stared at his wife for a moment, sadly shook his head and went back into the kitchen. Millie followed and was surprised when she saw the supper preparations. "Oh, Spud. How nice. Are those venison chops? I haven't had any for a long time." She came to him for a kiss. But Spud just grunted and turned away.

Millie tried again. "How did it feel to be a movie star? Was it fun?"

"Yeah, Daddy, tell us about being in the movie," Timmy urged, tugging at his father's pants leg. "Did you shoot any bad guys?"

"Nope," Spud said and retired to his chair in the living room. He sat there, in stony silence, staring straight ahead while Millie and Timmy begged him to share his adventures. Millie became exasperated.

"Spud, I know you don't like my new hairdo. But does that have to spoil everything?"

He just looked at her and didn't answer.

"Think about me," Millie said. "My hair is so easy to care for now, so easy to wash. And it doesn't get in the way, especially when I'm at work in the newspaper office."

"The newspaper office," Spud said, spitting out the words. "That's all you really care about. You don't give a damn about what I think. Only the newspaper, the damn newspaper!"

Millie angrily threw up her hands and returned to the kitchen. Timmy stood in the doorway, looking from one parent to the other. Then he quietly went into his room. Millie fought back tears as she put the potatoes on to boil, made a green salad and then fried the chops. She noticed the wine glasses on the table, but she didn't get out the bottle of burgundy. Dinner was a silent, sullen affair.

CHAPTER FORTY-FIVE

"*SETTLER-BANNER.*" MILLIE ANSWERED THE PHONE on her desk at the newspaper office.

She listened a moment to the voice on the other end and then said, "Sure. Just a second." Millie left her desk with the telephone receiver in one hand and the mouthpiece in the other, trailing a long cord. At the front counter she set down the mouthpiece and with her free hand began going through a card index file. "Here it is, Missus Valdez. Let's see, your subscription isn't up until September. You don't owe anything until then. Yes. We'll send a bill. Thank you." Millie sighed as she hung up. Thank goodness Mrs. Valdez wasn't canceling her subscription or had a past due account. If only there were more like her.

Millie was now doing everything around the newspaper office. She waited on the counter, answered the phone, took want ads and kept the subscription lists current, read proof, wrote her column and the social news, and did most of the general reporting. She worked four days a week, Monday through Thursday, after she got Timmy off to the second grade. He was able to have lunch at Grandma Sarah's on San Lorenzo Avenue because it was just three blocks from the school. In the afternoon he'd come to the newspaper office where his grandfather kept him busy with simple chores. Timmy was learning the difference between leads and slugs, and he knew about ems and ens, and how to use a type stick. With his grandfather's instruction, Timmy had nearly mastered the type case and could handset a headline in forty-eight point. Sometimes he'd stand on a hellbox, so he could reach the forms on the composing stone, where the pages of type for the previous edition of the newspaper were laid out. To "kill" them out, Timmy would separate out the handset type, saving it and all the leads and slugs and throw the lines of lead into a hellbox so they could be melted up again into bars, called "pigs" for the Linotype. Although Fred wrapped his grandson in a printer's apron many sizes too large, he'd manage to smear ink on every uncovered spot. Millie would have to scrub him with that strong yellow soap Timmy hated. He'd do his best to wriggle away. Fred would laugh and declare, "That boy has the makings of a real printer."

But Timmy soon would get tired of being a printer, especially when grandfather handed him a broom, and Millie would have to bring out the coloring book to appease him. But most days she could leave work about three in the afternoon and take Timmy home after school so he could climb the pepper tree in the backyard, or organize a stick horse rodeo with his friends.

With Millie and Timmy gone for the day, Fred would watch the front office and try to get his editorials written. He was now seventy, but he still came to work every day, puttered around the back shop, and made his rounds on Broadway, visiting with the businessmen, picking up an ad or two, some envelopes to print, or make notes for some newsworthy story. Most mornings around nine-thirty he'd be at McGuire's Fountain having coffee with Al Carlson, Les Hables, A.B. McReynolds, Harvey Burns and some of the other "old-timers," as they called themselves. Fred didn't much like the appellation for himself, but he was an old-timer. He'd been there almost from the beginning of the town and he liked to look around and take pride in what he'd helped accomplish in King City.

The board sidewalks had long since given way to asphalt and cement, and Broadway, where wagons had once been mired in mud, or travelers been covered with dust, was now a handsome, wide, well-paved thoroughfare with big shade trees along the sidewalk. The state highway went right through town, bringing travelers' dollars which were a boon to the business community. Most of the wood-framed structures with false fronts had given way to modern, cement block buildings with plate glass windows.

Fred liked to stand at the intersection of Third and Broadway, the commercial center of town, puff on his pipe, and look at the imposing Monterey County Bank building on the northeast corner, or the equally impressive Bank of America on the southwest corner. Designed in the beaux arts style, their two stories marked with paired pilasters along the side and columns in front, with high windows and classic facades, they stood like bastions guarding the center of town.

"Wasn't much here when I started *The Settler*," Fred Godfrey would tell anybody who'd listen. "Two hundred people, some shacks along Broadway, a couple of two-story wooden hotels and a store or two. But anybody with half an eye could see this town was a comer, filled with live wires who wanted to do things first class."

Fred also liked to remind people that there was no irrigation in the valley when he'd first started publishing *The Settler* and writing about the problems caused by the lack of water. "There wasn't a dairy, an orchard or a vegetable field in the entire Salinas Valley when I came here. When I suggested irrigation they thought I was a loony."

Every day at noon Fred walked down Third to Bassett and on to San Lorenzo for lunch. He often reminded himself that when he'd built his house this area was considered "out in the country," Now the town had extended far past San Lorenzo and most of the streets were paved, or at least, graveled.

In the spring when workmen were putting down a cement sidewalk on San Lorenzo in front of Godfrey's house, Fred had guided Timmy's hand into the wet cement and helped him write the year, 1930. "That'll be there when you're a grown man and you can show it to your kids someday, Timmy," he told his grandson.

Fred enjoyed the short walk each noon, anticipating Sarah's good lunch, feeding his pet duck Oscar, and playing with his grandson. He took his big gold watch from its pocket in his vest, flipped the back open, and checked the time. Just right, five past twelve. Oscar would be waiting.

He turned the corner of Bassett into San Lorenzo and looked across the street. There was Oscar, the fat mallard duck, standing on the front lawn, quacking at Fred. Oscar had joined the family at Thanksgiving two years ago. A subscriber had brought the duck in a crate to the newspaper office. "Fred," he'd said, "I'm a tad short of cash. But I thought you might like a duck dinner for Thanksgiving in exchange for my subscription?" That was just fine with Fred. But then he discovered that he just couldn't bring himself to take an ax to the duck, and pretty soon Sarah had named the bird Oscar, and Fred was digging worms for it in the backyard. Now it had become a noon-time ritual. Oscar was always out front, waiting for him, and quacking furiously if he was late.

Millie kept the office open during the noon hour. The two printers went home for lunch and so did Bobby. But with Spud off on the truck all day, and Timmy at his grandparent's house, Millie usually skipped lunch. A Coca-Cola kept her going and sometimes she'd share a snack with Timmy when they got home in the afternoon.

One of her jobs was to prepare the tear sheets. Advertisers such as Hitchcock's Drug Store, Tholke's Men's Store, Fanning's Cash Store, Tynan Lumber Co. received full copies of the paper. So did some of the other local advertisers, but they also needed copies of their advertisements to send to the manufacturers so they'd receive their advertising rebates.

Millie would tear out the ads for the H-A-F Co., King City
Mercantile and Reel Joy Theatre. Then copies of all the automobile ads had to be sent to the Detroit ad agencies, and there
were a lot of them these days. Buicks were sold at Johnson's
Garage, Fords at El Camino Motors, Old's Garage had the
franchise for Essex and Hudson, Sunshine Motors had the
Star Car, King City Garage sold Studebakers, Chevrolets were
at Earl Enfield's and L.E. Chaney was selling Dodge Brothers'
autos. Most weeks they were all represented in the paper, so
Millie had a bundle of tear sheets to send off. She didn't mind.
It meant *The Settler-Banner* was finally showing a profit, in
fact, becoming prosperous.

Strange, she thought. With all the news in the big city
papers about business failures thanks to the 1929 stock market crash, King City was doing well. Some of the farmers were
complaining about dropping farm prices, but the truth was
some were higher than ever. *The Settler-Banner* reported that
the famous King City pink bean crop was estimated over one
million dollars, and Jim Kelly's lima beans on the Salinas
Land Co. averaged 2,483 pounds per acre at thirteen cents a
pound for a healthy profit. The barley market rose eight cents
to $1.75 per hundred weight. Land in the Mission district now
sold for the unheard of price of $500 per acre, and Bob Diaz
said 613 head of cattle were shipped from the stockyards in
King City and San Lucas in one day at the top of the market.
This prosperity spilled over to the business firms in town so,
generally speaking, times were good. Bob Godfrey didn't think
Wall Street's problems would ever hurt small towns in the
West. But Millie's father wasn't so sure. She considered that
strange. Her father was usually the cockeyed optimistic and
Bob the realist.

Millie had just finished the tear sheets and was licking
stamps for the envelopes when her brother opened the office
door and stepped inside. She looked up and was struck by
Bob's strange expression. He just stood there, his mouth working, trying to find the right words to tell her.

"Your Uncle Tim has been arrested."

339

CHAPTER FORTY-SIX

For Tim Cleary the day started as so many others had through the years. He was sitting slumped over his kitchen table when the first rays of dawn sent a weak shaft of light through the window. The remnants of his supper lay scattered on the table, where his head also rested, cradled in his folded arms. An empty whiskey jar lay at his feet. And beside him on the table was the small, metal box.

He'd returned late the night before from a trip to Alvarado's in San Ardo, where he'd replenished his supply of bootleg whiskey. Tim had been keeping his car at the home ranch in Long Valley. Oscar Bauman had made it too much of a hassle to drive down through his place to the Pine Valley road. So Tim Cleary would ride horseback over the hill, leave his saddle horse in his nephew Pat's corral, and use the Long Valley road. But the padlock on Bauman's gate at the county road finally became more than Tim Cleary could stand.

That happened the morning he found his own gate open, and a dozen of Bauman's cows eating the hay he kept for his horses. Tim had driven them out, cursing the animals and their owner. He'd saddled up and ridden down to Bauman's place, intending to accuse him of an act of spite—of opening the gate and turning the cattle into his yard. But the house by the road was empty. Tim rode into the yard, looked around, called out Bauman's name, but got no answer. By that time his anger had cooled and he reined his horse toward home. But he looked over at the gate, studying the big padlock and the chain for a few minutes.

The next day Tim had driven to King City to consult with Joseph Crandle, the lawyer who'd just hung up his shingle outside the Reel Joy Theatre building where he now rented an office. "What's my standing under the law?" Tim inquired. "Don't I have a right of way across that land?" Crandle said he would check it out.

340

Within a day, he had an answer for Tim, who had returned to Crandle's office at the appointed time. "Well, Mister Cleary, according to the county recorder's office there are no liens on that property, no recorded right-of-way. None existed when your father owned the land. I suppose it wasn't thought necessary, being all in the family. But I did find at the title company that there was a written agreement allowing you access across the property as a condition of the bank sale to Mister Bauman. There is also such a thing as an easement by implication or necessity. In other words, your continued right to use the road was implied in the sale, there being no intent to leave you landlocked."

"Well then," Tim declared with a relieved smile, "he can't keep me out. I must have that agreement letter around somewhere."

"On the contrary," the lawyer said. "He can keep you out. If you let him! I'll admit this may sound strange. But the fact that there was an agreement to allow you to pass demonstrates that Mister Bauman gave permission. Under the law permission can be revoked. You indicate that he has refused you passage and placed a lock on his gate. In order to assert your right to pass through you must force entry, maintain your prescriptive right."

"Force entry? What do you mean by that?"

"You must remove his lock, or take down the gate, and enter the property by a hostile act. If you do that on a regular basis, you will have established your right-of-way," Crandle explained. "By placing the lock and retaining it there to obstruct passage, I'm afraid Mister Bauman is establishing the road as private, not public."

"By God, are you telling me that the only way I can get my right-of-way across that bastard's land is to force the lock?" Tim was dismayed. "That doesn't make a damn bit of sense."

"That's the way the law is written," Crandle stated.

A bewildered Tim Cleary left the lawyer's office and walked up Broadway. At the end of two blocks he'd made a decision. By

341

God, if that's what it takes, that's what he'd do. Determined to defend his rights, Tim crossed the street and entered King City Mercantile. He purchased a heavy-duty bolt cutter.

After gassing up his car, Tim drove down to San Ardo, where he made his usual visit to Alvarado's. With a new supply of Mason jars in the back seat, Tim turned into Pine Valley road and drove up the canyon as dusk settled in. It was dark by the time he parked in front of the locked gate. There were no lights showing in Bauman's house. Bastard must still be gone, Tim thought. He took his time, first sampling the latest batch of jackass whiskey from the Lockwood still. Then, with the lights of his old Dodge illuminating the gate, he brought out the big bolt cutter.

He clamped the jaws around the stout chain securing the gate and applied leverage. The chain finally gave, the cut link parted, and it slipped to the ground with the big padlock. Tim spit on it in disgust. Then he replaced his bolt cutter and had another drink, savoring his work. He opened the gate and drove through. "I should leave the damn thing wide open," Tim said aloud, "let his cattle out onto the county road." But he just couldn't do that. Closing gates behind him was an ingrained practice, learned in childhood. Tim drove on up Coyote Canyon to his cabin.

He fed the colt in the corral, checked the water, making a mental note that he'd ride the young gelding over to the ranch in the morning to pick up his own saddle horse. Then he filled his arms with kindling and firewood and went into the shack. Tim built a fire in his cook stove and put a pot of water on to heat. He was hungry and looked for something to cook. Not a bit of meat in the place. Have to get some venison, he thought, glancing at the rifle hanging on the wall. At least it's deer season now. He'd be legal for once. That is, if he had a license and deer tags. Tim savored his little joke.

Tim fried some potatoes. He found some bread and cheese and washed it all down with the rest of the whiskey in the fruit jar. He opened a second jar and sat there thinking. He knew he drank to kill the pain of remembrance. Sometimes it took a lot of whiskey to numb his brain, to shut out the memories. But other times it was as if he couldn't remember why he hurt so much. It had been so long, the memories would slip away, become gray, shadowy things on the periphery of his mind. Tim would have to reinforce them, bring them to life in bright color so they'd hurt. He'd open the little metal box on his night stand and go through the letters, read the faded clipping, stare again at the picture of the beautiful, young girl in the wedding dress, the girl he'd once thought was his, remember how it felt to hold her in his arms, to kiss those lips.

Tonight was such a night. Tim crossed the little room and picked up the box, carrying it to the table. He sat down, the box beside him, and took a long pull on the jar. He raised the lid, lifted out the letters and the yellowed clipping, and began his ritual. He read and remembered, drank and thought, and finally sank into sodden unconsciousness.

The morning sun slanted through the single pane of glass in Tim's cabin and focused its glare into his eyes. He moaned as he moved his arms to ward off the light. The pain broke into his stupor. He came slowly awake. Stiff and sore, he was cramped from the hours his arms were folded beneath his head against the table. His whole body ached. He sat up, blinking and rubbing his watering eyes. He rose and stretched, and suddenly had an overwhelming urge to relieve himself. Tim staggered out the door and around back.

He returned to the cabin and slumped down on the door stoop. The colt nickered, but Tim ignored the animal. He needed a drink before he could start another day. He rose, stumbled against the door jam, and lurched into the cabin. He found his supply of jars and pulled the lid from one, tipping the glass, feeling the strong, raw taste against his tongue, letting the whiskey roll down his throat, the heat of it spreading through his veins. Tim sat down again at the table and rubbed his eyes. He became more aware of the emerging sunlight, the morning sounds of dove and quail, the colt calling to him.

Tim put kindling into his stove, got the fire burning, and dipped water from the bucket into the coffee pot. He was reaching for the can of coffee when he thought he heard the sound of a shot. He listened, trying to place the sound. In his numbed state he wasn't sure from which direction the shot had come, or if he'd truly heard a shot. He waited. But all was quiet. Tim set the coffee pot on to boil, sat down again at the table, his head in his hands and waited.

Then a shout intruded on his consciousness. Tim raised his head to listen. "Hey, Cleary! Hello in there — !"

Tim slowly walked to the door, opened it and looked out. "Huh?" He was bewildered. Was somebody out there? He couldn't see anyone.

"Hey, Cleary," the voice called from the nearby hillside. "I shot a buck over there, but he ran into your place and dropped by the spring. I want to go get him. Okay?"

"Huh?" Tim stood on the steps, confused, squinting against the early morning sun.

"Cleary! Can't you hear me? Just a minute. I'll come over there."

Then Tim made out the figure coming toward him. *That god-damned Bauman! What does he want? The son-of-a-bitch is on my property.*

"Bauman, get the hell off my property!" Tim finally mustered the strength to yell.

"Wait a minute, Cleary. All I want to do is pick up my deer over there. I'm coming up to talk to you." Bauman continued walking toward the gate. It was then that Tim realized he was carrying a rifle. *Bauman is coming to get me.* Tim felt a tense wave of panic.

"Get away from my gate!" he shouted. "Stay out of here, Bauman!"

But Bauman had his rifle in the crook of one arm and was opening the gate. Tim stepped back into his cabin and took the thirty-thirty rifle down off the wall. He returned to the open door just as Bauman came through and closed the gate. Tim levered in a shell. He had Bauman in his sights as the man came toward the house.

Tim's finger tightened on the trigger. The report echoed in the canyon. Bauman took two staggering steps toward Tim. He dropped his rifle. Arms outstretched, he took another step. "My God, you've killed me," he whispered. Bauman fell forward in the yard.

Tim lowered the rifle and watched him fall. He stood there, incredulous, looking at Bauman lying in the dust. The sight seemed to sober him. *Dear Lord, what have I done?*

Tim walked slowly up to the inert body. He stood over Bauman, just staring at him. He walked around, studying him from different angles. The dust next to Bauman's mouth didn't move. He wasn't breathing. There was no doubt in Tim Cleary's mind. *He's dead! I killed him!* Tim shuddered with the awful realization.

Tim returned to the house and put the rifle back on the wall. He found his hat and stood on the cabin steps as he put it on, never taking his eyes off the dead man in his yard. Tim caught the colt, its skin quivering, eyes wild, still nervous from the shot. Tim soothed the horse and slowly brushed him off, stopping frequently to look back at Bauman's body, willing the man to get up, to walk away. He eased the hackamore over the colt's nose, smoothed the blankets, and lifted up the saddle.

Tim led the horse into the yard, giving Bauman's body a wide berth, but watching the whole time. The colt snorted and shied sideways. When he was clear of the yard, Tim swung up into the saddle. He gave a last look back, then headed the colt up the trail toward the ridge and Long Valley.

Lord, forgive me. I killed a man. Lord, forgive me. Tim whispered it aloud as he rode. "Lord, forgive me, please forgive me."

Pat was doing the morning chores when his uncle Tim rode into the yard at the home ranch. Tim unsaddled and turned the horse into the corral with the others. He slowly approached his nephew.

"Patrick," he said in a low, halting voice. "Please call the sheriff. I've killed Bauman."

"You what?" Pat was astounded. He didn't understand. "What happened? Are you sure? How?"

But Tim didn't answer. He walked up to the house and went inside. In the kitchen he sat down at the table and put his head in his hands. Buck and Seamus had already left for the day, but Honora and Kitty came into the kitchen. Pat repeated what Tim had just told him, and the two women looked at Tim with a mixture of dismay and compassion. Pat went to the phone hanging on the wall.

He rang for central in King City. "Please put me through to Sheriff Abbott in Salinas," he said.

Tim was still sitting there, his head in his hands, when the sheriff arrived three hours later. Tim looked up at him. "I killed a man," he muttered. He stood and held out his hands and Carl Abbott seemed embarrassed. But he put on the hand-cuffs and led Tim Cleary to the sheriff's car. In answer to every question, Tim simply said, "I killed a man!"

* * * * *

Millie sat staring at her typewriter. For more than an hour she'd been writing a few words, or a sentence or two, and then ripping the copy paper from the roller. Her mind wouldn't work, and if the words did come into her head her fingers couldn't type them. How could she write that Timothy Patrick Cleary had been arrested for the murder of Oscar Bauman?

"You have to cover the story, Millie. You're the reporter," her father said. "And keep in mind," he warned her, "that you must include everything, leave nothing out. People know of the family connection and they'll be watching to see if we give complete coverage. Play it just as you would any other local murder, no more, no less." Fred Godfrey looked sternly at his daughter. He knew how much she cared for Tim Cleary, probably more than any of his blood relatives did, and he knew how

346

much Timmy loved his great uncle, but neither of these factors could get in the way of *The Settler-Banner's* obligation to its readers.

"Oh, Dad, it's so hard to write this," Millie said as she tearfully rolled another sheet of paper into her Smith Brothers typewriter.

"I know, I know," Fred said, patting his daughter's shoulder as she began to type.

The city papers had already shouted the news from their front pages, especially *The Salinas Index*. A copy sat on Millie's desk. *South County Recluse Murders Neighbor,* read the big, black type. *Timothy Cleary, a loner who lived in a tiny homestead cabin in a secluded south county canyon east of San Ardo, shot and killed his neighbor, Oscar Bauman, 47, yesterday. Cleary, 68, is a member of the once-prominent Cleary family of San Lucas, brother of the late supervisor, Will Cleary.*

Millie was trying to find a different lead, another angle to the story. She wrote, *Timothy Cleary, 68, of San Lucas, was taken into custody by Sheriff Carl Abbott last week, accused of the murder of Oscar Bauman, 47, the neighboring property owner in Coyote Canyon, northeast of San Ardo, who was found dead of a rifle bullet in the yard of Cleary's cabin. It is known that there was bad blood between the two men. Although Cleary would not speak in his own defense, there is conjecture that the shooting was in self defense.*

Fred reading over Millie's shoulder, said, "Millie, whose conjecture? The sheriff's or yours?" She looked up at her father. "Who knows there was bad blood?" he asked. "You? Or did someone in authority say so? This is supposed to be an objective news story, not an opinion piece."

Millie sighed. "Yes, Dad. I know what you mean. I'll try again and just stick to the facts." She pulled out the copy paper from her typewriter and rolled in another sheet. Fred left her alone while she struggled.

Millie rewrote the lead and added: *Cleary would not speak in his own defense and his attorney, Joseph Crandle of King City said it was too early for him to say what plea would be entered. A grand jury hearing is scheduled for next Thursday in Salinas.*

It is believed that the shooting occurred early Friday morning and that Cleary rode horseback to the home of his nephew, Patrick Cleary, in Long Valley. The sheriff was called from there, and Cleary voluntarily turned himself in. The county coroner, Sheriff Abbott, and a party from Foor's Mortuary in King City drove to the Cleary homestead in Coyote Canyon to examine the scene and retrieve the body. They would make no comment on what was discovered.

Sheriff Abbott did state that he'd turn his findings over to the district attorney, who would determine whether or not to ask the grand jury for a murder indictment.

The deceased had purchased his ranch property about six years ago. He lived alone and it is not known at this writing if he leaves any survivors. Funeral services are pending.

Millie didn't add anything about the Cleary family as the Salinas newspaper had done. "They feel bad enough, without the newspapers rubbing the family's nose in it," she told her father.

They played it under a banner across the top, *Man Killed in South County Shooting.* Underneath was a three column headline in smaller type. *Tim Cleary Arrested for Murder of Bauman.* The story ran down the right hand side of the page.

Her eyes were still puffy from the tears she'd shed while writing that day and she felt particularly fragile that evening when Spud came home from work. She was completely unprepared for his reaction. Usually he saved *The Settler-Banner* for his Sunday reading, but he reached for it the moment he came into the house. Millie watched him while he read it, saw the familiar tightening of his lips, the furrow cross his brow, his jaw set. But he didn't say a word, just finished the reading and let the paper slip to the floor.

He stared into space and she waited for him to speak. Finally he looked up and asked, "Why? Why, Millie?"

"Why what, Spud?" She was puzzled.

"Why the big black headlines? Why did you have to embarrass my family like that?" He glared at her.

"Good Lord, Spud! I didn't embarrass your family. What on earth do you mean?" Millie could feel the hurt and anger rising in her.

"The sensationalism! All over the front page like that. You're worse than the Salinas paper, for godsakes!" Spud's words shot out like daggers, each one hitting its target.

"Spud, listen." Millie tried to be reasonable. "If we didn't give it a big headline and cover it like any other story, people would say it was favoritism because of my last name. This is big news. The paper is on the spot. I'm on the spot. Can't you understand?"

Spud gave his wife a withering look. "No, dammit! I can't! You know damn good and well that Bauman has been needling Uncle Tim since the day he moved in," Spud declared. "I'll bet, sure as hell, it was self defense. Bauman probably came after him. Uncle Tim probably had to shoot him. Why didn't you put that in your story?"

"I can't write what I think, Spud. That's just conjecture. I have to wait to get a quote from one of the authorities."

"Authorities hell," Spud growled. "You damn newspapers are just out to embarrass my family, anything to sell papers." There was a bitterness in his voice that Millie had never heard before, not even in that awful time when Spud's father died and the Clearys were told they were going to lose their land.

"Oh, Spud." Millie pleaded. "How can you say a thing like that? I'm part of your family. I love Uncle Tim. You know that." Millie couldn't hold it in any longer. She went, sobbing, into the bedroom. Spud slammed the kitchen door on his way out to check on his home brew in the garage behind the house.

Millie decided to take the next day off. She was in no mood to write personals and social news, or even be around the newspaper office. What she needed was to get out in the hills, maybe a horseback ride with Kitty or a visit with her and

Honora. She called and told her brother she couldn't come to work. "Sure, Sis, take a break. See you tomorrow," Bob said. She was grateful for his understanding.

She telephoned the ranch and heard Honora's voice. "Who? Oh, it's you, Millie."

"I was hoping to drive out there today and visit with you and Kitty, maybe take a horse — "

Honora interrupted. "Not today, Millie. It's not convenient!" And with that she hung up the phone.

CHAPTER FORTY-SEVEN

SPUD AND MILLIE HARDLY SPOKE as they drove to Salinas. They were on their way to visit Tim Cleary at the county jail. But they didn't talk about it. The few words they'd exchanged since Tim's arrest steered clear of the subject. Spud was grimly quiet and Millie hurt so deeply by the family's rejection that she could hardly think of anything else. Fortunately, their new Model-A Ford purred along at fifty miles an hour, so the trip only took an hour. Millie spent the whole time silently praying that Uncle Tim would understand that her reporting of the story was just her job.

Two guards brought Tim Cleary out from the cell block into the visitor's room. He looked so thin and frail, so diminished in his jail garb, so tired and haggard. Millie thought he'd aged twenty years since she last saw him. The sight of him made her want to cry. But she mustered a smile and gave Tim a hug. He didn't return it, just stiffly endured it. He shook hands with Spud and the three sat down at a table, facing each other. No one spoke.

Finally Millie asked, "Uncle Tim, do you want to talk about it? I could write your side of the story." Spud frowned at her with irritation.

But Tim just shook his head. "Nothing to say. I killed him."

Spud changed the subject. "Had any visitors, Uncle Tim?"

"Yep. My brother, Dan, was here. Said some prayers. Hope they work."

"Yes, Kitty called Father Dan," Spud explained. "He said he'd come right down."

Tim just nodded.

Millie reached out and took his hand. He let her hold it and seemed about to say something to her. But he didn't. So she spoke. "I had to write about it, Uncle Tim. For the paper. Did you see the story?"

"Nope," Tim said, fatigue registering in his voice.

"Do you want me to bring you a copy?" Millie asked tentatively

"Nope!" He was emphatic this time.

Spud wished Millie would stop mentioning the newspaper story. "Is there anything we can bring you, Uncle Tim?"

Tim Cleary thought a moment and then said, "Well, it would be a comfort to have that tin box from my cabin."

Millie and Spud rode home the same way they had come to the jail, in silence. It was punctuated only once when Spud said, "You'll have to get that box for him, Millie. I can't take another day off."

"Sure, Spud," Millie said softly. And the silence again engulfed the Clearys.

Next morning was Friday, Millie's regular free day. As soon as she got Timmy off to school Millie drove the Model-A out to Tim's place. Millie felt a strange uneasiness as she slid the latch board in Tim's wooden gate, swung it open, and drove into the deserted yard. She shut the gate and looked about as she slowly walked to the cabin. Where had the shooting taken place? Where had the body fallen? Where had Tim been when he shot?

Millie found the quiet around her eerie. No horse nickering in the corral, no quail calling on the hillside. Millie stood for a moment on the stoop, took a deep breath, and pushed open the door.

The place was in disarray. Every other time she'd been there, she'd been amazed at how neat and clean Uncle Tim always kept his little cabin. But now the table was cluttered with spoiled food, potatoes, moldy cheese, crusts of bread, a dirty dish. Potato peelings were scattered on the floor, a chair lay tipped over beside two empty fruit jars. A pot of coffee had boiled over onto a greasy frying pan standing on the stove. The whole room was dusty and disheveled looking.

Then Millie spotted it. There amidst the clutter on the table stood the little tin box. It was open. Millie could see it contained a bundle of envelopes, and beside it lay a newspaper clipping, worn at the creases from years of handling, yellowed with age. The box and its contents were just as Tim had left them. She wondered if he'd been looking at them just before the tragic shooting.

Millie resolved not to read them. They were too personal. It would be prying into Uncle Tim's private life. She decided instead to clean up the cabin. She started a fire to heat up water and cleared the rotting food from the table, careful not to disturb the box and its contents. She swept the floor, washed the few dishes, scrubbed out the frying pan, straightened things up. All the while her eyes kept straying to the little tin box and the clipping beside it. Her resolve left her. It was there on the table, open, in plain sight.

She picked it up and studied it. She saw the photo of the beautiful, blond Amy, lips parted to receive her bridegroom's kiss. Millie saw the penciled words written on the margin, hardly legible after all the years. "Thought you should know. A friend." Millie's heart went heavy with Tim's pain as she read the story. How awful for him to find this out about the girl he loved and read about it in a newspaper clipping, sent anonymously.

Millie took out the packet of envelopes. She knew they contained letters. She could see they were from Amy Barnes, but she chose not to read them. They were too private. But there was a paper folded beneath them and that she did look at.

Millie carefully unfolded it to see that it was a sales agreement. She was incredulous as she read that Timothy Patrick Cleary had received of Tanana Mining Company two hundred thousand dollars in payment for all rights to that certain hard rock mining claim known as Coyote Mine on Cleary Creek in the district of Fairbanks, Territory of Alaska. On the margin, in Tim's handwriting, was a notation. "Took out over a million in gold. Lost it. Letter of credit burned in S.F. fire."

In shock, Millie slumped down on the chair. Dear God, no wonder the man drank and shunned people. He'd lost the girl he loved and his fortune. How terrible!

Millie's hands shook as she refolded the piece of paper, replaced it and the letters, and put the clipping on top. She closed the box. Uncle Tim's precious box. His life was in there. If people only knew, realized what he'd suffered, they'd understand Tim Cleary.

Millie would write it. She'd make the world know about the pain he'd been trying to ease when he drank, about the memories that haunted him. But how could she write the story without betraying that she'd looked into his precious box, betrayed his confidence?

She had to find a way, the right words. If she showed Uncle Tim as a sympathetic man, made the readers understand him as a human being in pain, that he's basically a good person, perhaps Tim's family would appreciate it. She'd be accepted again. She missed their love and understanding. Particularly Aunt Kitty's. Maybe this was a way back to the Clearys.

Millie couldn't wait to get to her typewriter. But first she made some stops near San Ardo and she called at two homes near San Lucas. She visited with several people who had known Tim Cleary in his youth. It was late afternoon when she arrived at the newspaper office. She went straight to her typewriter. The words flowed across the paper.

Usually this column concerns itself with child development, brightened occasionally by the funny things children say and do. Sometimes my own son, Timmy, is the subject and his antics are made to represent most all youngsters.

But today I'll tell you about another Timothy, known to the world as a recluse, a proud, hard, unbending, often bitter, old man, consigned to self-exile in his mountain shack, taking solace in his solitude, and sometimes comfort in his whiskey jar.

Today he sits in a cell in the jail in Salinas awaiting trial, accused of murder.

This man was once young, handsome, friendly, filled with good humor, a successful farmer with a wonderful future. I know him as Uncle Tim, a kind, gentle person, caring and nurturing with my son, that spark of humor still alive deep within his soul.

What happened? What destroyed this promising life and sent this man into seclusion from the world?

Perhaps the answer is known only to Timothy Cleary. The rest of us may only surmise. But the answer may lie in a little tin box he keeps by his side, in the memorabilia it contains. No one knows, for Uncle Tim is a private person who has shared his pain with no one.

But there are many in our area who remember the Tim of old, those who went to school with him in Long Valley, shared youthful games, enjoyed his companionship on cattle drives, at brandings, who worked on his harvester crews, and knew him as a helpful neighbor when he farmed near San Ardo. Some recalled his cheerful nature, and remembered his enjoyment of those early-day San Lucas dances and social affairs where his laugh was joyful.

I've visited with some of those people, elderly now, but with vivid memories and stories to tell. I've asked them about Uncle Tim, the man accused of murder. Several people remembered a beautiful, young, blond girl whom Tim planned to marry. He was building a house for her on his farm when he discovered she'd married someone else. Tim Cleary was the sort of man who gave his heart but once, and then totally.

Some said that he answered the call of gold in the Yukon and he was gone eight years. Some claim he struck it rich, very rich, and returned a millionaire. But, if that was so, what happened to this fortune? Uncle Tim has told no one.

Others recall that he returned to his homestead in Coyote Canyon in 1906, shortly after the San Francisco earthquake and fire, and that it was rumored he'd been present for that awful event. What part did that terrible time play in his past?

Whatever the forces that made a recluse of Timothy Cleary, they didn't make him a bad man. Surely, he was a lonesome man, a misunderstood man. I know that he had differences with his neighbor, Oscar Bauman. Uncle Tim told me of those problems. And I am sure that these were not his fault entirely.

Perhaps the authorities will unravel the mystery of what happened in Coyote Canyon that tragic morning. I hope so, for Uncle Tim won't speak in his own defense. I believe, that were he to do so, we'd find that mitigating circumstances would prove Tim Cleary didn't kill Oscar Bauman with malice aforethought.

Timothy Cleary is not a murderer!

Millie placed the copy on her father's big roll top desk. Fred Godfrey looked up from the proof he was checking, leaned back in his chair and read what his daughter had written. After a few seconds he stopped, looked up at Millie questioningly, and then back at the copy. She waited for her father's verdict.

"Millie, that's an excellent bit of writing." Fred placed the copy back in front of him. "But do you really want to run that?"

"Yes, Dad. Those are my opinions and it will be in my column."

"Well, as far as the newspaper goes, it's fine. You can put your opinion under your byline in your own column. You haven't seen any evidence and the trial hasn't started. But how about the Clearys? How will they take this?"

"Oh, Dad. That's just it. I'm sure they'll appreciate it. I'm trying to make readers see Tim Cleary in a different light, maybe sympathize with him. And I suggest it was self defense. That's what Spud wanted."

"I don't know, Millie. Old Jeremiah was a very private person and I think that rubbed off on them, except for Will. Now that he's gone, I don't think the Cleary family appreciates their private matters being made public."

"Well, it can't be helped. Tim Cleary did shoot that man."

"Holy Jehoshaphat, Millie, you've been in this business long enough to know that they always kill the messenger who brings bad news."

"I know. But this is different, Dad."

* * * * *

"Yes, Naomi. I'm about through here. I'll stop by." Millie hung up the phone, frowning with concern.

It had been Naomi Cleese on the phone, Timmy's teacher and she wanted to talk with Millie about the boy. Millie was worried as she hurriedly walked the two blocks over to San Lorenzo School. She quickly found her way to the second grade classroom.

Millie sat in Naomi's chair, while the teacher leaned across the desk. "Timmy's become quarrelsome. He's been in several fights at recess. And his school work has dropped off. He was one of the best students and never a disciplinary problem, Millie. Suddenly he's become one. I hoped you might have an answer?"

Millie knew. But she didn't want to discuss it with the teacher. "I'll talk with him, Naomi," Millie promised. "See if I can find out what's troubling him."

"I do know one thing, Millie." Naomi Cleese hesitated for a second. "He's bothered by the Tim Cleary business—the murder trial. I think some of the fights develop from the other children taunting him."

Millie nodded. "Yes, I know kids can be cruel. But there's not much we can do about that." Millie already knew that Timmy

356

was being taunted and teased. She'd found him crying after school a week earlier and he'd sobbed out the story.

"They asked me how come I'm not in jail if my name is Timothy Cleary." Tears had rolled down his cheeks. "They chased me home and threw rocks at me and called me a murderer."

What do you tell your child at a time like this? Millie wondered. Was there anything in those child development courses she'd taken to make this right for her little boy?

"Uncle Tim is my friend," Timmy cried. "Why'd he have to go and do that, and get put in jail?" Millie did the only thing she knew. She pulled her son onto her lap and cuddled him.

She thanked the teacher for her caring interest and left the classroom. Millie struggled to hold back her tears as she walked over to her mother's house. Sarah made a pot of tea and they sat at the kitchen table as she listened to her daughter pour her heart out. "The whole family is mad at me, Mom," Millie said, not whining, but genuinely hurt and distraught. "I can take that. But not Spud, too. He won't even talk to me. He leaves at dawn and has breakfast up town, comes home after dark and sits there in his chair, working on his tagbook, eats what I cook, and goes to bed. The tension is hurting Timmy."

"It's always the children who suffer when adults have problems," Sarah said. "You understand all that, Millie."

"But what can I do? Timmy's doing poorly in class. His teacher is worried. I just came from a meeting with her. And he's been sassy to me. He was never like that."

Millie sat silently for a moment. Both she and Sarah sipped their tea. Then Millie looked straight at her mother and said what was on her mind. "I'm thinking of leaving Spud."

"Leaving him!" Sarah was appalled. "Millie, that doesn't make any sense at all. Why on earth would you ever do that?"

"I just can't raise Timmy in such an atmosphere. It's the paper, my writing, not just Uncle Tim's arrest—everything. Spud just doesn't understand the newspaper business. He can't understand my job, what I write, why I write things or

357

how I write them. He seems to feel every story is an invasion of somebody's privacy. But he reads the paper, every word. They all do. As long as it's about somebody else."

"Millie, Millie." Sarah held up her hand. "Slow down. Let me ask you something. Do you love Spud?"

"Well, Mom, yes, I suppose I do. He's a decent, honest man. And he works so hard to provide for us. I sure did love him when I married him. I think I loved him from the day I first saw him when I was just a silly little girl. He was bigger than life, so full of fun and excitement. Things were wonderful when we were on the ranch. He was the kindest, most thoughtful, understanding husband a woman could have. We could talk about things, all sorts of things. He had ideas and opinions. We could argue and then laugh." Millie was still, sadly shaking her head, tears in her eyes. "But it all changed when we moved to town."

Her mother reached across the table, placed her hand under Millie's chin and raised it up. She looked full in her daughter's eyes. "Millie, you know the reasons behind Spud's personality change. This terrible matter with his Uncle Tim has simply driven him further into his shell. But Millie, underneath all that is still the man you married, the man you love. Give him a chance. He'll come out of it."

"I understand what you're saying, Mom, but will it be soon enough to keep from hurting Timmy?"

"Kids are tough. When this trouble is over, he'll bounce back," Sarah reassured her. She got up from the table and busied herself at the sink for a moment, thinking. Then, she sat back down across from her daughter. "Millie, I'm going to tell you something. Something very private about your father and me."

"What?" Millie asked.

"I left your father once." Sarah waited for Millie's shocked reaction to subside. "I was a bride of six months or so and I thought I had it hard. We didn't have any money. We lived in a hotel room. I couldn't buy clothes. Fred expected me to work at the paper. I'd been raised in luxury and I was a spoiled, silly girl. I'm not suggesting that you are any of those things, Millie. You're not. You certainly weren't spoiled. You're a sensible, mature adult. But I want to make a point."

She had all of Millie's attention. Her eyes were locked on her mother's. "Go on," she said.

"So I went home to my mother, thinking she'd understand and sympathize. But I got the shock of my life when she told me her life story. I'd just accepted the way I was raised, having everything, and when I came up against real life I wasn't prepared for it. That my mother's life had been any different never entered my mind."

"How had it been?" Millie asked.

"She told me about being raised in poverty in Ireland. About the sufferings of the great famine. She saw her mother and father starve to death. Had to leave them there, dead in the little cottage, and emigrate. Then after a horrible passage across the Atlantic, she was separated from her sister and never saw her again. She worked many years as a maid in Boston before she met my father. He took her to California and into his life of wealth. When she told me all this, I realized how well off I was. I came home immediately, and became the wife and helper your father needed and deserved."

"Oh, Mother," Millie said, reaching out and holding her mother's hand. "But this really isn't the same."

"I know," Sarah agreed. "But the point is that you don't have it so bad. Everybody has some adversity in life. My mother did. I did, just being made to face reality. Your father certainly did trying to make a go of our little newspaper against all odds. If you still love Spud it's your job to help him get through this bad time in his life. You pray about it, Millie. That's what I always do. God will give you the answer."

359

CHAPTER FORTY-EIGHT

M ILLIE DID PRAY, ASKING GOD TO HEAL her marriage. But if God was listening, it didn't seem that Spud was. He spoke to her only when necessary. And Millie was tired of being rebuffed. When she returned from Salinas, where she'd gone to bring the little tin box to Uncle Tim, she wanted to talk with Spud about it, but he cut her off.

Millie had entered the jail and asked to see Tim Cleary. The desk man had her sign in and asked about the box. Millie explained that it was a keepsake of Mr. Cleary's and that she wanted to give it to him. The guard looked in the box, saw the letters and papers, and said, "Okay. I'll take it in to him and tell him he has a visitor, Missus Cleary. Please wait."

So Millie waited. But it was only for a few minutes and then the guard returned. "I'm sorry, Missus Cleary. He said he didn't want to see any visitors today."

"But — " Millie was dumfounded. "Did you tell him who it was?"

"Yes, I did. I'm sorry, ma'am."

Millie was on the verge of tears all the way home. When Spud arrived after work she told him about it. "Why, Spud? Why?"

"Somebody probably gave him a copy of that damn column of yours." And that was the end of the conversation.

The next day the grand jury was convened by Wesley Baetchen, the district attorney, and *The Settler-Banner* announced that an indictment for murder had been brought in against Timothy Patrick Cleary. *Grand Jury proceedings being secret, both Baetchen and Sheriff Carl Abbott, who gave testimony, refused comment*, the newspaper reported.

Two days later the headlines said, *Cleary Pleads Not Guilty,* and the story explained that his lawyer, Joseph Crandle of King City, had entered a plea at the arraignment of *not guilty and of not guilty by reason of insanity,* and that Cleary had been bound over to stand trial. Trial was set for Monday, Sept. 16.

Millie had packed a small suitcase and took the early train to Salinas to cover the trial. She checked into the room her father had reserved for her at the Jeffery House. Bill Jeffery himself welcomed her, remarking how nice it was to have a member of the Cleary family in the hotel again after so many years. Tactfully, he didn't comment on the trial and Millie was relieved. She left her things in her room, freshened up, and hurried to the court house.

She was a bit flustered entering the packed courtroom, anxiously searching for the other members of the press assigned to the trial. She located a long table at the side, which had been set up for the reporters. The Cleary murder trial had attracted attention from all the major daily newspapers. Hand printed, cardboard nameplates tacked to the edge of the table indicated spaces for Max Morgan from *The Chronicle*, Sally Hanfeldt of the *Oakland Tribune*, Porter Jenson of *The Examiner*, and several others whose bylines Millie recognized. She was somewhat hesitant about taking the empty chair, but Porter Jenson invited her to sit, and scrawled out a nameplate. When he stumbled over the name *The Settler-Banner,* he asked Millie, "Where is it?" Millie explained she was from King City, and he nodded.

As soon as Judge Horace Bishoff had entered and was seated Millie took out her notepad and pencil. She looked around and saw Uncle Tim seated at the defense table, his lawyer, Joe Crandle, next to him. Tim was no longer in his jail garb, but wore clean, ranch clothes. Tim, who had been tall, straight and slender, now looked smaller, stoop-shouldered and skinny, his shirt and Levis too large for him. Millie assumed that Honora or Kitty had brought them up for him. She tried to catch his eye, but Tim didn't look her way. In fact, he didn't gaze around at all, just sat staring straight ahead. He didn't even react when the charges were read in the "Case of the People of the State of California and the County of Monterey against

Timothy Patrick Cleary." Millie looked around and found Kitty and Buck sitting with Pat in the back of the courtroom. She smiled and nodded to them but they didn't respond.

Most of the members of the jury panel were from the Salinas area and selection proceeded swiftly, except when the prosecutor thought someone might have known Supervisor Will Cleary, or been friendly with the Cleary family. "And were you ever befriended by Supervisor Cleary?" Baetchen would ask. Millie was surprised at how many people had to admit that they were once well-acquainted with Will Cleary.

"Do you believe that you are capable of rendering a just verdict in this case regardless of this acquaintanceship?" They all answered that they were, but several were excused anyhow. Crandle used only one of his challenges. He excused a woman who was well-known for her temperance views.

By the time the jury was selected Judge Bishoff ruled that the day was late and that the trial would convene in the morning with opening statements. Millie found herself in a group of reporters walking back to the Jeffery and discovered they were all staying there. She was invited to join their table in the dining room, and felt accepted into the camaraderie of newspaper people, enjoying the shop talk that flowed about her except when she was asked about the coincidence of her last name.

"Missus Cleary? Is your name just a coincidence or are you related to the accused?" Porter Jenson asked.

"My husband is Tim Cleary's nephew," Millie said.

"Oh, doesn't that make if difficult for you to cover this trial?" Sally Hanfeldt wondered.

"Yes, it does," Millie admitted ruefully.

"Well, why didn't your paper send somebody else?"

"There is nobody else," Millie said. She explained that *The Settler-Banner* was a small weekly and that she was the only reporter. "It's my job."

"Well, good luck, dear," Sally Hanfeldt said.

The next morning Millie awoke with a knot growing in the pit of her stomach. Today they'd hear evidence for the first time. She fervently prayed her theory that Uncle Tim had been forced to shoot in self defense would be proven right. But she knew that Tim had absolutely refused to testify in his own defense. He was not going to take the stand and tell his story.

Baetchen started off, telling the twelve jurors that they had before them a simple case of murder. A man had been shot down in cold blood, he claimed. A man who had approached Tim Cleary's home had found, instead of hospitality, a bullet in his breast. There was no question about what had happened. The defendant himself had repeatedly said, "I killed him."

Crandle's statement in defense was brief. "The witnesses we call will prove beyond a doubt that my client is innocent of this charge. Ladies and gentlemen of the jury, you will find that there was no malice aforethought, no deliberate premeditation. You will find that the death of Mister Oscar Bauman was not murder, only a tragic accident."

The prosecutor first put on the stand George Whistone of San Ardo, who stated that he owned a blacksmith shop and sold hardware supplies. Baetchen asked him, "And did you sell to Mister Bauman, on or about July 15, 1930, several items from your stock?"

"I did."

"And what were those items?"

"He bought a heavy chain and a padlock," the witness replied.

"Did you ask him what he planned to do with these items?"

"Well, yeah. I was curious. I guess I did."

"Now, Mister Whistone, please tell the jury in your own words what he said to you at that time."

Whistone looked around, up at the judge, and then at the jury. Baetchen nodded, encouraging him to speak. "Well, he said he was going to keep that son-of-a-bitch Cleary from crossing his land, lock him out once and for all."

Crandle had no questions. Whistone was excused. Baetchen called another south county resident, Bert Appleby, a farmer who lived down the road from the Bauman place.

"Mister Appleby, is it true that Mister Bauman told you that he was afraid of his neighbor, Timothy Cleary, the defendant here?"

"Well, maybe," the farmer admitted, looking at his hands. He obviously was uncomfortable being asked questions about Tim Cleary. But the district attorney insisted. "Remember, you're under oath, Mister Appleby. Did Mister Bauman tell you that the defendant had threatened him?"

Appleby reluctantly nodded his head and muttered, "Yeah."

"Tell us in your own words just what Mister Bauman told you that Mister Cleary had said to him."

"Objection, your honor." Crandle had sprung to his feet. "That's hearsay."

"Sustained," the judge intoned.

Baetchen nodded and turned back to his witness. "Did Mister Cleary ever tell you, Mister Appleby, that he was having trouble with Mister Bauman?"

"Well, yeah."

"And what did he say? Tell the jury."

"Well, old Tim don't talk much. Fact is, I don't see much of him. Hard to remember."

Baetchen was obviously becoming exasperated. "Mister Appleby, I remind you again that you are under oath. Now tell the jury what Mister Cleary told you?"

Appleby looked over at Tim and shrugged. In a low voice he muttered, "He said that goddamned Bauman can't keep me off that road. Clearys have been using it for seventy years. If he gets tough with me, I'll kill the sonofabitch!"

There was a collective gasp in the courtroom and a buzz of conversation. Judge Bishoff banged his gavel.

"No more questions," Baetchen said, returning to his seat, a smug smile on his face.

Joe Crandle got up and walked quickly toward Appleby. He stood facing the farmer. "Tell the court, Mister Appleby, just where you were with Mister Cleary when he supposedly uttered those words."

"Out on the road," Appleby said without hesitation. "I was fixing a fence one evening, and Tim there came along in that old Dodge of his. He stopped to say hello and offered me a drink."

Crandle's eyes narrowed, but he continued to stare at the man on the stand. "I see, Mister Appleby. A drink? A drink of what?"

"Well, whiskey, of course," the farmer answered. "Just a minute now. I got no idea where he got it. He just asked if I wanted a snort. Naturally, I refused."

"Whiskey, huh?" Crandle said. "And could you say that Mister Cleary was drunk when he made that threat about Mister Bauman?"

"Well, yeah. Old Tim was drunk most of the time." Appleby looked apologetically at Tim Cleary. Tim just stared straight ahead. "But it was hard to tell. He held it good. He was pretty much always the same."

Crandle moved closer to the witness. "But you did say he was drunk, Mister Appleby? Are you sure of that?"

"Yeah, Tim was drunk!"

"Do you think he meant it when he threatened Mister Bauman?"

"Objection!" The prosecutor was on his feet. "Question calls for an opinion, pure conjecture."

"Sustained. Restate your question, Mister Crandle."

"Did Mister Cleary appear to you to be in command of his faculties when you heard him make that threat, Mister Appleby?" Crandle asked.

"Nope! He was drunk."

Crandle gave a quick, satisfied nod. "No further questions, your honor."

Millie wondered about the testimony. It was obvious that the district attorney had established that bad blood existed between Uncle Tim and Oscar Bauman, that Bauman wanted to keep Cleary from crossing his land, and that Cleary had made threats about Bauman. But she thought that Tim's lawyer had done a fine job with that farmer when he got him to explain that Tim was drunk when he said those threatening words and that Appleby didn't believe Tim really meant it.

The next morning when she took her place at the press table, Millie looked back to see Spud enter the courtroom and sit with the family members. Spud had taken the day off to watch what they believed would be the final day of the trial.

The county coroner testified that he found the body, that Oscar Bauman died of a gunshot wound to the chest, that he'd been dead about six hours, which placed the time of death between six and seven the morning of Thursday, Aug. 7, 1930.

A ballistics expert identified the bullet taken out of the dead man at the autopsy as coming from the thirty-thirty Winchester rifle discovered on the wall of Tim Cleary's cabin. He produced the old rifle and entered it as evidence.

"Were there any shells in the magazine of the rifle?" the district attorney asked.

"Yes, there were four."

"And how many shells does the Winchester thirty-thirty hold?"

"Five."

"Therefore, it is obvious that one shell had been fired. Is that not correct, sir?"

"Yes."

"And you established that the missing shell was the one discovered near the steps to Mister Cleary's cabin, and that the bullet was found lodged in the chest of the deceased?"

"Yes," the witness agreed.

Crandle had no questions and Sheriff Carl Abbott was next on the stand. He testified that he'd gone to the scene the day of the murder and found the body laying inside the gate to the yard at Cleary's homestead cabin. He also testified that he had entered the cabin and found it in disarray.

"As if there had been a struggle?" the prosecutor asked.

"No. Just a mess," Abbott corrected him. "As if it hadn't been cleaned up for several days."

"What else did you find inside?"

"Just the rifle," Abbott said, "and we found the expended shell just outside the cabin door."

Crandle stepped up on cross examination. "Sheriff," he asked, "was there anything else in the cabin of particular significance?"

"Well, yes, I think you could call it significant that there was a case of fruit jars filled with jackass."

"Jackass, sheriff? Perhaps you'll explain that term to the jury."

Abbott nodded and smiled at the jury. Everybody knew what jackass was. "It's a term for bootleg whiskey, like rot gut," he explained.

"And was it a full case, sheriff?"

"No, it wasn't. There were two jars missing and I found them on the floor, empty."

"Thank you sheriff. Now when you drove out to Mister Cleary's homestead that morning, how did you go, by what road?"

"We took the Pine Valley road, of course."

"And in what condition did you find the gate to Mister Bauman's property, the one across the road Mister Cleary used? Was it locked?"

"No, it wasn't," Abbott said. "The chain had been cut. It was laying on the ground with the lock. Right by the gate."

"Now when you arrived at the homestead and found the body, did you discover anything by the body?" Crandle asked.

"Yes, we did. A rifle."

"What type of rifle was it, sheriff?"

"A small hunting rifle, a thirty-two caliber Remington pump," Abbott said.

Crandle paused a moment, looked over at the members of the jury, who were all listening intently. He turned back to the sheriff.

"And had that rifle been fired?"

"Yes," the sheriff replied.

There was a flurry in the court room as reporters exclaimed to each other and hurriedly jotted down their notes. People in the courtroom all started talking at once. Judge Bishoff pounded his gavel for order. When the room settled down, Baetchen approached the witness.

"Sheriff Abbott, you say the rifle had been fired. Can you tell the court if there was any evidence of a bullet having been fired at Mister Cleary, any bullet hole in his cabin, for instance? Or did you discover an ejected shell by the body or anywhere near?"

"No."

"Can you explain why there was a shell missing from the magazine of the Remington rifle?"

"Sure, there was a dead deer, a forked horn buck, just up the canyon from the cabin, not far from his spring, inside Mister Cleary's fence line."

"And how did you discover that dead deer?"

"Buzzards," Abbott said. There were gasps from the people in the courtroom and there was a buzz of conversation. Millie was frantically writing, trying to keep up with the testimony.

Crandle then put on the stand a series of south county people who testified that Tim Cleary was an even-tempered man, never one to invite trouble, a man who kept to himself, a man of good character except for an occasional drink. He rested the case for the defense and stepped aside for the prosecutor's closing argument.

Baetchen insisted that Oscar Bauman had simply come to Tim Cleary's gate to enter and bring out the deer that he had killed. He dramatically recreated the scene as he believed it to be, claiming that Cleary, who hated Bauman and had threatened to kill him, now took the opportunity to carry out his threat.

"When Mister Bauman came to his gate with a simple request, to pick up the deer he'd shot, Timothy Cleary took aim and fired a bullet point blank into his chest."

Crandle waited a moment after the district attorney had returned to his table. Then he rose and walked to the jury box, spread his hands and apologetically admitted that Tim Cleary had been drinking heavily, as testified by the empty whiskey jars found in his cabin. "When Bauman approached the cabin, Cleary saw that he had a rifle. In his befuddled state, Mister Cleary thought that his neighbor had come to shoot him, to get revenge because Mister Cleary had cut the lock off the gate. Timothy Cleary was filled with fear," the attorney stressed, pointing at Tim, who sat at his table, head down. Crandle turned back to the jury box. "He simply saw an enemy with a rifle and believed he was protecting his life. This is absolutely a case of self defense, mitigated by Mister Cleary's intoxicated state at the time. Gentlemen of the jury, this shooting was a tragic accident. I remind you that there was no malice afore-thought, no premeditation. I ask you to return the only verdict that is fair and just in this case: A verdict of not guilty."

The jury deliberated less than an hour. As they filed back into the courtroom, Millie tried to read the face of each member. But she couldn't. She watched Tim sway slightly as he stood to hear the verdict. He stared straight ahead. She held her breath.

The judge spoke loudly and clearly. "Mister Foreman, has the jury reached a verdict?"

"Yes, we have, your honor," the foreman replied firmly.

"And how say you?" Judge Bishoff asked.

"We, the members of the jury, find Timothy Patrick Cleary not guilty!"

Tim heard it, but his expression didn't change. He simply stood still as the courtroom came to life around him. He seemed bewildered as Crandle shook his hand, and members of the Cleary family came quickly over to surround him, Kitty and Honora trying to embrace him, Spud and Pat shaking his hand. Tim appeared uneasy, confused, unable to grasp that he was a free man. Millie stood by the press table, watching, longing to make herself part of the family, to share in the joy at the verdict, but she was afraid of more rejection.

As they filed out of the courtroom, she joined Spud and walked toward their car just ahead of Uncle Tim. She turned to him, "Come with us, Uncle Tim. We'll give you a ride home."

But Tim Cleary gave her a long, cold look, walked on past her, and entered the car with his nephew, Pat.

CHAPTER FORTY-NINE

IT WAS A BEAUTIFUL MORNING IN EARLY MARCH and the hills on each side of town were forty shades of green, just like they said of Ireland, Millie thought, as she walked up Vanderhurst and headed for the newspaper office. This was the kind of morning that would once have made her burst into song. But Millie hadn't felt like singing for some time.

She managed to force a smile in answer to the cheerful wave of Pop Williams, who was opening his little candy wagon for the day, and thought, what a grump she was getting to be. She couldn't go on like this, she reasoned. She turned onto Broadway, and then down Third toward *The Settler-Banner*. Most days she could put her own troubles behind her when she sat down at her typewriter. She truly loved the newspaper, the ink smells in the office, the excitement of being involved in the town, the people she met and wrote about, the satisfaction she felt when the paper came off the press each week. But today she was morose and, no matter how hard she tried, she couldn't shake the depression she felt.

Spud, she thought. She couldn't reach him any more. Things had become worse since Uncle Tim's trial, not better. Her apologies fell on deaf ears. She'd written the words she thought would help matters, hoping that the family would appreciate her column about Uncle Tim. But they just thought she was invading their privacy again. And Spud had become the most distant of all. *How can I reach out to him if he won't forgive me?*

Millie missed being part of the close-knit Cleary family. But every overture she'd made had been politely refused. Christmas had been particularly difficult. Every year since she and Spud had married, they'd spent Christmas Eve with her parents and brother Bob and his wife, exchanged gifts, and attended Midnight Mass at St. John's. Christmas day was always spent at the ranch in Long Valley. When she asked Spud about it, he curtly answered, "We haven't been invited." Millie felt that remark like a knife in her heart.

Timmy was confused, too. The other children at school had stopped tormenting him, but his schoolwork hadn't improved. And he was continually asking to go to the ranch. Or to see Uncle Tim. He didn't understand why they weren't making their Sunday visits to the ranch. "I want to see Nana and Uncle Pat and ride the horses and play with Seamus," he pleaded.

And why couldn't they go to Uncle Tim's for a picnic? Millie didn't know how to explain. How could she make her little boy understand the complexities of people, how they hurt each other, even those they loved? And there was no way to make him understand the differences between newspaper people, such as her family, and the fact that they looked at the world differently than very private country folks, such as the Clearys. Millie wasn't sure she understood it herself.

* * * * *

Tim Cleary was sitting on the steps of his cabin, looking out at the green hills, absently listening to the quail chattering. It was what he did most days. There weren't any colts in the corral for him to work, only old Beauford to saddle up for a ride over the hill to the home place in Long Valley once in a while for dinner with the folks. The Dodge sat under the eucalyptus tree, nearly covered with leaves and dead branches. A flat tire was further proof it hadn't been moved for many months.

Tim didn't do anything. He didn't even drink. Tim Cleary hadn't had a drink since the day he was arrested. At first, when he was in the jail, he'd have given anything he had for just one sip. He imagined the raw liquor rolling over his tongue, down his throat, into his veins, numbing his brain. He thought constantly of the day he'd get out, if he did get out, and what he'd do for a drink, where he'd go for it, how he'd get it, what it would taste like. But gradually the craving left him. When he arrived at his cabin he was almost relieved to find that his stock of fruit jars had been removed by the sheriff. He had no urge to drive down to Alvarado's. Tim Cleary was dry. He was sober. And that was his torment.

At night he lay awake on the big bed he'd slept in since childhood, and thought. During the day he sat on the steps, and thought. And all he could think about was that he had killed a man. He stared at the spot where Bauman had fallen. Then he recalled that long-ago time when he and his father, Jeremiah, had run off the squatters from this very piece of land. There'd been a shot back then, too, several of them, and Tim had been so afraid his angry father was going to kill one of the squatters. But Jeremiah didn't. His shot was only to scare them off.

Tim sighed and rubbed his eyes, trying to erase the memories, trying to forget. He went to the corral and threw an ample supply of hay to the horse. He checked the water and made sure there was a full trough. Tim walked back to his cabin and found his broom. He gave the floor a good sweeping, cleaned and stacked his dishes, and neatly made his bed. He noticed his mail, which Kitty had brought over several days earlier. It contained some advertisements and his bank statement. He tore it open. Even after the check for his lawyer had been deducted there was more than ten thousand dollars in his account.

He picked up the little tin box by his bed and carried it to the table. Tim found his box of thirty-thirty shells and took down his rifle.

* * * * *

Spud came home early that night. Millie had just arrived from work and Timmy had run outside to play when Spud drove in. Millie heard the back porch door bang shut and went into the kitchen to greet him. He stopped in the middle of the room to face her. But he didn't say anything. She saw tears in his eyes. She waited as apprehension grew in her. Finally, he spoke.

"It's Uncle Tim. He's dead."

"Dead? What do you mean?" Millie swallowed hard, never taking her eyes off Spud.

"Kitty found him in his cabin about noon. Shot himself."

"Oh, Spud, Spud — !" Millie burst into tears and Spud held out his arms. She came into them with a heart wrenching cry. He held her, stroked her hair, patted her shoulder, tried to comfort her. Millie sobbed against his chest.

"I'm so sorry, so sorry!" she choked out the words. "Oh, the poor man!"

Millie finally raised her head and Spud handed her his handkerchief. She tried to dry her eyes, but the tears kept coming. "Why, Spud? Why?"

"There was a note. They turned it over to the sheriff. But Pat told me. It said that he just couldn't live with the knowledge that he'd killed a man."

"Oh, that's horrible." Millie sobbed quietly for a moment. Then she recalled Spud had said that Kitty found him. "How awful for her," Millie said, imagining the terrible moment when Kitty found him.

"Yeah. Pat came to tell me. Kitty had ridden over on horseback to visit Tim. She found him there at the kitchen table. Dead for several hours. She rode right back to the ranch and told Pat. He said Kitty was pretty upset. He came to town for the sheriff," Spud explained.

"Oh, Spud. The little tin box! They'll find it with those letters and things," Millie said, frantically.

"Won't matter," Spud said. "Pat said the little box was there on the table beside him. But it was empty. There was a pile of ashes in a bowl."

"Uncle Tim destroyed his memories." Millie's voice was hollow and sad.

"Millie," Spud lifted her head from his chest. He looked into her eyes. "There was something else in his note."

"What was that?" Millie asked.

"It was to you. Tim wrote, *Tell Millie there's some money in Monterey County Bank. It's for her and Timmy. The Coyote homestead is for Timmy.* Pat thinks it's like a will. The homestead patent was there on the table."

Millie pulled back from Spud and looked up at him. Her eyes opened wide and they were shining, not just with tears, but with the enormity of it, the meaning of Uncle Tim's gift. Spud stared down at her and their eyes stayed locked together for a long moment.

She tried to speak. "Spud — " But he placed a finger tip over her lips. "I know," he said. And there was something in his eyes that said he understood, and that everything was all right.

* * * * *

Clara Mertens, the widow of Joshua Mertens, sat in the library of her Green Street home in San Francisco. Dressed in mourning black, her habitual attire, Clara's blond hair was mostly gray now, although she was not yet forty years old. Her lips were set in a firm, thin line and her eyes, once merry, looked sadly out of a face that held little of its former beauty. Her black dress was worn, not for the loss of her young husband, killed in action in France, but in memory of an Irish rebel whom she'd never fully understood, whom she'd known only for a short while before he'd returned to Ireland to give up his life for the cause to which it was dedicated.

Clara's gaze fixed on a stack of newspapers on the library table, copies of the *Salinas Valley Settler-Banner*. She was still a subscriber, but she hardly ever read the paper. She'd have them thrown out, but first she'd glance through the latest issue on the off chance she'd recognize a name.

Timothy Cleary. There was a familiar name. *Funeral services held for Timothy Cleary.*

Clara remembered Timothy Cleary, the recluse who lived up Coyote Canyon. She'd seen him in San Lucas a few times, but he always avoided her, never would speak to her. She'd always wondered why.

Private graveside services were held Tuesday for Timothy Patrick Cleary, 68, who passed away Saturday at his Coyote Canyon home of a self-inflicted gunshot wound. Mr. Cleary was buried in the family plot in King City cemetery.

Last fall Mr. Cleary had been judged not guilty in the tragic shooting of his neighbor Oscar Bauman.

Never married, Mr. Cleary is survived by three sisters, Mrs. Joseph (Peggy) Carrigan of King City, Mrs. Charles (Annie) Phillips of Bitterwater and Mrs. Buck (Kitty) O'Keefe of Long Valley and two brothers, Seamus Cleary of Long Valley and Father Daniel Cleary of San Mateo, who conducted the graveside rites, and a cousin, Mrs. Christopher (Constance) Baxter, of San Francisco. He was the brother of the late county supervisor, Will Cleary. He also leaves several nieces and nephews.

Clara carefully read the story and put the paper aside. Bauman, she thought. That was the man who bought the Cleary ranch. And Connie Baxter was the wife of her attorney. She hadn't realized the connection.

But Timothy Cleary. He was a strange man. What tragedy made him into a recluse who'd kill his neighbor and then take his own life? Clara wondered about it for a moment.

Then she dropped *The Settler-Banner* on the stack of papers and rang for a maid to throw them out.